500 YEARS IS A LONG TIME TO FORGET...

# INSOLATION

# BRADLYN WILSON

Solstice Publishing - www.solsticepublishing.com

# Insolation

## By Bradlyn Wilson

Hey Lance, great job today! you are great to work with!

Bradlyn Wilson

## Dedication

For my parents, who have always encouraged me to chase my dreams.

# Chapter One

It was darker than humanly imaginable. Stuffy hot air floated around, so humid and thick that it felt as though it could be cut with a knife, like warm butter on a hot day. The black was encapsulating and overwhelming, as though a person was floating and being crushed all at the same time.

In the dark, her eyes were playing tricks on her. She blinked furiously trying to make sense of her surroundings, to comprehend if she had gone blind or if she was in hell. A pit formed in her stomach as she struggled to digest her predicament. The only thing she could hear was the ringing in her ears that threatened to make her head explode. The quiet was deafening. Uncomfortable. Unimaginable.

There was a tightness in her chest, as though someone was wrapping their hands around her ribcage and pushing down, trying to shove the air out of her lungs. She tried to take a deep breath, but found herself coughing in the hot air as it poured into her lungs. She started to panic and felt her breath quicken. Her hair and skin was sticky with sweat; she could feel the tiny hairs on her back stuck to the ground she was laying on.

*Calm down, I need to calm down,* she thought, unable to stop the panic rushing through her veins. She reached up, hoping for a large empty room. The darkness was growing, consuming.

She reached an arm up hoping to get a clue of where she was. Her hand hit cold concrete before she could even get her elbow off the ground and her heart sunk. She started to run her hands all around her and soon realized that she was in a jagged and rutted enclosure similar to a coffin. The realization that she was going to suffer a slow and excruciating death as she suffocated and starved, drying up like a warm raisin, slowly sunk in. Tears prickled her eyes. She felt the warm water pour down her temples and clink onto the hard ground.

Then she did the only thing she could think of. She started to scream, as loud as she could.

She flailed her hands against the concrete, banging harder and harder until her arms started to get raw. She could feel them stinging as the concrete wore away at her skin. She didn't stop, though. She kept banging and screaming until she felt the warm flow of blood ooze down her elbows and onto her chest. She started scratching furiously at the rock above her.

She laid her arms back down, resting for a moment. She tried to see something, straining in the dark but it was no use. There wasn't a single speck of light for her retinas and lens to latch onto.

Unable to give up, she dug her nails into the ground and started kicking. Unexpectedly she felt immense pain through her abdomen. Everything froze as visions flew through her head, but she could only make out a feeling: resentment.

She was terrified as she moved her hand slowly towards the source of the pain. Her fingers trailed over her waist and down towards her groin. Just below her belly button, she felt the warm handle of a knife. She traced her fingers around the blade and realized she had something resembling a chef's knife lodged straight through her abdomen.

She let out a bloodcurdling scream.

She started to feel herself hyperventilating, the blood vessels in her lungs narrowing as the carbon dioxide levels in her body fell. Blood slowly stopped moving to her brain and she felt herself getting lightheaded. She started drifting into a hazy state, filled with dreams that felt like old memories.

She was certain she was going to die. That's when the sounds started.

She started to scream louder.

# Chapter Two

She was eight and playing in the harsh red sand. She looked up, saw the small grey house, and smiled. They were the only things for miles but that didn't scare her. Instead, she was excited about being in the middle of the desert.

She looked up and saw her grandpa rush out of the house. His grey hair stood on ends. His skin was the colour of burnt leather from so many years out in the desert. His round glasses were almost falling off his nose.

He stopped dead in his tracks and stared at the blazing sun. There wasn't a cloud in the sky.

She burnt her eyes looking up to see what her grandpa was studying intently and turned her face back to the dirt. There were small shrubs around her and she looked just in time to see a lizard run across her leg. She smiled at him as he licked his tongue onto her sweaty calf.

She turned back to her grandfather, suddenly realizing what he was looking at. Half the sky was dark. The sun reflected off the metal and the grooves were clear. It was bigger than anything she had ever seen. Bigger than any city she had ever been to.

"Hadley, get in the house," her grandfather yelled, his normally soft drawl harshened by panic, without taking his eyes off the ship.

Hadley got up and dusted herself off. Her white dress was stained orange.

She walked towards the house and as she did, her grandpa put a hand on her back and walked into the house with her. He spun her around by the shoulders and knelt in front of her. She looked at the scar that made up the left side of his face; loving it, she always traced the lines when she sat on his lap. But he never let her lift the eye-patch.

She reached up and put her hand on his cheek. He put his rough hand over hers and smiled.

"Kiddo, you remember how your mom said that you were going to have to stay here for a while?"

"Yeah, her and daddy had to go on a trip." She knew this. He had told her so many times over the last few days. It was as though he thought she was dumb.

"Did you see that ship?"

She nodded slowly.

"Your mom and dad are on that ship. And kiddo, they aren't coming back."

She didn't understand.

"What?"

"I'll explain when you're older—but they wanted you to know that they loved you very much and if things had been different then you could have gone with them. But they weren't and so it's just you and me now."

Her grandpa wasn't making any sense. Her mom and dad always left, but they always came back. Always. They would be back in a few weeks; of that, she was sure.

She wrinkled up her nose. Her eyes were stinging but she was determined that she wasn't going to cry.

# Chapter Three

Hadley screamed with all her might, every ounce of energy she had left going into the piercing scream she was allowing out of her lungs. It was echoing around her like fireworks going off inside her head, but she could hear the rumbling around her and had to hope someone was hearing her. A brief thought that this could be death danced through her brain; she hoped if it was death that it wouldn't last forever, and that she would have release from this prison.

She took a deep breath in, pausing to listen, to strain to hear any sign that she might soon be freed.

"Help," escaped her lips. The first word she had uttered since waking up in this nightmare.

She hasn't expected anyone to hear; it was a soft whisper to ease her pain and frustration.

"We're coming, hang on!" someone yelled back.

A shudder ran through her spine as she inhaled another breath of warm hot air. She felt a knot of electricity form in her stomach. She waited patiently, pounding her hands slowly onto the concrete on top of her. She hoped that it would be enough to lead them to her. She had no idea how far underground she was.

Without warning, light poured over her face. She shut her eyes tightly as her retinas tried to process the sudden influx of sensory action. She squeezed them tighter, feeling pain through her face. She inhaled the cool fresh air, and started sputtering as her lungs adjusted to the increased oxygen around her and tried to exhale the dust particles.

She braced herself for what and who would be there when she finally opened her eyes.

"Are you ok?" the same voice as before asked.

Hadley opened her eyes. She looked up and saw two figures silhouetted against the harsh yellow sun. She blinked, trying to make out their features. They were standing a couple feet over her head and were on top of the jagged rock that surrounded her.

"I said, are you all right?" the taller figure half shouted down, it was man's voice. His tone was gruff and strained, as though he had just woken up.

"I'm not sure," Hadley replied, unable to think of anything else to say.

"Can we pull you out?" the female said in a musical voice.

Hadley ran her hand down her body and felt the knife. She ran her hand across her hip, onto her back, and couldn't feel the other end sticking out. She figured she had a better chance if she got out of the hole.

"I think so," she replied, reaching her hands up as she maneuvered her torso into the short tunnel above her.

The two people above her reached down, gripped her bleeding arms around her wrists, and pulled. It was almost an instantaneous relief when Hadley was freed from her turbulent tomb and she lay on the ground, watching her hands shake just inches from her face. She tried to pull her eyes away from her cracked and bloody palms; her nails were nothing more than bleeding nubs on the ends of her worn fingers.

The two others watched her meticulously. They were studying her to see what would happen and figure out if there was anything they could do. Hadley started to rock back and forth.

The woman looked at the man. "I think she's in shock."

"She'd have to be..." the man countered with a shrug.

"She was stabbed!" the woman exclaimed.

"She'll be all right."

Hadley tried desperately to pull herself together. She closed her eyes again and began meticulously calming down what seemed like a nerve at a time. Eventually she exhaled and looked at the people who had saved her.

"Thanks." She smiled; it was the only thing she could think to say.

"No problem," they said in tune.

They remained staring at each other in silence for what seemed like an eternity.

The man grimaced, pushing his perfectly shaped eyebrows close together. His grey eyes studied Hadley. "Who are you?"

"Hadley Evans, who are you?"

"Paxton Avery, I go by Pax," he said with an air of self-worth as though his name should mean something.

He knelt down slowly, pushing his blond unkempt hair out from in front of his eyes. He gave her a smirk.

"Nice to meet you Hadley," Pax smiled as put his hand on her shoulder, "now this is going to hurt…"

Aggressively, Pax grabbed a hold of the knife handle piercing through Hadley's stomach and pulled. She glimpsed it slide out from between her abs, and the blood flow from it. Paxton pulled the shirt off his back swiftly and tore off the sleeve; he wadded it up and pressed it against her bleeding stomach. He tore the bottom ring off the shirt and tied it tightly around Hadley's waist, compressing the wound. This was the first time Hadley realized she wasn't wearing anything but a pair of non-descript white underwear and bra.

Then Pax held up the knife, or what was left of it.

"See, it wasn't that deep."

"How did you know how to do that?" Hadley asked through clenched teeth.

"Five years in the military as a doctor after high school; I've seen my fair share of battle wounds," he said nonchalantly before a grimace spread over his face.

The woman stared daggers at Pax, taking a step back. "How do you know that?"

"Honestly, Vanya I didn't even know I knew that until it came out of my mouth."

"Don't lie to me Pax; after the last 2 days I thought we were in the same boat."

"Vanya, I swear, that's the only thing I've remembered."

Hadley watched them go back and forth. Vanya was a thin woman with long flowing red hair. Her eyes struggled to focus and there was an indent on the top of her nose where her glasses should be. She was terrified.

"I thought I could trust you," Vanya squealed at him taking a step back.

"Vanya, calm down, I haven't lied to you."

Hadley moved her arms over herself, trying to cover up her indecently exposed body. She saw the black bruises covering the majority of her body. As she started to relax, the pain began to intensify.

Hadley had to ask, "What are you talking about? You can't remember anything…?"

"Can you?" Vanya asked in horror, her eyes widened and her breath quickened as she panicked.

Hadley thought for a moment, trying to figure out anything about her life that she knew. She knew that the sky was blue because the particles in the air scatter sunlight as blue light more than red. She knew about research she was undertaking and a thorough knowledge of the planet. However, when it came to herself and her experiences it was as though she was a memory card that been wiped clean.

"I…I…"

"Where were you born?" Paxton asked.

"I don't know; where were you born?" Hadley countered.

Vanya piped in, "What do you do?"

"I have a PhD in Environmental and Evolutionary Sciences; I basically combined the two to see how humans interact with the environment, as well as how they contribute to global warming."

"Where did you get that PhD?" Pax quizzed.

"I..." Hadley paused. "I'm... I'm..."

"You don't know?"

"No..."

Vanya smiled sadly, "Neither do we..."

Hadley looked Vanya straight in the eye. "How is that possible?"

"Have you looked around?" Pax replied.

She hadn't, with everything happening right in front of her face she hadn't taken a second to look at the bigger picture. She looked at the pile of rubble that lay beneath her, the remnants of a building that had long collapsed and she pondered how she had become a part of it. She looked up and saw the building on which they stood was one of many that were disintegrated.

Some steel structures still held on. The windows had turned into fine powder below their sills. There was no sign of vegetation, grass or trees. It was a crumbling concrete jungle. It seemed as though the three of them were the only people left in a deserted world.

"So you have no idea what happened here?" Hadley inquired skeptically. Pax and Vanya shook their heads.

Vanya opened her mouth as though to make a suggestion but decided against it. Instead Pax spoke. "We've been wandering around for 2 days. We haven't found water or food and it's becoming a problem. I would love to sit around here but we're headed towards the other end of town in search of anything."

A wave of pain rushed through Hadley's entire body, radiating from her head. She looked at Pax who was waiting for an answer, suddenly her stomach started churning and she vomited on her feet.

The vomit kept coming and coming. She continued to dry heave until there was less than nothing in her stomach, but her body wouldn't stop convulsing. Hadley put her head on the warm concrete below the setting sun and waited, either for death or the end of her body's rejection of the air.

"We have to find water," Pax exclaimed, "if we don't... well it won't be long before the severe dehydration sets in for you Hadley, and the vomiting is making it worse. Vanya, we also can't go on much longer."

Hadley looked at Pax. "I think I'll die now...," she whispered beginning to close her eyes. The blood was soaking through the makeshift bandage on her stomach and she was starting to feel lightheaded.

"Nope. No one is dying today. It's probably a concussion," Pax declared as he scooped Hadley up into his arms. She laid her head on his shoulder as she gave up trying to fight.

The sun was beginning to set and the sky was blazing a fiery combination of reds and golds. The last bit of the day was slowly fading into the jagged horizon. The wind started to shift as they walked off the building they were on. Hadley felt the hairs on her arms stand on end and she began to shiver. Pax held her closer, his warm chest moving up and down beneath her. He was starting to panic a bit but wouldn't let it show. He knew that would send Vanya off the deep end and he needed their group to stay together. If it was the last thing they did.

They walked and walked, finding nothing but demolished buildings. It seemed as though it was never going to end. Then, almost suddenly, they got to a bit of the city that looked almost in one piece, even though only a few windows remained.

They saw a mannequin in a half broken window as they crossed the street and Vanya almost yelled out, thinking it was another survivor. She bit her lip as she realized her mistake and Pax gave her a sympathetic look.

Then Hadley saw it, the sign lying on the ground; she barely made it out against the glow of the moonlight. She tried to speak but her voice came out as a squeak, her lips were so dry that they were cracking and blood was pooling in the corners. With all the strength she had left she hit Pax's arm.

"Huh?" he exhaled alarmed.

"Serva," she replied.

Vanya's face lit up. "Did you say Serva?"

Hadley raised a shaking finger towards the sign, and they all saw it. Pax started to walk faster, almost into a run, causing Hadley to bounce up and down in his arms.

They ran into the building, which was cold and damp. Pax walked with conviction until he found the store they were looking for, above it the sign read "Serva- For all your nutrition needs".

Hadley held her breath as they walked through the doors, but the store was almost completely empty. A thick layer of dust coated the shelves.

"Can I let you down?" Paxton asked Hadley, his eyes piercing into her soul.

Hadley nodded her head and he placed her feet back onto the ground. Without another word the three of them started to scavenge the high aisles.

The box was on the bottom shelf tucked away in the back corner when Hadley saw it. It was small and almost hidden beneath the dust. She reached for it, holding her breath. With the palm of her hand she wiped the thick grey particles off the label and read 'H2O Nutrition Patch- Activity dose. Use after heavy exercise. Equivalent to 2 litres of H2O. 100% 2-hour biodegradeable packaging. Easy skin absorption."

Immediately she pulled the tab on the box and opened it, revealing a hundred or so quarter size packets.

She placed the box carefully on the shelf and grabbed a packet. Tearing open the package she pulled out the nutrition patch and stuck it to the underside of her tongue.

It was almost instantaneous that she started to feel hydrated again as the nutrition patch worked through her body, distributing the hydration through her.

"Over here!" she yelled as the moisture in her mouth returned.

Vanya and Pax almost ran down the aisle and she handed them both a patch. They both tore them open and popped them in their mouths. Relief washed through the group as they realized they were going to live.

"Find anything else?" Hadley asked.

Pax shook his head and shrugged empty handed. "Thank god you found the water."

Vanya held a small tube. "I found malnutrition patches that are each equivalent to two days of meals."

Pax started laughing. "Could we honestly have gotten luckier?"

Vanya joined in laughing as she opened the malnutrition patches and placed one on the inside of her arm. Hadley reached in and grabbed one too, placing it carefully on her arm. She didn't join in laughing with the others.

Pax studied her. He was good at reading people but couldn't figure her out, or why he got this powerful feeling that he knew her before today. He couldn't help but notice how see through her clothes were, but he immediately felt like a pervert for even thinking that.

"We need to find you some clothes, Hadley," he mumbled, then quickly added, "I think a storm is coming and I don't want you get pneumonia after everything else."

Hadley gave him a puzzled look but nodded either way.

# Chapter Four

Deeper within the Serva building there was an open concept department store, or what used to be one. The empty shelves and unstacked racks showed it had been rummaged and sifted. In one aisle the shelves had been knocked down and destroyed. Under the coat of white dust, the massive dark red stain peaked through. Hadley looked at it and grimaced.

They walked deeper and deeper into the store. Hadley saw the now vertical *women's wear* sign and walked that way. She looked around at the emptiness and started to rummage with what was left. Luckily she was able to find a few pieces of clothing including a warm jacket.

Vanya was also looking for a few more items, and adding them to a dusty bag she had found on the ground. Pax had wandered over to the men's section and was slowly wandering through picking things up in his arms.

Hadley noticed a pile of pants and grabbed the ones on the bottom; there was only a tiny line of dust to remove and she did so with a brush of her hand. She opened a drawer that used to lie beneath a display and pulled out new undergarments. She slowly slid down her panties and pulled on the new ones, then fastened on a new bra. She pulled on her slightly dusty pants and a large knit sweater. She finally let out an exhale.

"Do you really think there isn't anyone else?" Hadley asked Vanya, who was bent over shovelling underwear into her bag.

Vanya looked up, biting her lip uncomfortably as her eyes widened. "I…I really don't know…" she sighed.

Hadley just nodded her head slowly, unable to think of anything to say. She walked away from Vanya and down a long forgotten electronics section. Everything was smashed and a symbol of an Earth with two intersecting V's was spray painted on the wall.

Hadley picked up a small quarter shaped object and tried to press it; momentarily a holographic image appeared above it. A screaming woman stood in front of a nuclear cloud. Before she could blink the image was gone and the quarter tablet started buzzing until it squealed and died. Hadley placed it gently on the shelf, her eyelids beginning to sag and the after effects of her stressful day wearing down on her body.

Unexpectedly she felt a hand on her shoulder, the hefty fingers of a strong man pressed deep into her back. She leapt into the air involuntarily and swung her hand until it made contact with something hard. She felt the crunch as she recoiled back.

"Fuck, Hadley!"

Hadley looked up and saw Pax. He was holding a smashed and bleeding nose. A fiery look flashed through his eyes. His muscles tensed as his breath quickened for a moment. He closed his eyes and let out a small whistle through his teeth as he clenched his jaw tightly.

"Oh god, Pax, I'm sorry, I didn't mean to… it must be the anxiety."

"Don't worry about it Hadley." He said with a smirk that made her smile, as he adjusted his nose somewhat back into place. He clenched his jaw through the pain but didn't say anything about it. She watched the way he did it, the restraint he exercised and felt oddly sympathetic towards him. He locked eyes with her and they stood staring at each other. Hadley felt a pang in the pit of her stomach. She could feel a long lost memory struggling to break free in her brain; she tried and could feel it becoming clearer.

Vanya came out of nowhere behind them and broke the moment. The small memory Hadley could feel disintegrated into shattered pieces inside her brain. They broke their gaze and Paxton looked at a shelf, almost too intensely. He pondered the moment they had, wondering if Hadley had felt the same pull between them.

"I found the abandoned bedding area; there are a couple mattresses… at least we won't have to sleep on the floor…" Vanya pretended that she hadn't interrupted them and pretended as though she hadn't seen the look Hadley and Pax were giving each other.

Pax gave her a curt nod.

Vanya turned on her heel and led them down the dusty aisles until they got to a circle of biodegradable mattresses; a few had long warped and melted, but a couple looked as though they still had some spring in their cushion.

Hadley grabbed another water patch and popped it under her tongue as she felt the familiar sense of thirst, the dryness in her mouth. The nutrient patch was still absorbing into her body. As before, it was almost immediate that the thirst went away and she felt a wave of exhaustion.

She could no longer lift her arms and flopped onto one of the beds. It erupted in a cloud of dust around her but she didn't care. She laid her head on one of the display pillows and watched as Vanya carefully dusted off the bed in front of her. Pax watched her in disdain.

Vanya crawled slowly on the bed and Pax followed her. He wrapped an arm around her as she started to sob. Hadley felt an uncomfortable pang of jealousy as her body longed for human touch. She rolled over and closed her eyes, immediately falling into a deep sleep.

# Chapter Five

2083

Pax had shut off the car and they were sitting with the top down in the back seat. They parked far off the beaten track beneath a row of apple trees that were sagging from the weight of their fruit in the late summer. Hadley swung her legs slowly back and forth as she watched the leaves rustle in the wind. Every once in a while one would come loose and float softly onto the dusty grass beneath them.

They watched the hustle and bustle of the town below from their hideaway, their own place of seclusion. People running around in their own lives, preoccupied with their own well-being.

Pax's arm was tight around Hadley's shoulder, and she rested her head on his shoulder. Neither spoke, for fear of what the other would say. The sky turned from oranges, to red to purples. Pax's shoulders gently lifted up and down as he breathed.

"Are we going to talk about this?" he said shortly.

"Talk about what?" Hadley sighed pulling away.

He moved away from her so his grey eyes could stare into hers. "Do you still love me?"

"Of course, I have since we were twelve. But that's not enough. We know that. There's no point." Tears welled up in her eyes as she struggled to keep in her punishing emotions. She didn't want to do anything to ruin this evening, which would be a perfect memory, a sad end to a fading fairy-tale.

"What makes you so sure?"

"I just know." She thought about their last few months, the magical last summer they had. She had cherished every moment. Memories welled up. The night they had spent on the beach looking up at the stars talking about her parent's trip, and how much she didn't know about them. Pax had always been good at talking about the hard things. He had a way of bringing up her parents so she could remember them even as the few memories she had faded.

She thought about the day they had driven to the mountains and spent the week camping, just the two of them. The way they had hiked through the evergreen forest.

The idea of university and the future had been looming over them for the entire summer. Though excited it was the end of everything they had known for the last years of high school. It was a constant reminder of the end of everything.

"Marry me," Pax almost demanded. Hadley took a deep breath. This was not the first time he had asked. At the beginning of the summer he had elaborately proposed after a grand dinner in their favourite spot in town.

Hadley cringed as she remembered what she had said, how she let him down gently in front of their friends and family. Though she still loved him, she knew that their relationship wasn't supposed to make it in the real world. It was the stuff of fairy tales, and sadly all fairy tales end.

Hadley looked at him, knowing she had asked him to propose at the end of the summer again. But the last two months had just solidified her views that ending everything was the best idea.

"I love you. To the moon and back."

"Then spend your life with me."

"I can't. We can't—" Hadley said as she looked away. The last few colours were starting to fade into a completely violet sky.

The tears ran down her face; she didn't want to control her emotions anymore, she wanted him to see how much this decision had hurt her. She didn't even blink them away; she just let the warm drops run down her face and fall onto her lap. She looked at him through watery eyes.

They sat in silence for a while, just staring at each other. Pax ran the tips of his fingers slowly up and down the side of her bare arms. "Please don't do this." He pulled Hadley into him, both their foreheads resting on each other's shoulder. They were a tangle of arms and bodies.

Without thinking he started to unbutton her shirt. She watched him do it, but just let it happen. He had a casual way about him but she always felt the electricity between them. Her breathing quickened as she felt her pulse throb through her chest. He slid his hand across her body, pulling her shirt off and unclipping her bra.

Hadley pulled hard at the bottom of Pax's shirt and brought it over his head. She could feel how hard he was through his pants as she reached down and unzipped his jeans.

She pulled herself close to him, feeling his hard muscles against her, his strong arms around her waist. She was becoming desperate

"I need you right now," she whispered.

They separated momentarily and took off the rest of their clothes. He sat back down and she swung her leg over him and with one motion he was inside of her. She moved up and down quickly, arching her back under the apple trees. They shared moments of ecstasy, both breathing harder and harder.

He lifted her up and quickly changed position. He laid her onto the back seat of the car and kissed her gently and passionately. He paused and looked down at her, her hair falling across the leather seats as she bit her bottom lip.

"Let's make this last," Pax whispered, kissing her neck. Hadley gently smiled as she ran her nails across his back.

He made slow, smooth deliberate movements. She bit her lower lip feeling the sensations starting to build in her body.

"Let go," Hadley whispered.

They both came together in a moment of bliss. He laid there, still inside of her, both of them trembling. He pulled back slightly and they lay in the seat with their feet dangling outside of the car. Pax pulled a blanket from the floor and wrapped it around them, pulling Hadley into his chest. He didn't want the moment to end; he was dreading morning.

Finally, when the moon was starting to go down, they got dressed. Then they drove back into their small seaside town. They both looked at the quiet buildings that hadn't woken up yet. Hadley looked at the small bakery where she had spent her time after school working before heading to the ocean for sunset.

Pax didn't even look at Hadley as he drove her home. He pulled up to the house, silently parking in the driveway then he got out of the car determinedly. He quickly opened Hadley's door and let her out, grabbing her hand to help.

Pax intertwined his fingers with hers beside the car. His jaw was clenched as he tried not to cry, to let his emotions run away on him. Hadley looked up at him.

"Do you want to come in? My grandpa's not home," she suggested. But he took a step back and just shook his head, looking at his shoes.

"No Hadley. This is the end," he said sternly, before he wrapped his hand around the back of her neck and kissed her passionately. The heat between them in the early morning light was invigorating and intense. She pulled away breathless.

"I love you," he said, practically to his feet.

Hadley placed her hand gently on his cheek. "Good luck at West Point. You're going to be the best doctor they've ever seen."

"I know," he laughed. For the first time in days he let his sarcastic playful personality out. He had been too scared that it would cause everything to break if he hadn't taken it seriously. Only now did he realize that everything was already broken. He continued. "Good luck at Harvard, you're always the smartest person in the room, and hopefully someone else is a little bit smarter than you there. Give you some competition, Had."

Hadley smiled a true genuine smile. "Doubt it Pax."

"I guess this is goodbye. I'll see you around I'm sure." Pax gave her a hug.

Hadley walked to her front door as Pax got back in his car. Neither of them looked back. They were off to bigger and better things, on their own.

They were already strangers.

# Chapter Six

2584

Hadley woke up in the darkness and looked over at Vanya and Pax who were breathing in sync with each other. They seemed to fit so closely together, despite only knowing each other for what she assumed was a couple of days.

Quietly Hadley pushed her feet onto the ground. Every piece of her dream felt real. The way she had felt about Pax felt real. The pain she felt leaving him, it was all real. Realistically, she knew it wasn't.

She walked out of the bedding area, and came to a turn that led her towards what must have once upon a time been the main entrance to the store. Huge door frames remained, even though the glass didn't.

The small white tiles were tinged yellow and cracking across the floor. A chandelier laid shattered into a million pieces. Everything was covered in dark brown paint chips that were peeling off the walls and ceiling. Pillars surrounded the entrance had kept their glassy smooth marble appearance. Hadley listened closely and could hear the pitter-patter of the rain starting outside.

She walked towards the door frames and leaned against one, letting her head sag to the side. She was still exhausted but the restlessness and intrigue had taken precedent and she needed more information. She was thirsty for it.

She caught a glimpse of herself in the puddle that was forming in front of her. The moonlight lit her face, giving her a ghostly tone. It was the first time she had seen herself and she winced when she did. There was a gash on her head that was large and bruised. She ran her hand across it and was relieved that it wasn't deep.

She had another cut down one of her cheeks. Her light hair was matted and covered in dust and blood. Squinting to see, she noticed one of her eyes was bloodshot. The veins were thick and the red was vivid against the blue and white with the black center misshapen.

She felt she looked much older than twenty-six.

Hadley heard something ahead of her and looked up struggling to see. The rain was coming down harder and harder and it was creating a fogginess that wafted through the street.

A stocky man walked down the sidewalk opposite her; he had an automatic machine gun in his hand, ready to fire. He hummed a soft harrowing tune as he walked, looking in all directions.

For a moment they locked eyes, but without thinking Hadley dove behind a pillar, frightened more than she ever had been. She caught his reflection in another. He was staring at the spot where she had just been, trying to figure out if he had actually seen someone or if it had been a figment of his imagination.

Hadley watched as he inched closer, shining a light from the end of his gun over the inside of the entrance. She held her breath, only able to hear the falling rain, and she watched as his reflection got closer and closer.

She waited for him to see her, hoping he wouldn't.

Then he stopped looking towards the pillar, and he saw her outline.

"Hey there! UN! Come out with your hands up," he shouted.

Hadley didn't have to think, she just ran. She ran towards the mattresses, weaving in and out of the aisles.

"GET UP!" she squealed hoping that Pax and Vanya would hear her. They were just standing up as she got to them.

They saw her frenzied look and the man running behind her and sprinted towards the Serva. Hadley followed, knocking over shelves as she went. They ran past the Serva and out onto the flooded street, twisting and turning through the streets until they ran into another building.

Pax looked around and decided to run up the stairwell; four floors up they paused and sat on the ground, waiting. But no footsteps came. Hadley peaked out of the broken window and didn't see anyone below on the street. Half the building was gone and two feet over it was a freefall onto the pavement below.

"Why—" Pax started to say loudly giving Hadley a disapproving look.

"There was a man carrying a gun walking around outside. When he saw me, well he looked like he was going to shoot," Hadley whispered urgently.

"Let's go see him, maybe he knows what's going on," Vanya whispered.

"I don't think we want to do that," she whispered, shaking her head. Her stomach gave a lurch.

"Why not?" Pax asked.

"I get this feeling he isn't the type to help us."

Paxton nodded; he was starting to understand her fear. "We will wait for the coast to be clear then continue on; at least we know we aren't the only ones out here."

"We don't know if they are good people though."

"In the apocalypse is anyone?"

Vanya twitched. "Why do you think it's the apocalypse?"

"Vanya, have you looked around?" Hadley asked, an air of discontent straining through her voice.

"I know but…" Tears welled up in Vanya's eyes and she looked away shaking.

"Had, we have to stay united…" Pax warned.

Hadley walked towards the other side of the building alone. Pax put his hand comfortingly onto Vanya's shoulder as she sobbed. Hadley shook her head as she watched the rain pile down. A while later Pax walked over.

"It doesn't help to be like that to her Hadley."

"I know, I mean I don't even know why I said that, I... It's just... I don't even know." Hadley was flustered.

"We're all on edge, so it's fine," Pax said as though his opinion was the most important.

Hadley grimaced at him but bit her tongue.

"Let's all get a few more hours of sleep."

In the morning, they woke up with the sun. Hadley opened her eyes and felt Pax's arm around her. She lifted her head off his shoulder and wiggled to relieve her total body stiffness while pushing her heels forward. She felt the stretch through the back of her legs. She reached towards the sky and felt the cracks run down her spine. She tilted her head casually to one side and the crack rang through to her ears. Sleeping sitting up was no fun.

She took a look at their surroundings in the daylight, realizing how differently it all looked in the morning sun. The rain had stopped and as Hadley looked out into the street she saw the puddles start to dry. The windows were long blown out of the building. The floor they were on looked as though it had been partially vacated before it was blown to bits.

Hadley noticed a broken bottle close to her and a chainsaw lying cracked in two. The walls were surprisingly intact but many of the support beams were crumbled in many places. Had looked up and saw pieces of the roof falling down. *So much for stability.* She sighed having no ideas on what to do next.

"Hey—thirsty—water—" Hadley said when she saw Pax's eyes open. Her lips were cracking again and she could feel the sawdust coating the back of her throat.

Pax also looked dehydrated as he dug into his bag and threw her a water patch. Hadley slid it under her tongue and felt the slow release.

"I know. Me too," Pax said as he also popped one in his mouth, scooting his arm out from around her. Vanya had rolled over and was lying in the fetal position on the floor, her chest moving up and down in a peaceful manner.

It was strange, she had known him for less than a day and suddenly they were relying on each other for survival. Hadley suddenly felt a pang of guilt for how she had talked to both of them. She got up and looked out the window cautiously. There was no one in sight, just the destruction they had seen the day before.

"We should keep moving," Hadley said to Pax, who was putting another nutrition on his arm.

Pax nodded. "When Vanya wakes up Hadley, there isn't a rush. We're probably going towards nothing."

"Pessimistic much?"

"Coming from the queen of happiness and good decisions?"

"Point taken." Hadley scrunched up her nose, unable to think of anything else to say.

After a long uncomfortable silence Pax said, "Did we know each other before this?"

Hadley's eyes widened, "I had the same thought…"

"Weird isn't it? Not knowing anything about our lives."

"Are you having dreams?" Hadley whispered, knowing she sounded crazy.

"Everyone dreams, Hadley, it's a physiological process, especially after trauma."

She looked at him, unimpressed, until she saw he was joking. A smirk ran over his face, and he again felt oddly familiar.

"But yes and flashbacks?"

"I thought I was the only one…"

"The only one?" Vanya said waking up. A sadness spreading across her face as she once again realized she had interrupted a moment between Hadley and Pax.

"Flashbacks," Pax said simply.

Vanya smiled, relieved. "Oh right."

Pax handed Vanya a couple patches and they got up. They made their way back out onto the street. There was a long amount of nothing where they walked through more rubble and destruction. No sign of any other human.

The rain from the night before evaporated in the hot morning sun, typical of a concrete jungle. Before long they were sweltering in the heat. Their water patches were going faster than they would have like. Hadley kept looking under anything for a sign of life.

Then they saw it: a fountain, completely disjoined from everything else around it. It was completely intact and cool blue water ran through it. All around it was destruction and piles of exploded concrete.

The fountain was carved into the shape of a man and woman beneath a tree. They had their hands interlocked. The woman held her hand like a gun against her mouth. Her lips pressed against the base of her index and middle finger. Her thumb was pressed against her temple. The man's hand was clenched in a fist over his heart. There was plate beneath it that read "In the future we entrust protection of the earth. 2095." Underneath someone had written "We will not be silenced; they will not take our minds. We promised only peaceful revolution. But it's us against them." Hadley thought this inscription was odd, it must have had some significance but she couldn't figure it out and to make matters worse the man and the woman looked vaguely familiar.

The water looked clear as day. The sunlight danced on its ripples. They walked up to it mesmerized. Hadley knelt beside it and took a scoop in her hand. It smelt like fresh water. She brought it up to her lips and sipped. She felt the cool water run down her throat.

"How do you know it's safe?" Vanya hissed.

"We don't," Pax said with a pretentious shrug.

Paxton sat down beside Hadley and took a drink. They spent a few moments taking in as much water as they could. Vanya eventually gave up her fight and starting drinking too.

Then there was a crash behind him and a voice, "We finally found you three."

Hadley turned her head slowly, still hunching over the fountain and saw a figure standing there.

He smiled, holding his gun, "Good afternoon Dr. Evans. Everyone will be so glad we found you."

# Chapter Seven

The man was tall and thin. His glasses were slightly askew on his face and he had a sympathetic smile on his face. His green eyes blazed and he took a step forward.

Hadley jumped to her feet, followed by Pax and Vanya who slowly retreating backwards looking for an escape route. The men and women with guns started pouring into the square around them like ants retreating to their nest.

The three of them stopped looking around.

"Hadley there is no reason for you to be scared of us," the man said meekly, re-holstering his gun and putting his hands up in front of his chest. He meant it as a sign of cooperation but with the 50 or so other guns pointed directly at them they couldn't take it that way.

She stared at him, not uttering a word, her eyes searching while her mind played games. A familiar tingle shot up her back and through her chest and her heart quickened. *Adrenaline*, she thought.

"Captain, just grab them!" another man said, the same man Hadley had run from the day prior, as he turned the corner beside the man. Hadley caught the new man's eye and he gave her a scowl.

"Shut up Jeremiah, always rash." The captain shook his head and waved a dismissive hand towards Jeremiah who took a step backwards.

Hadley glanced at Pax who had puffed out his chest defensively. Vanya was shaking in fear her hands raised just above her hips, pleading silently for no one to hurt her. The captain took a step forward. Paxton defensively stepped in front of both women. Hadley shook her head, outraged. She side stepped beside Pax, while Vanya quivered behind them.

"Don't be afraid of me," the captain said. He raised his hands even higher to symbolize he really meant peace. He looked straight into Hadley's eyes as though he could see into the depth of her soul. Hadley glared back, careful not to break the eye contact they had established.

"Why shouldn't we be?" Pax replied. He glanced from Hadley to the captain.

The captain crinkled his nose and pressed his lips into a thin line, obviously debating what he should say. He countered smoothly, "I am not here to hurt you. We have been looking everywhere for the two of you. I know you don't know who I am, but we will do everything we can to help you remember."

Hadley narrowed her eyes to signify that she meant business. "How do we know that's true?" she retorted with more coldness than she meant to.

"I guess you don't," the captain shrugged. He still didn't look away from Hadley, barely even noticing anyone else was there. It was exhausting holding someone's eye contact for this long, but Hadley wasn't going to be the first to look away. She was bound and determined.

Out of nowhere something changed and his gaze became unsettling. He knew something they didn't. Hadley opened her mouth and started to say something when she felt hands around her. They were strong and rough, and held she couldn't break free.

Hadley started to thrash around, trying to loosen the solid grip she was held in. She looked to her side and saw two large men, well over six feet and triple her size holding her. She tried to wriggle but it didn't work.

Vanya had subdued to the man holding her and was standing completely still as her hands were cuffed behind her and a bag was thrown over her head. Hadley watched and felt her hands get clammy.

Pax was doing a good job fighting off his would-be captors. He was standing in the middle of a circle of large men who were ready to pounce. Two already lay on the ground writhing in pain.

A man jumped towards Pax, swinging his arms and smoothly Pax took out his legs. As he did two others jumped in but Pax was too fast, his fists hitting them hard as he jumped in the air sending them both sideways. Pax was winning and the unconscious count was pilling. Then a small woman stepped out from behind a big man. She held a small metal tube and aimed it at Pax. Five small metal objects, the size and shape of tacks, flew at Pax. They adhered to his skin and clothing, then erupted in a flash of blue light.

Pax ended up twitching on the ground. They rolled him over and tied him up, pulling a bag over his head.

Hadley wanted to scream as she watched Pax's defeat but she knew she had to continue fighting. Jeremiah came over and grabbed a hold of her arms, dismissing the other two. They both looked at him obviously puzzled but they just shrugged and walked away. Hadley didn't understand why he would take over from two noticeably bigger men. He was muscular and strong, but he was a couple inches shorter than her.

Jeremiah pulled her arms together, causing a pop in her shoulder. "You're stubborn Hadley."

"Wouldn't you be?" Hadley spat back.

"I was, but calm down. We're here to help."

Hadley continued to fight against him. She got a good kick into his shin but he didn't even flinch on his grip. A man came by and pulled a bag over her head but Jeremiah just kept a firm grip and forgot to hand cuff her. The bag made her feel claustrophobic and sick as the memory of being trapped under the rubble resurged. She tried to suppress it but her stomach did flip flops and she could feel the vomit try to make its way up her throat.

Hadley struggled as they walked; unable to see, she tripped over her feet constantly. She thought that if she was being dragged to her death there was no way she would go quietly. So she became dead weight and tried to make it hard for Jeremiah. However, he was stronger and didn't notice; he just dragged her shins across the ground.

Hadley kicked and squirmed and felt another set of hands on one of her arms. Two of them dragged her along, hardly noticing her effort to break free. They struggled to hold onto her limbs sometimes but never let go.

Finally, she got one arm free and without hesitation raised her elbow to her eye level and brought it back hard behind her. There was a sickening crunch at her shoulder level as her elbow made contact with something.

Both sets of hands momentarily let go and she removed the bag from her face. She started to run, avoiding the other soldiers that were trying to grab her. Someone shot a metal cylinder at her and she watched as the tacks exploded over her shoulder against a wall. With one glance back Hadley saw she had broken Jeremiah's nose. He clutched at it, blood drenching his shirt. He started to run after her, one hand on his face.

She looked away and ran, faster than she ever had before. The muscles in her legs burned as they propelled her forward. She didn't even pause to look back, hearing the echoes of footsteps near behind her. She swerved and ran down a narrow back alley.

The streets were cobblestones and the whole alley was red brick buildings, or at least what was left of them. The bricks lay in heaps on the sides of the street. The one at the end still had windows, remarkably. They were in the older part of the city, headed towards the suburbs. Hadley glanced around as she continued bolting down the street. She ran past a door and slowed for a moment as she saw the same symbol she had at the Serva. This time it was modified though; instead of just the symbol right under the top of the circle was a number four and a Roman numeral one. Three letters were stamped above the symbol RFE. A fleeting memory returned as she ran, but as fast as it had come it was gone and she was running past the symbol.

Hadley turned for another glance to see if her momentary slowing had caused her to lose the distance she had gained. Before she could turn her head all the way backwards the air was forced from her lungs.

"You really don't have to be scared," she heard the captain whisper in her ear as they tumbled forward. She glanced backwards as they both fell forward. His hands were wrapped tightly around her sides. Soon enough his entire weight was on top of her. She just caught a glimpse of Jeremiah whose nose she had broken breathing heavily to the side watching them fall.

Both the captain and Hadley rolled down the cobbled street. Hadley felt her arm twist in an odd direction and the crack rang through her ears. Her entire side was scraped brutally by the stone and she was left lying on the ground. The air was pushed out of her lungs as she felt a body on her back. Moving her eyes backwards, she saw the captain kneeling beside her with a hand on the back of her neck and his knee between her shoulder blades.

"Jeremiah how in hell did you let her get away," the captain grunted.

"She broke my nose sir," Jeremiah said sheepishly, staring daggers at Hadley.

Hadley kept squirming through the pain. The captain leaned forward and hissed into her ear, "Can you stop running? You can't get away, and even though you don't know it, you don't want to."

"Fuck you!" she yelled.

Jeremiah was shaking with rage as he held her arms back and tied them tightly together. He tied them tighter than he needed to, letting his anger take over. Then he tied her legs in two places so there was no way she could run.

The captain threw a bag over her head. In one swift movement he threw her over his shoulder and started to walk.

"Where are you taking us?"

"Shut the fuck up. You've made this day difficult enough Hadley. You'll see soon enough."

Hadley knew she had made a mistake in running but it was her only choice and she wasn't going to feel bad about it.

# Chapter Eight

Hadley was thrown to the ground in a hurried frenzy. Since her hands were tied behind her back, her shoulder and cheek broke her fall as she landed face first on her side. She landed on the same side as her road rash and felt the pain radiate through her body. Everything was still dark since the bag was still over her head.

She struggled against her restraints but it was no use. The bag was blocking everything from her vision. She squirmed on the ground like a worm. Finally, she brought herself into a seated position. Everything was quiet.

Unexpectedly, she felt the bag being pulled off of her head then she realized someone was in the room with her. She looked up and saw him, with the same knowing look in his eyes. She stared at him. His captivating green eyes were ablaze.

"Fuck you," Hadley whispered as she pursed her lips.

"No thanks, not today," he played.

The colour rushed to Hadley's cheeks and she bit her lip. His tone had completely changed since coming into this room. He no longer wore the military garment of the field instead his thin shirt was buttoned unevenly. His glasses still sat crookedly on his nose.

"Hadley, I'm Captain Neil Kane. But call me Kane, you always have," he said as a matter of fact as he bent to a one knee kneel in front of her. His auburn hair was longer on the top and short on the sides. He had it slicked to one side.

Hadley studied him, trying to figure out who he was. His cheekbones were high and his nose was long. He was attractive, and dangerous but had a scholarly look about him. Kane wasn't much older than Hadley and he definitely wasn't what you would expect of an army captain. He was strong looking but he was, hands down, a scientist.

"How do you know my name? How do you know me?" she asked timidly. She heard the edge in her voice as her speech heightened near the end of the sentence. She hadn't wanted to show fear or dismay, but both had come out in her voice. She cocked her head to the side and waited for his response. Just as before, they continued with strong eye contact, a pull growing between them.

"I know all about you," he replied softly as his eyebrows flicked upwards.

"Yet, I know nothing about you." Hadley felt the anger growing inside her and struggled against her restraints. The muscles in her arms started to cramp.

Kane stood up and pulled a small pocket knife from his trousers and walked around behind her. He cut off the restraints holding her arms. Then he knelt back with her and cut her legs loose.

Hadley pulled her arms forward and rubbed her wrists gently. Her one shoulder was completely dislocated. Kane looked at it and sighed. He flexed his jaw bone as he figured out what to say next.

"Give me a second to explain. You do know me; you just can't remember," he said softly, so much so it took her off guard. She didn't say anything; instead she just studied him waiting for him to say more.

"What do you know? Or think you know?" he asked, trying to keep his voice steady.

"I don't know what I know. The last thing I remember was explosion after explosion. I know what I was studying at school. I remember school but only bits and pieces. I think I know everything before... or maybe nothing before," Hadley blabbed. It all came out in a meaningless blur that she hadn't even thought about.

Saying it out loud was scary, as if the words she was saying were out of someone else's mouth. *How could the last few years be such an empty blur?* she thought to herself, finally feeling the fear.

Kane purposely put his hand on her good shoulder. He leaned closer, and she felt the heat of his hand radiate through her. He gave her a reassuring nod and asked sympathetically, "Do you know about the UN's SPaDI program?"

In the back of her mind, a light switched on but it was too far to get to. She knew the name and the rest was on the tip of her tongue, but she couldn't make sense of it. She didn't like the uneasy feeling that she was getting, and unable to formulate words she just shook her head no.

Kane nodded supportively. He squeezed her shoulder a couple of times. "Hadley, you were the first person on the exclusive team. I recruited you myself in your third year of university. The same year a prominent group of academics and experts at the UN decided that if the world was going to end that we wanted a fighting chance to restart it, thus SPaDI. It's the UN's Scientific, Political and Defensive Initiative."

"Why though?" Hadley asked.

"It's a long story, and I'll tell you everything over time, which I know is a frustrating answer," he stated dryly before he decided to continue. "When we gave up that climate change was going to destroy everything well we started to recruit a group of the most intelligent students across the globe we could find in various fields. Then the planet would have a chance. A small one, but a chance. What we didn't expect is that the effects of climate change would lead to biological warfare that would turn into nuclear warfare and a full-fledged global crisis."

Hadley just looked at him, unable to form words.

"We should have known. We should have, really. The resources were becoming scarce. Anyways, now we've been trying to find the last living members of the initiative. Luckily you were the last living pinger."

Hadley felt herself start to shake uncontrollably. She was dehydrated, cold, hungry and bleeding. Those things, along with being confused, made her feel like she was going to throw up again. She was swaying back and forth.

"So what's left?" she choked out, scared of the answer.

"There are twenty-four students from the initiative left. There are less than a few million people alive and every major governing body except the United Nations has fallen. Eighty-seven percent of the world is uninhabitable. Hadley, we are the resurgence."

His eyes met hers. She was absolutely terrified.

"What year is it?" she asked slowly, feeling her brain becoming foggy and tired.

"2584."

Right. She knew she should have known that. She raised an eyebrow slightly before falling to the side, her eyes rolling back into her head.

# Chapter Nine

2106

"150, 160, 170…." Hadley's watch counted through her implanted earbuds. "Target heart rate reached."

Hadley slowed her pace to a light jog, twisting around the corner of the forested dirt path she was running on with Kila, her Labrador whose tail wagged in the wind. Hadley looked around and enjoyed the peace that surrounded her. She had taken the week off of work with SPaDI to rent a cabin in the woods and enjoy some time away from the hustle and bustle of city life. Spending the first bunch of years of her life with her grandfather in the middle of the desert meant she had learned to love the outdoors.

The sun was beating down through the bright green leaves as the hot summer day came to an end. A drip of sweat ran down Hadley's brow and into her eye. She stopped to wipe her forehead, lifting up her already soaked shirt to do so.

"It's hot today huh Kila?" Hadley said bending down. She took a small water bottle out of her running belt and coaxed Kila over, who immediately opened her mouth. Hadley squirted the water into her mouth.

Kila walked to sniff a tree, her tongue hanging out of her mouth. Hadley watched as she bent her head forward. She stretched out a back leg as she did so and her tail wagged even more so. Then, she walked around the tree and squatted to pee on it.

Then Kila came back to Hadley's feet. Hadley balanced on her toes to pet Kila's neck. Kila rolled on her back and expectantly looked up for a tummy rub.

Hadley stood up with one more pat on Kila's head and began to walk. There was a crunch behind her. She turned an ear bud out to listen and vaguely heard the sound of a gun's safety turn off.

"Hadley!" someone shouted behind her. She didn't even turn around to see who had called her name, because she knew who it was. Instead she just rolled her eyes and started to run, ducking into the thick forest, off of the trail. Kila could barely keep up to Hadley until she started to really run, jumping over logs.

Hadley ran through the trees, winding through them like an obstacle course, praying not to catch her shoelace on the ground and end up on her face. She glanced back to make sure Kila was still with her and couldn't help but smile seeing she was right on her heels even though they were running away from someone. Kila had no idea why they were running so fast.

They both jumped over a tree log and scampered down the edge of a ravine. The water was shallow and flowed slowly through the woods. Hadley looked around and saw a hollowed area of moss and branches; she dove into it completely out of breath. *Why am I always running from something?* she thought shaking her head to herself.

Kila started to lick the sweat from Hadley's bare leg.

"Hadley! Come out! We've been trying to get a hold of you!" The voices were closer than she would have liked. Hadley held her breath and pulled Kila closer to her. She could hear the footsteps getting closer; she knew she would be found soon.

Then her phone started to ring in her ear. "Paxton calling," her watch said. Hadley clicked a button to ignore it.

The footsteps kept coming her way.

"Had, stop ignoring my calls!" the person yelled.

"Pax?" Hadley said instinctively, immediately covering her mouth with her hand.

The footsteps came around in front of her and she had nowhere to go. There in the blazing sunlight stood Pax and Kane.

"Oh, well hello," Hadley said smoothly.

Kane shook his head despairingly. "Why do you always run?"

"Why are you here, Kane? You should have sent Pax alone, or really anyone else."

Pax gave her a look. "You didn't answer his question Hadley."

"You know how it's been this month, since the Odyssey TNB mission went down. How was I supposed to know that you weren't just another group of paparazzi?"

"You didn't even look Had," Pax said with a smirk.

Hadley tried to hold her tongue, but failed. "Oh come on, my life has been hell. Give me a break."

"We know, but Hemmer needs you in the lab, it's urgent."

"Fuck Hemmer!"

Pax held out a hand to help her up. Hadley begrudgingly grabbed it and hoisted herself to her feet. Hadley looked at them both staring at her awkwardly. "I'm not going back to the lab yet; we can video call him from the cabin. He can take it or leave it."

Kane grumbled but didn't say anything; Hadley shot him a look before saying, "I still hate you." A wave of anger rushed over her. The colour drained from Kane's face as he fiddled with his hands and the small metal band that wrapped around his finger on his left hand.

"I know," Kane said miserably.

They walked back to the cabin, in silence for the following hour. Inside, Hadley went to the bathroom. She showered off, taking her time.

"Hadley, it's been 20 minutes, Hemmer is getting impatient."

Hadley turned off the shower and grabbed a towel, starting to dry her hair.

"Let him wait."

"You're impossible," Pax laughed from the other side of the door.

"Pax, you've known that for years," Hadley joked, smiling to herself.

She grabbed a thin dress off the hanger, which was almost transparent and worked perfectly with her tanned skin tone. She pulled it on and walked out into the humid, almost ancient cabin. The wood that built it was decaying and it was built into the trees.

Pax and Kane stared.

"Where's the holo?"

"All set up for you."

Hadley grabbed the sensors and stuck them to either side of her head. She pressed call on the small box sitting on the counter and was transported into Hemmer's office. She was slightly opaque and went to sit in the chair in front of him.

"Hemmer, you wanted to see me," she stated plainly.

Hemmer looked up from his computer and smiled. "Thanks for taking the time Hadley, I know you're on vacation."

"This couldn't wait until I was back?"

"Maybe it could, but I was looking at the initial findings of your research before you left and was too excited to wait."

"It's not finished yet Hemmer, and it might not be."

"It would be a revolution though Hadley, change the world, for the better."

Hadley scowled at him. "That's the plan."

Hemmer spun a rock on his desk that acted as decoration. "Can I have your passcode to see the rest?"

"No Hemmer, not now. Maybe when it's done."

"Maybe?" Hemmer glared at her.

"Yes, maybe. If I think it's worth it to you."

Hemmer stood up and leaned forward. "That's not your call Hadley! Maybe you don't understand how this works, but I have every right to every piece of research that happens in this facility."

Hadley just looked at him indifferently. "Hemmer, I'm not my mother. I'm not going to let you do what you did to her to me."

"I told you, you don't have a choice."

"We'll see Hemmer," Hadley said, smiling.

Hemmer's blood was boiling, Hadley could see it, but he took a deep breath and said, "We will revisit this as your research progressed; until then I look forward to reading your lab reports."

"Thank you Hemmer," Hadley said as she ended the call with a press of a button on her head.

Back in the cabin, Hadley was fuming, she immediately ran at Kane, viciously like an animal. He took a step back and Pax grabbed her around the waist.

"How dare you! After everything, you gave him my research specs?"

"It's my job."

"Fuck you Kane!"

Pax stepped between them and looked Hadley in the eyes. "Had, you know he had no choice."

"But after what happened with my parents? With my mom? How dare he!"

Pax nodded towards Hadley and looked back at Kane who was staring sheepishly at his shoes. "I think you better go man." Pax shrugged.

Kane nodded and left, feeling worse than he already did. Paxton held Hadley in his arms as she cried.

# Chapter Ten

The lights were bright; she could feel the harsh warm light through her closed eyelids and could still feel the visceral pain from the memory. She blinked them open and all she saw was the large beams of light above her head, and instinctively closed her eyes.

After a moment she reopened them. She turned her head from side to side and saw she was in a perfectly square white room, with grey faded tiles on the ground. She tried to sit up but her arms, legs and torso were strapped down to a cold metal bed.

A door opened somewhere above her head and she craned her neck back to see what was happening but she couldn't get her head back far enough.

"Who's there?" she coughed, suddenly realizing how dry her throat was.

"Hello, Hadley," a sickeningly sweet woman's voice said.

Hadley thrashed around trying to get up. The woman suddenly appeared above her. She was older and friendly looking with yellowing teeth which she had set into a forced smile.

She looked at Hadley and said in her high pitched voice, "Lay still and this will be over soon enough."

"Who are you?"

"Dr. Emily; I am in charge of pinger health and need to do an initial assessment on you, since it's been so long." She smiled more.

Dr. Emily walked to the side of the room and pressed a series of buttons in a panel on the wall and as she did so a large machine descended from the ceiling. It was large and rectangular, exactly the same size as the bed Hadley was laying on, who watched amazed.

The machine descended and clicked into place around Hadley, encasing her in a steel box. Hadley's palms started to sweat and she tried desperately to wipe them on her clothing.

Then the lights started, and Hadley watched amazed as an image of her body appeared before her. She didn't feel anything as small lights scanned her whole body. She watched as the red lights flashed back and forth over her, scanning every minute detail. It was terrifying to see the inside of her body appear in full three dimensions in front of her, but she couldn't help but grow more amazed.

Hadley saw a blue circle in the middle of her forearm. Her pinger, she assumed. There were red circles around all the places she was bruised. She saw black lines across her ribs and nose and assumed they must be broken.

The majority of her bones appeared in a steel grey with a few scattered in a soft pink. She looked at her stomach and lower abdomen, which appeared in a dull purple, significantly distinct from everything else.

The metal box lifted itself off of Hadley and the 3D image of her body projected into the center of the room. The restraints unclipped themselves and Hadley pushed herself to sitting, continuing to study her body, which was standing before her.

"Hmmm," Dr. Emily exhaled out loud, a puzzled look spreading through her forehead as she walked around the scan.

Hadley raised an eyebrow, "What is it?"

Dr. Emily walked over to one part of the scan and put her hand over it. "You haven't had all your bones replaced with titanium. It seems strange they would leave a few."

"Titanium?"

"Yes, over the years we have integrated as many technologies as we can to make you untouchable… immortal if you will, or as close to it as we can get," she said as a matter of fact, she tilted her head to the side staring, "and this is strange."

"What is?" Hadley fidgeted becoming uncomfortable.

"I haven't seen this in a very long time, not since the Family First Act of 2066."

A brief glimmer of a memory flashed across Hadley's mind. The name of the act made her think of her parents, always hunched over a computer typing furiously, making notes. She gave her head a shake.

"Oh well, must be nothing, I'll send it to the lab for further analyses along with your blood samples."

"So we're done here?" Hadley exclaimed almost too excitedly.

Dr. Emily smiled softly. "Sadly not, just a couple more things."

A tray emerged from the wall on a set of wheels; it roved its way towards Hadley and stopped by her left arm. Dr. Emily quickly grabbed an alcohol swab and rubbed it furiously against Hadley's arm.

"You're right handed correct?" Dr. Emily asked as she grabbed a large syringe filled with a cloudy grey liquid.

"I think so?"

"Good because this one causes tenderness in the arm in which it's administered." Dr. Emily shrugged as she dug the needle into Hadley's arm and started slowly pressing the syringe.

Hadley winced trying not to move. "What is it?"

"A healer for your broken bones and other injuries also will probably make you feel drowsy for the rest of the night."

Hadley felt the warmth crawl through her arm and into her chest. It made her start coughing uncontrollably.

She waited as it ran through her whole body as though she could feel its pathways through her blood. The holographic image started to change and she watched as everything became a shade of pale green. The black lines on her ribs and nose started to fade. It made her feel numb and helpless.

Dr. Emily pulled out the needle and placed it on the table; Hadley thought it was over. Then, without warning, the doctor grabbed what looked like a gun off the table and shoved it against her neck. She heard a click and instantly the pain ran down her side.

"I'm sorry," Dr. Emily cooed with a mischievous grin. "I don't like to warn people about that one, it never gets better, and you just have to bear it."

Hadley clenched her jaw and waited, breathing slowly through her nose.

Dr. Emily grabbed the last injector off the table. It looked like an epi-pen. She flipped it over between her fingers grinning. She popped off the cap and came back towards Hadley, who struggled to back away; her limbs were so weak she could barely move.

"What the hell is that one?"

Dr. Emily just fixed a smile on her face as she raised the injector slightly above her shoulder and brought it down with all the force she could muster into Hadley's chest.

"Insurance," she said simply.

The pain seared through Hadley's whole body and everything went dark but not before she saw Dr. Emily chuckling and the alarm sound on her holographic body image.

# Chapter Eleven

2083

Hadley was wringing her hands together as she looked around the library filled with women in cocktail dresses and men in suits. She felt out of place between the books and dark mahogany, where before she had always found sanctuary. She had been asked to come to this mixer by Kane and had begged for Anna to be allowed to come too. She didn't like going places with Kane it made her feel uncomfortable even though she hadn't been his student for six months.

Now Anna was off flirting it up with some handsome man in a navy suit with a pink tie she had 'accidentally' bumped into as they had walked in the main door. Hadley rolled her eyes just thinking about it, but smiled knowing it was just Anna's personality. She remembered vividly her first day at Harvard, which happened to be the first day she met Anna.

She had breathed in the warm fall air, admiring all the seemingly ancient buildings, whose structure had withstood the hands of time. She had looked around and the excitement bubbled within her. She was finally where she had always dreamed, Harvard. She clasped the cold metal handle of an enormous suitcase that rested on the cobbled street.

Harvard currently was the top international school in the world. The 2070 referendum for consistent education, where education became a global economic resource formulated for success of the best meant it was harder and harder to get into the programs. Hadley was one of the few who had secured a spot for the next class.

She pulled out her holographic phone. It was the size of a coin and she opened in to reveal a holographic map. Hadley walked down the path pulling her suitcase along and got to the dorms. She walked in and a woman approached her. "Are you looking for a room miss?"

She had rainbow hair and was holding a holographic tablet.

"Hadley Evans."

She nodded and started to scroll with the touch of a finger, "Room 42B. Your roommate's name is Anna." She pressed a button and a small chip the size of a pin head popped out of the tablet. Hadley held out her hand for it but the woman grabbed her wrist. She placed the chip onto Hadley's wrist who watched as it absorbed into her skin, disappearing, attaching itself to her program.

"I didn't realize they were programmable now," Hadley cooed.

"New this year!" the woman exclaimed with a smile.

Hadley felt the smile spread across her face, unable to hide her excitement about the small things.

Everyone was implanted with a program at birth. They were small, and left a small bump under the persons less dominant wrist. Everything you needed was added and since they were made of semi organic material when a piece was useless it was absorbed and deleted. Microscopic threads wound their way through a person's entire body, so taking it out would lead to a painful death. That's what the government had planned. There were black-markets claiming to be able to do it, but no one was ever certain they worked.

Hadley remembered asking her grandpa what would happen if someone lost the arm in an accident if the person would still die. He just nodded his head slowly, and had to explain that they were meant for perfect human beings only. The government had decided that those who ended up crippled were a burden on society. It had only been 20 years since science had gone far enough to start altering the human body. People got their bones replaced with lightweight titanium and organs could be grown in a lab.

Hadley flexed her fingers, feeling the familiar warmth of adding to her program. "Thanks," she said with a nod and hurried down the hall. It was filled with people from every country imaginable. A pretty even mixture. Hadley passed one girl who looked vaguely familiar but she brushed that notion aside.

The stairs creaked as she made her way up to the fourth floor. The hardwood was worn and showed its age. Harvard had kept some of the original wood decor and they had worked tirelessly to protect it after wood was declared a protected and sparse resource.

She smiled down at her shoes. This was the happiest she had ever felt in her entire life. This was what she had been working for, for the entirety of her education. She finally opened the door onto the fourth floor. People were hustling around, but the noise was noticeably less than on the main floor. She found room 42 and heard the lock click as she brought her hand to the automatic latch. The automatic door swung open the perfect amount for her to bring her stuff through.

Hadley walked in and saw a girl sitting on her bed, four or so books sprawled out around her. Her hair was tied up in a messy bun on top of her head. Her glasses took up half her face and she was deep in conversation with herself.

'Hi," Hadley said gently as to not startle her. Unfortunately, she still jumped anyway.

"Hi!" she exclaimed jumping off the bed. She ran and took Hadley's hand, shaking it furiously. "I'm Anna and I'm from France."

"Hadley, Canada."

"I'm so excited to meet you. I've been dreaming about my roommate!"

"Me too." She could tell Anna and her were going to be best friends just by their co-loving of books and their excitement to be there.

"I'm in Neurobiology with a specialization on genetics and genetic infections."

Hadley rattled off her own major, "I'm double majoring in Climatology and Neurobiology with a focus on climatological impacts on human evolution."

"We are literally going to be best friends."

And from that moment they were.

Hadley smiled remembering it all, how much they had been through over the time since then. The heartbreak, the late night study sessions, the girl's nights out and the world slowly ending around them.

Hadley walked up the marble staircase. She looked around the entryway and marvelled at the pristine statues. One of them stood right beside the door and towered over the young adults making their way in.

She turned sharply to continue down the hall and almost ran into someone. She didn't look up instead she just looked at her shoes. "Sorry," she murmured apologetically before side stepping around them, trying to avoid making a scene or starting a conversation. She pulled down her too tight skirt.

"Hadley! Hey!" a friendly chipper voice said. Hadley let the words bounce around in her head. It was a voice she knew only too well and turned around in slow motion, lifting her head from her scuffed shoes.

"Paxton?" His name got choked in her throat.

He stood there beaming in his lieutenant uniform, medals hanging from his lapel.

"Hi, Babe." His eyes got wide immediately and he clenched his jaw.

Without thinking Hadley practically spat at him, "Don't call me that. I haven't seen or talked to you in almost a year!"

"Sorry. Force of habit." He flexed the muscles in his jaw.

She looked at her feet, the words caught in her throat. "I didn't mean to snap—"

He shook his head at her. "I think you made your point pretty clear. Same old Hadley."

"What's that supposed to mean?"

"I only came here tonight hoping to see you. I was invited and almost turned it down, but I had to see you. You haven't responded to any of my emails."

"Pax—" Hadley looked into his grey eyes, searching for a hidden motive that she couldn't find. "We said we were having a clean break."

"That's easier said than done. Especially when you're thrust into war. Thinking about you was what kept me going. I knew I needed to see you when I got back from my deployment," Pax said grabbing a hold of her elbow.

"What happened to your degree?" Hadley said taking a step back.

"Didn't you read my email?"

She sheepishly looked away to the chandelier hanging off the roof in the distance, remembering how she had set all his emails and contact to go straight to junk, "I must have missed that one."

"I finished my first 2 years in an accelerated program in four months before I was deployed for the last nine."

Hadley gaped at him, a smile spreading across her cheeks. "Show-off!"

"You could have done it."

Hadley shook her head. "No, I couldn't have. Here I thought I was the smart one."

Pax laughed, a real laugh for the first time in a long time.

Out of nowhere Hadley felt a hand on her shoulder and turned her head around, still laughing. Kane had a gloating smirk on his face behind her.

"Hadley, introduce me to your friend." It was a demand, not a request, though Hadley was sure Paxton thought he was friendly enough. She was the only one who could tell the small change in Kane's voice, especially when he was talking to her. She only hoped this wouldn't become a fight later.

"Professor Neil Kane, Paxton Avery," Hadley muttered.

Pax held out his hand, which Kane took, giving it a hard shake. Kane studied him for a moment as they let their hands fall back to their sides.

"Ah, you are our West Point Medical student. I've read all about you. You are impressive, maybe even more than Hadley here," Paxton just stared. Kane continued, "I'm on the invitation committee and head the scientific research."

"Nice to meet you," Pax said each word slowly trying to keep his voice level.

Kane slid his hand onto Hadley's lower back. He rubbed his palm up and down, making sure Paxton saw. Hadley clenched her hands into fists and dug her nails into her palms to avoid shuddering.

"Come sweetheart. There is someone I need you to meet." Kane put pressure onto Hadley's back and guided her forward.

Pax was bewildered. Hadley looked over her shoulder and gave him a shrug as she furrowed her brow.

"Hey! What was that?" Hadley said as she stopped and moved away from Kane.

"Babe, you were done talking to him." There was that word again, Babe—now she knew why it upset her so much. It was Pax's word for her.

"Says who?" she spat.

Kane raised an eyebrow. "Weren't you? Now come on."

Kane left it there. He had the last word. Hadley followed him grudgingly as they walked up to a man with grey hair and menacing eyes. A man who Hadley had seen before but she didn't know where.

"Hemmer. This is my prized student, Hadley Evans. She will make SPaDI great."

"Nice to meet you, sir." She held out her hand and Hemmer just looked at it.

"I hope that you are as amazing as Kane here says—" Hemmer looked her up and down. It was an instantaneous dislike, on both sides. Maybe it was Kane's hand on her back, or maybe it was the way he held himself. In the end, Hadley didn't like Hemmer and first impressions were everything.

# Chapter Twelve

"Have a great rest of your day, and just call 9911 on your program if you ever need an appointment for any medical issue," a woman in her early thirties smiled sweetly. Hadley's head was spinning as she walked forward out of the office. A woman was waiting for Hadley.

"I'm Commander Alice Kimberly," the young woman said as Hadley walked out of the office. She was noticeably taller than Hadley, which was amazing considering Hadley's anything but short stature. She was bigger too. Her shoulders were broad and her body straight with just a hint of curves. She was in terrific shape and Hadley was envious as she looked down at her average frame. *Too much time in the books*—Hadley thought and giggled to herself. The woman's blonde hair was pulled up into a high ponytail that swung back and forth while she walked.

"Hi, I'm…"

"You don't remember me Hadley but I know you. I'm doing Kane a favour by escorting you to your room, but I won't have anything to do with you after that."

Hadley was taken aback; she said the only thing she could think of: "All right."

Hadley followed Alice down the hall. She practically had to run after her as she walked with such power. They got to a door and Alice unlocked it; they were at another, smaller and homelier door, which Alice also unlocked. She held it open for Hadley to walk through.

"Kane doesn't want you meeting the other participants until after the meeting tomorrow. So for tonight, you'll find a fully stocked mini fridge and everything else you could ever need. Sleep tight."

"What..." Hadley tried to ask a question but the door slammed in her face. She heard the distinct click of the lock going into place.

*Great!* Hadley rolled her eyes, turned on the light switch and looked around. It was small room with a bed and dresser. There was couch and a small kitchenette inside. A door led to a bathroom. Hadley went to the fridge and opened it. She was thankful to see it was fully stocked with solid food, something she hadn't yet seen since awakening in the rubble.

She grabbed an apple and a water bottle and walked into the bathroom, excited to finally have real substantial food, to relieve the longing she felt in her mouth. Looking in the mirror she saw once again a reflection that she barely recognized. She needed to get the dust off and even more she needed to get the blood off, which had hardened across her body. She felt fine now and flexed her muscles, seeing if there was any residual pain, but there was just a tightness and exhaustion through her body. Nothing that a good night sleep wouldn't fix.

She turned on the shower and took a bite of the apple. She chewed and heard the loud crunching in her ears. She tried but couldn't bring herself to swallow; it was as though she was chewing cardboard. Looking around as she continued to move her jaw she opened the lid to the toilet and spat out the apple chunks. She flushed it, watching the floating pieces of apple disappear into oblivion. She threw the rest of the apple into the composter.

She opened the icy cold water bottle and took a long gulp. The water immediately came back up. She spat it out over the mirror and sink. Her throat was completely raw and apparently her stomach was in no state to take anything in. The nauseated feeling reared its evil head. Water droplets ran down the mirror and over the metal frame around it.

Feeling determined to make at least some of the water stay in her stomach, Hadley took another slow gulp. She felt the cold on her throat, soothing her dry throat as it ran down, cooling her core.

After a moment the mirror started to fog up from the shower. Hadley watched the steam settle over the mirror and sink. She slowly peeled off the layers of clothes that were stuck to her from the sweat, blood and dirt. Reaching out a hand she watched the water roll off her palm, in tiny droplets and eventually stepped into the bolting stream. The water ran red down her legs. She watched it flow over her and swirl in the bottom of the grey stone shower.

Hadley took the bar of soap off the ledge and started to scrub. First she scrubbed and scrubbed ignoring the pain, watching tiny gravel flecks fall from her arms, sides and legs where she had road rash.

She scrubbed until her whole body felt nothing and she dropped the bar of soap onto the ground and watched it bounce and spin until it stopped near the drain.

The water left a speckled pattern across her non-bruised skin. Suddenly her knees started to shake and she could feel the tears. She fell back against the side of the shower and let her knees give out so she could slide down the wall to sit on the ground.

She let herself cry with her head between her knees. She just watched her tears mix with the water that was flowing over her. It all ran clear, having washed away everything that had happened over the days before.

The water eventually ran cold.

Even as she shivered under the icy stream her body released emotion, her sobs turned into short gasps, from a pain hidden so deep within her soul that it was eating her up.

Unable to stand, she turned the shower off and crawled out. She grabbed a towel off the shelf and wrapped herself in it as she slowly drifted off on the floor. She left her bed perfectly made.

What seemed like moments to Hadley but was actually hours later, there was a heavy handed knock on the door.

Hadley opened her eyes, wiping the crust from the corners. She blinked in the morning light that flooded the room from the artificial window that shows a mountainous sunrise. She got to her feet, still shaking and went to the door. She pulled the towel tighter around herself before she casually opened it, surprised that it was unlocked. She looked up to see Kane.

He was standing with his back against a wall, and had an eyebrow raised. He carelessly flicked his eyes up and down Hadley. Judging, always judging.

Hadley raised her eyebrow at him and bit her lip feeling the red rush to her cheeks.

"Hi Dr. Kane," she breathed.

"Hadley, it's just Kane."

"Neil then?" she joked, before realizing that she might have overstepped. Her eyes got wide and she fidgeted uncomfortably.

"My mother was the only one who ever called me Neil," he stated playfully though with an edge that suggested he'd rather keep it that way.

Hadley tilted her head. "Well, Kane," she tested how the words felt on her tongue. "What do you want?"

"Oh, right!" he exclaimed as though the last few moments had completely baffled him. "SPaDI."

"What about it?"

"The meeting is in 15 minutes," Kane shrugged, "I came to escort you, and Vanya who is next door." Kane tilted his head to the left to suggest a direction.

"Ok."

"Get changed, I'll get Vanya."

Kane gave her a crooked smile and walked to the left. Hadley shut the door and looked around, trying to find clothes. She went to the dresser and opened it to find neat rows of perfectly folded grey clothing. She let out a subtle groan before picking up a flowing grey dress, which she pulled over hemp undergarments.

She went to the bathroom and looked in the mirror. She was surprised to see everything was completely healed.

She opened the vanity and grabbed a hair tie out which she used to twist her hair up into a high bun. With a shrug she went back to the door, beside which she found a row of shoes. She slipped her toes into a light white flat.

Kane was standing outside the door with Vanya in tow when Hadley emerged. Kane gave her the once over and started to walk without a word.

Vanya looked frightened out of her mind. Hadley didn't have the patience to deal with her at that moment and they all walked in silence.

The walls were flat and grey, with subtle blinking lights and control pads everywhere. The doors were steel and had small plaques denoting what they were. It was a sterile and uninviting environment.

They had a glance of a large open atrium where you could feel the natural light bleeding in but it was short lived before they headed down a ramp into the basement. The lights flickered an unnatural white and Kane led them into a large lecture theatre.

"This was part of a very old university," Kane said simply.

Looking around the wallpaper was peeling and the dusty red seat cushions had long needed replacement. There were hundreds of seats but only a few at the front were occupied. Dark wood adorned the room and the steps down creaked. A table was set at the front with coinets. The latest version of a coin tablet, which was the size of an old-fashioned coin but expanded into a genius supercomputer.

Hadley grabbed the one with her name on it and sat down in a seat beside Pax. He was already fiddling around on his coinet and was in his own little world. He didn't even look up until Vanya sat on the other side of him. He placed a hand gently on her forearm.

Kane sat down on the other side of Hadley, she turned to him. "A little more warning would have been nice. You know Alice could have told me when she locked me in the room last night," Hadley hissed stubbornly.

Kane looked at her and shrugged. He turned his attention back to Alice who was walking in and gave her a wave. She glared at Hadley. Hadley started to wonder what she had done to Alice but suddenly the lights dimmed and a projector turned on.

A man stood in front of it, and Hadley knew instantly who it was.

A man from her dreams, or her nightmares.

Hemmer was alive and well.

"Good morning everyone; for those who don't know me I am Doctor Isaac Hemmer. I am a former Vice President of the formerly known United States which dissolved to create a more peaceful society," he said confidently, he was a natural leader. Hadley found herself listening intently to him despite her distaste, and a nagging feeling in the pit of her stomach. "I am pleased to announce that we have found all of our live pingers. I know that it is unfortunate how many we have lost but the 24 of you are the future. As of today we can start to change the world. Now if you'll turn your attention to the slideshow some of your questions will be answered. Which I know will be a relief to those of you who have been here for the last month."

*People have been feeling like me for a month, with no answers,* she thought. Hadley was astounded and she could feel the anger boiling inside of her for them, for herself. She looked around the room thinking that she would have gone crazy feeling how she did for a whole month, without any answers. *What had they been doing? Sitting locked in their rooms?* she thought.

The presentation started and it rolled through pictures as Hemmer disappeared into the shadows. It started with a time-lapse video of increasing smog over New York and London. It also had a time lapse of rising oceans on the West coast. Everyone watched in horror as the city of Los Angeles crumbled into the sea. It took only 156 days Hadley noted from the date at the bottom of the lapse.

The San Andreas Fault cracked and the oceans steadily rose, causing total destruction of California's coasts. For what seemed like comic relief the video then panned to Disney World in Florida getting swallowed by the sea until all that was left was the top of Expedition Everest. 60m of building crumbling into a raging ocean.

From there, the video moved into pictures of the pingers at their schools. Hadley saw a picture of herself smiling with another girl with light brown hair; their arms were around each other in front of the Harvard sign. There was a picture of Pax in his army uniform at West Point. Hadley glanced at him and smiled. He was lost in the slideshow. The pictures moved to them working in rooms like the one they were in now. Then there was a picture of a group of them. There must have been over a hundred young, successful and brilliant young adults. A group that had turned into nothing more than a skeleton of what they once were.

The pictures turned dark and grey again. They were shown a picture of a nuclear bomb go off and the unmistakable outline of the Eiffel Tower in the background. The next picture was the bombing of Tokyo. There was a satellite photo of the world. It showed almost 20 nuclear clouds going off at the same time.

Hadley put her hand over her mouth and took a deep breath. Tears threatening to trickle down her face, she blinked them back.

The pictures moved to people in cities that were dying of sickness. Hadley saw one lady with blood running from her eyes and felt overly sympathetic; the woman's eyes spoke to her soul. The next showed a little boy whose stomach was bloated and his skin was yellow and covered in boils. A family laid dead in their home next. Flies covered them. Hadley blinked back tears. The people's face forever burnt in her memory.

Doctor Hemmer appeared on the screen. He gave a little cough and started to talk. He explained that pingers were the unofficial title for the researchers hired for the Western SPaDI project. They were called that because everyone had a microchip inserted in their arm for when the world came to an end and they had to find them. There had been safe houses set up throughout the continent for our safety and to ensure the lasting of the project. They knew they couldn't save everyone. The SPaDI project took brilliant young minds that had a knack for innovation and scientific improvement. It was an intense screening process but they had found a large group of students who wanted to make the world a better place. The students and graduates were chosen to start campaigns and studies on the future and they wanted young minds. As he talked pictures started to roll by showing people working on scientific and political projects. They were smiling and working together. Hadley saw a picture of herself and Vanya with the girl from the Harvard picture. The pictures were of a different life she no longer remembered; they seemed a million miles away.

The lights flicked back on as the video presentation ended. Hemmer walked up in front of them. Hadley noticed that Alice was clutching at Kane's hand.

Hemmer began to speak again; it was so quiet in the room that you could hear a pin drop. "Now, the world has changed. We no longer live in a peaceful society; there are revolutionaries out there that have profited from the destruction. They are called the RFE's or Revolutionaries of Free Earth. They will use the weak to get what they want. So we need to start as soon as possible. In the binder in front of you, you will see listed your supervisor and list of four projects. Once a week we will have group meetings where we will have to vote on some tough issues. As for now you will also start an extensive mental and physical training program in the mornings to ensure everyone is prepared to go into the field." Hemmer nodded as he finished his speech to a silent room.

Everyone stayed in their seat. Hemmer walked out of the room and there was a click as he left.

Hadley was the first to look around, at the crying and pale faces around her. Without thinking she stood up and started walking up the stairs.

"Where are you going?" Kane yelled from behind her, he was on his feet, his hand still in Alice's.

Hadley just looked at him. She couldn't get the image of the little boy out of her head. More so, she couldn't shake the feeling that she could have stopped it. All of it.

"For a walk, what do you want from me?" Hadley practically spat at him.

He just looked at her, and then sat back down.

"You're all dismissed until tomorrow," he said gently to the rest of the room.

Hadley could have waited for the others to stand up but instead she rushed out of the room, blinded by the pain of what she had just seen and still blinking back tears. The rustling of the room long behind her.

# Chapter Thirteen

Hadley practically ran down the halls, retracing her footsteps back to her room, and finally collapsed on her bed. She stared at the grey symmetrical tiles on the ceiling, trying to remember anything.

Forcing the memories to come back started to give her a headache and was seemingly no use. If anything from her past was going to come back, it would take time, not mental determination. She knew that from the dreams she had been having.

There was a small tap on the door. At first Hadley thought she was hearing things but then it got louder. She got up with a sigh and went to the door placing her hand on the knob but not turning it.

"Who is it?" She breathed.

There was a silence, a pause as though the person was deciding what to say.

"It's me, Pax," Hadley let out a breath, feeling the air leave her lungs. Then she opened the door.

Pax was standing in front of her; he swept his hair out of his face with a swish of his head. His grey eyes staring into hers. He pushed past her and walked into the room.

"Hey!" Hadley protested.

Pax sat on the bed with a slight bounce and looked back at Hadley. She closed the door slowly and sat on her dresser. They were silent. Hadley started to tap her fingers against the dresser, looking away from Pax.

"So," Pax paused, "how have you been doing with everything?"

"Meh," was all she could manage to say. She continued to avoid eye contact, feeling uneasy, especially remembering the memories that had slowly been returning to her.

Hadley bit her lip, "Pax, can I ask you something without you thinking I'm crazy?"

"Shoot," he teased with his crooked grin.

"Have you remembered anything? I've been having dreams, and I…"

Pax cut her off. "And you don't know if they are real or not?"

Hadley inhaled sharply and looked at him, searching. "Yes," she breathed.

He got up and walked towards her, intensity in his eyes. He grabbed her waist and without hesitation he kissed her.

Their lips entwined softly, he gently swept her hair off her neck as he moved his hand to the back of her head. Hadley moaned as she smelt the faint peppermint of his breath.

There was a familiarity in the kiss. Something that couldn't be faked. A feeling of warmth and friendliness. Hadley pulled away, her heart racing.

"Did you feel…?" Pax asked, unsure of his words.

A nod was all that Hadley could do, as the heat rushed to her cheeks.

"We were something…" Pax grabbed her and pulled her close into his chest. They stood in silence before he left. Neither of them able to say anything else they got lost in a feeling that they couldn't place.

Hadley lay down and let herself doze for a moment, trying to activate her memory again.

A while later she woke up in a cold sweat and was breathing hard. Her heart was beating out of her chest. She looked around trying to orient herself; the lights had faded so everything looked different.

She looked down at the grey quilt and groaned. Exasperated she got up and grabbed the grey housecoat off the door. *They really needed to get some clothing that wasn't so monotone or itchy*, she thought. But she knew clothes and dye were hard to come by.

Pulling the robe closer towards her body she opened the door and carefully peered out. The long hallway was abandoned and the only thing she saw was a picture of a fruit bowl. She had gone the other way down the hall a couple of the times and the other way led somewhere else entirely she could just tell. She tiptoed down the hall towards the source of the light. The marble floor was cold against her feet and she noticed the black and grey swirls that looked like ripples through it.

This hallway was different from any other she had seen since coming to the SPaDI complex. It was as if it were inside a home. But a presentation ready, perfectly designed home where people weren't actually meant to live.

There were monotone pictures hanging on the wall. They showed landscapes, fruit bowls and animals. Hadley raised an eyebrow at one showing a cow grazing in a field and just shook her head.

She walked past at least 10 doors until I got to the end of the hall. She turned and was in a large living room, which was surprisingly comfortable. There was a table in the corner that had a large bouquet of pink roses on it. One petal had fallen to the floor and was all alone. The roses stood out against the grey scale of the rest of the room.

Hadley turned her attention to the couch where Vanya was sitting and chatting to another girl. It was the most comfortable that Vanya had been since they had met. The other girl was short with a blonde pixie cut. She had hard features and a tattoo of an arrow ran across her collar bone.

"Hi," Hadley choked, getting their attention, feeling rude at interrupting. She hadn't realized how dry her throat was again, and had to find out why that kept happening.

She stood there uncomfortably rubbing her feet against the cold ground sliding the top of her toes back and forth.

They both turned towards Hadley. Vanya had a startled smile on her face, while the other girl was just happy as can be.

"Hey Hadley" said Vanya. "Come sit down."

They motioned for her to sit and she slumped into a chair across from them. She pulled one knee up to her chest. The blonde looked as if she knew Hadley.

"I'm sorry I know I should probably know you but—" Hadley tried to get the words out but they got jumbled.

"No worries, it took me almost all month to get my brain all sorted out and even then it's as if you don't get everything back." She reached out her hand, "I'm Jinni. Sorting out what is real and what the neurons inside your brain want you to think is real is the hardest part of all this." She smiled. Her voice was girly. It made Hadley smile, with the contrast between her look and her attitude.

"So everyone was fuzzy?" Hadley asked.

"Absolutely, it is actually crazy. When this part of the war started a few years ago we didn't expect this. Then everyone was chaos and all the plans in place went to shit. Hemmer and Kane were luckily able to keep some control. But they had sent us out on missions, and the rest is history. They have been looking for you, Vanya and Pax the longest. You three had the last remaining active pingers, so it's no wonder you are the most confused." Jinni sighed.

"The world was destroyed. We are a few of the lucky ones that are still alive. A few memories were jumbled. I can't imagine what everyone else is doing who didn't have the support of SPaDI and a few video diaries. Also the dreams, oh my god the dreams. They just drive you nuts. I once had this dream about Hemmer— Dear god!" Jinni continued to ramble rather too optimistically.

Hadley smiled at her, for the first time feeling slightly at ease. "Video diaries?

"Kane and Hemmer will show you them in the next couple of days. It's a diary we all made in case this happened—" Jinni shrugged.

"Everyone felt this way, and Jinni was just telling me that it gets better," Vanya stated blankly.

"Glad to hear it." Hadley smiled as she wondered what she had said in her own video diaries. She felt anxious about finding out.

"It's crazy though, what the world has come to. There are revolutionists running around with what they think they remember. It's chaos out there. Be grateful we found you before they did."

Hadley was astonished and confused. She had so many questions and shifted nervously wanting to ask Jinni about her encounter with the doctor and everything that had happened since she got to the complex.

"Also don't feel bad about Dr. Emily. She is a friendly enough person who hates her job. We also haven't seen anyone leave conscious after their first dose. But the shots do help to clear things up." Jinni replied as if reading Hadley's mind.

"What?" Hadley asked alarmed.

"Vanya was just telling me about her experience. Everyone goes through some initial injections. Then every few weeks after that. They are new vaccines to combat new illnesses caused by the biologic weapons. Also one of them is a genetic enhancer. It doesn't change anything it just allows for your genetics to become resilient to the earth. It's like evolution, but faster. I was shown a video where a group of us came up with it."

It all was starting to make sense. "As long as I wasn't the only one who passed out." Hadley laughed uncomfortably as she revealed a weakness.

Jinni suddenly jumped to her feet. "I'm honestly a terrible person! I haven't shown you around, either of you. You probably feel like a guest, instead of it feeling like your home again... Kane and Alice are terrible at this stuff."

Jinni grabbed Vanya's hand and pulled her up. Hadley got to her feet. They went through the whole area. It was a large dorm that was sectioned off from the rest of the base. There were 40 rooms in total. Jinni informed them that they had built three sections but enough of the pingers didn't survive to even fill one.

There was a large kitchen, numerous bedrooms with en-suite bathrooms, a pool, a technology room, a living room and a fitness center. The whole complex was huge and it was unimaginable to think it was inside another building.

They walked back to the bedrooms as they chit chatted about what they knew and what they didn't. Vanya was a geologist and Jinni was in Nanotechnology. They had all started Ivy leagues and excelled until either Kane or Hemmer had recruited them to SPaDI.

They laughed at the fact that some government officials had decided to leave the world in the hands of some above average students.

They finally got back to their rooms and said goodbye. Hadley was genuinely happy and was grinning as she flipped on the light in her room and took a look around with a new optimism. There was a computer and tablet on the desk. Other than that it was plain furniture. She went to the bookshelf and was surprised to see her favourite books and every book imaginable on climate change and neurobiology.

Finally, she turned off the light and fell asleep somewhat content, but still unable to shake the feeling that something was wrong. Something was very wrong.

# Chapter Fourteen

2083

A light flashed slightly as the professor spoke loudly and words sprang across the board. An overview of the glaciation of the world was illuminated on the board. As he spoke the number of glaciers slowly shrank and then grew as millions of years passed in a blink of an eye. The continents were shifting back and forth.

Already a few chapters ahead of the class, Hadley was twirling her stylus in her hand. She tapped her bright pink toes on the granite floor, which had grey flecks running through it. She looked up and watched Kane move through the classroom. He was excited and passionate, his voice peaked as he talked, and his full body moved with his voice. He looked at Hadley and gave her a smirk.

She continued to play with her stylus, unable to concentrate on anything, her body buzzing. She caught the end of her stylus on her ring and had to admire how it shined in the fluorescent light. The white gold band was twisted like leafs with a sapphire in the middle and a wave like pattern encapsulating the stone.

"The longest ice core to date is around 3500 m long. It is important to note that the longest cores come from Greenland and Antarctica."

The bell rang and Kane stopped, looking at the class.

"All right we will continue this lecture on Wednesday. Remember if your paper says to see me, please stay after class."

Hadley looked down and there was a note attached to her paper. She was practically grinning from ear to ear.

*Please see me after class.* Hadley took her time cleaning up her books and tablet, careful to make herself look busy, while really just shuffling everything around on her desk. She watched everyone else file out. Soon she had everything in her bag and the room was empty except for her and Kane.

Hadley watched him close the door. He pulled the blinds closed to the lecture theatre. He did everything with such determination and his muscles flexed as he did it.

"In my office?" He asked with a smile raising his eyebrow. Hadley nodded feeling her heart start to flutter.
He motioned her to walk in. It wasn't even two steps into the office when Hadley dropped her bag on the floor and stood beside a bookshelf facing him.

"You wanted to see me Professor?" She said in a school girl voice looking him straight in the eyes. He stepped forward authoritatively and he wrapped his arms around her waist.

"Call me professor again," He said as he brought his lips down on hers, kissing her passionately. She felt electricity throughout her entire body and wrapped her arms around his neck.

He moved his lips smoothly down her neck, kissing slowly towards her collarbone. She arched her back, letting her hair cascade down her back and over the bookshelf behind her.

"Oh professor," She moaned, knowing how absurdly dumb she sounded. But he was hard in a second and she could feel it against her skin.

The bookshelf was jagged against her back but she didn't even notice as he lifted her up against it so she had her legs around his waist. He took her top off in one swift motion as she unbuttoned his shirt.

She ran her fingers across his abs as he worked his mouth down towards her breast. She exhaled sharply feeling his hand move downwards.

# Chapter Fifteen

2584

Hadley woke up with a sharp bolt. Her heart racing and her stomach in knots. She was hot and sweaty. The fan on the ceiling glowed in a faint moonlight that was coming from the artificial window. Hadley sat up and looked around, the electric sensation of Kane's hands running over her body still burnt in her mind. It felt so real.

"That was not real, you can't dream about him—everything has your head all messed up" She said out loud to herself to even out her breathing.

She remembered what Jinni had said about her ridiculous dream about Hemmer. She felt her heart beat steady and tried to keep herself calm. Slowly she lowered herself back so she was lying down again.

She knew it was just a dream but as she fell back asleep she looked at her finger where the ring was. She felt the base of her finger and it was calloused, as if a ring should go there. The picture in her mind was so vivid that she was sure it was real, and she couldn't help but wonder what had happened to it.

It took her a long time to fall back asleep. The moment before she finally fell asleep all she could see was Kane's face. She gave a shudder and rolled over hugging her arms around her chest.

It was morning before she knew it and the sun was coming up. She got up, ready and was out the door. Hoping that the day would be better than the ones previous.

They were told to meet in a large gymnasium type room. It was the size of a small stadium and reeked of dried sweat and floor polish. It was Hadley's second full day at the complex and she was still trying to figure it all out. They were all standing around when Hemmer and Kane walked in. Hadley watched Kane, he was wearing a black t-shirt that showed off every inch of his torso and she couldn't help but get a little breathless at his abs conrtacting. He looked incredibly attractive with his hardened features.

Kane was followed into the room by a group of straight faced soldiers, or at least that's what they seemed. They were non-descript. You couldn't tell them apart if you weren't looking closely. They walked in time with each other and besides than their legs and arms, they didn't even move.

The room was silent, as Kane and Hemmer stood in front of them. "All right everyone, we are going to begin today with the start of an intensive program. We're going to first do some basic physical assessments," Kane sighed, extremely frustrated. "This is to get you back to where you were before the last bombs went off. Let's start with a few cardio exercises and some strength training that I hope you are still able to complete."

There were a few muffled groans from around the room. But everyone got into a line. Hadley looked ahead of us and saw that the far end of the gym was a large obstacle course.

"What are you waiting for?" Hemmer shouted.

Everyone looked at each other then started to run. Single file they ran after one of the soldiers who took off to lead them. There was a tall parallel wall that they had to climb up; at the top there were ropes to rappel down.

After that, there was an army crawl, and then it got harder. There were monkey bars, and rope swings, high balance beams and it all ended with shimmying across a bar 20 meters in the air. Everyone was struggling.

Hadley finished the obstacle course and struggled for breath. Her lungs felt like they were on fire. She doubled over and tried to breathe in as much as she could.

"Get some water, 5 minutes!" She heard Kane yell. Everyone started to move towards an upright cooler filled with water bottles. Paxton, who was quite a few people ahead of Hadley, made his way back through the crowd and handed her a water bottle.

"Thanks," she said taking it and opening the spout. She took a long drink, finally feeling the burning in her lungs start to diminish. Sweat poured down her brow.

"How are you doing?" Pax asked her. Hadley just shrugged at him while she raised her eyebrow. "Me too," he laughed.

"Time's up, water down everyone. We're going to start some of the assessments" Kane said and everyone groaned.

Hadley felt Vanya grab her arm, who smiled and said, "I thought that was the assessment." Paxton looked at Hadley and laughed, then he whispered, "Was that not assessment enough or is he purposely trying to torture us?"

Hadley snorted and gave Pax a wicked smile before she looked across at Kane's stern look, which from out of nowhere was mirroring Pax and Hadley's thoughts.

Hadley wiped her brow and watched a droplet of sweat fall off of her forehead and land in a perfect circle on the chestnut coloured floor.

"All right everyone we will start with some basic exercises to get those hearts pumping. We will be coming around to work with you and monitor your progress."

Hadley watched Kane walk towards her group with another man. People were gathered in groups around Kane's helpers as they split up into natural patterns. Kane whispered something to the man and walked to another group. He gave Hadley a look and then walked away.

Their group leader was one of the men who had restrained Hadley when they found her. She frowned at him and rubbed her arm where he had death gripped it, though it no longer hurt. "My name is Lieutenant Jameson Martyn. I've been with you since the beginning and was a top agent when the FBI was still an agency and when the United States existed. I will be helping Kane with the assessments."

*The FBI was destroyed?* That was never a possibility she had considered. Jameson pulled out a coin and pressed it bringing it to life. The small coin turned into a full holographic projection tablet.

Jameson pressed a button on the holographic screen in front of him and small dots of light flew over the entire group's heads. They created circles with a counter in the middle.

"Let's start with burpees guys! On your mark, get set, go. You have one minute!"

They started to go as fast as they could after being thrown straight into it. Hadley jumped as high as she could, squatted and jumped her feet back, push upped and then started again. By the second one she had run out of breath and gasped for air. But she kept going; she kept up with Vanya who seemed to be struggling as much as she was. Hadley watched as the bubble above her head slowly climbed, she was one of the worst in the group.

After the minute was up they moved on to push ups. Then planks. Then on to mountain climbers. Hadley knew they were assessing fitness level, but she felt like she was going to keel over and die.

They moved to sit ups. "All right, go!" Hadley heard Jameson say, his loud voice echoing through the room. Kane came back as they got to the thirty second mark. He walked through the group and knelt down beside her.

He placed a hand on Hadley's stomach. "Come on Had, use those core muscles. I've seen you stronger than this." His touch sent a tingle up her spine, and she almost gave her head a noticeable shake in order to wipe the feeling of his hands on her.

"I...am...trying," Hadley hissed trying to get air. Kane said nothing in return and stood back up as the minute ended.

Then she practically passed out, she lay on the ground, dizzy, trying to catch her breath. For a moment she wished she was back under the rubble. But just for a second.

# Chapter Sixteen

Her bed was the most comfortable place in the world, and as she laid in dreamless sleep for the first time in days she didn't know footsteps were coming towards her door. Even when they arrived she didn't realize that the tapping was someone purposely trying to get her attention. She rolled over, covering her ears with her pillow, thinking that the pipes were shuttering again.

Then someone said something, and it piqued her interest. Hadley slowly opened her eyes, becoming annoyed at constantly waking up in the dark.

"Hadley! Wake up already!" A giggling girlish voice yelled.

Hadley rolled her eyes and went to the door. In front of her stood a group of gaggling giggling women. Even Vanya was smiling from ear to ear.

Jinni was giving her a fake condescending look, "took you long enough."

"I thought you were just some machinery; I was ignoring it," Hadley laughed.

"The guys found some great things in the complex tonight, and after the torture Kane put us through today it's worth any consequences." Jinni laughed pulling Hadley's arm.

The door clicked shut behind her as she was pulled down the hall in just a t-shirt. She tugged at the bottom, and was glad that it was long enough to cover her bum.

"Come on," Vanya whined, noticing that Hadley was holding up the group who were eager to get where they were going. Hadley picked up her pace, as they practically ran down the hall and emerged onto the pool deck.

Pax stood with his shirt off, in a grey bathing suit that matched the other men and held a clear bottle filled with a dark brown liquid. He turned around as the women entered and smirked, "took you long enough."

Jinni rolled her eyes, "we couldn't wake up Hadley."

Pax looked at Hadley with a gleam in his eyes, "so you're the one ruining the party."

"I just wanted to let you guys sweat."

Pax laughed from his stomach, throwing his head back, "get changed so we can get this party started."

The girls laughed as they headed to the change room. Each of their names was hung on an individual change room and shower. Hadley walked into hers and the lights went on. They were tiny but she had a row of bathing suits, caps, goggles, fins, and nose plugs waiting for her. She pulled on a two-piece grey athletic suit that fit perfectly.

She reached for the handle of the door and was sprayed with a thin mist, a message blinked across the door *sanitation fluid, for pool health.*

She was the first girl back out onto the deck, and wondered what was taking everyone else so long. The guys were leisurely sitting around on pool chairs and Hadley slid onto the one beside Pax who was in the middle of telling a thrilling tale, or so it seemed. He went quiet as Hadley sat down.

"Looks like you are trying to make up for your tardiness earlier?"

"Nah, I was hoping to be last, but apparently I'm fairly quick."

"Here," Pax grinned handing her an open bottle.

She grabbed it willingly. "Where did you get it?" Alcohol was strictly banned in the complex for safety reasons; it was also very rare to come across nowadays. Factories that produced alcohol were huge targets during the war as they created huge blast sites. *Or at least that's what they told them, probably to keep the horny adults under control.*

Pax clenched his jaw, and looked side to side as though about to reveal a secret, "I stole it if I'm being honest, but from where, you'd have to kill me to know. I'll never tell."

Hadley gave him a playful punch in the arm and shook her head. The other girls finally emerged from the change rooms, one by one and soon the party was in full swing. Everyone was laughing, drinking, and feeling relatively normal.

They were in a beautiful Olympic style pool with a hot tub and surf tank. The roof was a digital skylight, showing a night sky. Around the edges it was all modern and sleek.

Vanya got to the edge of the pool and uncapped the bottle she was holding. She took a long swig. Then she lowered the bottle she started to cough. She handed it back to someone then jumped in the pool and Hadley quickly followed her in.

Pax jumped up and was on Hadley's heels, he splashed her as she surfaced. Hadley splashed him back. For the first time they felt like didn't have a care in the world. The alcohol didn't last long but they soon felt the effect of it.

The boys started to jump off the diving platforms in the craziest ways they knew how. A few of the guys swam up to Hadley and introduced themselves. Jeremiah, Stephen and Joey.

All three of them were engineers. Jeremiah constantly had a look on his face like he had swallowed something sour. He was huge with short army cut black hair. Hadley was instantly intimidated by him. He was easily three times her size and she studied him closely before it dawned on her who he was. He was the stocky man she had seen her first night awake and he was the man whose nose she had broken.

Her face instantly went red as the realization set in.

"Umm. I'm really sorry about your nose—" Hadley said without thinking. She smiled shyly at him, not knowing how else to continue. He studied her for a moment.

"No problem. You were scared; it's to be expected. I'll remember not to let my face get too close to your elbow again though." He gave a stifled laugh. Hadley gave him a smile and turned to the other guys he was with.

Stephen and Joey were more than friendly. Stephen was a scrawny guy with unkempt blonde hair. Joey would have been conventionally attractive if it weren't for the dreadlocks and facial piercings. His tattoo took up one whole arm and his torso. There was a dragon shooting fire along his collarbone. It made Hadley smile as she studied the intricate details.

It made her look down at her own arm; the tattoo had been bothering her, since she couldn't remember why or when she had got it. She pushed her arms gently through the cool water until her thoughts were interrupted.

"Starting to make sense of everything Had?" Stephen asked politely.

"I think so. Slowly," she replied with mediocre enthusiasm.

"It will take time," Joey added softly trying to be helpful. All anyone ever said is it will take time, and this was starting to push on Hadley's nerves.

Everyone started to get riled up again. Vanya screamed as Joey plunged her underwater. Hadley giggled and floated backwards with her ears in the water looking at the sky. She felt relaxed with her head spinning from the liquor they had hastily drunk.

Suddenly, something grabbed her leg. She screamed as she tried to both kick and flee at the same time. Glancing up momentarily, she saw Stephen laughing hysterically. He was full of himself until Hadley splashed him in the face. He spit out some water and lunged forward. His whole body weight came down on her pushing them both underwater. Hadley pushed away from him and moments later they both came up sputtering. Both laughed so hard they could barely breathe. Combined with being underwater they both struggled to catch their breath.

Stephen had a boyish gleam in his eyes. "Good one," Hadley chortled.

"I thought it was a good idea," He retorted.

Everyone thought we had a brilliant idea and started to throw each other through the water. Jeremiah on the other hand just stood in the water near the edge and watched. Hadley made eye contact with him once and the look he gave her sent chills through her spine. So she looked away and tried to forget it.

She dove under the water and enjoyed the relaxing sensation of the cool water washing over her body. She came up beside Vanya who was talking to the other girls.

"Hey," Hadley said to announce her presence. Vanya smiled at her meekly.

"Hadley! This is Marcia." Vanya motioned to a girl with curly brown hair. "Caitlyn."

A blonde with pale features gave Hadley a smile. Her teeth were practically the same colour as her skin. She had grey eyes, and when she didn't have any emotion, she almost looked poetically dead.

Vanya introduced one more girl as "Syb". The third girls had long flowing dark hair and skin the colour of dark chocolate. She was stunning, easily the most attractive of the group.

"Hi there," Syb said, her voice radiating coolness. Syb was intriguing and she looked as though she was full of secrets.

"What do you do Syb?" Hadley asked as everyone continued to drunkenly squeal through the pool. Vanya swam towards Pax, who was finishing a bottle and a glaze had spread through his eyes. Vanya kept trying to get close to him, but he was resisting. Hadley chose to ignore them and turned her attention back to Syb.

Syb looked at Hadley with dismay, "I keep forgetting you don't remember anything Hadley."

"Do you remember?"

"I was the first one they found after the last attacks," She sighed, "I've been here almost 3 months. I'm also the only one left in central intelligence. I left myself a roadmap. So I remember most things."

She beautifully dove underwater and surfaced a few feet away. She gave Hadley a half smile and said sadly, "Let me know when you remember Hadley, or maybe by then you won't talk to me anymore."

The night sky above them started to change to dawn and they decided that we should probably get out of the water. Hadley grabbed a towel out of a cabana and tied it around her chest. Behind her she felt Pax's hand on his hips. They were sheltered from everyone but it still made Hadley uncomfortable.

"What are you doing?"

"After that kiss Had, I don't want to stay away from you."

"Vanya's been after you all night, have you talked to her?

"Why would I?"

Hadley gave him a stern look. He was being ridiculous. He had to talk to her before she could go any further with him but he was drunk and she didn't feel like arguing with him. He kissed her hard, and she barely moved her lips. It took her off guard.

"Come to my room after you change?" He winked and walked away. It was a rhetorical question. Hadley shook her head and went to change, with no intention of ever going to his room.

# Chapter Seventeen

2584

The Earth lab was in a far corner of the complex and it took Hadley and Vanya almost twenty minutes to get there. Granted, they got lost a few times and had to keep referring to the virtual maps on the wall, they eventually got there.

With a swipe of Vanya's wrist, they were inside and saw Kane sitting on a table studying the immense holographic screen in front of him. Numbers were flashing along with graphs and charts.

"What is all that?" Hadley asked.

"I'll explain in a second Hadley, thanks for finally showing up you two," he noted in disdain. Vanya shrunk back and tried to stutter something.

"It's not like this is an easy lab to find Kane."

"I keep forgetting you two don't know anything," he was annoyed. Hadley's blood was beginning to boil.

She looked past him for a moment and saw that the top number on the screen was global carbon dioxide levels. She had never seen numbers so high, and her eyes widened.

She looked back at Kane, composing herself slightly, but her words came out like fire, "You know Kane, it's not as if we chose to lose our memories. So back off. Do you remember EVERYTHING?" She stressed the last word, basically spitting it at him.

"No," he admitted, turning back to the screen, leaving the conversation there.

"So what are we doing?" Vanya piped in after a moment.

Hadley raised her eyebrow, waiting for a response. Kane exhaled.

"You two are on my team, as you always have been. We need to look at how humans and the earth are interacting geologically. As you two are the only Earth Scientists left," Kane said in a happier voice than either girl had ever heard. "Slash neurobiologist— I don't know how you possibly came up with that double major." He added to Hadley with a smirk, but there was an edge in his voice. Judgment.

"Now," he continued, "let me give you the thirty second tour, so you can get your bearings."

Finally, Kane was doing something thoughtful and Hadley smiled to herself. He motioned them to follow him.

There were computers everywhere and a large table in the middle of the room. There were doors leading to offshoots of the lab leading to specialized research areas such as air pollutants, weather forecasting and storm analysis. Hadley looked to one side and saw 3 large glass tubes extending to the ceiling. They each had to be 2 meters in diameter.

"Those," Kane said seeing Hadley's intrigue, "Are simulators, you use the control computer in the corner and you can run 3 virtual earths' at once. For example..."

He went to the controls and starting typing on the holographic screen, turning the virtual dials 3 separate fields of corn appeared. He twiddled with a few buttons, and different weather occurred in each tube. One was a drought, one was too much rain and the other was the control.

He turned another dial and time sped up, almost exponentially, until only the control remained.

"See," he said with a smile, wiping everything clear and continuing the tour, "Play around with it when you have a spare second."

On the other side of the room there was a metal surface that was at least 10 meters wide with lights blinking consistently. Two stairs were attached to the side.

Numerous projectors pointing into thin air above it. Hadley stared at it puzzled, so puzzled in fact she forgot Kane was speaking.

"Am I boring you Hadley?" Hadley looked up at him and blushed. Looking him in the eye made her think of her dream and she felt the colour creep up her face.

"No sorry Kane—" She said looking at him briefly.

"I was going to save that for last, but I think we've covered almost everything and since you seem so interested. That piece of equipment you were staring at is a state of the art Earth simulator. It takes real time data from satellites and GIS, then projects it into a globe. Watch—" He took a remote from his pocket and pressed a button. An earth started to slowly project in pixels above the metal surface. Hadley and Vanya watched in awe as finer and finer details started to develop. Every piece of Earth was perfectly displayed on the floating orb.

Before she realized what she was doing she walked to the earth and looked at it absolutely dumbfounded. The oceans took up more area than she had ever seen or even imagined. Places she used to know as Los Angeles, Florida, Italy, Vancouver, Sydney were just gone. There were no white spots to indicate ice and half the land area was black. *Nuclear warfare does that that I suppose.* Hadley thought.

The earth as they had known it was gone. Completely and utterly changed. *How was it that the world I knew had changed so greatly in such a short time, there is no way this could have happened in even the entirety of my lifetime*, she was baffled into silence.

Kane motioned for them all to step onto the platform after him. The three of them walked up and stood beside the globe, that looked perfectly real until a pixel gleamed in the light.

Hadley put her hand out and touched the globe. It spun from her hand. She watched as a major hurricane approached North America from the north east. She waved her hand through the projected cloud but it didn't change. "Why is there a cyclone in the North Atlantic?" she asked Kane puzzled.

"Current changes and the effects of an intense El Niño for the last few years. The teleconnections are through the roof and with no ice and a relative change of ocean temperature and air temperature of previously unimaginable proportions—" He paused, "Well we are here to see if we can find a way to slow down the intense weather."

He started to pace in front of them, circling the globe. His voice was strained as he kept talking, "You see we have seen an increase of tropical storms, blizzards, rainfall, droughts— every extreme you can think of— we need to look at every climatological possibility"

"So where does that leave us?" Vanya asked. She didn't look up from the globe. She just wrung her hands together.

"The amount of destruction that the nuclear war had in combination with already increased temperatures due to global climate change will soon lead to so much carbon dioxide in the air that we will be plunged into another ice age— One like the planet has never seen before."

"Let me show you something," he continued. He reached out and placed his hand over the hurricane. It grew bigger around them, staying in the confines of the simulator, just a step out.

Before Hadley knew what was happening they were in the eye of the hurricane, standing in the middle of the ocean as an eerie calm settled around them. She looked forward and saw the spiralling winds coming closer and closer. The salt water below it violently thrown into the air.

"This spot used to be covered with hundreds of meters of ice. But I guess we were all born too late to do anything about that. The leaders of the world didn't believe this would happen, everything really started to go downhill in 2017. They figured they'd be dead far before it happened. For the most part, that's true," Kane mumbled sadly, "Hemmer's colleagues did this to the planet. The Industrial Revolution that allows us this technology and everything we know, did this. The most we can do is try to survive. We've got more than they ever had to work with, and there's still little we can do. If only the climate summit in 1988 had opened the eyes of the world, we wouldn't have lost the majority of the species and humans on earth. If only the Intergovernmental Panel on Climate Change had been believed. If only protestors had just worked together and believed that Climate Change was real. But never mind that."

Kane pressed a button and they were sent spinning back into the lab. The hurricane no longer approaching them. Hadley just stared at him, dumb founded.

"How long?" she asked, picking up his underlying meaning.

"A month, maybe two—" He looked grim and she knew exactly how he felt. Stopping anything would be almost impossible. There was next to nothing they could do, except let the earth rejuvenate itself but they were still willing to try. They had every possible technology on earth at their disposal, and with that in mind they might find a way.

They started to work, analyzing the numbers, graphing the changes.

*But was there really any way to stop an ice age?*

# Chapter Eighteen

Hadley got up early the next day, sleep had evaded her and her eyelids were drooping. She stood in the empty kitchen of the complex, mindlessly watching her oatmeal bubble in the pot. She grabbed strawberries and walnuts and started to chop them into small pieces.

The picture window was mimicking her mood and the clouds were drizzling a sad grey rain. "Oh come on," she said into the air as she turned off the heat to the stove and moved her pot to the side. She grabbed a ladle and spooned the oats into a clear bowl, sprinkling the walnuts and strawberries on top.

She grabbed a mug and poured herself a cup of tea. She put all the dishes she'd used to cook into the automated environmentally friendly washer and composter and walked out of the kitchen. Someone had walked in as she left, but she hurried out only hearing the faint tap of their footsteps.

The bedrooms were cold and harsh, Hadley couldn't imagine eating her happy breakfast there and so she headed to the pool. She walked onto the deck and all she could hear was the soft ripple of water hitting against the sides. She smiled as she watched the small waves in the water.

Her food was still hot and she let it sit for a moment to cool as she sipped her lemon tea. She opened her coinet and started to browse.

She started to peruse the climate change websites. Looking for anything to solve the dilemma. She browsed through the ancient NOAA website and the CMS as she read the first article that came up. *Canada- the First CO2 free nation. Decades after the Canadian government shut down the oil sands they have become the first nation to run completely on renewable and clean energy. As of June*

*13th, 2087 all power throughout the 62-million-person country will emit less than 1%.*

Suddenly she saw a new message notification, highlighted in yellow in the corner of the screen.

*New Folder Added: Video Messages*

Her heart skipped a beat. She was going to finally hear from herself. Hear her own thoughts on everything that had happened, and maybe get some clarity. Hadley opened the folder and found only two files. She clicked the first file and watched the video load on the screen. The minute she saw the room it was filmed in, memories started to come back hazily. She tried to figure out what was happening.

It had been a clear sunny day, and Hadley was absolutely furious. She was ready to slap Hemmer and Kane. She still couldn't understand what she was doing there; she had agreed to meet them to talk about a compromise.

"Sit her there," Kane said to his minion who was grasping Hadley's fore arm roughly.

"I thought you wanted to talk Kane. What the hell is this?" Hadley sighed.

Hemmer walked in jollily sipping a cup of steaming coffee.

"Morning Miss Evans," he said gently.

Hadley just stared at him.

Kane turned on a tiny 4K Camera. "Hadley we need you to film your video diary, that's why I got you to come here. The world, well it... it doesn't look good Had."

"I told you not to call me that," Hadley whispered, the nickname hitting her like a cold bucket of water.

Hemmer pursed his lips, "Say what you need to Miss Evans." The minion with Kane loaded a paralytic into his gun; Hadley heard it click into the chamber.

Hadley rolled her eyes, but it was easier not to fight with them.

She looked directly at the camera and started to talk.

"Hey Hadley. If you are watching this, it means the worst has happened. It means that war has erupted and you have lost sight of what has happened. We saw this day coming. We knew it would happen eventually.

I need you to remain calm. Stay collected. Remember that the SPaDI project is the only way. The RFEs are against you. Hemmer and Kane know what's best. Listen to them and Jeremiah and Vanya. Also remember to love Pax. You always have and he loves you too, he's your best friend even if he makes mistakes sometimes.

I promise to give you more information in the next year or so to make this transition easier. Keep your head up and spirits high.

I also know you probably look like me right about now. This fat lip was from self-defence and army training which you are probably restarting now. See you tomorrow?" She looked away from the screen to Kane and Hemmer and for a moment the smile fell off her face.

"Is that the right ending?" She said. They nodded happily. She looked back at the screen blankly and pressed a button so the screen went black.

Then the minion shot her with the paralytic, even though she had said exactly what she knew Hemmer wanted her to say.

It had hurt. Hadley remembered that, she had been emotionally and physically hurt by them more times than she could count. That day had been different though because besides everything, Hemmer and Kane had been protecting her. If only she remembered what from.

With a sigh of relief Hadley kept eating her oatmeal. The SPaDI project was good. Reassurance from herself was helpful. Though the video might have been the most awkward thing she'd ever watched, she knew no one liked watching themselves on camera.

She should love Pax. That was a strange thing to grasp, who she should and shouldn't love. Though Hadley knew it was herself that had said that, she didn't even know the woman on the screen anymore. She barely knew anything and at that moment she barely knew Pax. She couldn't help but think that maybe once upon a time she had loved him, and deep down she maybe knew she still did. However, at that moment she couldn't focus on that.

Love was something she couldn't deal with. Not on top of everything else.

In the distance an alarm bell rang, signalling it was time for work. With a groan she got up and unconsciously started to fiddle with the sleeves of her jacket which were slightly too short. The clothes at the complex were organic, biodegradable and itchy. Though good for the environment and the world, Hadley couldn't help but think they made them ill-fitting and itchy on purpose or someone in laundry had a sick sense of humor. Hadley laughed at the ridiculous notion and she dumped her dishes into the washer as she walked through the kitchen. Her clothing was far from something she should be thinking about, because really, the ice age was coming.

She pulled at her sleeves as she walked down the long hallway to the Earth lab. She scanned her program with a wave of her wrist and heard the faint ding as it unlocked. She pulled the heavy glass door open and it was almost silent. The door softly closed behind her with a ping and a click as it relocked itself. She made her way into the lab, dropping her coinet and earbuds on a work station. She looked around for Kane or Vanya but they weren't there.

They had turned on a few of the world class measuring devices overnight to get an idea of the atmospheric conditions. They were analyzing the air quality outside, Hadley looked at them spin as they pulled air from the long tubes attached to the ceiling. She glanced at the graph on the screen. It seemed the numbers had reduced in the past year but marginally.

She wondered if that could be a good thing, if something was destined to change. A glimmer of hope radiated inside of her. So much so that she had to remind herself that slight atmospheric composition changes were likely on these scales. The computer was massive and was pulling in everything it could. It basically did the leg work for the lab. Charting the day's numbers against everything humanity had ever known to record.

Carbon monoxide, nitrogen dioxide, ozone, particulate matter, sulfur dioxide, carbon dioxide and hydrogen sulphide were the key measurements they were taking. These, especially the carbon dioxide levels, gave them an indication of the health of the air and what the atmosphere could potentially do over the coming month.

Atmospheric levels are important to how long the atmosphere will be liveable. They were getting close to the point where going outside would cause death almost instantly. There were still also high levels of radiation in the air from the nuclear war, which had to be added into the equations. Even with radiation injections the air was far from safe and the gamma rays could cause huge health risks.

Hadley continued through the lab, needing to ask Kane a question about the data and talk through some options that had been swirling in her head. She was thinking on a small scale, and as much as she tried her mind kept going to survival tactics rather than ice age prevention. As it would.

The timeline of everything seemed skewed in her mind and she needed exact dates and more data, which was only on a password protected server. She got to the door of his office and just as she was about to open it she heard yelling coming from inside.

"What do you want me to do?" She heard Hemmer yell inside the lab.

"Nothing!" Kane said exhaustedly. He sounded as though he had completely given up.

"You had your choice. I told you we could implant it so she could remember you. You made the decision. It's not my fault you feel that wasn't best now." Hemmer said anger radiating through his voice.

"I know—but I didn't want to risk it with—well you know…" Kane trailed off. Hadley peered through the crack in the door and could see him leaning on his desk. His hair was disheveled and hung over his forehead. He looked up and she jumped back from the door.

"You cannot do anything now. You cannot under any circumstances tell her. If you do everything will be ruined. We agreed on our plan, we have the same goals. You just don't get the girl. Kane, though I hate her, what you did was inexcusable," Hemmer said sternly.

"You know why I did that…" Kane whispered.

"Diplomatically, I can't admit that. Think of how that would look." Hemmer shook his head in reproach.

Hemmer walked to the door and she took a step aside. The door opened and he walked out looking Hadley straight in the eye. The color drained from his face but he didn't give anything away. "Miss Evans." He said curtly and continued to walk away. *Who had they been talking about?* She thought.

Hadley was still reeling when she walked into the office. Kane looked like he had seen a ghost when she walked in and tried to hide his dismay, pushing his hair back gingerly. Hadley could only focus on her heart pounding in her chest. It was so loud in her ears she was worried that Kane would hear it.

"Hey Kane," she said putting on a smile.

"Hadley," he said curtly, "we need to start the write up. Do you mind inputing the numbers from the last week of ocean level numbers into the computer? The system was broken today and they printed out onto the holographic disk. They need transferring onto the main system." He thrust the holographic chip into her hand.

"Sure. Umm— I need the..." Hadley started to ask him about the password, but he walked away. Brushing straight past her without a second look. He caught up with Hemmer and they left the lab.

Now alone, Hadley took the holographic chip and went to her station. She opened it into a massive pile of data into the air just above her. She turned on two of the computers and linked them together, and then she waited for the login screen to load. Once it did she logged in and opened a spreadsheet. She started imputing the numbers. They were ocean readings from a series of buoys floating around the planet. They sent back a satellite data reading every 4 hours as they floated through various ocean streams. For each reading they imputed salinity, temperature, density, wave height and ocean height from each buoy. It was tedious work.

The numbers started to fuse together, and Hadley turned and looked around at the lab wondering who Kane's mystery girl was. It sounded like he loved her, which confused Hadley as she had seen him holding hands with Alice.

Kane walked back in silently a while later and began working with the globe simulator. Hadley swiftly started to imagine him grabbing her and kissing her on this desk. He would pull her hair as he kissed her neck. She physically shook her head to get the thought out, ever since her dream she couldn't look at him the same. She looked up and caught his eye in the reflection in the glass in front of him.

She turned around sharply, holding her breath, praying he hadn't noticed.

She returned to imputing numbers, letting her thoughts drift to something else. After a few hours she heard someone open the door.

Hadley looked up, Kane was staring at her.

"Yes?" she asked.

"It's past 8, Hadley; you haven't left that desk in almost 12 hours."

Hadley looked at her watch and her eyes widened, "Where was Vanya all day?"

"Working with the ecology team."

"Oh." Was the only word that Hadley's brain could spit out of her mouth.

"Good night Had, see you tomorrow." Kane gave her a smirk and left the room.

Had.

That was the only thing she had heard.

The only thing she wanted to hear.

She packed up, on cloud nine. A heat growing within her, an impatience to know everything about him.

# Chapter Nineteen

It was dark, as it seemed to always be. A warm hand clamped down over Hadley's mouth. She opened her eyes, struggling to breathe, trying to scream. She thrashed around underneath the weight of another human, trying to focus on what was happening around her.

She was startled to see the carefree silhouette of Paxton sitting over her, giggling to himself absolutely amused by his actions.

"What are you doing?" Hadley whispered amused. She pulled the sheet up to cover her pajamas. Her hair was still wet from swimming earlier. She felt uncomfortable; Pax could see her, all of her. Hadley's cheeks grew hot and flushed as she pulled herself further under the covers.

"I want to show you something," he stated plainly. He was staring at her dreamily. It was taking all the restraint he had to keep looking at her beautiful face.

"What are you talking about?"

"Get dressed!" he exclaimed exasperated.

"Get off me and I will"

He pecked her forehead and jumped off the bed. Hadley got up slowly and grabbed some clothes out of the drawer pausing for a moment to stretch her legs. Pax was watching her intently.

"Get out!" she said as she threw a pair of socks at him.

"Ok, ok," he said laughing and shaking his head as he left the room and closed the door behind him.

Instantaneously he grabbed her hand, winding his fingers through hers. They were off, down the winding halls.

"Where are we going?" Hadley asked as he pulled them into the main hallway.

"Have patience," he laughed.

Hadley hated how he always found her so amusing. It was as if everything she said was a joke. But she knew he didn't mean it in a bad way. He was carefree and cocky. They reached a stairwell and started to ascent. It was a long time before they got to the top of the stairs. When they finally did, they emerged outside.

"I thought we couldn't get outside!" Hadley exclaimed.

"We're not supposed to," he said with a raise of his eyebrows. He had a twinkle in his eye like a kid in a candy store. He had that rebellious side to him which made Hadley like him even more.

The night was clear and bright, a deep midnight blue fluttering around. The moon was a crescent and the stars shone more brilliantly than had ever seen. The city lights were far below and they were the highest point as far as the eye could see. Hadley looked all around her and could see galaxies clearly with her bare eyes.

It was breathtaking; it was the most amazing sky she had ever seen.

"This is amazing."

Hadley sat in the center of the roof and looked up at the sky, tracing lines through the constellations. Pax sat down and put his arm around her shoulders, pulling her into his chest.

"I know right," he replied, "I found this place when I was supposed to be looking through old UN political documents. Is it safe to be outside?"

"Currently yes, we've been injected with Anti-Radiation and our lungs configured to deal with the higher amounts of greenhouse gases and chemicals in the atmosphere. But not forever."

She leaned closer to him, wrapping herself deeper into his chest. Maybe it was just because he had saved her but she always wanted to be near him. He looked at her, his grey eyes glowing in the moonlight. He moved closer and she didn't pull away, she couldn't get close enough. She looked into the depths of his eyes. The greys and silvers swimming around his pupils looked like they could house the world.

Their noses were almost touching and they were both still. She held her breath, listening to the silence between them. She closed her eyes and he kissed her lips. Hadley inhaled sharply, catching her breath, pulling away slightly so they were still sharing the same air but could look at each other.

He reached his hand up and cupped the back of her head. He pulled her into him, one arm around her waist and they kissed again. Their mouths opened so their teeth and tongues were whirling together.

She brought her hand to his cheek and ran her fingers against the harsh stubble on his chin. He pressed closer to her and lowered her onto the ground. His weight pressed against her body when he aligned himself right over her. They kissed for a long time before they both pulled apart. Breathless, yearning.

"I've been waiting a long time to do that" he said quietly right into Hadley's ear. Their arms were wrapped around each other. They kissed gently.

"Is that why you brought me up here? To take advantage of me?"

He smiled and laughed. He pushed himself off of her and lay down on the ground next to her. She curled up close beside him with her face on his chest and they watched the stars. The stars shifted through the night sky until a pale pink was glowing over the horizon.

"Do you think everything they are telling us is true?"

Pax leaned on his elbow and grimaced, "What do you mean?"

"I keep feeling like we're not being told everything."

"We're probably not," he said simply with a shrug.

Hadley was taken aback, "And you're okay with that?"

"Had, look around, Jesus, everything is destroyed." Pax chortled, "We have a roof over our heads, food and the occasional bottle of whisky. At this point they aren't doing anything bad, so I'm just going with it."

"But…"

He was getting frustrated and said too loudly, "We weren't going to survive much longer on those water patches Had. I'd rather not die; I don't know about you."

"Jesus Pax, this is our past we're talking about! I didn't mean to offend you, but I don't know about you I want my memories, and I need the truth." There was ice in her voice.

Pax stood up and brushed himself off, "Let's get back inside."

# Chapter Twenty

Staying up all night hadn't been a good idea, Hadley was slowly realizing. Her eyes were drooping as she walked into the gym, ready for another day of strength and combative training. She couldn't even look at Pax, feeling so differently than him. She couldn't understand how he had been so cavalier about their past.

Kane came into the room, followed by a group of soldiers.

"Shut the hell up!" he yelled to the room. Everyone was instantly silent. The anger that resounded through his face was radiating through the room.

"All right," he continued, composing himself and toning down his voice, "we are going to work on real combat and self-defence today. We've given the last two of you a couple days to acclimatize and get back into the groove of working on the important things in your field. But we have to face facts. The RFE's are delusional and misguided. They think they know everything, but what they know is wrong. We know they will resort to violence and we need you prepared. Sadly, there aren't enough of you left for anyone to be disposable."

Kane stated pacing in front of them. Hadley looked around the room and everyone was slowly starting to form a cohesive unit.

"All right everyone please watch!" Kane muttered stepping up onto a padded platform behind him. He was followed by Jameson, Hadley let out a low groan, her body still hurt from the burpees the last time they were in the gym.

Kane and Jameson fought, and they fought well. They moved like trained soldiers. Each anticipating the others next moves. Jameson swung to punch Kane in the face. Kane moved grabbing his arm and flipping him over his shoulder. Jameson was on his feet before he could hit the ground. Jameson kicked Kane's leg out then grabbed his arm bringing him to the ground. Jameson's hands went instinctually towards Kane's neck before Kane tapped out. Jameson had clearly won.

Kane got back up and dusted himself off. "If you can beat me like that we have nothing left to learn," Kane smiled at Hadley, giving her a subtle look.

Hadley was paired with Stephen, which was better than Jeremiah. She thanked God for that. After pairing them up Kane said, "You might work with everyone you might only work with a few people, remember in the real world you can't anticipate who you are going to fight. You just need to be able to win."

Hadley and Stephen started to fight, making small uncoordinated movements around their mat. Everything was going well for Hadley until Stephen got an upper cut straight to the side of her face. She saw stars as she fell onto the ground onto her stomach, the air pushed out of her.

"Hadley! I'm so sorry—" Stephen said kneeling beside her in a panic. She rolled onto her back clutching her face, trying desperately to get enough air. Pain radiated through her abs.

"It's fine," She laughed trying to shake it off, "real people trying to kill me wouldn't take it easy."

With Stephen's help Hadley got to her feet, she brushed herself off and moved her hips back and forth feeling out her body.

"Do you want to keep going?" He asked unsure of how to proceed. He never liked stopping an exercise halfway, he was a follower and an overachiever. He had a panicked look in his eye though. He had definitely never hit a girl before and from his expression Hadley guessed he had never actually hit anyone before.

"Yes," she nodded defiantly with a smile, "I can't tap out in the real world."

Hadley raised her hands to shoulder level, gripping her fingers into fists. She bounced a bit to get rid of the built up pressure in her limbs and get blood pumping back through them. Her head was aching but she was nowhere near giving up.

Stephen went in for the first offense. Hadley blocked his wimpy punch and brought her foot up into his side. He stumbled a few steps then came back at her, realizing she was going to give it all she had.

His fist hit her stomach, hard, and she was sent reeling backwards but stood up quickly. They kept fighting until they were both out of breath. They looked at each other doubled over and called it with a chuckle.

"Stephen, try with Captain Martyn," Kane said as he walked up to them both standing up. He motioned Stephen towards Jameson who had a glare in his eye.
Stephen grimaced and laughed as he walked away. Hadley knew he was going to be pummelled and it was probably because Kane had seen him taking it easy on her.

"Ready?" Kane said raising his hands in front of his chest as he stepped onto the mat.

"I guess," Hadley said with a shrug feeling concerned, she knew it was going to hurt. She raised her arms. He took a step forward and lunged. Hadley stepped back barely avoiding his punch.

Kane was out for blood.

"Keep your arms close and flex your muscles, keep everything tight," Kane said. "Now take a shot."

Hadley lunged forward and tried to punch him in the face. He stepped out of the way and grabbed her wrist and pulled so she stumbled into him. Her back pressed up against his chest. She could feel his pecks against her shoulder blades. He was warm and damp with sweat and she inhaled a combination of spearmint and pine.

His arm instantly caught her around the waist to stop her from falling. She lost her breath momentarily and neither of them moved. Chills ran down Hadley's spine; there was electricity between them and she knew he could feel it too.

Kane jerked and flipped her onto her back on the floor. He brought his fist high into the air and she closed her eyes expecting the worst. Hadley heard the hit but didn't feel the pain. She carefully opened her eyes to see his first was indented into the mat just millimetres from her face. His fist was clenched so tightly that it was turning a shade of grey.

He stood up and helped her up. "Keep going," he said as he took a step away from Hadley. She watched him and decided to try a different tactic. She lunged forward and he dodged, she was faster this time and didn't let him catch her.

Kane nodded, "Good, you're remembering. Trust your body; it's done this a million times."

Hadley noticed that her teammates were gathering in a circle. The pressure was on. She waited for Kane to make his move and he did. So she dodged his fist as it went straight for her face. She ducked and turned. He caught her but not before she brought her elbow back into his stomach. He held her for a second before letting her go.

"I could have killed you—" he whispered menacingly into Hadley's ear, her skin was crawling from his cool breath on her neck.

He didn't let go of Hadley yet though. His arms wrapped tight around her as he said to the whole group, "If I was an RFE, Hadley would be dead. I'm stressing the importance of this."

Kane stood back and pushed her forward with a lurch. He stood up straight brushing himself off and called out, "All right, you can have the afternoon off. I don't know what you all did last night but the majority of you look like you might die on me. Get some sleep."

"Half a day off! My god!" Vanya said as she skipped up behind Hadley who was nursing a broken ego. She was bouncing with excitement. Hadley was still thinking about the peppermint. Her dream about Kane flooding back into her memory. The way he held her against his chest gave her goose bumps.

"What are you going to do?" Hadley asked in monotone.

"Hmmm, I know who I would like to do..." She uttered under her breath stealing a glance at Jeremiah.

"Vanya!" Hadley burst into laughter, her eyes went wide and she blushed.

"Oh don't play coy; I've seen you and Pax." She gave Hadley's arm a light hit.

"What?!' Hadley played innocent, wondering where Vanya's sudden confidence was coming from.

"Right." She said abruptly and walked forward to Jeremiah. Hadley watched her put her arm through his as they walked out the door. She just laughed and watched Kane start talking to Jameson and the other captains in the room.

Hadley rushed after Pax who had stopped right outside the doorway.

"I thought you weren't talking to me," he sneered.

Hadley looked at him, "I just got my butt kicked, and I'm over it."

"Maybe I'm not," he started to smirk.

"Oh come on!"

He grabbed her and pulled her into a corner. She was taken aback and bit her lower lip. He kissed her lightly, and then brushed a piece of hair off of her face.

They walked back to the dorm together, smiling to themselves. As they approached Hadley's door it got awkward. She didn't know what they were doing, if they were saying goodbye.

Pax cleared it up by saying nonchalantly, "I'm going to hit the gym, but grab lunch with me after?"

Hadley just smiled and nodded as he walked away towards the gym. She stood outside her door for a moment before deciding to go to the pool. A place she now considered her sanctuary.

The lights came on as she opened the doors and walked out onto the deck.

"Hello Miss Evans," a voice said, it was something that was new.

"Hello?" she called into the emptiness around her.

"They finally fixed me, I'm the voice activated controls for the complex; can I interest you in any sounds or lighting arrangements?"

Hadley laughed. "Yes, give me a soft seaside wind in the late afternoon."

The statement even sounded ridiculous coming out of her mouth. But the lighting and sound effects started.

Hadley turned on her tablet on a lounge chair and decided to open the second video diary, just in case it was different than the first.

Again she saw herself sitting on a chair, with blood running down her cheek.

"Hey Hadley. Me again. But I guess you could have guessed that.

Any who! Hope everything is coming back to you. I hope you have started to get some memories back. Is that the right thing to say? Who knows?" She shrugged and brushed a piece of hair out of her eyes, but it got stuck in the blood on her cheek. Her eyes flicked to something behind the camera as she tried to get it out.

"Umm. Well trust Hemmer and do as he says. Listen to Kane. He was always a mentor and almost like a— umm— father figure?" She was super unsure of herself as she said the last part as though she was reciting it from a script.

"So you should know that Kila, our dog died yesterday. You probably remember her but don't know what happened to her..."

The Hadley on the screen just kept talking about nonsense until Hadley turned off the entry. She was frustrated and was hoping for more information, anything real that she could grasp and hold onto.

She promptly deleted the files.

Swimming was a great way to clear her head and she decided to take a swim. After changing she hopped into the deepest part of the dive pool and let herself sink a few meters to the bottom.

She sat there underwater looking up at the flickering lights that passed through the water above her. She closed her eyes, seeing how long she could hold her breath. She kept going until her lungs yearned for air and she pressure started to push on her head.

Then she remembered something.

It had been months ago. She was running through the streets as they burnt around her. The bombs had dropped years before but the world was still on fire.

She had awoken long before she should have and knew she had to flee.

She ran until she saw the pile of rubble sitting there, she climbed down a hole as deep as she could and lay down. She had been wearing a yellow dress and she peeled it off leaving her in her underwear. A small wooden box clutched in her hand. She opened it and smiled.

Then without hesitation she rolled it up in the yellow dress and stuffed it into a crack in the concrete as far as her arm could reach.

In the other hand she had an injector; she pulled off the cap with her teeth and dug it straight into her thigh. Then she went to sleep.

Hadley's eyes widened as she remembered and she pushed off the pool bottom. She made it to the surface, coughing out the water in her mouth. She swam to the edge, grabbed her towel and rushed to change.

With her hair still wet she ran down the hall and started hammering on Pax's door.

He opened it, and stood there in a white towel, his abs gleaming under a coating of water droplets. He was drying his hair with a smaller towel. Hadley bit her lip and her cheeks flushed.

"Oh, couldn't stay away?" He said in a sultry voice.

She pushed through into the room and turned around, after he closed the door and said quietly, "I remembered something…can you help me?"

He just smiled.

# Chapter Twenty-One

Hadley peered out of Pax's door an hour or so later. She was breathing heavily, her heart racing as the adrenaline pumped through her body. She was ready to find the small wooden box and find some well-deserved answers.

She felt for the paring knife she had hidden and slipped it into her sock. The hallway was dim but the lights gradually turned on as she peered out. She hid behind the slit in the door and looked out, waiting for whoever was coming.

There were two sets of footsteps, stumbling along down the hall.

"That was fun," Vanya said with a giggle.

"Mhmm it was, wasn't it?" Jeremiah replied devilishly. Jeremiah pinned Vanya against a wall his fingers tracing along her arm, along to her elbow. They started furiously making out, hands all over each other.

"I just want to get out of this place, go home," Vanya said as Jeremiah kissed her neck.

"Soon babe, soon," he replied against her neck. He pulled her shirt over her head and moved his hand to her chest.

Pax started breathing over Hadley's shoulder, watching with her.

"In the hallway?" he breathed exasperated into her ear. Hadley had to stifle a laugh.

"I know, I know, but I'm getting sick of waiting. I feel like we are just going through the motions. Just doing the right things to the right end," Vanya said.

The right end? Hadley strained to hear every word the two were saying. What was she talking about? It sounded as though they had a dirty secret. Hadley pressed her back harder into Pax knowing they definitely didn't want their conversation overheard.

"Everything has to be perfect; you know that, Hemmer wants to do it right this time around. He needs ALL the information." Jeremiah said. He grabbed Vanya's hand and pulled her into his room. They were gone.

"What was that about?" Hadley whispered to Pax.

"No idea," he shrugged. "Strange though wasn't it?"

Hadley grabbed the rest of her things, her coinet, and a small backpack filled with a bottle of water and some food patches.

"You're adorable when you're nervous" Pax laughed as he stood waiting by the door.

"You're not nervous?"

"Meh, what's the worst that can happen?" He was chill as always.

His hair fell over his eyes in a carefree sort of way. His silhouette was distinct against the wall. They stood by the door for a moment ensuring there were no more sounds. Hadley rested her ear cautiously on the door waiting for absolute silence. When they were sure there was no one around they rushed quickly out of the dorm. The halls were empty and deserted.

They rushed to the roof through the winding halls. Hadley held her breath hoping that they wouldn't be caught. She breathed in the cool night air as they emerged through the door onto the roof.

It was natural, not fresh, but natural, and a nice change from the indoors of the compound. Hadley hadn't noticed how sterilizing the interior of the compound was.

"You're sure we won't die from radiation out here?"

"Oh now who's the nervous one?"

Pax gave her a punch to the arm. "Shut up." He laughed.

Hadley gave a chuckle. "We will be fine for about 4 hours, and we will definitely be back in our beds before that."

She looked up at the cloudy sky, which had an eerie yellow glow from the moon. The clouds looked radioactive and were exuding brightly coloured light. As she watched them shift for a moment sending streaks across the sky she knew they were the product of the gas levels in the sky and that a terrible storm was brewing tonight. *Great!* She thought. *We couldn't have picked a less intense night.*

The lack of ozone and increased greenhouse gases meant that more charged particles were entering the atmosphere as a result of solar winds. These were colliding with the oxygen in the atmosphere creating the lights through the clouds in the sky, like the northern lights that used to be a treasured phenomenon that people chased around the globe. Slowly the magnetic poles had shifted and the lights fluttered into nothing. Occasionally they could be seen hovering over areas of Antarctica.

"What now?" Paxton asked with a crooked grin.

"You start that way and I'll go the other." Hadley said with conviction, pointing to a ledge right in front of them.

They started at one edge and started to look for any way down to the ground. The ground didn't seem too far below them, but that was always thought standing staring over the edge. Hadley started to get frustrated at the lack of a way out of the compound and she calculated the probability of survival if she were to jump.

It was low.

As far as the eye could see the roof extended. Splitting up was good to cover more area but still it was seeming more and more like a fool's errand. Hemmer wasn't one for missing things. He missed the open door but he wouldn't have left a way out. Not one Hadley could find. The more they looked the bigger and bigger the roof seemed to grow. Like the Universe continually expanding.

At last she saw it, just as she was about to give up, in the far corner of the eastern section of the roof, a ladder leading down the side of the compound. We were at least 100 feet up at that point and the ladder led to a platform below. Hadley looked down and to the sides and saw no cameras or people. She threw her leg over the edge and put her whole weight on the ladder. It held. Thankfully.

The ladder was old and the paint was peeling off the fading copper. As she grabbed the rung she felt the paint dig into her palm and she held on tighter knowing a tight grip was the only way not to fall to her death below.

The temperature was noticeably dropping, at an alarming rate. Frost was starting to form on the metal rungs, freezing the paint into tiny ice crystals. Hadley's breath was forming a small loud in front of her face. She watched as the tips of her fingers started to turn white.

"Come on!" She yelled to Paxton as she poked her head over the top of the railing.

The wind was howling in her ears and that was all she could hear. Her hair started to fly around her head and she couldn't see anything. She hoped that Pax had heard her, but her hands were freezing and she started to descend.

Almost a minute later, and 20 or so rungs Paxton leaned over the rail. He looked down at Hadley completely shocked.

"Are you crazy? We were just scouting tonight Hadley. Come back up so we can think this through."

"Never mind that Pax, this might be our only chance! Now what are you waiting for?" She laughed her voice electrified with excitement.

He shook his head but swung his legs over and started to climb after her. The ladder started to shake and they both held on.

"Dammit," Paxton breathed, his knuckles going white from hanging on too hard, "remind me you owe me for this Hadley."

Hadley laughed. The ladder was definitely less sturdy with two people on it and she could feel it vibrating beneath her. Her hand slipped for a moment and she let out a quiet yell.

"You okay down there?" Pax yelled back concernedly.

"Fine, how about up there?" she yelled back, not skipping a beat.

"Fine!" he said gruffly, she could imagine the eye roll that went with the statement.

They kept climbing down the ladder; it took longer than either thought to get near the bottom. The cold dark air started to whistle as it blew faster and faster. The storm was picking up steadily.

Then, to make matters worse, the rain started. It pelted against their faces and obstructed their vision. The rain drenched Hadley in seconds. Lightning streaked across the sky. Combined with the lights it was creating a masterful artwork of the sky. They started to move faster and faster as burgundy and gold splashed above them. They were so close to the bottom but still so far.

Hadley put her foot on a rung and it collapsed along with the last 20 feet of the ladder. She screamed as she dropped down barely managing to hang on by one hand to a frigid rung above her.

"Pax!!" She screamed trying furiously to grab on with her other hand. She could feel her hand slipping and started to panic. She screamed Pax's name again. It was met with silence.

She tried to look up but her vision was so impaired by the rain so she looked down and saw the ground far below her. Puddles already forming.

She knew that she wouldn't make it if she fell but the rain was making the rung impossible to hold onto. She dug her nails into the metal, trying to get any grip she could. She scrambled and thrashed trying to hang on. The muscle in her arm tearing as it strained itself.

Finally, she felt her hand slip off the rung. She closed her eyes and expected to fall.

She didn't feel it; her body didn't move. She looked up and Paxton was holding her arm. She exhaled as he hoisted her up.

Pax used all the energy he could to hoist her up. She clung to him, unable to stop shaking or to let go. He held her tighter than he had held anyone before. He knew he had almost not made it.

His arms were almost crushing her and her nails were digging into his back. But neither of them let go. They were breathing in sync and their heart beats were at the same pace. The warm tears burnt Hadley's eyes and poured down her cheeks onto his shirt. The rain came down harder and harder. They were dripping wet and their skin was freezing to the metal.

Pax whispered into Hadley's hair, "Let's go back up."

She pulled away from him and looked around. There was a pipe a few feet away from the ladder. She watched how it led downwards into the blackness below. Without thinking she reached out and grabbed it.

"What in the world do you think you are doing?" Paxton said pulling her back to him.

"I'm not giving up that easily," Hadley smiled weakly as she wiped the tears off her cheeks. Then without thinking she jumped for the pipe. She almost overshot but managed to hang on. She shuffled down it like a fireman, holding her breath the entire way until finally she felt her feet hit the pavement. She looked up to see Paxton looking down in disbelief.

"You're crazy woman!"

"Come on you chicken!" Hadley laughed up at him, regaining her rhythm. The rain was pounding her face and for a moment she was unable to understand where her courage had just come from. It took him a few moments before he grabbed the pipe and was on the ground beside her.

"You are absolutely insane!" He pulled them together in an embrace. They both laughed basking in their adrenaline and stupidity.

"Let's go, we will figure out how we're getting back in later," Hadley said grabbing his hand as they walked down the street keeping our eyes peeled for any sign of the pile of rubble he had pulled Hadley out of.

"So much for scouting." Pax laughed.

It was difficult to distinguish street names because so much of the city was destroyed. Some still had their ancient road signs. All the digital and holographic signs no longer functioned so they had to rely on looking at buildings that might have any distinguishing features.

Before they knew it, the sun was starting to come up and they still hadn't found anything they recognized. They started to jog checking every street as they went. Hadley had her coinet out and was slowly marking her way through a map she was drawing in a GPS app. They were making a grid of the city, but the city was bigger than she could have ever imagined.

Then in the distance there was a faint outline of the Serva that had saved their lives. They started to run towards it.

They heard voices ahead of us as they rounded a corner and before they knew it they ran straight into a group of people. They were not their people either. Hadley was starting to get frustrated at running into unfriendly people in the streets. She wished they had slowed down in time to not let them see them.

*RFE's*, she thought at last. She could tell by their colourfully eccentric clothing, which was a mix of bohemian chic and eco-friendly.

The pair stopped in front of the group. The rain was pouring down and a thick musky fog was settling. The rising sun cast an eerie glow on the pavement between us.

Hadley looked at one in particular, a heavy set tattooed man. He was easily a foot taller than the rest around him, he was tanned and rugged.

Their eyes locked for a split second, Hadley could see the grey in his eyes.

"Hey!" one of the RFE's yelled.

"GOVS," another one shouted.

Pax and Hadley started to back up; trying to go up the street they had come from. It was too late. The street was filled with RFE's. Who were looking more unfriendly every minute.

# Chapter Twenty-Two

"What are you doing here Gov's?!" the tattooed man said stepping out from the crowd; he had a bun tied on the top of his head. He was amazingly tall and built. His face was covered in scruff but you could still see his sharp features and high cheekbones.

"Wrong place, wrong time," Pax said lightly, trying to ease some tension.

The tattooed man's face remained cold as ice. A few men and women around unlatched their guns, and it was almost instantaneously that Pax and Hadley had twenty pointed straight at them.

"Just kill them already," a woman screamed in the crowd.

Hadley made eye contact with her and saw her curly hair drenched, her bones poking through her skin. She looked on the verge of death. Her eyes sunk into the back of her head.

Arms grabbed Hadley and Pax. They struggled to get free but couldn't. Paxton was struggling against four of them. He took a swing at the closest and a fight erupted. Limbs started to fly and punches were thrown. Pax seemed to be keeping up and more men and women started to go at him, until he was lost in a sea of people. Hadley stood watching in horror.

Then a gun shot rang out.

When it settled, Pax was laying on the ground unconscious. Bleeding, luckily from his bicep. He wasn't dead, yet.

The man with the bun came closer to Hadley. He stood less than a foot away. His height was menacing this close.

"How long have you been at the complex?" He breathed into her face, studying. Calculating. His eyes were making rapid movements though his jaw remained set. There was a gleam in his eye. But before she could analyze it further it was gone.

"A few weeks now—" Hadley whispered. She glanced downwards and saw he was holding his gun a few inches from his side. His hand was shaking but he was holding it as still as he could.

"Did they give you the injections?" He got closer than she ever thought possible. Hadley tried to back up but couldn't move; there was a small army behind her. The closeness and disruption of personal space was making her head dizzy.

"Yes," she whispered looking down. A pain rushed through her chest at the thought of the injections. His warm damp breath tingled on her cheek, his eyes ablaze.

"There's nothing we can do!" He threw his hands in the air and walked away. Without even looking at Hadley he hissed, "Hang them, we need to send a message. Hemmer thinks he's too powerful."

"Stop!" Hadley yelled fiercely. She didn't know what she was going to say next but the thought of the hangman's noose lingered in her mind. The man did pause for a moment, but he didn't look back.

The guards threw her to the ground. She felt the knife she had stashed in her sock dig into the side of her leg. Though she didn't dare move until she saw an opening. She knew she would have just one chance to get herself free.

The two guards closest to her were having a conversation, obviously not thinking Hadley was much of a threat and she wasn't realistically. She was surrounded by twenty people all of whom were carrying guns. One pull of a trigger and it would all be over.

Hadley moved slowly, making small unnoticeable movements as she brought her hand to her ankle. She held her breath hoping no one would spot it. She moved slowly to bring her knee up and her hand to her ankle. It was a tedious and painful process, moving slowly enough to not be spotted. She stopped every time there was the smallest glance her way. Fear driving her every movement.

Two men tied two nooses in perfect circles made of thick hard rope. The thought of having that tied around her neck before making a hard fall would lead anyone to feel nauseous. They got another two men to help and the ropes were strung up. The nooses were left on the floor. One-man drug unconscious Pax directly beside the noose. Hadley watched in horror and they kicked him repeatedly trying to bring his around. His face was unrecognizable. The rain-washed away some of the blood but he was still bleeding heavily. A pool of red formed around him on the shattered concrete. His nose was a crushed blob on his face.

Finally, Hadley grabbed hold of the cold handle of the knife. Without contemplation she jumped up and grabbed the woman closest to her, who happened to be the thin woman who was screaming for her death. She was small and Hadley had her knife at her throat. She pressed just hard enough to not puncture her skin, even though a piece of her wanted to draw blood.

The RFE's were around them immediately but Hadley was already making her way to the edge of the circle. There was no one behind her now.

"Hey!" The woman screamed, obviously terrified. Hadley felt a pang of guilt, she didn't like hurting anyone. But it subsided when she remembered they meant to hang her.

The man with the bun was obviously impressed. Though also thoroughly annoyed.

"You are going to let us go or I swear to god I will kill her," Hadley said looking him dead in the eye. She didn't blink and she held her ground.

"You're a fighter," he said nodding his head. He walked up to the pair.

"Stay back." Hadley took a step away from him, and his eyes never left her face.

"Let's make a deal gov. You let her go and I'll let you go." He shrugged.

"I'm not going without Pax." Hadley stomped her foot stubbornly. *Childish move,* she thought as she did it.

"Oh princess," he mocked, "You are not in any position to bargain. You see if you kill her, then I'll just kill you."

He made a good point. Hadley was going to have to save her own skin. "Fine." She pushed the woman forward and started to back away. But the man walked past the woman and towards Hadley.

Before she could turn to run he grabbed her arm and kicked her feet out from under her. Hadley landed hard on her back, the wind knocked out of her stomach. He put his entire weight down on top of her. The knife fell from her hand and he grabbed it bringing it to her neck.

The rain came down even harder. Sheets of it surrounded them. Lightning flickered through the morning sky. The mud and water Hadley was lying in were creeping over her neck and face. She struggled to breathe as he pressed his large frame into her chest.

"What's your name princess? I want to know who I'm killing today," he said with a devilish smirk. Constantly mocking.

"Hadley, Hadley Evans," she spat in his face.

# Chapter Twenty-Three

The tattooed man was stunned, completely and obviously. Hadley was confused as to why.

"Had?" he whispered, he thought he was imagining her. The face beneath him wasn't real, just a figment of his imagination he tried to reassure himself. A cruel trick by the govs.

"You know me?" She gasped under the weight of his massive frame.

It was as though they were frozen in time for a split second. Then he had the knife right back at her throat, pressing so hard that it drew blood.

"You're not real, you're just my imagination," he hissed through clenched teeth, looking away from her face.

The blood was starting to drip down the side of her neck, diluted by the rain it ran into the cool mud she was sinking into.

"Do you know me?" she screamed at the man.

He slapped her, hard. So hard her mind went dizzy.

"You're not Hadley!" he screamed into her face.

His blood was boiling and he was losing focus. He kept blinking trying to figure out what was real. He recoiled slightly bringing the knife off her neck.

Hadley took the chance to bring her knee up hard into his groin. She used every bit of strength she had and the man rolled onto his side in a ball, tears in his eyes.

Hadley scrambled up, pushing herself out of the mud which had suctioned her into it.

She looked around frantically for Pax, for the Serva, for the rubble. For anything.

The rain was coming down harder and harder, and the fog had created a low cloud. It was so misty Hadley could barely see a few meters in front of her.

Then she felt a hand on her ankle. The tattooed man had grabbed her, she tried to kick him off, but his hand wrapped around her leg as he tried to pull her down.

She struggled not to fall. Then from out of nowhere someone kicked the man in the face. His grip loosened enough for Hadley to start to run; she felt a hand on her arm.

"Let's go!"

She looked back and saw Pax, or what was left of his face. It just looked swollen and broken beyond recognition.

"Are you ok?" Hadley yelled as she ran. She saw the pile of rubble and ran up it.

Neither said anything as they searched for the spot where Pax had pulled her out. They finally found it, in a stroke of good luck.

Hadley reached down into the nook, and didn't feel anything. She looked at Pax, almost defeated.

"What?" he sputtered through his broken teeth.

"I—" Hadley didn't know what to say, they had almost gotten killed trying to find something that wasn't there.

"Maybe it shift...ted?" He continued to sputter, blood still pouring from his demolished nose.

Hadley had no choice but to jump into the hole that had been her tomb. She peered around in the dark, wet cavern and looked. She reached her arm into the nook and felt around. Just as she was about to pull her arm out and give up, her fingertips brushed against something soft and smooth.

"Anything?" Pax yelled down.

Hadley reached as far as she could, practically putting herself into the nook, and grabbed. She brought her arm out and saw the dress, wadded up over a small wooden box.

She stuffed the thin fabric into her jacket pocket and looked at the box. In the dark, she could barely see it. It has what looked like tiny dots carved into the wood in a tiny zigzag pattern.

The latch opened with no problem. Inside the box was a thin silver chain. On the end were a key and a ring. The ring was the one she had remembered wearing when she was in Kane's class.

The key was engraved, but in the dark Hadley couldn't read it. She clambered out of the hole and sat trying to make it out.

"What did you find?" Pax asked sitting beside her.

"A key, and a ring," Hadley said showing him the box and its contents.

Pax just nodded, he was in so much pain and talking wasn't making it any better.

Hadley grabbed her coinet out of her pocket and turned on the light function. It illuminated the key and she could see that what the engraving said.

*1908 Evvelynn Street. Box 96.*

"What are we waiting for?" Pax hissed.

Hadley got to her feet, and typed the address into the coinet. It was only a few blocks away.

Hadley and Pax stumbled down the rubble in the fog and started to walk, following the map on the coinet since the fog was so heavy.

The rain started to lighten, but that just made the fog worse and worse. It got to a point where they couldn't see anything around.

Hadley's heart almost jumped out of her chest as she was notified they were there.

1908 Evvelynn Street. It towered into the air above them, completely made of dense dark stone that was intricately carved.

It was an old bank, a historic building. A little sign attached to the cement block in front of it that read it was established in 1902.

One of the marble pillars was broken in two and laid spread across the doorway. They hurdled themselves over it. The room was dark and the sunrise cast a spine-chilling glow over the cracked white marble. They ran up the marble stairs and through the teller's door. The gate was hanging by one last hinge and gave an unnaturally loud creak as they opened it.

Hadley paused and looked around. There was a spiral staircase leading into the floor and a half wall surrounded it. She took a leap of faith and charged down the stairs. The metal stairs clanged as they hustled down them.

They were in the vault, and it was filled with safety deposit boxes. Hadley ducked through the open vault door and into the crumbling room. It had obviously been hit by a bomb and raided. They both frantically searched for safety box 96. All the boxes were tarnished metal. Hadley spun around casting the glow of her coinet over as much as possible as fast as possible.

Then she saw it. It was on the bottom row tucked away from the rest. It had no damage whatsoever and was a gleaming sterling silver, as though it had been placed there after the bombs. Hadley took the chain out from around her neck that held the key and the ring slowly, and looked at it. She walked to the safe and knelt down. She ran her palm across the cold metal. She brushed her wet hair off her face.

She fumbled to try to get the key into the lock.

It was quiet, besides the fiddling of a key against the metal.

"Hurry, sun is coming up" Paxton urged not helping her nerves.

Then the sound started, it was loud, and droning.

"Is that..." Hadley muttered, trying to open the safety deposit box faster.

"Helicopter," was all Pax could get out.

She finally got it open. She turned the key slowly and opened the door. She pulled the safety deposit box out. She pulled the top open, and saw the last thing she'd ever expected.

A picture says a thousand words.

Then there were lights behind them coming down the stairs. Hadley thrust the entire contents of the box into the inside pocket of her jacket, there wasn't much. Then she stood up and threw the safety deposit box into the far dark corner.

Arms were on her, and they were being led out of the bank before they knew what was happening. Kane stood in front of a helicopter looking disapprovingly at her.

"This was a bad choice Had."

"But it was the right one for me," Hadley retorted as a man pushed her into the helicopter.

They watched the city disappear below them as they flew higher over the city.

# Chapter Twenty-Four

2228

Hadley had been pacing back and forth and back and forth in her room for almost 5 hours. The walls were looking surreal, as though she was being dragged into another world. She was seeing shapes in the generic grey paint that clearly weren't there.

She studied the way the light made the shape of a man and woman on the wall. As she got closer, the light changed and they disappeared. She placed her hand on the wall where they had been a moment ago.

She was frustrated. She was more than frustrated; in fact, she was livid. She couldn't believe she had been so stupid. Subconsciously she must have known what she had wanted the simulator to show. She must have known this was what she was trying to create.

Hadley slammed her fist into the wall. The outline of her fragile hand made an impression in the drywall.

She was at the lab before she knew what she was doing. She walked in and it was eerily quiet. Every computer was shut off.

Hadley looked at Biobot. "Hey wake up!"

"Hi Hadley. I can't do anything for you—"

"I know. But you can tell me what they have saved and printed."

"The genetic coding and the virus statistics, along with all the results. They have almost everything saved in various places."

"Did they copy or take the control key?" She held her breath for his answer.

"They never asked for it—"

"So they have it?"

"They don't even know there was one."

Hadley smiled beside herself, absolutely relieved.

"Can you help me hide it?"

"Yes Hadley. That is in the scope of things I can do. They forbade me from letting you change or delete any of the viruses."

"Loophole, I love it!" she chuckled.

"Hadley, I know what we created and I know what they will do with it. So I don't want it getting out either."

Hadley smiled at the Biobot as they began working. She started a long process of hiding the control. She needed it in a place she could find it but they never could.

She had no choice but to leave clues: lots and lots of clues.

She spent hours and hours with Biobot hiding everything to do with the control in a place she would find it and erasing his memory with his help. Finally, she sat in a chair and Biobot was scanning her brain. It was tedious and completely experimental. But they highlighted the exact pinpoint in her brain where the memories of the control lay. All except the starting point.

She walked into their living quarters and Anna was cutting her apple into eight perfect slices like she did every time she ate an apple. She had exactly a tablespoon of peanut butter in the centre of her plate. Hadley just smiled at her when she saw it.

"Same as always," Hadley joked.

"You know it Hadley." She returned a genuine smile.

She placed the apple slices around the plate and picked it up. She walked to the table and sat down. Hadley sat across from her at the table. The complex had been empty these last few days since the missions had gone out. Anna and Hadley were the only ones left in the complex by sheer dumb luck.

Hadley couldn't wait any longer. "Anna I found the pinpoint in my cerebral cortex that houses the activation information. I hid it, the activation information. They won't find it. As long as you erase her memory."

Anna stopped mid bite. She stared at Hadley dumbfounded. After a moment, she continued to chew and finally swallowed the apple piece. "And I thought I was smart. You always show me up." She smiled.

"I need you to destroy it." Hadley reached a hand forward and grabbed hers.

"That could kill you Hadley, or damage the rest of your memory."

"I don't care. Under no circumstances can anyone get it. You know what Hemmer is thinking about doing with it. That's why we put the controls in place. That's why I'm the only one who knows how to activate it."

Anna took another bite of her apple slice and pondered what Hadley had just said. "This is crazy Hadley. We put the measures in place so that we wouldn't have to resort to drastic measures like these."

"Look at what he is doing with the memory serum!"

Anna studied her hands intently. Her eyebrows furrowed close together. She was thinking through every possibility. Exactly like Hadley knew her best friend would. "Fine."

"Thank you." Hadley squeezed her hand.

"Let's just do it before I change my mind." She stood up, leaving the majority of her apple untouched. Hadley just followed.

They walked to the biomed lab. Hadley followed her into one of the procedure rooms. They opened the biobot and Anna put her fingerprint onto the scanner. Hadley's data came up immediately, just as she had saved it.

A little green dot was blinking in the left side of Hadley's cerebral cortex. It was the size of a one-hundredth of a pinprick. The biobot started to talk. "We will insert a particle laser through your skull and laser away the few particles responsible for the particular memory you want to erase permanently. Hadley, are you sure you don't just want to use your exemplary memory serum?"

"Biobot you know memory serums may have a cure eventually."

"That is true Hadley. But I must inform you of the risks of this procedure." her thoughts drifted to the man she loved as the biobot listed every tiny thing that could go wrong with the procedure. Hadley thought about his hair and his eyes. She had to give her head a shake.

"Ready?" Anna asked. She was holding a pen like instrument in her hand.

"Go ahead!"

Anna placed the end of the instrument just above Hadley's left ear. Anna pressed a button and Hadley heard the laser start to cut through her skull. The pain was blinding but she didn't move.

"Do you want local anesthetic?" She asked.

"You know I don't believe in that."

"Just checking."

Hadley heard the laser stop cutting and the cord of the second laser unravel. The cord, like a snake, entered her brain. She could almost feel it squirming around inside her brain though that could have been her imagination. On second thought, it was definitely her imagination. Finally, everything was silent as the laser found its target.

The biobot spoke, "Anna you have to press the red button now."

"Ok." Anna whispered and she pressed it.
Hadley felt a tingle through her spine, but nothing more. Like that, the memory was gone and she smiled, relieved. The laser recoiled and she felt the instrument stitch up her head.

"Thanks Anna," Hadley whispered feeling nauseous.

"Anything."

She stood up her stomach in knots. She ran to the recycling basket and puked. Her throat burned. But relief came shortly after the dry heaving ended.

"Are you okay? Do we need to check for more neuro damage? Biobot scanned—but—"

"No," Hadley managed a weak smile, "I just haven't been feeling well the last few days—who knows."

Hadley stood up from the ground and they walked out of the lab. The activation procedure was safe. No one knew anything anymore. Hadley was ecstatic.

Until that is, the news came the day after she had erased the activation information. Russia had released a deadly super virus in various places across the planet and already death tolls were in the thousands.

Anna and Hadley were watching the news when Hemmer burst in. "WHAT DID YOU DO?!"

"Nothing!" She jumped away from him.

"I can't activate your virus. I can't fight back."

"Maybe something went wrong?"

"No—you did something!" He motioned and three men emerged from the shadows behind him. Two of them grabbed Hadley and she was hauled out of the room while the other held Anna back.

Hadley was thrust into a chair and biobot started to scan her brain. "There appears to be a scar that wasn't there before."

"You erased the memory!? How!?"

"I'm not stupid you know Hemmer."

"How do I get it?!" Hemmer was screaming in her face. His hot breath made her cheeks red.

"You will never get it!" Hadley spat in his face.

"Take her to cryosleep—we will wake her up when this is over. Then we can figure it out and get the Russians back for this."

# Chapter Twenty-Five

2446

Hadley was puzzled by what Hemmer wanted. Why he needed her so urgently. She walked into the lab and it took her a second to understand what was happening.

Hemmer was standing over Anna who was tied to a chair.

"Hadley. Nice of you to join us."

"Hemmer what is going on?" Hadley asked before she saw that he was holding a gun with a silencer.

"I have word that the Asian United Nations plans to invade the Western United Nations in the next month. They are going to declare full-fledged nuclear war."

"That's not possible…" She said holding up a hand to calm him down.

"We don't know what's possible anymore." He was shaking with rage. His eyes were like fires in his face.

"Hemmer you know that Asia stands no chance." Hadley said calmly.

"They will really stand no chance if you give me the activation sequence."

"I can't do that, even if I knew it I couldn't give it to you."

"I will shoot Anna if you don't!" He pointed the gun at Anna. There was sheer panic in her eyes.

"Hemmer, stop this!"

"She doesn't know it," Anna cried out.

"I'll give you to the count of three. One…"

"STOP!" Hadley screamed, "You saw her brain scans!"

"Two."

"Hemmer you can't have it." Anna whispered.

"Anna I'm sorry, you know I don't have it. Hemmer STOP!"

"I know Hadley, it's okay."

"HEMMER STOP!" Hadley screamed.

"Three."

It was as though the next few moments played in her head in slow motion. She watched as Hemmer pulled the trigger. The bullet travelled slowly into the back of Anna's skull. The blood splattered forward as the bullet carried on into the wall. Hadley felt the warm blood hit her, soaking her face and t-shirt. She fell to her knees.

She couldn't comprehend.

"Now you know how serious I am. Get me the information, or someone you care more about will be next."

Hemmer wiped the barrel of his gun as he walked away, neither care nor consequences in store. Hadley cried for an eternity on the floor, clutching her best friend in her arms. She was hysterical until finally she wiped her face and went to find Saul. This was the last straw.

# Chapter Twenty-Six

Paxton and Hadley sat behind a large mahogany desk in an enormous office. Most of the room was glass and it had a 270-degree view of a large area of the complex. It looked like a bird's nest; you could see everyone's movements.

Hadley studied a man typing furiously on a computer at a small desk in the corner. He was the oldest person she had seen since being here, and had to be in his mid 80's. She wrapped the blanket she had been given around her shoulders, shivering since she was still soaked to her bones. Her hands were tingling as they regained feeling. She flexed her fingers looking at her white knuckles.

There was an antique tea set in front of them on the desk. One of the luxuries that Hemmer must have thought himself privy to. The thin porcelain had gold and blue flowers running over it. Hadley grabbed the teapot with shaking hands and poured the tea into one of the cups. She grabbed the saucer and cup and took a sip. The hot liquid poured down her throat and instantly warmed her.

"Want some?" She asked to Pax. He just shook his head barely able to open his mouth. His entire face had become a mess of dried blood.

They both jumped as Hemmer walked into the room, or more like exploded into the room. He slammed his fists onto the table. It made Hadley jump so high that the hot tea she was holding crashed onto her lap. The liquid ran down her legs. It burned but she hardly noticed. Her cup clinked to the ground and rolled across the floor until it hit the window and stopped with a thud.

"What do you think you were doing?" he yelled with an emphasis on every individual syllable.

"We—" Hadley couldn't think. She had not formulated an excuse or a reason or any story to tell Hemmer. She didn't want to have to have an excuse; she wanted freedom, though this egalitarian world seemed to lack that.

"You could have died, or worse been tortured until you told them something! Do you know the ramifications of that?!" He yelled into Hadley's face, basically ignoring Pax.

"I didn't know we couldn't leave," Hadley said raising an eyebrow, taking a different approach. She knew she was crossing a line but she couldn't help but say it. The looked in his eyes was worth whatever came next.

"You dumb stupid little girl, I knew from the moment I saw you, you would be trouble." Hadley heard the slap across her face before she felt it. Her cheek stung and got hot and she could feel her eyes start watering but she forbade herself from crying. This was the second time she had been slapped in a matter of hours.

"Stop it!" Paxton wheezed through his broken teeth, standing up. Two guards walked into the room and pushed him against the glass wall.

"You are under my command, do you understand," Hemmer sneered inches away from Hadley's face.

"I just want more answers—" she said throwing caution to the wind. He yanked one of her arms and pulled her to her feet. He twisted his hand into her hair and threw her face first against the desk. He brought his face close to her ear.

She could feel his angry breath through her hair. He had his arm pressed into her back. Her cheek pressed against the cold mahogany as her blood boiled.

"You can't handle more answers! There is nothing else you need to know. Other than you are on the winning side and we are fighting a war against a militia revolution! The RFE's are confused, delusional and reckless! We have the ability to save this planet. Do not hinder us! Kane believes in you, but I could kill you right here. I will destroy everything that gets in my way." His words burned into Hadley like a hot brand. She felt him let go. Then he turned to Paxton, "Same goes for you. Now go see Dr. Emily before you die."

Hemmer walked out of the room slamming the door so hard that it rattled the walls. Hadley ran into Paxton's arms. He held her for a moment as she held in the tears. They were both shaking and confused.

The guards motioned them out of the office. As they did Hadley glanced at the man typing in the corner and he briefly looked at her with a smile. The wrinkles around his old eyes scrunched together and he immediately went back to typing. He was so small Hadley couldn't help but keep studying him as they were led out.

Once back at the dorm she gave Pax a short hug and kissed him on the cheek. His scruff was rough against her lips. The warmth of his skin left them tingling.

Pax headed towards the doctor's office.

Everything was unusually quiet in the complex since it was the wee hours of the morning.

They went our separate ways without talking and left each other with nothing more than one last meek smile. Hadley walked into her room and turned the shower on. She took her jacket off and went back to her bed. She pulled up the mattress and put the jacket underneath.

The bathroom mirror was foggy, and she wiped one spot off to see her reflection. Her hair was matted in blood and mud. She stopped looking and peeled off her layers. She stepped into the hot shower stream.

The red filled the bottom of the shower. She stood there until the water started to get colder and the digital temperature screen gave her a *'you've used your daily hot water allowance'* warning.

She had a cut above her eye that wouldn't stop bleeding, so after she dried off she headed out to the common area in search of a first aid kit.

Vanya was reading a book in the living room when she walked in. She looked at her in terror.

"What happened to you?" she said stunned. Hadley caught a glimpse of herself in the mirror and saw a black eye and fat lip had formed. She had scratches all over her arms.

"Long story…" Hadley said exhausted as she sat down on the couch. "Do we have anything I could put on this cut?" Hadley took the cloth she was holding on the cut off and watched as the skin flapped open and blood streamed down her face.

Vanya looked at Hadley's face for a moment and left the room. She came back holding a small box the size of a box of cards.

"First aid kit," she said when she saw the puzzled look on Hadley's face.

She opened the box and grabbed a thin spray can. She pressed the button and Had felt a cooling sensation. She grabbed a small bug like tool out and put it on the end of the gash. It was reminiscent of a beetle. It had six little legs and even two antennas. Hadley watched in her reflection as it turned green and skirted across her face stitching up the wound, whilst spraying it at the same time. The tiny sensors inside of it made the stitches a precise science. It turned red and stopped at the end. Vanya pulled it off and put it into the case.

"Good to go!" she said smiling. Hadley smiled back as fast as she could.

*The RFE's could have killed me tonight, what was I thinking?* She thought with a shiver.

"Are you all right Hadley?" Vanya asked placing her hand over Hadley's.

"Fine," Hadley smiled meekly.

The noose lying on the ground was an image that would be burnt in her memory forever.

# Chapter Twenty-Seven

They were back in the lecture hall a day later, everyone was murmuring about Hadley and Paxton's adventures. Hadley was avoiding eye contact with most of the other pingers in the room who seemed to be staring at the back of her head.

Kane was talking, his voice was strained today. "In exactly two weeks we are going to start our main batch of fieldwork. We are working on teams as of now and will be sending you out to give information to the RFE's. We want their leaders to contact us. As you all know the fate of the world lies in us forming a cooperative society. We have very limited time for this."

This spiked Hadley's attention, she was used to daydreaming during these meetings, because they seemed to have no relevance to her. Kane caught Hadley's eye and hiccupped in what he was saying. She smirked at him. He looked away and kept talking.

Hadley sat up a little straighter in her seat, wanting to hear his plan for the people who had tried to kill her.

"Until now we have not talked about the RFE's in depth. We wanted to make sure everyone was feeling normal and the same before we brought down the hard truth on you all."

Hadley could sense the anticipation in the room, her own heart was pounding. Everyone's heads bobbed up a little higher. Pax adjusted himself forward in his seat.

"The Revolutionaries for the Free Earth or RFE's are a group of people that want freedom above all else on this planet. They will do anything to get what they want. This is unlike ourselves that want to unite the planet and make earth a sustainable and safe place. It is thought that the RFE's had powerful people in government and they initialized the war to put the planet in a so-called "restart". We have intelligence for some of their "Cells" and hope to go out in the field to make contact with them. At first it will not be dangerous, just giving some flash drives and other information. Persuade some of the lesser committed to change sides."

Hadley stared at him shocked. She glanced around and saw similar expressions on everyone's faces. The anger started in her chest and moved throughout her whole body.

*They knew who destroyed the planet! They knew who started this war and killed everyone and we were just sitting here playing scientist?!* Hadley could feel the anger boiling inside of her. She looked at Pax beside me and he wore the same face. She wanted to hurt them for what they did to us. They would pay one way or another.

This was WAR.

She walked in a daze to the lab. One of the lab offshoots was analyzing small samples of water from the oceans and Hadley decided to look at the results. She also wanted a place to be alone with her thoughts, so she set herself up in the back corner and watched the monitors pull water from their submerged computers and analyze it.

Vanya had decided to go back to the apartment for a while before coming to work and Kane had disappeared. It didn't matter though; Hadley no longer felt the need to work on their Earth climate model. She knew that nuclear winter was coming but no longer cared about stopping it. She knew what was out there, she had seen it firsthand. The realization had set in. They were never going to save the planet with the RFE's still out there, the people who resorted to violence and had started the war. They were against the govs and no matter what anyone did they would stand in the way!

Hadley decided to turn her attention to improving her skills in the field. The planet needed to restore itself and they needed to work together to make it a place for generations to come.

But there she sat in this lab room pretending she cared.

So she got up and went to a weather simulator. She watched a miniature tornado swirl around in the tube that sat in the middle of the room. She pushed a dial up that made it climb from a class three to a class five. For fun she dropped some houses and cars into the simulator, with the press of a button they appeared out of thin air. She watched as the tornado flung the plastic houses against the tube. They shattered into pieces as they hit the glass then they dissipated into a pile of pixels. Hadley pressed a button so it started to rain, lightning streaked across the tube.

She didn't hear Kane come into the room until he was standing right in front of her, staring at her through the tornado and pouring rain. She jumped and pressed stop on the simulator. She took a step back and looked at him.

"Bored of our research already?" He smiled.

"No, it's just that, it doesn't seem productive does it? With them out there we will never implement any of it. And it's not like we can stop the storm." She shrugged frustrated.

He smiled. "You're different you know."

"Different from what?" She raised an eyebrow at him.

He searched for the words, "Than when you got here I mean."

"Oh?" She could tell he wanted to say more but couldn't find the words.

Hadley walked over to him. He took a step back and leaned against a table with his hand holding him up. Hadley gently put her hand on his. He didn't pull away.

"You really want what's best for everyone in the world," he stated quietly.

Hadley bit her bottom lip, warmth growing in her stomach. She couldn't help but think of her dream again, the one she couldn't seem to shake. It felt so real.

"You are different from the person I met when I first got here too. You don't scare me anymore," Hadley said softly as she got closer. She took shallow breaths because she was shaking. She looked up through her eyelashes at him. He was even more handsome up close.

His free hand went to Hadley's waist. He pulled her towards him so their hips were touching. They stood there for a second, making sure they both knew what was happening, before he brought his lips to hers. They were breathing the same air. Then he kissed her. She moved her hand to the back of his head. It was electric and dizzying.

He picked her up and leaned her onto the counter. She felt his weight on top of her, grasping at every inch. He kissed her neck as he ran his hand down her side to her hip. His hand moved to the clasp on her jeans. Unconsciously she twitched, a picture of Paxton in her mind.

"Is everything okay?" he asked.

"Yes," she said pushing his hand back to her waist. She kissed him and he smiled.

"Should we wait?" he whispered in her ear before he kissed her again. She just shook her head and wrapped her legs around his waist and they were lost.

*Father figure my ass!*

# Chapter Twenty-Eight

2447

Hadley was sitting wrapped in Paxton's arm. They were both shaking. She could feel the tears running down her face and his. She couldn't bring herself to look at him. She could feel by his trembling he was as upset as she was.

They were sitting in a dark room that was under construction. They were hiding against a framed wall under a painter's tarp. They were on the top floor of a building rising hundreds of meters into the air.

A nuclear cloud appeared perfectly framed through the window behind them. Hadley watched in slow motion as the cloud erupted in the air. The surrounding areas blasted out of the way, as though in slow motion.

"What have we started?" She heard Paxton whisper.

She still couldn't bring herself to answer she knew it was her fault. She took a small box out of her pocket and started to carve holes into it.

Then her coinet erupted with a call. Kane was calling. She immediately pressed ignore.

Then an unknown number appeared.

"Maybe it's Saul." Paxton said glancing at her coinet.

"Maybe," Hadley said.

She picked up the phone with a, "Hello."

"Hadley, is that you?"

"Yes?"

"Are you safe?"

"I'm not sure."

"You weren't in the blast radius?"

"No, but I can see it from here."

"Are you downtown?"

"Yes."

"Are you headed to the safe house?"

"We needed to get rid of a GOV tail, but Pax and I are headed there soon."

Hadley glanced at Paxton with a meek smile. He placed his hand on her arm.

"Please be careful, we don't want anything to happen to…"

Hadley cut him off, "I know how important this is Saul. I'm not going to mess it up like everything else."

"I don't think that."

"You said it last night."

"I was just worried."

"Don't be. In a few months this will all be over and you won't have to see me again."

"You know that's not what I want."

"Don't you?"

Hadley hung up; she didn't want to hear his excuses or reasons for constantly putting her down.

# Chapter Twenty-Nine

All of them were back in the gym for final physical assessments. Hadley could feel that her body had become harder over the last few weeks. She was in peak physical shape, she didn't even know how, but they were taking supplements every day and she had built muscle like crazy. Hadley was able to move faster, stronger and more precisely, knowing her opponents move before them. But she still didn't know what would happen to if she didn't pass. She knew what she needed to do though. Her muscles still hurt from their adventure a few nights prior and she had been so busy with prepping for this assessment that she hadn't been able to look at the content of the vault.

It frightened her to look at everything, she felt like everything was unravelling, and she had just made a decision about her movement forward.

She looked around at their group and they looked like a synchronized army. Jinni came up beside her. "You ready for this?" She asked nudging Hadley in the side. Her hair was dyed pink today and she was laughing. Hadley looked at her knowing Jinni had nothing to worry about today. She was always the best.

Hemmer walked in without Kane. "I will be running the assessments today. Remember, you passing this is crucial. We need to be able to trust your bodies to survive out there. Also if I deem you unfit to continue your involvement will be terminated. Those are the facts."

Hadley's heart dropped into her stomach, she felt like she was sinking into the floor. Hemmer had had it out for her since day one, and the fact he was here without Kane was bad news. He had threatened to kill her already.

Pax gave Hadley a sideways glance. She had a lump in her throat.

Hemmer pulled out his tablet. He opened it with a flash and started at the top. "First up we have Hadley, against Jeremiah."

Jinni looked at Hadley in disbelief, actually everyone did. Hadley was just stunned. She just stood there staring at Hemmer for a moment before Vanya gave her a slight nudge. She couldn't think as she stepped up on the raised platform. Everyone had confused faces, except Jeremiah.

Jeremiah smirked at her, a devilish grin. Kane always put them with even opponents, though that wasn't the case in the real world. It worked better in a controlled environment where you didn't have the option to run.

Jeremiah could beat Hadley with his hands tied behind his back. Hadley put her hands up preparing herself. She flexed her arms and bent her knees. She tried to feel the world around her. She set herself in a balanced and poised position.

"All right, and you may begin," Hemmer said with a smirk.

Jeremiah raised his eyebrows and lurched towards Hadley. He punched sharply with his left arm and she narrowly dodged his hand. He jab-jabbed and she managed to avoid him with fast footwork. But he was beginning to understand her tactic.

"You can't just keep running from me forever."

"Watch me," Hadley countered.

He punched right but she was ready for it. He had put all his weight into it and she took his footing out with her heel. But he grabbed her wrist as he fell. She somersaulted, landing on her back. She twisted onto her stomach and attempted to push herself up but Jeremiah was quicker. He pushed her back down and grabbed her hair. He pulled her neck back sharply.

"Told you."

"Fuck you Jeremiah."

Hadley squirmed under him but he was bigger and stronger than her. She heard the crunch before she felt it as he smashed her face against the ground. She saw the ground twice more as her face hit the pavement.

Just as he was about to do it again, Hadley brought her elbow up sharply into his face. He receded for a moment, and that was all she needed to get back to her feet.

She could taste the blood in her mouth but wasn't about to give up.

"You always go for the nose, don't you?" Jeremiah almost laughed as she started to get up.

"Mostly," Hadley said as she ran towards him, she jumped, wrapping her legs around his neck. She spun, placing her hands neatly onto the ground and flipped him onto his back.

Like a ninja, she was on top of him and brought her fist neatly into the side of his jaw. One of his teeth cracked, her pushed her off and just as he was about to bring his fist into her face someone yelled.

"Enough!"

Hadley stared up at the ceiling for a moment unable to lift her head but when she did she saw Kane. He was shaking his head in the doorway. He was livid. His eyes were shooting daggers at Hemmer.

"I will remind you Hemmer that I am in charge of this portion of the SPaDI project," Kane said calmly.

"I will remind you I am in charge of you," Hemmer said laughing. Kane stared at him as he took a step forward with fire in his eyes. He was scary when he was angry. Hemmer laughed at him and handed over the tablet. "Kane, I saw what I needed to anyway."

"Thank you," Kane said as Hemmer left the room, "Get off of her Jeremiah, I'm glad you can show off your brute force on someone a fraction of your size. Hadley you need to work harder, not everyone will be Jinni's size. Frickin' ridiculous."

Jeremiah got off her back. He marched away. She pushed herself up and walked off the platform.

Embarrassment was the only thing she felt. There was a trail of red drops on the floor as Hadley wandered back to find a first aid kit, her nose was bleeding profusely.

She grabbed the match size box and inserted a smaller beetle into her nose. It went at it, fixing everything with a click and a crunch. Then it sauntered onto her cheek with a ding. She grabbed it off and it turned red in her hand. She placed it back in the box and grabbed a towel off the shelf. She wiped the blood off.

"Ok next up, Jinni and Vanya," Kane shouted. Everyone was quiet again.

Hadley couldn't decide whether she should stay or leave. She turned back around to watch the fight. The two girls smiled at each other and started to fight. It looked choreographed. They were both so good. They moved faster and faster until finally Vanya had Jinni on the ground. There were cheers from the group.

The fights went on; Hadley barely paid attention to who was fighting who. She didn't want to see what her face looked like now. She knew it was becoming more and more a disfigured mess. She just stared at the ground, looking at the brown flecks through the tiles.

The fights finally ended. She felt like she had stood frozen in place all day.

"You are all good to go, expedition teams will be announced tomorrow," Kane yelled.

Hadley waited behind everyone as they clattered loudly out the door. Paxton even caught her eye but she looked away. Soon Kane and she were the only people left in the room. She looked up at him with anger. Kane looked at her, unmoving, uncaring.

"You could have died; you are being a stupid little girl!" Kane half shouted at her across the gym.

Hadley didn't know what she expected him to say, but it wasn't that. He walked up to her and grabbed her waist. He kissed her hard, it wasn't passionate it was out of need. For the first time she was scared of him.

She turned her head and pushed him off, "I could have taken Jeremiah! I don't need you to save me! He wouldn't have killed me. It was just a test."

"You don't know what Jeremiah is capable of. You don't know what anyone is capable of given the right circumstances."

"Kane, you're always right aren't you?"

"You always need saving Hadley. You always have. You can act big and tough, but you are just you. That's just a small insignificant girl who is intelligent beyond her years. You belong in a lab inputing data, not out in the real world. That's all."

"You fucking asshole! I don't need you or anyone else. I'm strong enough on my own."

He came at her again. She stepped away, he grabbed at her, catching the edge of her shirt, ripping it.

"Stop it!" she practically screamed. He didn't even blink. He started to undo the buttons on her jacket and exposed her sports bra. He pulled her in sternly and started to kiss her neck. She pushed away.

She could feel his fingers grasping at her hips. His fingers moved south. Then he saw it, the chain had come out of her ripped top and was gleaming in the florescent lights. He stopped. He stared for a moment then he grabbed the chain and pulled the end up to his face. He looked at the ring dangling from the end. He let go of her completely, as if burnt.

"Where did you get this?" he whispered a look of panic on his face

"Nowhere. I just found it on the ground," she said nervously through gritted teeth. He stood up staring dumbfounded at her. He backed up slowly.

"Who else knows you have that?" he hissed.

"No one, just me," she said pulling the halves of her shirt together and standing up. She slowly backed away from him putting some space between them.

Without another word he walked out of the training center. He took one glance back and was gone. She fell onto her knees, sat down and cried.

Then she composed herself.

*What does he think I know?* She thought. Then she ran. Faster than she ever thought she could back to her room to see the contents of the safety deposit box.

# Chapter Thirty

The first thing she saw was a picture of her and Paxton wearing red RFE t-shirts. This was the photo she had seen when she had first opened the safety deposit box. She couldn't understand how it could be real; it had to be photo-shopped.

She studied the logo and noticed it was the same one that was spotted throughout the city. The circle with the V's. Hadley had seen it the first day she had woken up.

Next there was a poster with her face on it reading VOTE FOR FREE EARTH. Then there was a piece of paper with another address *90 Hummingbird Court*. This time there was a coin stuck to it.

The last piece of paper she pulled out was a handwritten note: *Hadley, you need to remember, you need to follow the clues. Remember, you have done it before. Don't ever forget who we are against.* It was her handwriting. She just stared at it. *Follow the clues?* She thought.

She pushed herself up and with the papers in one hand she walked to Pax's room. He never locked the door and she went straight in. She crossed her legs beside Pax's torso and nudged him with her free hand.

"What is it?" he said groggily rolling over to face her. But he kept his eyes closed.

"Wake up!" she whispered nudging him again. She poked him in the side and he twitched.

"It's the middle of the night Hadley," he said absolutely annoyed, still without opening his eyes.

"Come on!" she said shaking him.

"Come back to sleep," he said burying his face in the pillow. He waved his arm to dismiss her.

Hadley let out a frustrated sigh putting her hands in the air. She set the papers down beside her and pushed herself onto his back straddling him.

"Wake up," she whispered seductively into his ear laying her torso flat on his back. He turned over to face her with his eyes wide open. Their hips were touching and she could feel his excitement growing.

"I'm awake," he half exclaimed

"Good! Come see this," she said pushing off him and regaining her sitting position beside him. She gathered all the papers in her hands and waited for him to sit up.

He gave a huff, "you've got to be kidding!"

He got into a sitting position adjusting his crotch uncomfortably and sat face to face with Hadley. He gave her a stern look. She rolled her eyes and laughed.

"Finally."

"It's a good thing you're cute or I wouldn't put up with this—" he garbled.

Hadley thrust everything from the deposit box into his hands.

He studied it for a few minutes. They let the silence wash over them. Hadley didn't have a clue where to start or what to say. Pax's face turned down, deep in thought. He just sat staring at the picture of the two of us in RFE t-shirts.

"What do you think it all means? Do you think we were actually RFE?" Paxton said looking at Hadley concernedly.

"We can't have been— look at what they've done."

"What Hemmer has said they've done," he pointed out. It wasn't like Pax to say anything bad about Hemmer or Kane or the GOVs.

"All I know is that I need the truth. The whole truth."

"And nothing but the truth," he teased in a deeply serious voice. "How do you know it's not a trap?"

"I don't," she said with a shrug, "but I have to find out. If it is a trap it was very well planned. They hid the first clue in my tomb. So if they are going to kill me at least they've worked for it. But I have this feeling in my gut—"

"So when do we go?" Paxton smiled.

"Let's give it a few days Pax. Let everything cool off and let Hemmer think that we are following the rules." As she said it she could feel the excitement. She was smiling from ear to ear.

The anticipation of this adventure made her forget everything that had just happened. She grabbed Pax's face and kissed him. He rolled on top of her on the floor and they got lost in the moment. The papers scattered around, almost forgotten.

# Chapter Thirty-One

She couldn't find the strength to take the ring off from around her neck. She was drawn to it in an unnatural sort of way. The cold metal was soothing as she felt it pressed against her chest.

The earth simulator was showing increased storms. Every single continent was experiencing torrential weather. Hadley was inputing numbers but it was all no use.

She took a sip of her coffee and almost choked as she watched Kane saunter into the room. He was acting as though nothing was wrong.

"Kane," she said melodramatically.

"Vanya is running errands. Can you come to my office for a moment? I need to show you something anyway." He grabbed her hand lightly and led her back to his office. It was large and colourful. A projected 3D globe spun around on his desk, a miniature version of the one in the lab.

He closed the door behind them. He went behind his desk, sat down and pulled out a photograph. He handed it to Hadley.

Before she even looked at it she said, "You're not going to apologize?"

"I'm truly sorry about the other day. It was all these feelings and emotions. I don't have anything I can say."

Hadley peered into his eyes and decided to take him at face value.

"I found this in one of the old files," he smiled sitting on his desk motioning to what he had just handed her. She looked at the photo and he pulled her backwards into his arms.

Her back was pressed into his chest; she could feel his heart beating.

She looked down at the photograph and it was of the two of them. They were holding up a globe. His hand was on her back and they were both smiling. Hadley tilted her head backwards to look at him, "Do you remember this being taken?"

He shook his head, "No, I wish I did. But the war made lots of things blurry."

He turned her around and kissed her. She felt his strong arms around her and kissed him back. She felt something when she was with him. There was a feeling in the pit of her stomach, what kind of feeling she wasn't sure exactly.

Either way they didn't stop. She knew she had to choose one of these men soon enough. For now, though, she didn't know anything about their pasts, she didn't know anything at all, and therefore she felt like she couldn't make an educated decision on the matter. Maybe it was a coward's decision, but it was the one she was sticking with.

They heard the door open outside in the lab and stepped apart awkwardly. Hadley opened the door with a final glance over her shoulder and went out into the lab.

"Hey Hadley," Vanya cooed. Hadley's face flushed a bright red and she looked at her feet.

"Any progress on the storm?" she asked mindlessly.

Vanya laughed, "I still don't believe it's possible to stop an ice age."

"Me neither, it seems a ridiculous notion, but at least we will have all the information and can make predictions about the length and severity."

"To the order of a few hundred thousand years. Look at the Cryogenian ice age. It lasted over 200 Million years."

"But the little ice age only lasted around 10 thousand. Humans as we know can survive another few thousand years. We can ensure that. Look at how far we've come."

"The conditions are different than the times before, we may not even get them close. We could doom everyone if we're wrong."

"Honestly Vanya, we can never be worse off—just ill prepared."

"Hadley, look at what humanity did to the planet. Even before we were born, they were filling the oceans with plastic and the air with $CO_2$ and hydrofluorocarbons. Slowly eating away at the atmosphere and the ocean until there was nothing left. No one cared, should we?"

Hadley nodded at her slowly and shrugged. The Earth had been to hell and back, humanity had ensured that. The planet was supposed to be a self-sustaining ecosystem that could continue on for millions of years, starting and restarting, self-regulating. If it had known what the first hominines—the first real ancestors of the humans that developed in the eastern region of what is now the United Nations of Africa—would do, maybe it would have tried to destroy them, much like the dinosaurs. Though that was caused by an asteroid.

With that, they went straight back to work, leaving the conversation unresolved and unfinished. But the ideas of evolution and planetary resetting danced through the back of Hadley's mind.

Kane kept Vanya and Hadley working late for the majority of the next week. So much so Hadley barely had time to think about getting to the newest address.

It was the early morning when Hadley finally got up to make herself another cup of coffee; she stared through Kane's open door as he sat with his face between his hands. Hadley poured an extra cup and walked into the room.

She set down the coffee on his desk and he looked up at her.

"I'm sorry," he said gently.

"You don't have to be," Hadley murmured, unable to find the right words to say.

"I do; I mean everything is my fault." He realized what he said after he said it.

"What?"

Kane looked into Hadley's eyes, "everything that has gone wrong here was my fault. Losing you was my fault."

She just stared at him. "Do you remember something?" she asked gently.

"I just had a brief glimmer of a memory..."

Hadley held her breath, waiting for him to say what he remembered.

Then the bell rang. It was just a loud droning, going on and on.

"We better go," Kane said getting up, drinking his cup of coffee in one go and starting to walk away.

"Kane!" Hadley said hurrying after him, "We are not even close to being done with this conversation."

Vanya joined them for the walk to the auditorium but Kane didn't say another word about what he was hinting at. Hadley sat down beside Pax and a few minutes later the presentations started.

First everyone explained what they were working on and what was happening. Then finally, Kane got up on stage.

"We are nearing a point where we are at a crossroads. A storm is coming that will change everything again. We need to adapt, to change, in a way that we haven't before. We have all lived through a lot. This will be the worst," Kane said strolling in front of the meeting room. "It is important that starting today we make a plan for our upcoming course of action."

There was a murmur from the room, a soft whisper that was gradually growing stronger. Kane demanded attention at the front of the room, though everyone couldn't help but wonder the magnitude of what he was saying. The information he was giving was intense, and isolating, but he said it in a way that made Hadley believe this was not the first time they had encountered such a dire situation.

"The storm you see here is coming faster and harder than we could have imagined. There are events happening worldwide that are causing catastrophic damage." Kane continued waving his hand in front of the holographic projector. An image of the earth appeared around him. The storm swirled behind his head. He held out a hand and zoomed in on the continental United States. For comparison, he opened the globe with a wave of his hands so it laid flat filling the entirety of the front of the room. The storm swirled violently, and the eye of the most massive portion was by far bigger than the anything you could imagine. It looked unreal, and frighteningly it wasn't.

"So where do we start?" Jeremiah piped in watching intently.

"We can't stop the storm; we can only prepare."

"So what are we going to do in the meantime?" Jeremiah pushed further. He felt helpless and was overcompensating by being pushy.

"We need to resolve our conflict with the RFE's first of all. The human race relies on as many people living, especially after 2066. Once we do this everything else will fall into place. Every project everyone has been working on for the last bunch of weeks will be able to be implemented. Your teams are posted on the hologram in the front. Check them before you leave. These will be your teams for everything in the coming weeks. They will be like your family, treat them as such. Protect each other."

"How do you propose stopping the conflict with the RFE's?" Hadley asked finally daring to speak up. Maybe she was overstepping, but everyone turned around and stared at her.

Hemmer stood up, "We, Hadley my dear, will do whatever we have to." That was the end of the conversation.

That was all he could say, all he would say.

However, Hadley pressed harder, standing up despite her better judgement, "Hemmer you have said these are militants that we have no purpose conversing with. Why now?"

"To save humanity," Kane answered calmly.

"Sure Kane, that's great and all. But aren't we working hard to preserve a type of humanity that we want for the future?"

"Hadley, sit down," Kane urged, but she didn't even look at him, her eyes stayed glued on Hemmer.

Hadley took a deep breath and started to voice how she really felt. The anger she felt boiled over into her next statement, a noose swinging in the wind forcing her voice, "Hemmer, you have said, time and time again, that the RFE's are terrorists. It has long been known that we don't negotiate with terrorists. Why are we going to give them information?"

"You don't want to know."

"I have the right to know!" she screamed unable to control the volume of her voice.

"We are giving them information to see if any of them want to come back to our side. We are giving them the chance to live through this storm. To be on our side again." It was the first glimpse into Hemmer's humanity, and his insanity. Both had been buried deep within his soul. Hadley nodded and sat down, giving up her fight with him, understanding where he was coming from. Kane gave her a weak smile, almost thanking her for giving up. Everyone sat breathless for a moment, taking in the magnitude of Hemmer's statement. Taking in the fact that Hemmer really did want to save humanity, in his own twisted way.

After a few moments they got up. Hadley walked up slowly to the projector at the back that listed the teams. She had her fingers crossed that she wouldn't be paired with the one pinger she didn't trust.

She looked at the list: Team 1: Captain: Jeremiah, Vanya, Hadley, Fred, Kristen, Zeek, Olive, and Gunner

Hadley sighed, determined to make the best of a bad situation. By now word had gotten around about their escapades two nights ago and the fact that they had been out of the complex. Everyone understood why Hemmer had put her against Jeremiah during the fights.

The other teams read:

Team 2: Captain: Paxton, Stephen, Marcia, Cullen, Nadine, Alyse, Ernest

Team 3: Captain: Jinni, Joey, Syb, Benji, Caitlyn, Kryp, Daro, Marcia

Hadley groaned again, she caught Kane's eye but he looked away quickly. Paxton grabbed her around the waist and gave her a squeeze to stop her from saying anything. They walked out of the room ready to plan their next escape.

# Chapter Thirty-Two

Later, they didn't even pretend they were going to bed. They sat in Paxton's room with a map he had stolen. After they had left the meeting they each had gone to our own labs and worked for a while.

Kane didn't come back to the lab, a fact that annoyed Hadley immensely. Paxton had found the map while he was in the electronic archives and had copied it quickly onto his coinet. Though he was under strict supervision by Alice he had managed to snag it. Hadley definitely thought Alice had a soft spot for him.

Hadley took a virtual stylus and changed the colour to red. She placed an x on their location in the compound. She circled the exits leading out of the complex. There were 14 separate places to get out.

"Those are all patrolled," Paxton remarked, crossing out 10 with a black pen.

"This one I haven't seen this one before," Hadley stated circling it a second time.

"I didn't even know there was one there," Paxton wrinkled his brow in confusion.

Hadley said decidedly, "Well that's the one we should try."

Hadley got up and stretched her arms above her head. She headed for the door. Paxton blinked for a moment before he got up too.

It didn't take them long to reach the spot on the map where the exit was marked. Hadley looked at the abandoned hallway they were approaching and noticed it was under construction. There was a large yellow sign on it that read RESTRICTED. She pushed open a glass door and walked into a cloud of sawdust. Broken glass and nails crunched beneath her shoes as she walked further down. She tiptoed her way through. There were plastic sheets hanging through the hall. She pushed them out of the way as she walked. Single light bulbs hung from the ceiling, bare and alone, casting an eerie circle of light every so often and leaving the space between them dark. They were both leaving fine footprints in the thick dust, which was flying around them in soft pillows.

Hadley stopped suddenly to look in a lab. The top half of the door was glass. She wiped a spot clean and peered through the glass at a room that was frozen in time. The red streaks across the walls were what caught her attention most. The vials and equipment laid smashed on the counters and floors. The windows were cracked. A large red spot stained the floor and glowed through the dust. Hadley slowly grabbed the metal door handle and pulled the door open transfixed. Paxton grabbed her arm.

"What are you doing?" he whispered gripping her arm tightly while pulling her back. She just pulled away sharply and didn't answer him. The broken vials and equipment mesmerized her into a trance like state. She went to the wall and put her hand out. She didn't touch them but she could feel the marks. She let her fingers linger just above the wall, just over the long streaks. The drawn out streaks of a blood soaked hand running across a white wall.

An image of people being killed came to Hadley's mind, blood splattering through the room and the screams. She shuttered, crossing her arms. Pax just stood by the door watching her intently. He had set his jaw and was uncomfortable with the whole situation.

Hadley walked towards the other side of the room. There was a window. The first she had seen in the complex. She looked out onto the dark streets but with no streetlights she couldn't see very far in detail. The horizon was clear though. It was a broken and crumbled line against the full moon that was out tonight. She put her head against the window. Her breath was hot and humid and she watched the white mist cloud and disappear in front of her mouth. Her breath condensed on the hard cold glass.

"Remember when everything was easy?" she said in a singsong voice full of melancholy. She didn't know where the question had come from, but it felt true. Things must have been easier at one point in time, even if they couldn't remember everything.

"Was it easy? Or were we fooling ourselves?" Paxton retorted walking over to stand beside her. He put his hand lightly on her shoulder and ran the tips of his fingers across the top of Hadley's collarbone.

"It seemed easier didn't it?"

"Perhaps, or perhaps we just remember it that way," he said as he grabbed her hand. He squeezed it tight.

"I guess we don't even know if what we remember is real…" Hadley replied looking towards the horizon.

"We are going to find out eventually, but I don't think anything will ever be easy again."

Hadley let out a sigh knowing he was right. It was a harsh reality that she had been fighting with. Right or wrong. Hard or easy.

"Do you believe in fate?" Hadley asked bringing her hands to the window. She placed them lightly on the glass. It was cold and her skin left white condensation. Her hands seemingly imprinted for eternity onto the glass.

"I believe we make our own choices and that our choices lead us to where we are supposed to be. Everything happens for a reason and at everyone's core they are truly themselves. I believe in paths." He believed everything would work out. Always the pleasant optimist.

"Don't go soft on me," Hadley said unconvincingly and gave his arm a shove. "A war is coming. We have to find out what side we're on."

He shrugged, "I know."

They looked into each other's eyes. He looked the saddest Hadley had seen him since she met him a few weeks before. Pax couldn't make out Hadley's emotions, which infuriated him. Hadley knew that she should know more about him but deep down she believed she did. She just wanted to remember and to know with certainty. She knew he was a good person, but she felt like they were just scratching the surface with each other. Hadley trusted him fully and unconditionally but she never asked why she should trust him; she just knew that she did. That terrified her.

"We should go..." Paxton said pulling her away from the window. He wound his fingers through hers and she followed his lead out of the lab closing the door behind her. Though she wasn't sure she could ever put the feeling she got there out of her mind.

They walked until we got to the end of the hall. Every room was covered in red, long thin red streaks in groups of five, or splatters covering entire walls. Everything was broken. It was cold. Hadley couldn't shake the thought that someone was watching her, and she kept glancing over her shoulder, but destruction was all that lay behind. She pushed aside one of the plastic tarps and ducked under it. The doors at the end of the hall were boarded up and broken. They looked for alarm sensors but saw none.

"I think we are clear—" Hadley thought aloud. She took a deep breath and pushed the doors open, emerging into the night air. They walked in silence, both deep in thought for a long time. Hadley pulled out the map and looked at the streets around the complex. She finally saw Hummingbird Street. They followed the map until she stopped to look around in the middle of an intersection and saw a door with a red symbol drawn on it. It was the RFE symbol.

"This way!"

She practically ran to it, followed closely by Paxton. She reached for the handle but Paxton stepped in front of her. "Are you sure?" he hissed. Hadley pulled the coin out of her pocket. She saw a tiny slit in a pin pad to the right and put the coin in. She heard it clink as it rolled down a metal tube. The pin pad alighted and she heard the echo of the lock unlatching. The coin hit the end and was released back to her in a tiny trap door. She grabbed it immediately and slipped it back into her pocket, ensuring she'd have access again.

"Like I said before, I'm sure of nothing—" Hadley stepped around him and opened the door into the building.

# Chapter Thirty-Three

They walked in, hearing the door clink behind them as it locked back into place. They were in an office building. They waited a moment to let their eyes adjust. Hadley could see artificial light glowing at the bottom of a staircase. It made a thin line across the floor, the only light around. The staircase was long and narrow. So long in fact that they could only see the light at the end and the first step. From there it seemed to lead them into an abyss.

"This way—" Hadley whispered. She took a step and descended in the darkness, relying on faith alone.

They tiptoed down the stairs, carefully feeling each before actually stepping. They were almost at the bottom when there were creaks on the stairs above them. They stopped suddenly and listened. They both held their breath waiting; Pax had a hand lying gently on Hadley's arm. Nothing happened. Hadley motioned to keep going. They got to the bottom of the stairs and saw the light was coming from under a door.

At this precise moment she wished she had brought a gun. They walked to the door and as she was just about to open it there was a click behind her. So audible in the tight space it seemed deafening.

Hadley froze and turned around to see six guns pointed at her, all emitting tiny red lights that were scattered across their chests.

"What do you want?" a recognizable voice said in the darkness. Though Hadley couldn't put her finger on where she knew it from.

"I need answers—" Hadley stuttered bluntly, taking a leap of faith they wouldn't shoot.

"Who are you?" the man said in an exasperated tone. He rolled his eyes somewhere in the darkness.

Hadley thought of giving a fake identity but she decided against it, she had already told one of them who she was and he hadn't seemed to believe her. Above all else she was there for the truth and didn't want it under false pretences. "I'm Hadley Evans—"

"Sure you are—" the man laughed. Hadley furrowed her brows confused.

"I left myself a safety deposit box with this address in it and this coin—" Hadley tried cautiously. She pulled the coin out of her pocket in the dark and turned it over in her hand. The warm metal was heavy in her hand.

Someone turned a light on, on a tablet and the staircase was flooded with light. Then men standing holding guns took off their night vision goggles and lowered their guns.

"That's Hadley's coin; she's the only one who has one that colour," a tall man said in a professional tone in the back.

"I know," the man who had been talking said. It was the tattooed man from before. Hadley and he made eye contact that was uncomfortably personal.

"Do you know who I am Hadley?" the man said gently, his tone underlying with condescension and belittling.

"No," Hadley said simply.

"Great," the man said with an air of frustration.

"Should I?"

"That's up to you."

"What?"

"Exactly."

The conversation was going nowhere.

Hadley changed its course, realizing she wasn't going to get anywhere with this. "Do you know me?"

"I did. But that seems a lifetime ago now," he said sadly.

"So cryptic," Paxton chimed in with a laugh. No one else found his statement amusing, Hadley laughed inside her head though.

The man studied them both for a moment as though deciding how to proceed.

"Follow me this way," he said walking past them and opening the door into the room. The other men walked behind.

The room was a large foyer with many hallways shooting off of it. It was completely cement with extensive amounts of graffiti. It was extremely clean but there were too many people for the small spaces. But everything was perfectly in place. The smell was a combination of bleach, lime and smoke.

They walked down one hallway and into an empty room. The tattooed man opened a closet. Hadley gasped when she saw the wall was blown out and a metal gate was hanging on by a few hinges. The dark metal was old. Older in fact than anything she had ever seen since waking up. It was thick and heavy. It was ornately welded into an intricate pattern that reminded her of vines.

"This tunnel system was built in the early 18th century and originally connected the entirety of this area. Over time the system was walled up for security reasons. We have spent a large amount of time reconstructing it for our purposes."

"It's a good way to move around without anyone seeing you," Paxton noted.

"Where is it going to take us?" Hadley asked.

"To see what you came here to see. First though, and I'm sorry about this, but arms up!" the man said lifting his eyebrows with a smile. Hadley brought her arms to shoulder height. The tattooed man began his thorough pat down. Hadley glanced over and saw one of the other men patting down Pax.

The tattooed man took his time, but not so long it made her uncomfortable. He wanted to make sure they were unarmed. After he was done and his other man gave him a nod of approval the other five men dispersed into the rooms. The man went to a closet and pulled out two large metal bracelets.

He grabbed Hadley's left wrist and pulled up her sleeve hard. He put the bracelet on and turned her wrist over to latch it. The second he turned her wrist he inhaled sharply and held his breath. He looked at the tattoo on her forearm intently. She listened as he exhaled slowly. He clicked the bracelet closed; it perfectly covered her chip.

"You've seen it before? I'd love to know why I got it."

"I..." the man said, but then choose not to continue.

Hadley waited for an answer that didn't come.

"The bracelets cover any signal from your tracker and send the gov's a signal that you are on the street outside the complex. They also track you through our systems." He thrust the other bracelet painfully around Pax's wrist.

"Hey!" Pax exclaimed but the tattooed man paid him little attention.

The man then ducked his head and disappeared into the black tunnel with a wink. He was so carefree, it made Hadley smile.

She followed him. Keeping her head down, she felt her way by feeling the wall. The tunnel was long and dark. The ponytailed man seemed to go through effortlessly, probably because he had done it a hundred times. Hadley felt something crawl on her hand she jumped hitting her head.

"Ouch!" Shivers ran down her spine as she shook her hand to get whatever it was off; she didn't have the stomach to look. They kept walking though, attempting to not lose sight of the man in front of them. Pax was so close behind Hadley that she could feel his breath on her neck and it was giving her goose bumps.

They emerged into a slightly larger tunnel and saw there were offshoot rooms from this one. Each room had a gate but none were closed. It got colder as they got further into the tunnels. They passed by a group making a fire in one room. Hadley watched transfixed as a woman hit two stones together causing sparks. She raised a ball of grass to her lips and carefully blew until flames emerged. Hadley watched mesmerized at the primitive form of survival. Fire by rocks was something that hadn't been used in decades. As she watched, the fire turned to blue and to purple. Then the ball of flaming grass started floating. It turned in place before a loud popping sound and it turned into a black marble.

"Energy transfer technology production," the man said nonchalantly. Hadley was extremely impressed considering where they were. Turning a primitive form of energy into such a useful tool was impressive. It looked like magic. Hadley felt desperate to get back to her to ask how it worked. But she didn't want to push her luck.

They kept walking through a maze of underground tunnels. It was like the city had moved below itself. The path got narrower and narrower again. So they crouched lower and lower until they were crawling on their hands and knees. The wet mud was soaking through Hadley's pants and she was up to her wrists in cold thick mud. She had to forcefully pull her hand out with every movement. They started to crawl upwards and it got drier. Hadley kept crawling until she went to set her hand down and there was nothing. She fell forward slightly before her other hand, which was firmly planted on the ground caught her weight. She pushed herself out of the tunnel and stood up. They had emerged beside a deep black abyss of a gorge.

"It's usually not that muddy sorry— it's been raining a lot lately and we don't have the resources to block the water." The man stated plainly. Hadley and Pax both gave him a nod.

"Come on." He motioned forwards and they started shuffling sideways on about six inches of ground next to a dirt wall. The ground was firm and solid. Hadley slid her foot across it, concrete she decided. She grasped at the dirt with her fingernails trying to keep herself back instead of plunging forward.

The wall crumbled in her fingertips. There were a vast amount of sharp shale rocks and she was tearing up her palms trying to keep her balance. The presence of the tattooed man in front of her was profound, she knew exactly where he was without him saying anything.

Hadley could hear running water below but couldn't see anything. She peered down harder but it was no use. It was just an empty darkness. In front of her the man stopped his face lit by a small hanging light bulb over top of a three-foot circular platform. He put his hand back to stop her and she felt his hand on her stomach. She inhaled sharply as his large palm came in contact with her body.

"This is the hard part," he said calmly. His hand lingered for a moment against Hadley's abs and she shifted uncomfortably. He took notice and moved his hand.

"I thought that was the hard part," Hadley said with an awkward laugh, motioning to the ledge they had just trekked. Every single moment of that walk had seemed as though they were on the edge of death.

"You wish," he laughed raising his eyebrows again, "This was once a subway track but during the war a major water way broke through and has been running through here. It is over twenty feet deep and deadly. We haven't had time to connect the two halves of our system. That is why we are going through this crazy obstacle course." At least he realized this was the most intense thing Hadley had done in a while. "The only way across the river is this—" He listened for a moment "We had better hurry the rain is causing flooding and the water will be way higher in just a few minutes."

The man motioned to a singular thin wooden plank hanging above the river. There were two ropes tattered hanging parallel to the board. Hadley felt Paxton grab her arm behind her. She was pinned to the wall and her heart was beating a hundred miles per minute.

The man brushed Hadley's arm accidentally and then he grabbed the ropes with both his hands and stepped onto the board. Hadley watched as he slowly traversed the board. Keeping his feet steady, he took one determined step after another. She watched as he jumped onto the ground on the other side. He looked back and smiled.

Paxton pushed Hadley back and grabbed the ropes next, stepping over her. She almost protested but watched as he slowly traversed the river. Hadley watched the black water getting closer and closer to the plank, it reflected the single light. The bulbs light glowed in tiny ripples. The water was running down the walls and dripping from the roof.

"Your turn," Pax called back. She rolled her eyes and reached one hand up and grabbed one of the ropes. She rapidly grabbed the other steadying herself. She slowly lifted her foot, tensing all of her muscles. She put her foot on the plank steadily. It wobbled and vibrated. She took a deep breath letting the air fill her lungs and put her other foot down.

Then she took the first step across the thin beam. Then another, she started to walk faster. She was halfway there when she felt the water hit her foot she looked down to see the rapids licking at the plank. In an instant the plank was engulfed along with her feet and ankles. She kept her footing but the raging water was doing its best to get her off of the board, which was barely holding.

"What do I do now?" She looked at the man. His eyes were wide. He no longer had a casual air about him.

He put his hand into a fist and raised it to his mouth. He thought for a split second. With narrowed eyes he said, "Try to take another step."

"But—" Hadley protested.

"I don't know—" The man said. Hadley knew there was nothing else she could do but try to get to the end of the board. She lifted her foot and set it down again. For a split second she thought she had done it.

Then she felt herself fall as the board was carried off into the moving water. It was all in incredibly slow motion. She screamed as the water slowly got closer to her now horizontal body. She tried to hold onto both ropes for support but she felt her hand slip from the one upstream. She managed to hold on with both hands to the one rope as she fell into the water. The cold hit her like a thousand bullets. The air instantly left her lungs and her whole body tensed up. She couldn't make a sound as she struggled to hold on. Her feet fluttered behind her as she tried to push against the raging angry water. She hung on for dear life as the water rose.

The tattooed man stood at the edge of the water. His feet submerged assessing.

"What do we do?" Paxton yelled over the sound of the rushing water.

"Can you pull yourself up?" the man yelled. Hadley could only look at him; she couldn't say anything. Not even a retort to the dumbest question she had ever been asked. She made a mental note that if she ever got out of this mess to call him out for that.

She pulled with all her strength but finally felt her face go under. The water burnt as it flushed into her nose and eyes. She pulled up with all her might and managed to get a breath, which she held as her face went back under the water. The muscles in her arms were tearing as she dug her nails into the thick abrasive rope.

"I'm going to have to jump in, cut the rope and you will pull us back!" the man yelled at Paxton. It was all Hadley heard before the water pulled her further under. It was a peaceful sensation even as she struggled to hold on. For a moment everything was quiet.

Her lungs started to struggle to inhale. They had used all the nutrients and oxygen from the now useless air that filled her lungs and were desperate for more. Every muscle in her body urged her to breath. They were desperate.

One breath and it would all be over, a little voice inside Hadley's head sneered. She could feel her lungs burning. Her chest pressing with all its might. The dark cold quiet was encompassing.

She felt the splash beside her but it was too late.

Her lips parted and she took a breath.

# Chapter Thirty-Four

2228

The waves crashed against the rocks Hadley was sitting on. The hard grey boulders lined the water creating platforms that were perfect for picnicking and cliff jumping. The turquoise water below bubbled white as it hit the rocks. She looked down unable to see the bottom. She watched a school of white fish swim by; their scales glittered in the mid afternoon sun. They shone different colours near the surface.

Hadley watched as some gruesome waves approached, sent from a speeding boat passing by. She waved at the people onboard and they waved back before speeding off. As the waves crashed against the rocks she felt the sea spray across her skin. Though the hot sun combined with the gentle breeze and she was dry almost instantly. She felt her skin getting tough with salt and her hair blowing gently in the wind.

Hadley looked away from the water; past the path she had used to get down to the water and up to a small villa balcony. It was white and shone in comparison to the copper coloured house. The balcony door slid open and a man emerged; he was the only person around. The house was secluded and she felt they were the only two around. The man had a fluffy pink towel tied around his waist and even from her distance Hadley could see the beads of water on his tanned skin. She smiled as she looked at him and blushed, feeling as though she shouldn't stare, even though she knew she had every right. He was hers, they were together.

He caught Hadley's eye and she smiled and waved for him to come down, he shrugged and winked. Hadley smoothed her yellow dress and looked up at him before reaching for the back zipper. She slowly unzipped the zipper watching him watch her as he rushed down the path. She slid one sleeve off at a time letting them hang off her shoulders. Then without a glance around she let her dress fall to her ankles.

Even from the distance she could see the colour go to his face. He hurried down the path forgetting to close the door behind him. Hadley laughed out loud and turned to face the water. She stood in the wind for a moment before she stepped forward and dove into the water. The ten or so meter drop seemed to take forever. However, the water was refreshing as she slid through the cool surface and she took a moment before she surfaced. She looked around and saw she was surrounded by a swarm of colourful fish.

She swam for the surface, watching the sun sparkle on top of the water. The light twinkled and she felt as though everything was calm in the world, she revelled in the moment. The only care she had was using her body, her muscles, to push against a force she could beat, the rushing water. The earth was composed of forces that humans couldn't ever hope to understand fully. Though she tried.

Hadley looked up and saw the man. She used her arms to keep her up pushing them back and forth. She watched him take a running start and backflip into the ocean. He emerged seconds later feet from her. She laughed as he swam towards her. He grabbed her waist and she felt his body get closer. He kissed her hard, with a need only she could fulfill. She loved him so much and he was all hers. Forever.

He led her towards the ladder and they climbed up onto the warm stone. Dripping and wet they laid down together, the man's hair in his face, his tattoos running up and down his body.

"I love you," he whispered looking into Hadley's eyes.

"To the moon and back babe," she replied with a smile.

They kissed gently.

He pondered what to say next, looking at her body, "are you sure you want to do this?"

"You're my everything, and it's something I have to do."

"It will change everything Hadley."

"We'll have to be so careful; you'll have to hide from everyone."

"We've worked it all out."

"What if something changes?"

"Like what?"

He bit his lip and looked at her nervously, "Okay then."

Hadley almost squealed as a grin rushed across her face, "I love you."

They kissed again, letting the sunshine fade to a subtle golden glow around them. Completely lost in each other's company.

# Chapter Thirty-Five

"Hadley, Hadley!" the voices yelled somewhere in the distance. Hadley was being yelled at but the men who were yelling was far away, too far away and she had no strength to answer.

Pax knelt with the man who was dripping wet beside Hadley's seemingly lifeless body. He had grabbed her just in time, before she was carried away by the current but that hadn't stopped her from inhaling a large amount of water.

Pax had lost his carefree attitude and was almost shaking Hadley trying to get her to breath.

"Hell man! Is she going to be all right?" Pax asked.

"It's Saul by the way."

"What?"

"Move!" Saul said, as he bent forward and gave Hadley two slow breaths.

He then positioned his hands over her chest and began to give her chest compressions singing along in his head to a vintage song, 'Staying Alive'. He began to focus only on Hadley.

"What the hell are you doing?"

"CPR," Saul said simply to panicking Pax.

"That hasn't been taught since 2066."

Saul gave him a stern look and gave Hadley two more rescue breaths. "Oh yes, fucking Family First act."

"It was population control," Pax countered.

"It was wrong!" Saul shrugged firmly as he continued to do CPR.

"But they stopped teaching CPR because everyone's program was meant as a life support module;

able to save people from drowning, heart attacks... That was implemented the same year."

"To keep those favourable to the government, you nitwit. Anyways your program doesn't work down here," Saul said pointing at the bracelet he had placed over it.

"It was supposed to restart the earth."

"Do you think I live under a rock?" Saul said pumping on Hadley's chest.

Pax almost laughed, motioning to the ceiling above, "You do live under a rock."

"I know what was supposed to happen. But the stupid program is flawed and can't save you from a heart attack or bullet wound or stomach flu if it decided not to. It was artificial intelligence that got too complacent."

Suddenly, Hadley started sputtering up water. The hot water left her lungs and mouth. She rolled onto her side and vomited. It burnt as it came up her throat and through her teeth. She coughed over and over again, vomiting everything that she could possibly have had in her stomach. Finally, the reflex stopped and she wiped her lip on her sleeve. She remained lying on the ground in the fetal position.

She looked up at Paxton and the man. She hadn't realized how big the man was. He must have been at least 6'7". Being tall for a girl she wasn't used to feeling short and small.

"Thank you," she said to them both. They looked relieved when she spoke. Neither of them said anything for a moment.

"There is a blanket in the case just up there, can you grab it?" Saul said to Paxton, motioning up the hallway. Paxton just glared at him and walked towards the cabinet without a word.

"Why did you help me?" Hadley whispered skeptically looking into the Saul's crystal blue eyes that were shining in the dim light.

He stared into her eyes and stated plainly, "I wasn't going to let you die—"

"Wouldn't it have been easier that way? You tried to hang me a few days ago—" she suggested.

"It's complicated." He shrugged looking away for a moment before his eyes returned to hers, a sadness washing over them. They sat there staring at each other. He grabbed her hand giving it a squeeze.

"What's your name?" she asked after a pause.

"Saul," he said.

Hadley nodded. There was something comforting in putting a name to a face, the memory of the rocks and water swirled in her mind. She knew him.

Paxton grabbed Hadley's other hand as soon as he came back to her, but by then Saul had already let go. Hadley could feel Pax scowling at Saul before she even looked at him. He was radiating anger.

"We should get going," Saul said standing up.

"Can you walk?" Paxton asked, helping Hadley to her feet. He wrapped the blanket around her shoulders and pulled her close. She gently set her head on his shoulder but only looked at Saul.

"I think so," she replied.

"This way," Saul said, ducking into a small opening without making eye contact. Hadley went to follow but Paxton stopped her with a forceful tug.

"What?!" she hissed angrily.

"I'll go first," he said moving past her.

"What's your problem?" Hadley was exasperated and her throat felt as those it had been scalded by a hot iron. It hurt to talk but that didn't stop her.

Pax didn't even reply. He just glared and followed Saul. Hadley waited a moment feeling her blood begin to boil. She stomped her foot, let out a huff and followed.

# Chapter Thirty-Six

They walked in silence for close to ten minutes, through winding and twisting tunnels. Hadley felt caught in the middle. She was beyond angry at Paxton and couldn't stop thinking about Saul. She wanted to know his story; actually she wanted to know everything about him.

They eventually got to a heavy metal door that had numerous locks attached. Saul turned the knob and all the locks unlatched and they walked into a brightly lit room. It burnt their eyes, after being so long in the underground tunnels. Hadley closed her eyes tightly, feeling like it had been forever since she had seen real light. Slowly she opened her eyes to look around the room. It was circular. There was an archway leading to a bluish room where there were rows of beds surrounded by medical equipment. One of the beds at the back of the room had what looked like a glass dome over it. Watercolours swirled throughout it. Hadley caught herself watching a blue swirl that ran through it.

All of a sudden a grey hand pressed against the side of the glass dome. It was shaking against the liquid. The fingernails dug into the glass and swiped across it.

"What is— what the—" Hadley stuttered.

Saul turned around and looked from Hadley to the tank and back. "It's a medical treatment; it's hard to live underground all the time." He covered quickly and turned on his heel. Hadley had no choice but to follow. She pulled the blanket tighter around her shoulders, but she watched the tank as long as she could until she had to continue on and try to forget about it.

They got to a room filled with computers. Everything was facing one way and it was reminiscent of a classroom, though it was the size of a hockey rink. Hadley looked at a giant screen on one side that bore the RFE logo.

"This is impressive for an underground hideout," Hadley muttered impressed.

Saul went to a computer and started typing furiously. Hadley watched as the muscles in his neck flexed as he worked. "It's almost dawn so I'm going to make you a flash drive of what you need to know," he said over his shoulder.

Hadley and Pax had no choice but to stand there in silence listening to the typing. Hadley took a deep breath feeling her lungs reject the air and the burning returning. She began to feel unsteady and reached for the table beside her for support. The blanket dropped off her shoulders and onto the floor in a pool at her feet. She reached out for something more stable than the table and found Pax's arm.

Paxton grabbed her waist. "Had, are you ok?"

She just stared at him, unable to comprehend what he had just said. She blinked at him blankly. "Yes, I just need to sit down." She grabbed a chair and brushed his arm away from her waist. Then she folded her knees up under her chin and wrapped her arms around her legs.

She put her forehead on her knees and allowed herself to watch and regulate her breathing. She couldn't stand the look of Pax, his attitude was annoying and she needed to focus on herself for a moment. She slowly drifted off into a faraway place, a million thoughts running through her mind.

A good amount of time passed before she felt a hand on her shoulder. She looked up and Saul passed her a thumb drive.

"Thanks," she whispered weakly.

Saul also had a bottle in his hand with a dark red coloured liquid in it. He passed it to Hadley.

"Drink this, it will help."

"What is it? It looks like blood?"

"It is," Saul said plainly.

"What?!" Hadley screeched taken aback.

Saul laughed, a deep hearty laugh. The first time he had let his guard down slightly and revealed a true piece of himself, "Kidding, of course. It's beets and charcoal that give it the colour. It's our secret recipe."

Hadley laughed and bit her lower lip. Then she brought the bottle to her lips and began to drink. It tasted terrible but helped her start to feel better.

She slowly stood up with Saul's help after finishing the drink and looked at him through her eyelashes. Paxton's gaze made the hair on her neck stand up but she didn't look back at him.

"We put in all that effort for a thumb drive. You guys need to get on Wi-Fi in this complex," Hadley said to Saul who laughed. She knew that Hemmer and Kane would monitor any network so she understood why they had hardwired their information in such a remote spot.

Hadley stepped forward and gave him a hug. It took him by surprise but she felt him hug her back. She inhaled and smelt a mix of dirt, brandy and mahogany with a hint of spice. Then, lightning fast, she felt a slight of hand into her back pocket. It was instantaneous but after she could feel the imprint of a second thumb drive.

"Just for you," Saul whispered into her hair so no one could hear. Then he stepped back untangling their embrace.

"Thanks for this," Hadley said holding up the thumb drive Pax knew about.

"Of course," Saul replied curtly taking Hadley's hand in his. He took a glance at Paxton and then to Hadley. He let go of her hand but left a small piece of paper in her palm, which she stuffed into her back pocket, "Now let's get you back before we can't anymore."

They walked to a door and emerged outside into a surprisingly high place within the city. It had a clear, though small, view of the compound. Before Hadley could say anything more Saul was gone and Paxton and she walked in silence. They couldn't even look at each other they were lost in their own thoughts.

Hadley put a hand on her back pocket and felt the outline of a second flash drive. A drive Saul only wanted her to see. The anticipation was explosive.

# Chapter Thirty-Seven

2083

"Tell me the truth!" Hadley yelled bursting through the door into a room where Kane and Hemmer were talking. They were enjoying a cup of coffee and the sun was shining in through the windows behind them. Kids could be seen playing in a playground across the street.

"We are saving the world Hadley," Hemmer said calmly. He stood up, "Why don't you sit down?"

Hadley watched him pull out a chair for her but couldn't bring herself to sit down. She was buzzing with anger.

"We have come up with a thousand different ways. This isn't right. You can't do this," Hadley practically screamed and she could feel herself becoming more and more unstable.

"There is no other way," Kane said bluntly.

Hadley felt betrayed. She thought she could count on him and his betrayal took her by surprise. Like getting doused in cold ice water.

"I trusted you," Hadley whispered fiddling with the ring on her finger.

"You still can Had. We're doing the best thing," he said confused.

"For who, Kane?"

"Everyone."

"No Kane. You are doing what's best for the elite and the government. Since 2066 the government thinks that they are able to do whatever they want. Get rid of whoever they want."

Hemmer interjected, "Hadley, your mom was crucial to Family First."

"No Hemmer. You took her research before it was finished."

"It worked!" Hemmer sneered.

"Yes and there hasn't been any population growth since 2066."

Kane looked at Hadley with pity, "Which has saved the planet."

"For now, but at some point all of us will die and no one will be left. You didn't give my mom time to come up with a viable cure."

"I gave her all the time she had."

"Then you sent her to an exoplanet a thousand light-years away."

"I've heard she's still alive in cryosleep and doing well."

Hadley just looked at him astounded, trying to process that information, and stated plainly, "You took her from me."

Hemmer stood up, his face as red as a tomato. "We are working on amazing research here, everything from other planetary living to sustainable resources. Just because you don't agree with working on plans for the worst-case scenario, doesn't mean we are wrong. We are saving the planet, no matter the cost, even if that means getting rid of people in the process."

"It's murder."

"It's evolution."

"Forced evolution, there is a difference."

"Call it what you will Hadley, it won't change anything."

"I will fight you on this, till my last day," she hissed.

Hadley took off the ring and placed it on the table. Kane stood up. She walked out of the room and down the hall. She emerged outside and took a deep breath. Then she started running, for the first time in a long time she felt relieved. Not just relieved she felt unstoppable.

Defiance suited her.

# Chapter Thirty-Eight

Hadley was sitting in the lab twirling on a chair. She sipped at a cup of black coffee watching the earth spin in the simulator. So much of the earth was covered in black marks except for small green patches. She sighed.

She had changed, threw her hair up in a ponytail and had run from her room. They had made it back to the complex just in time to hear the wake up alarm. So she had taken two minutes and was out the door grabbing an apple on her way.

Even with her haste she hadn't seen Vanya or Kane all morning, they just hadn't shown up in the lab. She wondered where they were, but she didn't want them there. So she was, in fact, grateful for the privacy.

Hadley was thinking of things she could do and things she wanted to do. So she pulled up an internet search and typed "nuclear war" into the search engine. A message popped up: *You are restricted from this content.* She looked at the warning dumbfounded.

Hadley deleted the search character-by-character and typed in "Hadley Evans". She watched as the Internet browser ran its search. Just as the results popped up the whole computer shut down. "ERROR" appeared on the screen.

She stared at the black screen with the green words. She pounded the table with her hand and got up. She was about to walk out of the lab when she saw Kane's door open. She paused for a moment, contemplating the consequences of using it, before walking into his office.

She turned on the computer and was surprised it wasn't password protected. *Wow he's trusting—* she thought as she clicked on the Internet and typed in "Hadley

Evans" again. This time the search wasn't restricted. She clicked on the top result. She saw her picture at the top of the website; it was the picture of her that she had found in the box.

The first line read, "Leader and Founder of the Revolution for Free Earth. She was an inspiration in her time and we will celebrate the 100th anniversary of Death on May 14$^{th}$ of this year."

Hadley just looked at it, below it there was a picture of her, looking just a bit younger than she was now.

Death.

That word was what she focused on. She couldn't breathe. This had to be some sort of sick and twisted joke, she thought. She closed all the screens and cleared the history. Then she got up shaking as she ran out of the lab.

She ran until she got to the atrium. She looked around at everyone shuffling around completing their day-to-day tasks. She looked up at Hemmer in his office. He was sitting typing on his computer. He wore a calm facial expression. She watched him get up and stand looking out over the atrium. He fished something out of his pocket and she saw him answer the phone.

He talked casually as he scanned the atrium. She saw his eyes move towards her and she dared him to look. She couldn't look away. When he saw her their eyes met. She stared deeply at him. He smiled at her, a menacing smile, as though he could tell something was wrong.

The old man Hadley had seen in Hemmer's office walked to him and said something. The man's shoulders were hunched over and he walked with a limp. Hemmer nodded while he kept eye contact with Hadley. She finally broke and walked towards the dorm.

She was almost there when she passed Jeremiah. She didn't look at him but kept her head down and kept walking. She had just passed him when she felt an arm around her waist and a cold hand on her mouth.

Her feet lifted off the ground. She kicked as hard as she could but couldn't break loose. She made herself dead weight but he didn't falter. He pulled her into a small room and threw her against a cold concrete wall.

Hadley glanced down and watched him pull out a knife. He brought it up slowly until she felt the cold sharp metal against her neck.

"What the hell?!" Hadley hissed at him.

"This operation is mine to lead." He pushed the knife into her throat. She held her breath, too scared to breathe.

"Ok, I never said anything against you leading," Hadley didn't understand where he was coming from.

"You will not do anything to compromise our mission. We are saving the world! Do you hear me? Everything we have worked for starts tomorrow. You try anything, anything at all. I will kill you and— it will not be quick. Don't think I won't, you have no idea what I've done."

Jeremiah stepped away and slid the knife into his pocket. He laughed and started to walk out.

Hadley regained her breath and with the last bit of confidence she had she screamed, "Go to hell Jeremiah."

"You first," he called back.

Hadley watched him go, starring at the empty doorway, utterly confused.

After a moment she followed him out. No one had noticed him drag her into the room, no one bothered to care. Everyone in the atrium was still going about his or her business. Jeremiah walked towards Hemmer's office and so Hadley did the exact opposite. She walked back towards the dorm. Furious she slammed the door behind her once she got into her room.

She ruffled through her socks and found the pair in which she had hidden Saul's secret thumb drive. She pulled the small metal tube out of a thick pair of grey wool socks and held it in her hand wondering if she really wanted to see what was on it. Maybe it was better to stay in the dark, she thought. *Sometimes knowing less is easier—* she contemplated for a moment. Then before she could think it through anymore she untwisted the drive and pressed the green 'on' button. The drive immediately came alive. She watched as the flash drive loaded into thin air. The green bar on the side filled quickly; there wasn't much on it— *Download complete.* She watched as it opened around her, creating a screen in thin air as thumb drives did and she gasped.

There was only one thing on the drive, a slideshow and when it popped up she felt something get caught in her throat. It was a picture of Saul, sitting on a cliff. The same cliff she had dreamed about when she had almost died in the tunnel.

The picture changed to another, of them at a formal event. A picture of them sitting together at a picnic. Then finally a picture of her in a long dress.

*This couldn't be real—* she thought as she watched as if from a distance planet as the drive fell out of her hand. It fell in slow motion towards the ground, spinning as it went. It went slowly because it was so light it was like a feather.

She watched as the corner hit the cold concrete. The picture shattered into a million pieces all over the ground before disappearing completely. Hadley's hands were unmoving where they had lost grasp on the drive just above her hips, bent at a ninety-degree angle.

*What is going on?* Her brain screamed.

# Chapter Thirty-Nine

2228

The last moments of light fell over the city. Hadley watched as cars drove by. The snow was falling softly from above. The city was alive and buzzing. She stood on the white marble steps in front of her apartment building waiting for her car and driver to arrive.

She pulled her shawl closer around her shoulders over her dress. It was a red and floor length strapless ball gown. The crystals were hand sewn throughout the bodice that wrapped her hips lightly and the tulle skirt made her feel like Cinderella. Anna and Hadley had spent their whole afternoon getting ready and they both looked amazing by the time they were done. Hadley caught a glimpse of her reflection in the window of a car as it drove by. She smiled, for the first time in years she felt oddly pretty.

She looked around for anyone she knew but most people had made their way to the gala earlier and she was going to be right on time, not a second earlier than she needed to be there. A black town car stopped in front of her and a man in a suit got out. He wore a black hat and had a witty smile.

"Good evening miss, are you Miss Evans?" he said giving a small bow.

"Yes," she smiled trying not to laugh at his presentation. He rushed around the car as she walked down the last few steps. He opened the door and motioned Hadley into the backseat. He closed the door and hurried to the driver's seat. The car smelt of tobacco and leather.

The driver adjusted his mirror in order to talk to Hadley through it. Her thoughts were elsewhere and she jumped when he spoke.

"Where are we off to?"

"The Universal Science Awards Gala," Hadley said meekly. She opened her clutch to ensure she had everything. Her lipstick, her speech card that was formatted with multiple speeches, and an extra few bobby pins—

"So no date tonight?" the driver said making casual conversation.

"No, it's just me tonight," Hadley thought about that fact. She had had options. She really had. Pax and Kane had both asked her to accompany them, and she had politely turned both of them down. Though she knew she would still end up at Kane's table as he was on the board of executives for the Universal Science Society. He first hand approved the seating chart. Hadley rolled her eyes just thinking about it.

"Let me take you," he'd almost demanded.

"No," Hadley had replied.

"We could have an amazing time," Kane was grasping at straws.

Hadley gave him a stern look. "What about Alice?"

"We're separated."

"For now. You hurt me enough when you married her Kane. I don't want to do the same to her. It wasn't her fault she fell for you too."

Her last comment during that conversation had hurt him. She knew that saying it would stop his pestering and end it there. That didn't mean it hadn't felt terrible saying it. Hadley didn't want to purposely hurt him, the facts remained that she had loved him at one point.

Hadley had tried not to think about it. Stephen and Anna had left half an hour ago, they wanted to mingle at the cocktail hour. Hadley remembered Anna's pained expression when Stephen had gotten to their apartment to leave, "Hadley, this is your night, you should come with us." She was the sweetest person Hadley knew and Hadley knew the large role Anna had played in getting where she was.

Hadley had just shaken her head. Anna didn't press it further. Hadley took cute photos of them and shooed them out of the apartment. She had purposely gotten her car to come so she would arrive just on time and avoid mingling. She was happy, even if no one else could see it.

They drove through the snowy festive streets. It was just weeks before Christmas and everyone could feel the holidays in the air. Garlands and wreathes hung on the lamp poles. Twinkling lights glimmered through the streets, creating a sparkling glow in the snow. The car drove up to the museum and there was a red carpet down the steps. The Christmas lights twinkled around and there was still a small amount of people on the stone steps. A huge banner hung over the entrance with the Universal Science Society's logo and the event listed.

Hadley looked at the banner and the people standing on the stairs. They were photographers and reporters who had spent their night interviewing arrivals. However, they were all in private conversations when Hadley arrived, only small groups left that barely made a crowd. It was nearing event time and they probably weren't expecting anyone else worthy of a photo. Hadley took a breath just as her driver opened the door. He held out his hand and she took it. She stepped out and stared up the stairs.

"Thank you," Hadley said to him and he nodded before heading to the driver's seat. Hadley opened her coinet and tipped him generously.

"Thanks Miss," the driver said as he walked back to the driver's side.

Hadley waited until he drove away to start her ascent. She hadn't even made it two steps before she was stampeded by reporters. And here she had thought she would have avoided the commotion.

"HADLEY—HADLEY!" She heard all around. She smiled and kept walking.

"Hadley, how does it feel to be nominated for five awards tonight?" One reporter asked holding a microphone ridiculously close to her face.

"Amazing," Hadley smiled, a sad smile, and kept walking.

'You are the youngest person ever to be nominated? Is that true?"

"Yes, thank you," she said with a nod. She was so close to the top she could taste it. Their questions kept flying at her and she kept giving them short and sweet answers. She didn't feel like talking tonight. She felt the top of her dress start to slide a bit and tugged it up. The snow was coming down harder now and she pulled her shawl as close as she could. She didn't expect to win anything but the whole evening was still exciting. Her research and inventions were good. Brilliant maybe, but these awards were for the best on the planet. She felt she was far from that.

"You are here alone Hadley? No man in your life?" A voice said somewhere in the crowd. The high-pitched sound caught her off guard.

"Yes," Hadley looked around for the person who had spoken. "I have no one in my life presently. What would that matter anyways? I thought we dealt with the inequality issue over a hundred years ago." Hadley bit her lip at her outburst, embarrassed.

"It's rumoured that you were involved with your colleague Paxton Avery?"

"It is also rumoured that you are involved with your Professor. Neil Kane. He's on the board awarding the awards tonight." A man yelled; Hadley didn't know which one. He was lost in the crowd.

"Just rumours. All are just rumours. Kane has given me great guidance in the last few years. Paxton is solely a childhood friend, if anything a high school sweetheart." Hadley laughed before turning on her heel in terror.

How did anyone know about that? How did they know about Kane? Hadley thought as she hurried through the enormously decadent glass and stone doors.

She was greeted by a woman in a black dress and a man in a suit. Both were extremely preoccupied and kept speaking into their earpieces.

"Hi Miss—?" She waited for Hadley's answer as she scrolled a holographic screen not even looking at her. The woman was annoyed at how late Hadley was and that she had missed all of the cocktail party. Hadley could see that people were already starting to sit inside the ballroom. The woman tapped her foot as she rolled her eyes in disgust. "We are just about to start. Miss—?"

"Hadley, Hadley Evans," Hadley whispered meekly, so nervous she almost bolted back out the door. She didn't like making a scene.

"Miss Evans. My apologies for not recognizing you! So preoccupied, please forgive me." The colour drained from the woman's face and she tried to laugh off her mistake.

Hadley smiled at her genuinely. Really who should know me? She thought, the said, "no worries."

"You are at table three. Jackson here will take your shawl."

Hadley took off the shawl and handed it to Jackson. She shivered and smiled at them. They motioned her through a large archway. The arch sparkled with gold and white lights. There were hundreds of sparkling Christmas balls, wreathes and bows. She stood in awe for a second. Then she walked through the arch and was sprinkled with glitter that fell like snow. She twirled in place smiling.

Suddenly, she stopped spinning, absolutely joyful. She looked forward into the room and saw Pax smiling as he leaned against a wall. He was wearing all black, including his shirt and tie. His hair was combed back and he raised his eyebrow.

"Can I walk you to your table?" He smiled, his typical Pax smile. He looked brilliant. His suit fit just right and he was rocking the skinny tie look.

"That would be nice," Hadley said sheepishly. He held out his arm and she took it. They walked through the crowd and she felt so many eyes on her.

"What are they all looking at?" she whispered.

"You," Pax said as they got to her table. She saw her name card beside Kane's.

"Of course," Hadley said below her breath.

Pax grabbed her hand and pulled her towards him. He kissed her forehead. "Good luck Hadley."

She watched him walk away, looking amazing as ever. All eyes were on her for the first time in her life, and she wasn't sure she liked it.

The evening seemed to drag on. All through dinner Kane kept making small talk. For a few moments they had fallen into regular patterns but Hadley noticed the awkwardness that her rejection had caused between their normally easy banter. He kept making crude comments and demeaning her.

Just as they were finishing dessert she couldn't stand it anymore. She couldn't stand the way he was talking down to her. "This night is about me. Not you. That's why I wanted to come alone."

"And you couldn't choose—" Kane shrugged taking another bite of his chocolate cake.

"That's not fair," Hadley whispered.

"No it's not." Kane smirked condescendingly. Hadley rolled her eyes at him. She focused on her dessert and the conversation going on around them at the table.

Across the table she made eye contact with a man, his hair was tied up and the edge of a tattoo peeked out through his starched white collar.

Finally, the plates were cleared and the speeches started amidst a twinkling background. The head of the committee got up. "The world used to celebrate each year with huge awards for entertainment and film and television. But now on the 36th year of this event we know better." Hadley didn't pay attention as the speeches dragged on and on, she was too nervous and excited. Then, finally, the awards started.

Hadley immediately sat up in her seat. It was so abrupt that the man across the table raised his eyebrows at her. Hadley immediately went red and lowered her eyes to her lap.

The man who won the award for engineer of the year spoke for over twenty minutes about his influences. The wait staff came back to get drink orders and they weren't quiet about it; he was going on for so long. People kept trying to cut him off, but being quite old he kept going on and on and on.

"Champagne." Hadley whispered to one of the staff, and as she left Hadley called after her, "you know what bring the whole bottle."

Finally, Hemmer went on stage and politely put an end to his speech. After the man left the stage Hemmer took over the microphone.

"So I am here to present the award for New Scientist of the Year. Please turn your attention to the video behind me for the nominees."

Hadley watched as four faces went across the screen. Then she saw her own smiling face. The four other nominees were at least 10 years older and had been working in their fields for a lot longer it seemed. No one under 30 had ever won an award at the gala, not even new scientist, because the committees idea of new was actually experienced.

The first was a woman from China who had invented a miniature rocket that had made it to Mars with supplies for the colony there; it was noticeably smaller than the previous rockets and was a fraction of the cost. The second was an Englishman whose work with deep-sea fish was eradicating all sorts of diseases. The third was a professor from Harvard. She had invented a DNA tracking system that was far superior to anything that had been done before. The fourth was a man from Brazil who had revolutionized living in the space stations. Then there was Hadley with her research in biology and climate change.

She had reinvented evolution. It wasn't that impressive, she thought. She had just made natural selection a less natural process.

"And the winner is—" Hemmer opened the envelope. Hadley held her breath. "I am pleased to award this to a young woman who is tremendously smart and talented. She has made leaps and bounds over the last year in the biologic community. Congratulations Miss Hadley Evans."

Hadley stared at him shocked. Applause erupted around her. It took her a second to stand up. Kane stood as well and kissed her cheek as he moved her chair aside.

Hadley walked up to the microphone, holding her skirt to not trip. Hemmer grabbed her hand. A woman behind him handed him a gold figurine. He handed it to Hadley and stepped aside.

"Wow." she said looking over the hundreds of people in the audience. She pulled out her coinet and tried to open it. She was shaking from head to toe. "I never thought I would ever be receiving one of these. When I started at Harvard I never dreamed of where my life would lead. When Professor Kane asked me to work on this project I was oblivious to the huge contribution we would be making. I can't thank you enough Professor." Kane grimaced at being called professor and Hadley laughed in the back of her mind. "I would not be here without Anna or Paxton. Thank you both. And thank you to the society who thought I deserved this. The four other people nominated have done so much for the scientific community. Without them we would be nowhere. I hope to continue making advances in genetics and biology, this is just the beginning of my work on evolutionary genetics and the effects the planet has on human biology. Thank you!" Hadley blurted it all out.

It seemed too short. It was too short.

Hadley nodded and walked backstage. Anna was waiting for her. Anna ran over and hugged Hadley. Anna was crying, sobbing really, but her smile was spread over the entirety of her face.

"You did it!" she exclaimed. They didn't let go of each other for a while.

"I just can't believe it," Hadley barely got out through her grinning teeth.

Anna was overjoyed. "You deserve it Had. All of it!"

In the end, Hadley won three out of five awards she was nominated for. It was close to midnight when the awards ended and the wait staff quickly opened the doors to another ballroom. This one was decorated in green and silver. Three bars and multiple tables were set up. Hadley felt a hand on her shoulder and turned around to see Kane who was beaming.

"Care to dance?" he whispered.

"Sure," Hadley said half begrudgingly, but even Kane wasn't going to bring down her mood.

Kane grabbed her hand and helped Hadley to her feet. They were the first ones into the other ballroom. The full blues band started to play music reminiscent of the 1940s.

Before long the dance floor was filled with people and Hadley was twirling around with Kane without a care in the world. It felt right to be with him in that moment under the twinkling lights.

The song ended and they paused for a breath looking at each other.

"I still love you." Kane said simply.

"Kane, please." Hadley strained to get the words out.

"I know I hurt you."

"You can't even begin to imagine."

Hadley stepped away from him slightly.

"Let's try again."

"No," Hadley replied simply, "You broke me. I can't come back from that."

From out of nowhere, breaking the sharp air between them, Pax came up and politely asked Kane, "May I cut in?"

"I don't think so." Kane said smoothly pulling Hadley closer to him. She took a step back getting away from his grasp.

"You two had some time!" Pax whined.

Hadley just shook her head at Pax; she thought he was going to be above this.

"You two children figure this out and continue to treat me as though I have no say or opinions of my own. I'm going to get a drink." Hadley stormed off. She knew the moment away from them would only last so long. They would be running after her once they finished having a go at each other.

The bartender was enjoying his lull in business. Hadley walked up and put her clutch forcefully on the bar. She sighed and rolled her eyes.

"Bad night?" he said with a smile fit for a toothpaste commercial. His teeth literally gleamed.

"It wasn't—" Hadley trailed off, it had been perfect, well except for Kane's chatter in her right ear.

"Let me make you something to fix it." With that he started to work.

Hadley watched as he poured liquor into a shaker along with juice and some fresh fruit. He was captivating and she was over everything else.

"What are you getting?" someone asked beside her.

"Whatever he is making," Hadley laughed and looked over to see the man with tattoos and his hair in a bun who had been across from her at the table. He stood menacingly tall above her, even in her heels

"I'm Saul," he said casually.

"Hadley Evans," she disclosed.

He studied her while he looked her up and down. "Well Miss Winner, you're much shorter in person."

"Hey!" she laughed through feigned annoyance.

"So what? You win three awards and are leaving your night in the hands of a bartender?" Saul laughed.

"At this point it's my only option." The champagne had slowly melted her brain over the course of the evening.

"Why is that?"

"Do you remember the man sitting beside me at the table?" Hadley murmured with a casual wave behind her, where Kane and Pax were arguing.

"You two seemed cozy," he said sarcastically.

Hadley laughed out loud. "Was it that obvious?"

"How uncomfortable he made you?"

Hadley nodded as she bit her lip.

"Evans, you ordered an entire bottle of champagne to yourself."

"You saw that hey?"

"You were slurring your words on stage."

Hadley's eyes widened and the colour drained from her face. She whispered, "oh god, please tell me it wasn't that bad."

Saul laughed, "I'm kidding, you were perfect."

Hadley let out a sigh of relief. "Stupid men."

"I will give you that, our kind is the inferior breed. But we all aren't bad."

"I know—" She let out an exasperated sigh.

"Let's go then?"

"I can't just leave." Hadley persisted.

"Come on, take a risk. You can do whatever you want. You cleaned up tonight. It's your night." He had a childish gleam in his eyes. The sense of adventure intrigued Hadley as he held out a hand for her to grab.

"I don't even know you." Hadley blushed.

He winked at me. "You will. And you'll like me." Hadley took his hand and they were off. They were weaving through the crowd of people who were dancing through the ballroom.

"What about your drink?" the bartender called but Hadley didn't even look back.

Saul whisked them out of the ballroom and out the door as quickly as magic. They ran down the stairs as though Hadley was Cinderella and the clock was about to strike midnight.

Cabs were lined up on the street waiting for the event to finish. Saul held the door open and they both slid into the back seat.

"Where to?" the cabbie asked.

"The pier, and quick!" Saul said in his best suave English accent.

They were off in the blink of an eye. Racing down the snow covered streets, which sparkled in the moonlight. They got to the pier. Saul paid the cab driver and jumped out of the cab. He opened her door and helped Hadley out.

The cab drove away, eager to find other customers. Hadley and Saul however walked along the pier looking at the glassy water. The snow starting to fall harder and harder. Large, dense surreal snowflakes fell around them.

"Congratulations by the way. I hadn't told you that yet," Saul said as he took Hadley's hand gently in his.

"Thank you."

"You were the talk of the town tonight." Saul said genuinely.

"No, I wasn't—" Hadley replied quietly, quite embarrassed. She didn't like the attention normally, but she liked the way he was talking to her. It was different than she normally was talked to by the men in her life.

"Yes, you were, believe me." They kept walking up the snow-covered pier. Further and further over the water. The snow was slowly piling up around them and they were leaving small footprints. "You're freezing Evans!"

"I forgot my shawl."

"Take my jacket." He took his suit jacket off immediately and hung it over Hadley's shoulders. She pulled it tight around her shoulders.

"Thanks."

They kept walking, neither knew what to say. It had been a whirlwind, a spur of the moment decision and now they were standing seemingly the only ones on the dock.

"I just realized that I whisked you away in the middle of the ball Cinderella."

"I was happy to get away—"

"Even so I took you away from the dancing—" He jested turning on his Prince Charming.

He made Hadley blush and he knew it. He had the same twinkle in his eye. "I don't mind really—"

Saul took a step away from Hadley and bowed so low his nose almost touched the ground. "May I have this dance?"

"There's no music."

"Oh my dear lady, lest not be deterred by the lack of fair music," he said in a prim and proper English accent.

Hadley giggled as he took her hand. They started a waltz that he led with extreme grace and perfection.

"Where did you—?"

"I did all my schooling at a top finishing and boarding school in the UK." He said with a wink.

They continued to dance, lost in each other's arms. The snow flurrying around. The lights twinkling on the perfectly formed snowflakes. A moment of pure bliss.

*Maybe this was what love at first sight looked like,* she couldn't help but wonder.

# Chapter Forty

The sky was bright blue and there were no clouds in sight. Hadley could hear the super stallion helicopters with their propellers running before she was near enough to see them. They were military grade and were the newer version of the originals of the ones introduced in 1981. The military used the same plans to reconstruct three-hundred more a hundred and fifty years later. Each door was open. The dark metal of each glowed in the sunshine, a titanium alloy.

*Why did we have to make a show of flying all of a few blocks in these things?! The RFE's lived under us,* Hadley thought, *we could easily have done this mission with one person.* She sighed and rolled her eyes. She had to assume that it was Hemmer trying to show his power. She was starting to think he was compensating for something.

Hadley and everyone else had a gun in the holster on their hip. The leather jacket she was wearing was zipped tight in the cold air. She stretched out her legs, getting a feel of the tight pants she was wearing that at least were sheltering her from the cold harsh wind. From behind her she heard the order to move and immediately everyone was jogging towards the helicopters. Hadley was with her team, which thankfully included Vanya along with Jeremiah and Stephen. They hopped in the helicopter. Hadley felt weightless as it took off. The wind blew through the open doors and she felt her hair in her face.

"Scared?" Jeremiah hissed in Hadley's ear. She felt his hand on her lower back and flashed back to him threatening her, the cold knife on her neck was all she saw when she looked at him. His hand caressed the small of her back, there to remind her of his warning.

"Should I be?" Hadley retorted elbowing his arm away, hoping to give him a good bruise or at least hurt his ego a bit.

*This was a simple peace keeping mission. They were going to talk to the RFE's, going to give them the information and they were going to do what the GOVs wanted.* Hadley reassured herself.

Hadley felt the helicopter touch down and they piled out into an old parking lot. She could see the faded yellow lines under her boots as she followed Jeremiah towards the alley. Who had contacted the RFEs with this meeting, Hadley had no idea. All she could imagine was Hemmer sending a message to Saul who had replied with a big F-U.

As they moved through the alley they stayed in a tight formation, only holding their guns in the holsters. They had strict orders to keep this a peaceful meeting. They wanted to talk to the RFEs, to give them options and information. Hadley patted the thumb drive in her pocket that she had un-ceremonially been dedicated to give to them.

Jeremiah stopped in front of her so suddenly she almost ran into his back.

"Watch out," he hissed at her.

The entrance to the building they were going to approached and Hadley recognized it from the pictures of the mission plan. There was a red earth drawn on the door. Jeremiah nodded everyone forward. They walked towards the door with their hands in the air.

Even though the RFE's knew they were coming, they couldn't help but wonder if it all was a bit of a set up. Hemmer had always had it out for their organization.

"We are here to talk," Jeremiah said loudly.

The door remained closed and there was no sign of movement. The GOVs stopped in the middle of the street facing the building. They were about to move forward when Saul came out of the door followed by another two men.

Hadley inhaled so sharply she hoped no one in the group heard.

"What do you want?" he yelled at them, though his eyes flashed slightly to Hadley then away again. His long hair was down today and the wind was blowing it in all directions. He also wasn't wearing a shirt. For the first time Hadley saw his tattoo, it went over half his chest and down his arm. It looked like a lion or something from the distance they were standing.

"We want to give you some information, that's all," Jeremiah said.

"Why should we trust you?" the man beside Saul said.

"We told you that we were coming!" Jeremiah yelled completely annoyed.

"Go to hell Jeremiah!" Saul yelled at him.

"I've only ever tried to be your friend Saul."

"That's a load of crap."

Hadley watched the door open and seven other men and a woman walked out. The men stood in front of Saul. They formed a human barrier.

"We just want to give you a drive," Jeremiah's voice was deepening with a hatred even Hadley couldn't understand. Then suddenly he gave Hadley a shove with the butt of his gun.

"Fine," Saul muttered in the distance.

Hadley took her gun out of her holster, which prompted the men to raise their weapons at her. She carefully set down the gun on the ground and put her hands up in the air. Then she unzipped her pocket and pulled out the drive. She put her hand in the air holding the drive between her thumb and forefinger.

She started to walk forward. She could feel her heart quickening with every single step, both from anxiety and from excitement and anticipation. She walked keeping her eyes set on Saul. She started to get closer and could make out the features on his face. As she looked at him more memories flashed in her head.

She got to face him and could see by the look on his face that he had a lot of questions for her. They made eye contact that drew them both in.

"Did you see it?" he whispered.

"Yes." Hadley whispered back utterly desperate for more answers. She dropped the flash drive on the ground and they both scrambled to pick it up. Hadley finally was able to grab it and put it in his hand.

"What's happening over there?" Jeremiah yelled somewhere in the distance. He raised his gun and so did the RFEs surrounding Saul and Hadley.

"You are supposed to watch this—" Hadley said loudly, albeit unconvinced. She needed Jeremiah to hear her say it.

"I want to explain everything," Saul whispered, then said loudly, "I guess I'll decide if I want to. I'm still not sure this isn't a trap!"

"I need answers—" Hadley whispered desperately. Saul grabbed her wrist and placed a biodegradable message token into it. She knew the message would disappear if she didn't save it on a tablet. Hadley held it tightly as she walked back. She looked Jeremiah straight in the eyes as she did; he just scowled at her. The team's guns were up and pointed at the RFE's, cautious of any movement.

"How'd it go?" Jeremiah sneered. Hadley just shrugged.

"You watched me— it was fine. They said they'd watch it— we were just delivering a drive. In the end, it was almost as though we did nothing."

Jeremiah paused, "What?!" He stepped towards her and put his nose just centimeters from hers.

"This was the most useless, waste of time, energy and precious fuel. Why don't we do something that will actually help?!" Hadley rolled her eyes and began walking towards the helicopter.

"You stupid little bitch. You think you know everything. But you have no memories. You have nothing. You've always been the same Hadley." He was fuming.

"Jesus Jeremiah. You're an ass; I don't know what I did to you. Just get away from me. I did everything you said today. If there is something you remember that I don't know then you'd best tell me."

"You will continue to obey my directions, as your team captain I have the right, and privilege, to decide what happens to my team members, including termination." Jeremiah grabbed Hadley's arm forcefully, and they walked back to the helicopter. Hadley slipped the message token into her pocket and looked into the sky. Jeremiah pushed her into the helicopter.

Hadley pondered what was on the message, but she was too scared to even touch it in her pocket, but she could far from forget it was there.

They disembarked the helicopters back at the complex and saw the other two teams, who had just been running drills were already disassembling their guns back into the secure lockers. Two of the UNAG's were keeping a thoroughly brutal list of all the pieces on their tablets.

Hadley disassembled her gun quickly and handed them back to them with a nod. She turned away rolling her eyes at the bureaucratic system, that was completely outdated, though somehow remained rooted after a few centuries. Checklists and ranks, and then punishments were in store for disobeying the rules.

Humanity throughout history had flourished in this time of organization structure. Being a team, having leaders and knowing what to do without thinking was how wars were won in the early 20$^{th}$ century. A class system relying on ranks and superiority was what the world was built on, and somehow was the fallback every time something went truly wrong.

The thing with bureaucracy though is that it creates rebellion and chaos. Especially as many people end up ranked without earning their place and it also leads to abuse of power. Power that in life or death situations can turn ugly on a dime.

Rebellion was Hadley's strong suit, so every time they ended up organized like cattle she felt an urge to push back and do the opposite. The pinger program was brought in to fight every social stigma and thought that human kind had ever created. Somehow though they managed to fall right back to where they started and Hadley was really starting to get sick of it.

She saw Pax out of the corner of her eye; he had changed and was heading back to the dorm. He hadn't even looked at her since their escapades a few days earlier. Without thinking Hadley followed him, he noticed but ignored her and started into almost a jog.

It took him a few seconds to get into the dorm and so by the time they got to his room he had no chance of closing the door and locking her out. He immediately went to his bed and sat staring at the floor. Hadley clicked the lock in place and turned to him.

"Are you ever going to tell me what I fucking did to you?" Hadley said as she stood leaning against the inside of Paxton's door as he sat in bed.

"Nothing," he said. He was rubbing his sheets between his hands. He was avoiding eye contact with her.

"Really? You're going to tell me you've been acting the same all along?"

"I—I—" He couldn't even look up. Hadley was starting to feel the rage inside of her. She was red hot with anger. It had been an emotional tolling twelve hours. Hadley, without thinking, grabbed a book off of Pax's dresser and threw it at him. She barely missed his thick scull, and instead the hard cover book hit his bed frame and fell to the ground with a thump.

"I'm sorry—" He said hanging his head even lower, completely ignoring that she had just thrown a priceless and significantly sized book at his head, "Come here please?"

He looked up and patted the spot beside him to motion Hadley to come sit there. She took a moment to consider then reluctantly walked forward and sat down facing him crossing her own legs.

"I just don't understand." She stated plainly. The tears welled in her eyes. The warm drops blurred her vision and she tried to blink them back. One slowly trickled down her cheek and dropped like a raindrop onto the grey comforter.

"I was angry, at myself, and I took it out on you. You did nothing. But Saul and the way he looked at you— It made me so angry, because— because—" He looked absolutely devastated with himself. Hadley grabbed his hand and pulled it to her chest. She held it in both hands.

"I don't know Saul— I know you. It's all a little ridiculous."

"I love you Hadley. I think I have since the moment I met you. The moment I pulled you out of that rubble, and honestly before that, because we knew each other then." He looked her straight in the eyes and she struggled to find words to say.
At that moment Saul and Kane's faces flashed across her mind. Both of them held some part of her heart. She looked away as though he could see the guilty images crossing her mind.

Finally, she said with only slight hesitation, "I love you too."

He put both hands on her cheeks and kissed her passionately. She felt his tongue and teeth against hers. The only thing between them was pure passion and need. In that moment they needed and wanted each other more than they ever had before.

Pax reached down and grabbed her waist pulling her forward on top of him. Hadley wrapped her legs around his waist where he sat and in one swift motion her top was laying on the ground. She grabbed for his waist and lifted his shirt over his head. He pressed himself into her and brought his lips to her neck, nipping slightly along the crease of her throat.

# Chapter Forty-One

Hadley was spread out in bed awake, staring at the ticking clock that read 4:30 am. The room was chilly from the fact the complex was preserving energy and not heating at night. She heard the pitter-patter of the rain on the windowsill and knew she should turn off the window controls but Pax's arm was draped over her and she was too deeply invested in her thoughts to get up.

She desperately wanted to show Pax what Saul had given her. But instead she had kept it a secret, locked away in the deepest part of her soul. She saw Pax every day but she knew if her dreams had any grasp in reality her feelings might change. She couldn't fathom hurting him more.

Hadley turned her thoughts to the contents of the flash drive Saul had given both of them, the drive that he had used as a ploy to give her the real one. This fact made her nervous. She grabbed it off the bedside table; she was just able to reach it without disturbing Pax.

They had looked at it together when they had gotten back from the RFE complex. But it was regular propaganda anyone could find with a simple Internet search. Hadley rolled onto her side and opened it again, ensuring the brightness was turned down and it was on handheld size. She flipped through the pictures, wondering if she had missed something. If she typed in RFE she would have gotten a copy of the flash drive.

*Maybe that was the point*, she thought. Maybe Saul needed to talk to her alone.

Hadley pictured the drive that Saul had given just her and pulled out the piece of message tablet he had put in her hand. She held them close and thought about what was on them. She hadn't opened the message tablet yet, afraid of what it might say.

She couldn't lie there anymore and moved Pax's arm so she could get up, then she went to Pax's washroom and closed the door behind her. She turned on the shower and let the steam engulf the room. She held her closed fist up, digging her nails into her palm around the drive and looked down. Slowly she opened her fist and pressed the message.

*Hadley, you know we need to talk. Will be in touch.*

Hadley hadn't attempted to get out of the complex by herself and she didn't even know if it was possible anymore. Not without some higher power. Hemmer was watching her like a hawk. They knew they had gotten out before and they weren't going to let Hadley get out as easily as before.

As she stared into the depths of the mirror it came to her. Kane!

She had to find a way to use him to get what she needed. He had all the power, and it wasn't long ago they were on good terms— but could she even bear to look at him?

She jumped in the shower, to collect her thoughts and to warm herself from the frigid temperatures. She dried off slowly and wrapped her hair up. Then she wandered back to the bed and curled up.

Pax rolled over onto his other side giving Hadley room to squirm in with him. He flung his arm over and pulled her in close. She stared at the dark wall continuing to think. Kane didn't particularly like her the last time she saw him, but if she could just get his key card— she could go and do whatever she wanted.

However, she shuttered, thinking again about the last encounter she had with Kane. They had purposely avoided most contact since the incident. She shut her eyes, though her mind was reeling and tried to fall back asleep.

# Chapter Forty-Two

2072

Amy Burken was a brilliant scientist and researcher, even if Hemmer had drug her name through the mud after the Family First act of 2066. That had been a terrible year for her, except for her daughter's birth.

That day was the last time Amy ever looked at her research, and on the day her Hadley was born the virus was released by the UN. Though no one would say that, the official press release said there was a new strain of bacteria that was highly volatile and released when there was a malfunction in containment at a South American lab.

No one got sick, no one died, but slowly it dawned on people that no one was having kids. The internet started to go crazy with conspiracy theories as couples continued trying to get pregnant and fertility treatment rates grew. It was all futile. The bacterium was too powerful; more than Amy had ever imagined.

Hadley was the last baby born before the worldwide release, which was perfectly timed in 82 separate cities of mass population from London to Tokyo to Melbourne to Buenos Aires.

Now in her lab, Amy studied her computer, trying hard to figure out what was wrong with her cure for the disease she had invented. After years of work she thought she had finally figured out a way to undo, at least for a few, what she had done to them.

Kody, Amy's sister, was running her fingers through her perfect hair nervously and staring out the window at a dead man hanging out of his van. Then she saw them, the van approaching the building. A mass of men cascaded out and ran towards their building. Followed by a frustrated Hemmer.

"They're here Amy."

Amy started working harder, pouring all her samples in various combinations, over and over. Nothing was working.

They heard the footsteps outside the door.

"Dr. Burken, open the door please," It was Hemmer's voice.

Amy worked faster than she ever had. She didn't even know what she was combining. She heard the door start to creak open just as she saw one combination work. She threw it in for testing in the computer, which was almost instantaneous. SUCCESS.

She pulled it out and drew enough for two doses into a syringe. She ran to Kody and shoved the needle into her arm. She distributed half.

Then she ran to Hadley who was still sleeping in the armchair and gave her the second dose. She grabbed the marker on her notebook and wrote the words *Hadley, honey, it's in you.*

Then she stood back from everyone and put her hands up.

The forces pushed in and twenty red dots lit up her abdomen.

"Amy, Amy, Amy. We've been looking everywhere your flight is about to leave." Hemmer said sadistically.

"I know I just needed a few more things from the lab."

"Whose lab is this? It's not yours, yours is at the CDC."

"It's a friend's," Amy said quietly.

Hadley slowly woke up and looked at the men with guns. She was immediately frightened and started to cry.

"Mommy, what's going on?"

"Come here Hadley, honey. I have to take you to grandpa's now. Let's go."

Hemmer stood in her way. "Sorry Amy, one of my men will take her to her grandfather who is waiting outside. We have to go."

A man grabbed Hadley as she struggled towards her mom. But she was gone.

"Hemmer, you didn't even let me say goodbye."

"You had so much time Amy. I gave you every chance, now you're holding up pre-departure."

That was the last time Hadley ever saw her mom. She was carried, kicking and screaming down the elevator until she was placed gently into her grandfather's open arms. He hugged her close and bought her an ice cream as they drove.

Hadley's grandfather continued to drive until they got to the airport. Then they boarded a plane and were off to the furthest place they could get. A place of isolation and red sand.

# Chapter Forty-Three

Hadley didn't know if she ever did go to sleep completely after her middle of the night shower. She spent the next hours somewhere in a dream like state. When their quiet alarm went off at 6am, she shut it off immediately and slowly sat up in the bed.

Pax opened his eyes groggily. "Is it time for you to leave me already?"

"I'm afraid so—" Hadley slowly lifted the blankets off her legs and turned putting her feet on the cold hard ground. She shivered and Pax saw that. He sat up and grabbed her waist pulling her backwards. He locked Hadley in a bear hug as he leaned down and kissed the back of her neck. He pulled her back under the covers. She would stay there forever if she could and she really wished she could. Life would be so much easier in the little bubble that was that bedroom.

"If I—" He kissed Hadley, "don't go—" they kissed again, "soon, we—" he kissed her neck causing her to groan loudly as a warmth spread through her body, "will get caught!" Hadley said finally, spending the most time she ever had to finish a sentence.

She wiggled free of his grasp and hopped onto her feet. She grabbed her sweater off the floor and put it on. Then Hadley skipped to the door and with one look back she said, "Love you!"

He clasped his hands to his chest as if Hadley had shot him, "You're killing me!" he exclaimed, falling dramatically backwards.

"Sorry," she winked and was out the door.

Hadley walked down the hallway and turned towards her room. She got to the kitchen and went to the fridge where she opened it and felt the cool air rush over her. Thankfully it got rid of the warmth that had spread through her body and she gave her legs a shake.

She looked at the offerings and grabbed a vitamin iced tea and protein drink and an apple. She bit into the apple with a crunch and closed the fridge with her elbow. She walked into the living room as she continued her journey to her bedroom. She caught her reflection in the mirror, put her drink under the arm holding the apple, and smoothed down her hair, which was standing straight up.

"Hey—" someone quietly murmured a voice from the couch.

Hadley jumped so high she dropped her iced tea on the ground and stubbed her toe on a coffee table. The ice tea rolled across the floor and down the two steps into the living room. It was a biodegradable organic substance and it wiggled like jelly as it went.

"Ouch!" Hadley cried turning around. She saw Vanya crying on the couch. Her eyes were bloodshot and she had a bruise across her cheekbone.

Hadley knelt to pick up her ice tea, "Vanya, what's going on?"

"Jeremiah—"

"What about him? He didn't do that to you did he?! We didn't have combat training today—" Hadley exclaimed, mumbling as she tried to find the words. She didn't understand what Vanya meant.

"We're together— well we were together," she said simply, looking embarrassed at the ground. She rang her hands together.

"Oh," Hadley said as though surprised even though she had seen them together just weeks earlier. "Why did he do this?"

"He's got a bad temper," she mumbled, "Sometimes when he gets angry he gets physical, it's usually lamps, chairs, you know, but this time, well—"

"Did you end things?" Hadley asked slowly.

"Of course," she exclaimed, completely offended Hadley might have believed otherwise.

"Ok," Hadley sat down beside her and put an arm around her shoulders.

"I thought he loved me," she burst into hysterical tears

Hadley hugged Vanya gently, "He does, he just didn't show it—"

"Is Pax ever like that?"

"What?!" She played coy, but Vanya didn't buy it.

"We're all the smartest people in the world and you two aren't very subtle— and everyone knows smart people need more sex," she giggled through her tears.

"Well then—" Hadley shrugged no longer hiding anything.

They heard footsteps through the halls and Vanya hurried to wipe her tears. It was Stephen. He saw the look on Hadley's face and didn't ask questions. He just nodded at the two girls sitting on the couch and walked through.

"Let's go to the lab," Hadley suggested rising to her feet.

"Ok," was all Vanya could manage. She reluctantly got to her feet but her legs and body trembled like jelly. Slowly they walked to the door and to the lab.

Hadley scanned her wrist and they walked in. The Earth simulator was already going and half the computers were going through more data than she could read. The entire lab was in frenzy. Everything was beeping, scanning, and pinging. Kane ran out of his office in a panic carrying a full arm of old dusty textbooks. His hair was a mess and there was a long coffee stain down his offset buttoned shirt. His tie hung loosely. He didn't even notice the two women walk in as he spread two-hundred or so holographic pages across a desk. Hadley gave a little cough to announce their presence. He stopped what he was doing abruptly and turned his head slowly.

"I didn't expect to see you two here this early."

"We didn't expect you here either," Hadley sneered while raising her eyebrows. Vanya stepped behind her to shield her crying eyes. Hadley could hear her faint stifling and stood taller to block Kane's view, but he was distracted by what was in front of him.

"Since you are here you might as well help me!" he said frantically ignoring Hadley's comment.

"With?" She rolled her eyes. She had no motivation to do anything for him today.

"There has been a string of extreme weather patterns overnight; I fear we may be going into the ice age faster than previously thought. This could be bad, worse than we could have ever expected! I've been at this all night!" He was frantic. Hadley had never seen him lose his cool before this moment and she was almost frightened.

"What do you need?" Vanya whispered.

Vanya was thankful to have something to take her mind off Jeremiah and Hadley didn't blame her. Vanya's eye was swelling larger and was almost completely closed. Kane grabbed a holographic memory disk and did a sweep over half the files. They absorbed into it and he threw the small drive at Vanya.

"Start with these!"

Vanya looked at the disk in her hand and immediately went to her desk and started to work. Hadley watched her shoulders relax as she settled back into a comfortable routine doing something that wouldn't hurt her. Hadley could only smile meekly at her.

"And me?" Hadley stated more sternly than she'd intended. Kane took a step towards her trying to put a hand on her elbow. She took a step back and forcefully hit his hand away.

"Don't you fucking touch me, you no good—" She couldn't control her anger. She looked at Vanya, but she was lost in her work.

"Hadley please—" They stood locking eyes for what seemed like a lifetime.

Hadley had to break their eye contact and shuttered as she looked away. She watched the clouds billow and grow in the earth simulator, "You have no right to ask me for anything"

"At least let me explain—"

"2 minutes"

Hadley walked past him hitting his shoulder with hers with all the force she could muster. She walked into his office and sat on the desk dramatically crossing one leg over the other. He slowly followed her and closed the door behind him. He stood with his back to her, facing the closed door.

Hadley picked up his paperweight. It was a glass blob with lines of turquoise running through it. She turned it over in her hand as she swung her legs up and down, every time hitting her heels on the desk.

"Are you going to just stand with your back to me and hope I don't throw this paper weight against the back of your thick skull?" Hadley kicked over the chair sitting beside the table. Kane turned around slowly, tears in his eyes.

This was not what she expected and she was completely taken aback. For a moment, she wanted to get up and rush to him, hold him in her arms.

"I don't know what to say—" he whispered to his shoes. Without thinking, Hadley accidently dropped the paperweight. They both watched as it fell as though in slow motion towards the floor where it shattered into a thousand tiny glass shards.

Kane didn't even flinch. He hung his head lower in shame.

"You are the worst person I have ever met!" Hadley yelled standing up. Her voice was rising, the tears were boiling, and her whole body was shaking.

"More than you know," Kane's utter defeat made this all even worst. He knew what he'd done and that he couldn't do anything to undo it. Hadley wanted him to tell her that she'd deserved it. In some way that would have made it better. Seeing the shell of the man who had made a mistake. It made it hard for her to swallow.

"You are a pathetic excuse for a man," Hadley whispered, she walked towards him to get to the door, "Please let me leave."

"Hadley please—" He grabbed her arms and pulled her into him. She stood frozen, terrified. She looked over his shoulder unable to make eye contact.

He finally let go of her arms, as though burnt. She took a step back looking at her shoes. "I thought you were different, I felt a connection to you, and you just threw that away without a second thought."

"I know, it's just—"

"This isn't the first time you've done that though is it?" Hadley pressed hoping to get an answer.

Kane thought for a moment on what to say next. He decided to tread lightly. "Are you starting to remember things?"

"I didn't say that."

"You didn't not."

Hadley shrugged. "Were we together?"

"When I…?" He couldn't say it.

"Married Alice?"

"Yes," he said simply.

"Are you still with her?"

"It's complicated."

Hadley grabbed his hand in a moment of clarity and held it, "She loves you Kane. I can see by the way she looks at you."

"I know." Kane gave her hand a squeeze.

"Do you love her back?"

"I'm not sure anymore. I did at one point."

"Did you ever actually love me?" Hadley put an emphasis on the word actually. She wanted to know how he had really felt about her.

"I…"

Kane honestly didn't know. After all the time he still didn't know if it was love or control or excitement with Hadley. Or if it was a mixture of all three.

Hadley didn't want to hear anything else he had to say.

"I'm going to go now." She tried to push past him and avoid eye contact. The tears were already falling down his face. He grabbed her waist. Hadley felt her own tears run down her cheeks before she even realized they were falling. She fell into him and cried into his shoulders. They stood there holding each other, neither knowing what to do next.

After what felt like infinity, Hadley stepped back and stepped around him. She slowly turned the metal doorknob and opened the door. He stood like a statue with his back to her as he listened to her leave.

Hadley walked through the lab and Vanya didn't look up from her computer. Hadley saw the slow stream of tears running down her face in her reflection on the screen. She didn't even bother to brush them off. She let the tears dry on her face or splotch on the data she was going through.

She walked slowly down the halls with nowhere in particular to go. She stopped as she walked by the door Pax and her had previously used to escape. She opened the creaky door and walked into the demolished hall again. As though pulled by an invisible force she walked to the red splattered room. She knew it was blood but more than that she had this strange connection to this room. She was drawn to it; a distant memory she couldn't catch.

She went to the window sill and hoisted herself up. The window swung open outwards and she sat with her feet dangling out. The morning sun shone down on her face and she leaned her head on the window absolutely exhausted. Every muscle in her body hurt. She was completely emotionally drained.

She watched the sun rise higher and higher in the sky until it started to descend. She didn't care how much radiation she was getting or letting into her body. She just wanted to feel alive.

# Chapter Forty-Three

2228

The simulator wasn't getting Hadley's newest genetic pathogen right. No matter how hard she tried. She watched as the virus infected a small area and killed everyone, every time. She put her head on the desk.

"What do you want me to do Hadley?" The computer spoke.

"Try rearranging it again? And attack the hypothalamus. Also can we make it droplet and not airborne? Change the structure too." Hadley murmured. At this point it was tweaking. She had changed it so much in the last two hours she wasn't sure what it was anymore. She was just thankful the computer was keeping a data trail. She was throwing random suggestions at it.

The computer started to run the simulation. She didn't hear it ping out right away so she looked up. They had a globe in the simulator and she watched as the virus spread throughout the planet. It remained green though. It didn't kill anyone. Finally, the simulator stopped. All green but no SUCCESS popped up.

"What's the matter?" Hadley asked the simulator.

"I think you changed it too much from the original purpose. I will delete the data. This is not safe."

"Stop!" she yelled startled.

"What?"

"What did I do?"

"You created a virus that can be used as a ticking bomb. With this you can choose population groups specifically by genetics. You can then change their neuropathways, signals and chemicals. It is the perfect killer. For instance, you could choose every Caucasian woman of childbearing age with a certain level of Estrogen to no longer be able to breathe the current level of $CO_2$. You could kill everyone with the push of a button and there would be no cure."

"What?" Anna and Kane had walked in with Hemmer and they were all staring at the computer in shock.

"Give us another example—" Dr. Hemmer said stepping forward.

'You could target every man who is Caucasian and change it so their body will never allow them to have children. Or so their brain will clot and they will all die—" The computer said.

"Delete all the data," Hadley said at once. She practically screamed at the simulator.

"No. Do no such thing." Dr. Kane exclaimed. Hadley knew his voice overruled hers in the computers mind and everything suddenly came crashing down around her.

"Girl's please leave. Meet us in room 4." Kane said without looking at the two of them.

Hadley tried to protest but Anna dragged her out of the room.

"I may have just destroyed the world—"

Her eyes were wide, "I know. How did this happen?"

"I was throwing random virus changes at the computer. In no particular order."

Hours later, Anna and Hadley sat in a white room with three chairs and a table. They had been woken up in the wee hours of the morning and hauled to the room. They were sitting waiting for answers.

Dr. Hemmer walked in grinning from ear to ear. "You girls have done it! You have perfected the imperfect-able. You have made us have control of evolution."

Hadley inhaled sharply and said in a whisper that even frightened herself, "You have to erase it Hemmer. It needs to be destroyed."

"There is no chance of that!" He was gleefully giddy.

Hadley stood up, "I came back to work with you, not to do this."

"Hadley you gave me the greatest gift in the world. Though don't you fool yourself you came back because your little RFE project is running out of money and we have the resources you selfishly want."

"RFE is strong," said Anna and Hadley at the same time.

"It's for dreamers, and mark my words girls I will destroy it."

"You've said that before Hemmer," Anna smirked.

# Chapter Forty-Four

It was night now, and Hadley had dozed off with her cheek against the window sill. She stretched out and felt the feeling start coming back to her face. She wiggled her cheek trying to get rid of the implant she had created in her skin. She couldn't figure out what had woken her up. Then the light flicked across her face again and momentarily she was illuminated.

Her blood ran cold and she started to slowly bring her legs back inside. She looked down and saw three people standing below her wearing all black. One of them held a light.

"Evans is that you?"

Hadley was taken aback, there was only one person who called her that and without thinking she replied down, "Saul?"

"Hey!" he called back.

The window sill was only a few meters off the ground below and without thinking too long Hadley jumped. Her legs contracted as she hit the hard pavement and she stumbled. Saul was right there to pull her up.

"Well I'm not sure I expected that," a woman said beside Saul.

"Haven't we known Hadley is the epitome of unexpected for years now?" the other man replied with a low grumble in a thick Scottish accent.

All three of them laughed and Hadley gave them a weak smile. She didn't know the others beside Saul.

"Maggie," the woman said with an air of disdain. She smiled perfectly and tossed her red hair to the side in the wind.

The other man held out a hand, "Charles. Charles Dickens."

Hadley took his hand and shook it.

Charles continued with a laugh, "It's always strange to meet people you've known for so long and they don't remember you."

"I'm sorry," Hadley said embarrassed.

"No need," Charles smiled. "Hemmer is a bloody moron, I still don't understand what he hopes to achieve by putting memory inhibitors into his cryosleep chambers."

"What?" Hadley asked puzzled.

Saul suddenly grabbed her arm, pulling her attention away from Charles. He threw a metal cuff on her wrist, just like the last time.

"There's no time to talk about this here Charles. We knew we only had a short timeline when Hadley's program pinged that she was outside."

"Are you watching me?"

"Obviously," Maggie said with a smile.

Hadley didn't have a reply, but she smiled in spite of herself.

"It's only a few blocks Hadley, but we need to run. Hemmer patrols the sky with drones."

They started to run, weaving down the streets, mainly taking back alleys until they got to a small half sized door. All four of them climbed through and they were in a long shoot. Hadley wasn't expecting to fall and she let out a short scream and she got her bearings. The slide continued for a long time until they hit a large crash pad at the bottom.

"Jeez!" Hadley said, she looked around and could see they were in a room just off from the large computer room they'd been in before.

Everyone else was already on their feet waiting for Hadley to stand and she clamored to her feet.

They walked through the doorway and an alarm went off. It was quiet and dull.

"How long were you outside Hadley?" Maggie asked judgingly.

"I'm not sure. Why?"

"Radiation overload," Charles said nonchalantly.

"Dammit." Hadley rolled her eyes, she definitely had known better. But the soft wind had been cooling and felt great.

Saul went to a desk beside the door and pulled out a small syringe. He attached a needle and came up to Hadley.

"This really doesn't hurt, but I can't have you dying on me."

Hadley just shrugged and let him stick the needle into her arm. She didn't feel anything until half her body seemingly went numb.

"Am I supposed to—?" Hadley couldn't finish her sentence before she vomited on her feet.

"You always seem to be throwing up here," Saul joked.

"The last time I almost drowned," Hadley said with a grimaced as she glanced up at Saul from her bent over position.

Charles gave her back a slight pat, "Your clothes need to be washed."

Saul looked from Hadley to Maggie and said, "Can you take care of that Maggie?"

Maggie locked her jaw and rolled her eyes but nodded anyways.

This was the first moment that Hadley noticed how stunningly beautiful Maggie was. She flipped her hair to the side and fluttered her eyelashes at Saul. Hadley noticed Maggie almost completely ignored the fact that she was there.

Maggie grabbed Saul's forearm in assurance, "Of course Saul, anything! I'll even give her some of the perfume you like so much." She winked at him and the colour rushed to his cheeks.

"Mags, that won't be necessary. Just a shower and clothes."

"Come on," Maggie said, hoisting Hadley to an upright position. Then she started walking them down the hall.

She opened a door and they walked inside a bedroom. *Hers,* Hadley assumed. Immediately she rummaged in a drawer and pulled out a towel and a fresh set of clothes.

She handed them to Hadley, "If you give me your clothes I'll send them to the wash and you can have them back before you leave!" Maggie held out her arms for Hadley's clothes. Hadley looked at her confused. "There's nothing I haven't seen before."

So Hadley shrugged and undressed. She passed Maggie her clothes and wrapped the towel around herself.

"These do smell like radiation!" Maggie exclaimed, "Oh the bathroom is right through that door!"

Hadley smiled and walked into the bathroom. The shower was carved into the rocks. Small stones lined the bottom of the shower. She wiggled her toes across the stones. She grabbed Maggie's shampoo and opened the glass bottle. She smelt it and it smelt like apples and pears. It was amazing. The shampoo at the complex smelt like sterile cleaner. The government again didn't want anything to mess with their order and homogeneity.

Hadley showered as quickly as was reasonable, enjoying the smells and environment, and then dried off. She put on the clothes Maggie had given her which were slightly too small. But she squirmed her way into the pants, just barely able to do up the button. She looked in the mirror and hated her own reflection. She had barely healed scars across her face and arms. Her hair looked better than it normally did though. Magic shampoo apparently. She turned away from the mirror and walked out of the bathroom.

Maggie was sitting on her bed clicking her sky high pair of stilettos she had changed into. She was showing off everything in the skin tight dress she was wearing.

"You look great Hadley; I wish I was as pretty as you." She was completely genuine, which irritated Hadley slightly because of how gorgeous she actually was.

"Thanks Maggie. But I really don't think anyone compares to you."

"You are just being modest," she beamed. She got to her feet and put her hand on Hadley's shoulder. She moved with the air of royalty. She opened the door and motioned them both through. Back in the hall they walked towards the computer room.

"Nice set up we have here isn't it?" Maggie said attempting to make small talk.

Hadley looked around, "Yes, how many complexes are there like this throughout the world?"

"About eighty, give or take. We hear updates every so often. But radio silence is a must so the govs don't know where exactly the complexes are. There's also the matter of the rift between Saul and..." She stopped breaking eye contact.

"Rift?"

"I really shouldn't have said that. It's not my place."

Hadley nodded in understanding, they had a smart system. "But they know you are here in this city. Why don't they attack?"

"You tell me—" she shrugged.

# Chapter Forty-Five

Saul was hunched over a man, both of them looking intently at the computer. Charles was sitting on a desk to the side talking to a short girl wearing overly large glasses. Hadley and Maggie walked up behind them and they didn't even notice.

"So dinner one night?" Charles cooed to the woman.

"Charles—" she laughed.

Maggie gave Hadley a side eye and whispered, "Charles is the man every woman wants to be with here. Especially since his wife died last year."

Hadley's eyes widened, "What about you?"

"I only have eyes for one man." Maggie said sending a glance towards Saul.

"Oh," Hadley said.

Maggie just gave her a coordinated smile.

"Ahem," Maggie coughed. Saul turned around immediately and the man rushed to close the window on the browser. Before he did so Hadley saw her name on the screen and raised an eyebrow at Saul. He ignored it. The man turned his chair around and leaned back.

"Hadley, this is Elijah Roper." Kane said with a flick of his wrist.

The man had dark fuzzy hair that stood up in all directions. His skin was the colour of milk chocolate and flawless, it was gorgeous. He nodded his head at Hadley and reached out a hand, "Nice to finally meet you Hadley."
She shook his hand and smiled. He had a casual sense of being, of peace. He obviously did whatever he wanted and even though English was clearly not his first language, Hadley immediately liked him.

"I got here, after you disappeared—" Elijah continued, letting his sentence fade.

"Elijah, can you pull up the video on the screen?" Saul asked interrupting Hadley as she was about to inquire further.

"For sure boss man," Elijah turned with a solute and was immediately immersed in his screen. His fingers typed in a blur and the giant screen at the front of the room came to life.

A video popped up and the starting image was a picture of Hadley. Her hair was pulled up in a high ponytail and she was smiling wearing a RFE shirt. She looked as though she should be a camp counsellor. There were mountains and cabins in the back of the image.

"Ready for a whole new world?" Maggie whispered. Hadley nodded slowly unable to speak as if there was something caught in her throat.

Elijah hit play on his computer and mere seconds later the video started to play.

"Hi!" Hadley said on screen. "My name is Hadley Evans and I am the president and co-founder of Revolution for Free Earth or RFE. I am here to tell you that everything you have been told in the media and online is a lie. Granted, it did not start out this way but the Governments of the most prominent countries in the world have a belief that this is the only way. Restart or Die! It has been generations upon generations that we have known our consumption and waste production levels are sending this planet and the human race to extinction. The government will tell you they need volunteers to be sent to the moon and mars. Those are viable options, but not yet. They will tell you that the mass plagues and disease outbreaks are not government funded but they are. I am here to tell you there is another way. But it will only succeed if we all work together. So visit our website for more information and join RFE! I was one of the prominent minds of the SPaDI project, and so I actually know what I'm talking about. I started this organization and now it's grown to include a lot of people who care a lot. Be one of them. 'In the future'!"

Hadley looked around and saw everyone in the room was now looking at her. No one had watched the video; they had watched her reaction the whole time. She just stared at her own face, still plastered on the screen.

"Is that true?"

"Could we make this up?" Saul said sternly.

"When was that?" Hadley pried.

"The other video Elijah please," Saul said in a strained voice, hurrying it along. Suddenly another image of Hadley popped up on the screen.

She was covered in mud; her shirt was tattered. There was blood running down the one side of her face, actually it was pouring down. She was holding the camera and it was shaking all over, as though the ground was moving beneath her. She held it up to her face and spoke into the lens.

"Hadley! If you are watching this then you followed my, our...whatever... clues. Thank god they haven't taken all your brains away yet. Do not trust Hemmer or Kane or—" she paused out of breath, "Pax for that matter. You are the only one who knows the access code and you don't even know it. RFE is the only way. Stop Hemmer and Kane! Do not give them what they want. Do not help them. We've lost too much to give in now. That will mean the end—"

Suddenly, Hadley dropped the camera because someone came up behind her.

Big, thick arms wrapped around her and she glanced backwards and saw Kane. Hadley was able to hit him in the stomach and break free but he slammed his fist into her face. He threw her to the ground, in pure and utter rage. He continued to slam his fist into her face until she was spitting out blood. Hadley was able to get to her feet and started to run but Jeremiah stood in her way. He had come out of nowhere.

Hadley turned around to see Kane run straight at her, he threw her to the ground and pinned her against the broken glass on the floor. Hadley was kicking and screaming but gun shots ran through the air behind her so it was as though she was silent.

Kane pressed his forearm against her throat. She couldn't breathe and was struggling for breath. Jeremiah approached and Kane said something as Hadley tried to break free. Kane pushed his knee into her stomach. She started to scream as his arm came off her windpipe and was screaming at the top of her lungs but they weren't listening.

Then it got worse than Hadley ever thought it could. Kane's face was pure evil. It was sadistic. He straddled her legs and undid her jeans in one swift motion. His hand reached under her already shredded shirt and he grabbed her breast. He took a deep breath and said, "I'm going to make it so even your husband doesn't want you anymore."

"Fuck you Kane," Hadley said through the tears that were coming down her face.

He pulled her pants down with a quick yank and undid his jeans. In one swift motion he was right on top of her. There was a look of power on his face while silent tears ran down Hadley's face. Jeremiah held her down and Hadley couldn't do anything to stop what was going to happen.

"Stop! Kane please!"

"I'm going to hurt you Hadley like you hurt me."

"That was your fault!"

"I wanted everything with you."

"You threw it away," Hadley spat in his face, she tried to get free by it didn't work.

Kane reached his hand down to reposition himself and thrust inside of her. "I missed this," he said smiling sadistically.

He was getting off on watching her in pain, watching Hadley be helpless. It was what he had always wanted. He always wanted control, that's why he started dating his students.

He pounded against her. One thrust at a time. He pulled a knife from his jacket and she watched him cut open the front of her bra. He put his lips to her breast and the tears streamed down her face even more. When he pulled away her breast was covered in bleeding bite marks.

"Hope that hurt."

He came a moment later.

He pulled out, did up his pants and inched back. Hadley lay almost limp unable to move. He tore off her pants the rest of the way and threw them aside.

"Now your husband will only think of me when he sees you."

Hadley wasn't going to say anything but she managed a whisper, "You loved me once."

"That was before you—," he couldn't bring himself to say it.

Kane glanced at Jeremiah and they both looked out into the street.

"Cut her throat and parade her through the streets; let them know they can't win. Let anyone faithful to the government have a turn. I want this broadcast everywhere. We will make them know how badly we can hurt them." Kane said kicking Hadley in the face.

Jeremiah took a knife and slid it slowly against her throat, the blood pooling around her head as the light left her eyes.

Then, the video stopped.

Back in the computer hall, Hadley noticed she had tears running down her face. She quickly wiped them away and in her head she determined herself to kill Kane, if it was the last thing she ever did.

No one spoke or moved. Many of the girls in the room were also crying. Hadley looked to Saul and noticed he was facing away from the screen and had not watched the video.

"Too much?" she croaked barely able to speak to him suppressing the urge to break down again. She wouldn't be the victim they wanted her to be.

"I saw it once; you were live broadcasting to ensure that your message was saved; I don't ever want to watch it again." He shuttered.

Hadley curled her lip into a half smile that didn't do anything but say she appreciated that and she looked around the room and saw pitying faces looking back at her. Saul just looked defiant.

"Thank you for helping me understand, and not looking at me like the rest of them do." Hadley was really crying now, whimpering actually.

"It's not your fault and I'm biding my time until I can kill Kane—"

Hadley stared into his dark eyes, "Why do you care?"

He just shrugged. He wanted to tell her something but couldn't bring himself to and Hadley didn't press any further.

It took a while for everyone to calm down and get back to work. But they slowly did, typing slowly on their computers. The room was only full of typing and squeaky chairs.

"I need to sit down." Hadley sunk to the floor and put her head between her knees, the tears relentlessly running down her face now. She couldn't hold back. She rocked back and forth. In and out, in and out, in and out. She regulated her breathing.

She stared at the stone ground and ran her hand against the dust build up. It was as though she was covered in ice water. She was shivering. She felt disgusted in herself even though it wasn't her fault. How could she have let that happen?

Hadley felt arms around her and looked up to see the strong muscular form of Saul. His body basically encapsulated hers and she was fully enrobed in his arms. She leaned her head into his shoulder. She was lost for a moment thinking only about his breathing and her own, focusing on anything else but what she had just seen. Though more so the feelings it had stirred deep inside her. He was shaking with anger but trying to suppress it.

As the moments past, Hadley could feel eyes looking at their crumbled ball on the floor. Both of them couldn't seem to stop shaking. The tears started again down Hadley's face. She could feel him crying into her shoulder as he picked her up into a cradle.

Hadley glanced up through blurry eyes and saw Maggie staring daggers at her. Maggie's face was red and if it were possible smoke would be coming out of her ears.

Hadley moved away from Saul. She tucked her hair behind her ear and scratched at the side of her face. She started to chew on her lip.

Elijah evidently had run out of the room whilst Hadley sat crying and ran back into the room with a basket cradled in both his arms. He was so kind and had a big grin on his face. Hadley smiled brilliantly back at him. Maggie and Saul looked at each other as though she was crazy and again Hadley looked down.

"I got stuff to make Hadley feel better!" Elijah exclaimed as he stopped out of breath in front of them all. Hadley looked up at the bottom of the basket.

Saul got to his feet. "Elijah let's bring that to the conference room."

"All right!" Elijah exclaimed and was off without another word. Saul grabbed Hadley under her armpits and hoisted her to her feet. Hadley almost fell over when he let go, so he steadied her around her waist. They walked after Elijah, and Maggie followed a few feet behind them.

The four of them got to a small room with a board table. There was a small projector and a computer in the corner. The light coloured wood table stood out against the dark walls. A single light hung over the table and it rocked back and forth from the breeze of them opening the door.

They all sat down and Elijah started to unload the basket. He handed everyone bottles of water and juice. He threw them all organic chocolate bars, candy, chips and a full apple pie. Lastly he pulled out a homemade jar of ice cream. He was very pleased with himself.

Hadley looked at it for a moment in awe before she took a spoon and dug it into the ice cream. She swirled her spoon for a second and got a giant spoonful. She looked at the ice cream. This was something she hadn't had in a very long time and missed dearly. She popped the spoon in her mouth and savoured every second of it. Her eyes rolled back and she felt her body relax. When she opened her eyes they were all staring.

"What?!" she snapped

"Nothing!" they all murmured at various times.

"Are you all right?" Maggie whispered.

"I'm not sure I'll ever be all right." Hadley shrugged angrily. She could hear the venom in her voice.

"We didn't want to show you—" Elijah murmured, no longer his happy self. He looked like a twelve-year-old boy.

"Is that why you brought me here? To show me that video? Was it supposed to get me on your side?" Hadley stood up slamming her fists against the table.

Saul stood up. He was angry. "Do you think I like seeing that video? Every bloody time I have to watch it, I feel as though I am getting stabbed over and over and over again. You are on our side. Not theirs! You need to realize that!"

"Why do you care?" Hadley screamed.

"Because— because—" He sunk back down into his chair.

"Because?" Hadley practically screamed. She was sick of him not telling her whatever it was he wanted to.

"I can't tell you—" He whispered.

"You can't tell me?!" Hadley threw a muffin at his head and he moved just in time.

"You," he stressed the word, "made me promise not to."

Hadley stared at him blankly. She threw her hands in the air and turned towards the door. "I have to get back."

Maggie decided to join the conversation, "Hadley you don't understand!"

"What don't I understand?"

"I'm your husband." Saul said simply.

# Chapter Forty-Six

"I should go." Hadley said unable to think of anything else.

She stood up but couldn't bring herself to leave the room.

Elijah scanned the room and grabbed Maggie pulling her to her feet. She tried to struggle against him.

"We'll give you two some time alone." Elijah stated, pulling a basically kicking and screaming Maggie out of the room.

"She's not happy being forced to leave," Hadley said gently.

"No, she wouldn't be."

"Are the two of you involved?"

"We have been."

The statement hurt Hadley to her core and she looked down ringing her hands together uncomfortably, "Oh."

"You have to understand Hadley. I thought you were gone. They took you from me."

"You don't have to explain anything Saul," Hadley said convincingly.

Saul smiled at her, "I've missed you every day. Though I'm sure you don't remember anything."

Hadley started to unwrap a muffin because she couldn't bear the awkward eye contact. "I do remember the Science Awards. It's where we first met right?"

Saul's face lit up, "You remember?"

"Things are coming back slowly," Hadley said popping a piece of muffin into her mouth.

As if on cue, a quiet alarm pinged through the complex.

"Sunrise."

"I should get back," Hadley said standing up.

Saul paused for a moment, "You don't have to go."

Hadley smiled softly, "I need more answers from them."

Saul shook his head trying to not break down, "Can we ask you to do something?"

Hadley smiled, sensing a plan, "Anything."

Saul pulled out a coinet and opened a picture of a stunning woman. He showed it to Hadley and asked, "Do you know who this is?"

"No? Should I?"

Saul just laughed, "You should, but I know you don't. This is Liani, she used to be a major force in RFE until she went rogue. Our intel inside the complex says Hemmer is planning a visit to a GOV complex out West once the storms come in. Kane has been sending him updates and Hemmer has been communicating with the other GOV stations. I wouldn't hold it against Liani to try something. Can I ask that if you get the chance, kill her? She's trying to take down everything that both we and the GOVs have worked for."

Hadley was stunned and raised an eyebrow, "I can't kill her."

"If you remembered everything you would. So I guess I'm asking: do you trust me?" Saul smiled a memory obviously flashing through his mind. Something Hadley no longer remembered.

"I think so."

Hadley's statement made Saul grin from ear to ear. Then he said, "Just think about it."

Hadley nodded and Saul led her out. Then they heard footsteps behind them.

Maggie ran up to them. They knew it was her because her heels clicked distinctively. "Hadley, Hadley! Hadley!"

Hadley looked back and Maggie was waving her arms, "Hey Maggie?"

"Your clothes!" Maggie said placing a neatly folded bunch of clothes into Hadley's arms.

"Thanks," Hadley said.

"Oh Saul, Elijah needed you for something." Maggie said nonchalantly with a sarcastic look on her face.

"I better go then, you ok Evans?" Saul said looking into the depths of Hadley's soul.

"I'll show her the way out!" Maggie hooked her arm through Hadley's and started to walk down the hall. Hadley gave a glance back to Saul who eventually turned back.

Maggie was happy Hadley was leaving. She didn't want her anywhere near Saul. Her sympathy and kindness was out of jealousy. She led Hadley outside where they had entered.

"I'm not going to give him up as easily as you'd think Hadley."

Hadley couldn't think of anything to say and apparently didn't need to because Maggie went back into the complex shutting the door hard behind her.

Hadley was left alone on the street with her thoughts as she walked back to the complex.

# Chapter Forty-Seven

2228

"It would make this so much easier if the population of the planet was say one billion as opposed to ten—" Hadley said nonchalantly across a long boardroom table. Hemmer, Kane, Vanya, Jeremiah, Stephen and Pax sat at various places.

"You think so?" Hemmer replied with genuine interest. He studied her closely as he always did. She looked down at her notes fiddling with her pen.

"I didn't mean it as a genuine suggestion— I was nearly stating my frustration at the problem. We've been here for decades." Hadley fumbled and started to stutter. At last she composed her thoughts into words, "We've been at this for weeks and there is no climatological model that will not send the earth into the next ice age. We have so much smog. Half the ozone layer is gone. It's been years since the last ice sheet melted. In my lifetime I've seen almost every major coastal city destroyed. It's frustrating— there's nothing we can do but tell people to stop consuming. We've changed almost everything. But it doesn't seem to be slowing down. There's no way we can get rid of everyone—"

There was a moment of silence. Everyone just stared at her. She hadn't meant for that outburst to happen, it just had and she felt the color drain from her cheeks.

"Well put Hadley," Kane said genuinely.

"A lot to think about. You may have to start looking at other alternatives," Hemmer stated.

"Like what?" Vanya laughed as she popped her gum. She thought Hadley's idea was preposterous and was basically laughing at the fact Hemmer was taking any of it seriously.

"Shutting off all the power everywhere—" Hemmer suggested. Hadley hadn't thought of that before— she knew he was joking but it was a better last resort than killing off ninety percent of the population.

Hadley and Hemmer locked eyes and his eyes glittered. Little did she know that she had set off a chain reaction of ideas inside his brilliant brain and where those would stop she would never know.

# Chapter Forty-Eight

It was what seemed like a long time later that Hadley managed to find a way into the complex, through an open doorway on the far east side. It was cold and musky inside the room as she pulled the ancient looking door with dusty handles.

She grabbed the brass door knob and pulled it open. It led to a set of marble stairs. She ran up the stairs taking them two at a time and ran across the marble floor to the main doors. She looked around her and noticed the room seemed to have too many elements that didn't fit together.

The floor was a combination of pinks and whites glittering in the moonlight that was shining in through the picture windows on either side of a thick and heavy steel door. She slowed down as she walked towards the doors and felt something was wrong.

`Her brain flashed to the room filled with people, the doors were massive wooden doors and there were statues strewn about the room. Unconsciously she walked to a spot just to the left of the doors and looked down. There was a definite circle imprinted on the ground. It was about 4 feet wide.

She looked up expecting to see a statue. But of course it was not there which she knew before she even looked up. She stood looking at the architecture of the room. It was massive. The ceiling had to be at least 10 meters tall.

The ceiling was a biblical depiction of good and evil that appeared to have been chiselled in hundreds of years ago. Hadley looked at the artist's depiction of Satan. He was quite charming in his fiery oasis. His minions, demented creatures crawled out from the fire towards earth.

Oppositely, three figures stood surrounded by angels that extended down towards earth. She looked between the two and felt sadness for the people caught in the middle. They were helpless bystanders in a war that was bigger than them.

She looked away from the painting full of grief. *Who was looking out for the middle people in our war?* She wondered.

*Then again, no one had believed in God for hundreds of years.*

She sighed and opened the doors leaving the room. Something glittered in the corner of her eye as she walked through but before her body could stop her, the doors closed behind her. She tried to reopen them but they were locked. She went as far as to try her program and access to open it but it was futile.

She shook her head and started walking down the hall, reaching an occasional abandoned door every once in a while until she emerged just off of the main atrium. The door she came through had a huge sign that read: *access restricted.*

Pax came out of nowhere, giving her a puzzled look.

"Where have you been?" Pax asked running his hand through his hair. He raised an eyebrow towards the door.

"I honestly got lost."

"Right," Pax replied but he didn't press further.

"Where did Kane say I was?" Hadley inquired subtlety.

"Sick. He left it at that actually. I didn't press further."

"Of course he did," Hadley sighed

Pax looked straight into her eyes. "What's up Had?"

Hadley just shook her head for a moment, and then realized she needed to tell someone about everything that had happened. She needed desperately to tell Pax why she was being distant and cold. Why her thoughts were with a man that she barely remembered.

But she couldn't, she couldn't bring herself to tell him just yet. So, instead of telling him about what just happened and Saul's reveal, she started to ramble on and on about Kane. She went into a long ramble about Alice and his marriage, about Kane's advances and his distance. She went on about the way Kane had been treating her.

When she was finally done Pax was silent until he exploded, "What the fuck is wrong with that asshole?!"

Hadley hadn't expected him to react so viscerally. The expression on Pax's face scared even her and she retreated away from him a little. He noticed her shock and pulled her towards him taking deep calming breaths.

"Sorry Had— It's just— I just—." He let out a yell at the top of his lungs.

People turned to stare.

"We're in the atrium!" Hadley exclaimed as she instinctually clasped her hand over his mouth. His hair lay wildly over his eyes and she saw the rage leave his face. She uncurled her fingers from his face and kissed him gently. She kissed him with more love than she ever remembered kissing anyone.

"You know I love you don't you?"

"I love you too Hadley," he said nuzzling his head into her shoulder.

A ringing erupted around them and suddenly, though not really if Hadley thought about it, it was 8am. They were late for a meeting.

They practically ran through the atrium, winding their way through the desks trying to get to the conference room they were using for the meeting today.

You could cut the tension in the room with a knife as they walked into the meeting. Hadley was sure no one else in the room noticed. But Pax, Kane and Hadley sure did. Hadley and Pax took seats to the side, and quietly opened their documents off their coinets. Hadley was basically holding her breath, trying not to let out the deep breaths she needed. Her heart was pounding from the running.

Though as she sat there, all she could do was study Hemmer. He had more secrets than she could have in an entire lifetime. She deeply wanted to know what he was up to, especially since he was planning to send them West.

Hadley, tried to catch up by skimming through her notes, just to discover they were discussing grain and plant resources. Most of the world had radiation poisoning and thus the only sources of plants and animals had to come from heavily government controlled greenhouses.

Hemmer had a model greenhouse in front of him today. He was visually showing how the system was closed and no outside material was needed. Hadley was fascinated with the advance in technology. The greenhouse used only its resources and water and with the correct plants that's all it needed.

The water cycled through the system as though it was outdoors. The temperature was controlled to allow both condensation and evaporation throughout a twenty-four hour period. Cellular respiration and photosynthesis did the rest.

Hadley raised her hand, "How many people can each greenhouse sustain?"

Hemmer looked at her completely annoyed at her blatant interruption of his talk, "Each of the small can sustain 100 people per year, whilst the large are around 2500—"

"And how many did you say we have?"

"12 large and 60 small—"

"So around 100,000 people? That's less than a percent of the current world population"

"Yes Hadley, thank you for pointing out the flaw in everything. We realize that we can't sustain the population and are building as fast as we can," he snapped at her, a vein in his forehead popping out.

Hadley sat back in her chair. "Sorry—"

"I'm afraid Hemmer may poison you one of these days," Pax laughed under his breath nonchalantly.

Hadley didn't even giggle. "Me too actually."

"Maybe stay quiet for a while," he suggested and she nodded, realizing immediately that was best. When Hemmer stopped talking everyone started to get up.

"Hadley, a word please," Hemmer nodded to her.

Pax grabbed her arm and gave it a squeeze, "I'll wait right outside the door. Scream if you need me." Hadley nodded at him and swallowed. She walked to the front of the room and waited in silence while everyone cleared out.

"Do you want to be here?" he snapped at her walking forward.

"You know I do!" she said puffing out her chest triumphantly.

"You have a tendency to ruin morale—"

"I actually just have a tendency to point out the flaws in what sounds like a great plan on the exterior." She turned on her heel and walked towards the door.

"You don't want me as an enemy Miss Evans. Be careful—" The way he said it reminded her of one of her favourite classic movies, Harry Potter. He sounded a heck of a lot like Alan Rickman. Hadley remembered watching it with her grandfather, as he reminisced about old grainy films.

"I always am." Without another look she walked out the door and up to Pax who was leaning coolly against the wall. Half the time she thought he was better suited to be on a beach somewhere, drinking and surfing. Today she was just happy to have him waiting for her.

"I need to be careful," she whispered to Pax, letting the reality of what he said sink in.

"No shit Sherlock!" He laughed as he grabbed her hand and they proceeded to interlock fingers. Hadley smiled as they walked down the hall. But in the back of her mind Hemmer's threat stuck with her.

# Chapter Forty-Nine

It had been days since Hadley had talked to Kane and every night she thought about the way she could most hurt him. It almost saddened her, though it was mostly pity. He thought that her lost memories meant a new start for him. It would never be a new start.

She decided a swim would clear her head. She put on a bathing suit and walked to the pool, which was illuminated as though bathed in the early morning sun. The projectors glimmered off of the old stone ceiling. She looked at the water and dove in headfirst. She raised her elbow high out of the water and started to swim. She regulated her breathing and calmly swam back and forth.

Then she flipped over and swam back. She flipped onto her back and laid there in the middle of the pool looking up at the ceiling. The ceiling was exquisitely carved. She let her eyes wander around the leaves and trees that were carved into the ceiling. It was odd looking at the architecture in the pool. This room was decades older than everything else in the complex. Though maybe not as old as the marble entry way she had found herself in days before.

She brought her arms over her head and back down to her waist. The water rippled away and she faintly heard it splash over the edge. Somewhere in the distance she heard a door open and pulled her head out of the water continuing to lie on her back. She ran her hands through her hair pushing the water out and swung it over one shoulder. She turned around and saw Kane standing watching her. He was leaning against the wall with his arms crossed.

"Hi?" she half asked, trying not to show her hatred. She moved her hands back and forth to steady herself in the water.

He stared at Hadley for a moment in silence almost looking through the water at her, "I need your help."

"Ok?" She stayed where she was in the water and let her feet sink.

He was irritated and fidgety, "Hurry please!"

"Whoa, calm down." Hadley swam to the edge and pushed herself up. Kane watched her and threw her towel towards her. Hadley caught it and wrapped it around herself in a hurry. She wrung out her hair with her hands and tied it up into a tight bun on the top of her head.

"Let's go! You've been avoiding the lab for the last three days. And I'm sorry but we need to put everything on hold for a few hours and you don't have to like me, or talk to me, or even look at me, you solely have to work. The world is actually going into the extreme ice age we've been waiting for, but so much faster than we previously thought. We need to do something!" He rushed out of the pool and down the hall. Hadley quickly followed leaving a trail of water behind her. They rushed into their housing, through the kitchen and down the nondescript hallway. Hadley caught a glimpse of a bowl of fruit on the wall. Her least favourite painting. She turned to go to her room but Kane grabbed her arm and dragged her to the door.

"Can't I at least change?"

"You don't know what's happened now—" The strain in his voice was palpable. So she kept walking with him. Her bare feet left wet footprints as they went. They clapped against the ground making gurgled sounds. The floor, which was a light concrete was now painted black in places as it got wet.

They hurried down the hall. As they passed people Hadley got strange looks, which made her laugh. They must have been such the sight, Kane in a hurried frenzy and her practically running along behind him in a wet swimsuit.

"Are you going to tell me what's going on?" Hadley said breathlessly as they started into what was almost a jog to the lab. They reached the lab and Kane scanned his program and they ran in. Vanya was scribbling furiously onto a tablet.

"About time. I had wondered if you just gave up," Vanya said not looking up from her work.

The earth model was spinning at an abnormally fast pace. Hadley watched a large white patch get bigger and bigger. It was the size of Greenland and was sitting just north of it. It was a massive snowstorm and it was growing, engulfing the planet.

"What's going on?"

Vanya looked up from her work as she took a sip of coffee pursing her lips; the bruise around her eye was healing into a subtle brown and green. She hadn't even tried to hide it today. This was the first time I truly realized something was wrong. She saw Hadley and choked on her coffee. She spat half a mouthful onto the desk. "What are you wearing?"

"Kane didn't give me a chance to change." Hadley laughed

"I think we could have waited another five minutes Kane. She hasn't been here for days." Vanya laughed lightly teasing Kane. She was in fits and held her side while Kane just stared at her blankly.

"Never mind her attire. We have work to do."

"What's happened?"

"The storm we were watching the other day has doubled in size overnight and a new one has started just west of Australia." He stared at the girls intensely and then whispered, "It's time."

Hadley held back giggles at his attempt at a doomsday prediction, saying bluntly "Jesus Kane. Was that last part really necessary?"

He just rolled his eyes and went to his office. Hadley grabbed some of the info-chips and started putting simulations into the model knowing all the while that they should really be planning how to survive these storms not how to change the weather. She threw the info-chips into a pile on the clear table in front of the globe simulator. Working like puzzle pieces she attempted to fit the pieces together to either stop the storm or keep human kind alive. Each piece contained prediction and/or historic climatic data. Man had made leaps and bounds over the last four-hundred years, but this was too much. The storm was here, months earlier than anyone had expected and they weren't ready. The only thing they could do was see how it went and how they survived; they needed to predict its movement so they could figure out what to do next.

All of Hadley's predictions saw the storms continuing into the foreseeable and predictable future. The thing with ice ages is they were intermittent throughout the Earth's history. A series of positive and negative feedback loops that created global temperature and climatic variations.

Hadley shifted uncomfortably in the chair she was sitting on, typing like crazy into a computer. She pulled angrily at the bottom of her bathing suit that had continuously been going up her butt since it had dried almost six hours earlier. The armpits were digging in and when she moved the straps aside she could see the red marks the one piece was leaving on her body.

Kane's eyes were red and he furiously was shifting through a pile of ancient books and holographic information on the other side of the room. Vanya was fast asleep with one hand still clenched on her half full cup of coffee. Her other hand held the info-chips from her last failed idea.

The last few hours were spent putting solutions into the simulator. They had come up with nothing more than a way to freeze over the entire earth in a matter of days. This had made Hadley cry with laughter. At least she knew how they could make it worse. Hadley, Kane and Vanya were exhausted and frustrated. None of them could figure out any way to stop it. They were the only ones who could, and since they couldn't the world was utterly doomed. This had led Hadley to think the whole thing was hilarious. She was on the verge of tears from pain and laughter at any given moment.

She exhaled in frustration, half from the work, half from the fact she was still in a bathing suit that was so uncomfortable it made her wish she was naked. They had the technology to put a certain amount of heat, cold and gases into the air. But no amount of pressure or heat was going to stop this storm. They were too late. She desperately typed into her computer, changing the amounts of everything. But the storm continued to circulate in the earth simulator.

Kane, looked dishevelled emerged from his office after a brief entry to get something and then looked down at his watch, "Let's call it a night—"

"But, we can't we have no time!" Hadley exhaled, not wanting to give up. Kane got up and closed his tablet and it clicked into his hand. He slowly paced to the simulator and turned it off. Hadley couldn't do anything but watch the globe pixelate, and in a single flash of light it was gone.

"We've really done all we could manage tonight" Kane said in utter defeat. His eyes were jumping every which way. His brain was fried. He had resigned to failure.

Hadley had nothing else to say, "Ok". Nothing else was functioning in her brain except mathematical formulas that calculated atmospheric pressure and global warming. Kane put a hand on Hadley's shoulder briefly and walked to the door. He stood beside it waiting for her.

Hadley went over to Vanya and woke her up slowly. She shook her shoulder gently. "Vanya— it's time to go get some actual sleep." Vanya groggily opened her eyes, spilling her long cold coffee across her info-chips.

"Has the world ended yet?" She asked sarcastically as she stood up and stretched her arms high into the air. She reached down and touched her toes.

"Take six hours and we'll meet back here?" Kane said with as he opened the door. "At which point we will just figure out what the storm is going to do, and how we can best prepare the people on earth."

Hadley rolled her eyes albeit glad he finally figured out where his priorities should lie. Vanya and Hadley walked to the door and Kane held it open for them. Vanya hit the light switch on her way out. The door closed silently and the three of them took a moment to look through the glass at the few blinking lights still on in the lab. Then they all turned away in silence. Kane went right and the women went left.

Hadley turned one more time and glanced over her shoulder to see Kane sulk away looking at the floor.

Neither Vanya nor Hadley said anything on their walk through the dark hallways. Hadley occasionally glanced at Vanya and her eyes were skirting around, the dark bags under her eyes almost growing as they walked the short distance. Hadley scanned her program to let them back into the dorm and they both went to their separate rooms.

# Chapter Fifty

$P$ax was asleep in her bed snoring loudly and muttering to himself, Hadley smiled. He breathed gently and she watched his chest rise and fall, as if it was a lullaby.

She peeled off her swimsuit and threw it into the laundry basket. She grabbed a t-shirt off the floor and put it on. Then she opened her top drawer and pulled out a pair of underwear, which she slid into.

Finally, she was able to crawl into bed and cuddle up beside Pax. She brought the grey scale blankets up to her nose and stared at the flat ceiling with its indented lights. The tears ran down her face and before she knew it she was sobbing uncontrollably.

She was hysterical. Her whole body was shaking. She could barely breathe. Her breaths came in as short shallow gasps. Her tears soaked the pillow under her head as she cried looking above her.

Pax pulled her close, wrapping his arms tightly around her. He turned her to face him, "Are you all right?" He was both concerned and loving. She blinked at him in the dark through her tears.

"The world is going to end; there is nothing we can do about it."

"You will find something you can do," Pax pulled Hadley into his chest and she continued to sob.

"I— just— don't— know— what— to— do—" she chocked.

"Is there anything that would help you figure it out?" he whispered into her ear. The hairs on her neck stood up as he said it. He ran his hand softly across the back of her head.

"I honestly don't know Pax. I wish I had my memories."

"Me too," Pax sighed loudly.

They both lay in bed; though Hadley was exhausted she couldn't seem to get her brain to shut off. She was overly anxious and even though she knew she was struggling with anxiety she couldn't seem to change anything. The thought of the whole world being in her hands made her heart race and her palms sweaty. She tried to soothe herself and steady her breathing but it didn't seem to be any use.

"I have to go," she whispered into Pax's ear, he was already back asleep and just rolled over onto his side. She slowly got up out of the low bed and threw on his sweater, which he had carelessly thrown onto the hard floor.

She pulled the soft fabric close around her and walked out in bare feet. Her muscles pulled her to the only place she had been able to think lately.

The lab.

The storm was coming; she knew it was. She could tell by the neon sky and the billowing clouds surrounding the city slowly. She stared out the window in the broken lab she kept using as a refuge and saw the darkening clouds, even against the midnight sky.

Every day the sun seemed to get a bit dampened. Disappearing slowly. When it would return no one could predict. Hadley had spent days trying to find a solution to the storm and she had come to the conclusion nothing could be done. It had to run its course. They didn't even really have an idea what was in store for the planet. It was all mindless predictions; the smallest factor could change everything.

Her breath was causing condensation on the window and as she stood here she knew all Hemmer was thinking about was destroying the RFE's and if he did there would be less resistance. He was trying to find all their locations. Hadley had already disclosed the location of the RFE's in this city. They had worked so hard to disguise any exact locations. They were going to die and it was her fault. She felt sick about it, she wished in a dark piece of her soul she had never been driven to find out any answers.

The door clicked behind her and she turned around to find Hemmer staring questionably at her. "Hi Hadley, I'm confused as to why you're here."

"And where else should I be?"

"I thought you would be helping Kane or the team. Trying to find a way to survive this. It's a group effort Hadley."

Hadley rolled her eyes. "We can only run for so long. The world is going into the worst ice age in human history. Also we needed some sleep; I just wish my brain could shut off." She sneered sarcastically and shrugged, turning back to the window.

She hoped he would get the hint that she wanted to be left alone to wallow in her own self-pity. But he didn't, instead he came and stood beside her looking out over the colourful sky.

His wrinkled hands rested on the chilly window sill. He flexed his fingers and sighed. "You realize all I've ever wanted is peace right? To have the earth united."

"Sure." Hadley didn't look at him even though she could feel his eyes on the side of her head.

"The RFE's are like a cancer, a slow growing cancer. One that you can live with for a long time but it will eventually kill you, as all cancers do." He whispered the last part.

"If that's what you believe" *Why was he telling me this?*

"You have always acted the martyr. But really what is one life or a thousand or a hundred thousand for the sake of the planet and the human race?" His voice strained the last sentence.

Hadley looked at him and crinkled her nose. She tucked her hands under her armpits defensively, "You aren't god. You can't play god. How can you decide who lives and who dies?"

Hemmer sighed; he was tired of fighting. "It's my responsibility to act in God's best interest. He doesn't want the planet destroyed. Those who believe in God know he put us here for a reason and it wasn't to die out."

"So what do you plan to do? We have all failed at coming up with anything—" Hadley blurted out.

"No. You told me what to do once upon a time."

"I— what?"

"As of tomorrow we are shutting off all power to non-government buildings. The storm will freeze everyone else out. Natural selection. The weak get weaker and the strong get stronger. It saves our natural resources; it saves our lives." He stated calmly. He had no problem sacrificing the lives of thousands for that of the few. The few he believed were more worthy of living.

Before Hadley realized exactly what she was doing she slapped him. She hit him harder than she had ever hit anyone. Her whole hand stung so much she had to cradle it in the other. A small trickle of blood oozed from the corner of his mouth. He wiped it away with the back of his hand but it continued bleeding.

"I am saving your life. And in the end I just need one thing from you, one little thing locked away in that miraculous brain of yours. If we could get rid of you, that would be great. Because every time, your conscience gets in the way of what has to be done." He wiped his mouth on his hand again. Hadley was reeling so she slapped him again, using her other hand this time. He just laughed in her face, sickeningly happy. He kept laughing as he walked out of the room.

It had been no more than five minutes since Hemmer had sauntered out. Hadley was still staring at the place where she had the last glimpse of him. He had won, or at least he had acted like he had won, won something she was still unsure of. She had been trapped in her own head for months. She had no idea what was true anymore. She had no idea what side to be on. *What were either side fighting for?*

*He's going to kill them all.* She panicked, working out options in her head. It seemed like seconds before she was in the Earth lab. Hadley pulled up file after file after file.

Every time the files referenced RFE's she was blocked out. The computer errored and shut down. She was now on her tenth computer.

She slammed her hand on the current key board she was sitting at. She stared at the background of her desktop and watched the bubbles float back and forth. Then the computer screen blinked to life. She jumped back.

Lines of code started to scribble across the screen. Then an answer box popped up. Above the box was the question: What is your last name? Puzzled she typed in Evans without thinking.

YES! It blinked before the box reappeared with the question: Whose clothes did you borrow at the compound? Hadley typed in Maggie, getting more confused but started to get an idea of who she was talking to. Again it blinked YES! with a yellow happy face. The box appeared again this time with the question: Finally, who does Saul want dead? With a grin and a slight laugh, Hadley typed in the name. Kane.

The screen immediately started typing code again. Hadley watched as the lines and lines of white text raced across a black background. She watched it though it made her eyes go fuzzy. Finally, it stopped with a message: Press enter. She clicked enter.

A video box popped up. There sat Elijah. He waved with a friendly demeanor.

"Hi," she whispered into the mic. "Long time no talk."

"Oh hello, Hadley! I didn't think this would actually work."

"How is it working?" she asked suspiciously.

"We have been trying to hack in for months. We just needed an outlet in. Then we figured it was you going from computer to computer."

"And you apparently found one?" Her lack of computer skills gave her no insight into how they had gotten in.

"Yes." Elijah was ecstatic, "We—"

He was cut off by Saul pushing into the frame. Elijah's protests were loud in the back ground, his accent cutting through the air.

"Hi," Hadley said.

"Hey," he replied.

They looked into each other's eyes for a moment. Neither knew what to say to the other.

"I don't know how long we have until they find this connection!" Elijah whined louder somewhere in the background.

"Fine, fine Elijah!" Saul waved a hand to the side.

"Saul they are going to freeze you out!" Hadley blabbed. Verbal word vomit.

"What?" He was confused.

"The storm. It's going to lead to a full ice age."

"We know— we have similar systems to you, and have been monitoring it slowly" Saul replied grimly.

"They are shutting off power, everywhere that isn't government run!" Hadley exclaimed.

"We have back up supplies, we knew this might be coming—" Saul said grimly.

"For how long?"

"Hopefully long enough." He exhaled and changed his tone, "Now for what we need from you."

"Ok?" Hadley was surprised.

"Hemmer has a file. A file that would implicate him in everything that has happened. We need it, because if we survive long enough to adapt to the cold we need ammunition to take him down. Unfortunately, we know he saw you coming back that night. He will be after you and if we lose you this time I'm not sure he will let you live. You have to get the file and get to us. But be careful. And like you said the storm is coming. Soon you won't have a way out of the complex. Soon you will be trapped until who knows when."

"How do I get the file?"

"Meet me in the lab at sunset. You know the one. The one you're always sitting in. I will give you a jump drive and you need to plug it into Hemmer's computer."

The screen went blank. Hadley stared at it in awe. Her mind racing. She was sure he'd been watching her.

Hadley turned off the computer and she spun around on her chair to wheel herself over to the earth simulator. She turned it on and watched the major cyclone grow and grow.

She flipped on a holographic screen in front of the earth. She wanted to know what the stats were currently on the storm. She looked as the white letters appeared in thin air in front of her. Her mouth gaped open as she realized exactly what she was reading.

Oceanic temperature had increased less than previously thought, and was sitting at a 9.8C increase since 2000. But the winds were stronger than anyone thought possible, max wind speed was 563kph. Hadley looked at the data, it had long been known that for each degree of temperature change in the oceans, the max wind speed of hurricanes and cyclones would increase by 5%. Hadley didn't think winds of that magnitude were even physically possible, but as she was staring at the data, which told her there would only be destruction in its path. Nothing could survive the speed and severity of the storm that was coming straight for everyone she knew.

She reached up and turned the globe. She put the tips of all her fingers in the middle of Canada. She opened her hand and the area got bigger. The zoomed in area of Canada was getting pelted with snow. She watched as the differentiated temperature fronts converged into another storm system and the temperatures started to drop.

She zoomed out and zoomed in on Australia. An island a fraction of the size it once was. The west coast was completely wiped out. It seemed like the eastern cities had survived to a certain extent. They were experiencing a frigid draught.

Hadley sighed and zoomed out. She brushed her hand through the cyclone and watched it reset itself to the terror that it actually was. The clouds ever growing.

She was mesmerized by looking at the globe and before she knew it, it was almost noon. She checked the clock and realized she was going to be late for a meeting.

She walked to the conference room quickly, trying to avoid running, for fear people would start judging her, and luckily walked in just as a buzzer rang noon. Everyone was still fluttering about talking, and she sighed in relief as she walked towards her seat.

Vanya waved at Hadley as she walked in but immediately went back to talking to Jeremiah. Hadley tasted vomit in the back of her throat when she saw him.

A table had been set up with lunch at the back table. Hadley grabbed a plate and started to mindlessly put food on it including a sandwich and some grapes. She popped one in her mouth and crunched down on it, tasting the genetically modified food.

Hadley carefully put a carrot between her teeth and poured water in a glass. With her food in hand and her coinet open under her arm she went to a chair in the corner at the back. Completely opposite of the place she normally sat at meetings, which was front and center. She unlocked her tablet and started to eat her food. Subconsciously she noticed everyone sitting down and the quiet fell over the room.

Hemmer got up and went to the podium. "Hi everyone. I'm sorry to have interrupted your work and your lunch, though we have provided you with some great food at the back. As you all know there is a storm coming. We have approximately three days. The storm has grown exponentially Kane has informed me. So this afternoon we have to set up a rescue plan for our prime areas and people around this continent. I have talked to both the Continental European district and the Asia Pacific districts of our organization. They are already working to rescue their outposts. I know everyone has been working hard on the survival plan."

A map of the continents of North and South America popped up behind him and he continued after a pause, "So let's get started people."

He clicked a button and seven red dots showed up on the screen. Another ten showed up that were green.

"Okay so the seven here," he said motioning towards the northern ones that were highlighted in red on the map, "are the ones we need to make sure are going to have the supplies or be evacuated back here. The other ten are going to be fine."

Hadley rolled a grape between her two hands, ignoring the fact that Hemmer was planning to kill hundreds of thousands of people. It made her blood boil. She thought of all the other helpless people they were never going to save. But this was not the right time to stick her nose into it. She knew what Saul needed her to do and she couldn't draw any more attention. She lost interest completely as they decided which locations would be evacuated and which would have supplies dropped.

Jeremiah raised his hand, "I would like to volunteer to go to locations 1 through 4 and evacuate over the next three days with my team before the storm hits. It shouldn't take more than twenty-four hours of flight time to go between them."

Hadley looked at the map and saw that we were going to the North Eastern Region, right into the oncoming eye of the storm. *Of course Jeremiah felt the need to volunteer our team for the death trap.*

Hemmer smiled, "All right. Now we need supplies dropped."

Pax raised his hand. "I'll lead a group to go to 5 through 8." He had picked Central America.

Jinni spoke up next, "I'll lead my group to the rest." Jinni was the only female leader and probably a better leader than both Jeremiah and Pax, but she got the easy locations in South America because Pax and Jeremiah had taken the 'difficult' ones.

Even though every human was equal by 2100 in every possible way by the Earth Equality Act, some men had a sense of patriarchy passed down from the men in their families for generations.

"All right! All three of you need to get your teams together and strategize. You leave tomorrow morning at 0200 hours. It's not ideal to leave at night but it will get us to most destinations by sunrise," Hemmer said dismissively. That was all he had to say. An hour later and no one had questioned what was happening to everyone else living in those areas.

Hadley sat in her chair watching everyone leave. Hemmer, Kane and the rest of the leaders had left through another entrance. Everyone else was chatting and picking groups as they left. Hadley noticed Pax glance at her as he slowly gathered his things.

Soon they were the only two in the room. Pax stood still staring at her from the front of the room. She sat in her chair at the back. She got up and walked towards him. They never lost eye contact. Hadley was in the aisle and he put a chair between them. The smooth chair was like a steel wall. Though small it meant so much more.

"Pax—" she whispered gently.

"I love you." He said it simply as he spun a pen between his fingers.

"I love you too." Hadley was confused internally.

"We haven't talked in days; you've been avoiding me."

"That's not true."

Pax gave her a look, slightly moving the chair out of the way. Hadley took a step down getting closer to him. He just backed up, and raised his hands.

"Had, we'll talk after the missions," he said decisively.

Hadley just nodded; she knew he had made up his mind. Then he walked up the stairs and out the door.

Hadley turned and watched him go, and then Jinni walked in. She leaned against the wall and looked at Hadley.

"Always up to the same tricks Had."

"Excuse me?!" Hadley was startled.

"Everyone cares about Pax; way more than we care about you. You're always running off and making trouble." Hadley just blinked at her and she continued, "We get it though, we always have, but he acts like a puppy around you. He's so blindly in love with you, to his core."

"I know," Hadley said defensively.

Jinni nodded, a comforting look going across her face. "Just tell me one thing please," she asked.

Hadley gave a weak smile, "Anything."

"Do you know?"

Hadley couldn't be positive about what she was talking about, but only one thing came to her mind. She didn't want to admit it if Jinni was talking about something else. But how would Jinni even know?

Before Hadley could say anything else, Jinni just blankly said, "Do you know about Saul?"

"Yes." Hadley replied without thinking.

"I thought so." Jinni smiled weakly.

"How do you know Jinni?"

Jinni wrung her hands together, and Hadley walked towards her desperate for any information. Hadley was always thirsty for it since she got a taste, she craved knowledge. She needed any answers that anyone had. She didn't care who it was coming from.

"You don't know?"

"No."

"Saul's my brother Had."

Hadley was not expecting that, "Why aren't you with him then?"

"I've never agreed with him, or you. I liked the idea for a minute, but I never agreed with your tactics." Jinni stated plainly. Then she turned on a heel and walked away, leaving Hadley alone once again.

# Chapter Fifty-One

Hadley's long hair was blowing all over the place and kept whipping her in the face. She knew she should have tied it up, but it was too late now. She looked around expectantly and saw a figure pull himself over the ledge. His hood was up and he was dressed all in black. He brushed off his pants and stood up.

There stood the tall daunting figure of Saul.

"Hi!" she yelled over the whistling wind.

"Hi!" he yelled back.

Saul rushed towards her and grabbed her hand harshly. He thrust the flash drive into it. His hand was warm and his touch sent lightning bolts up her arm and down her spine.

"I'll be waiting when the helicopters land after your mission whenever that might be."

"How did you know?"

"Oh Evans, we know more than you think."

He winked at her and ran back to the edge of the building and jumped over. She gasped and rushed forward to see him rappelling down the side of the building. He smiled up at her with a wicked smile.

"Nice one!" Hadley yelled down to him.

"Always," he yelled back and disappeared into the impending darkness below. Hadley couldn't help but smile. The colour crept up her neck; she was blushing in the dark, completely alone. Her stomach was full of butterflies. She put her head down and ran back to the door.

She had about three hours until she needed to be at the helicopters for the evacuation mission and rescue plan. At that point she wouldn't be able to get into Hemmer's office until much later. Even now she had no idea if he would be there or how'd she'd get in. She was flying by the seed of her pants.

She ran down the metal stairs that lead to the roof and emerged into the hallway below. She walked towards the bird's nest. She got within distance and saw Hemmer was sitting in his office. He was slamming his hands into his keyboard, typing away on his computer. She sighed and sat in a dark corner, waiting patiently.

She waited and waited. People started to go back to their bunks, and the atrium became empty. She had a rough idea of how I was going to get into the office. *Who was I kidding?* She thought. It had never occurred to her that she would have to get into his office immediately after getting the flash drive. She knew the storm was coming but she assumed she would have a few days to get the drive into Hemmer's computer. *She probably should have thought this out.*

She watched the hands on the clock slowly move until he finally got up. She wondered if he had ever watched her for this long. The thought made her shudder. He turned off the light and closed the door behind him.

It occurred to Hadley almost too late that he was walking straight towards her. She dove deeper into the corner where she hid with her back pressed up against the wall and watched him walk by through the shadows. She waited patiently listening to his footsteps fade into the distance.

Then she went for it. She was at the door in no time and tried the lock. It was useless as she knew it would be; he had locked it.

She pictured what it would be like had she brought a bobby pin. Then she could have played a cat burglar and picked the lock. But alas, she had no small thin metal objects on her and even if she did she had only seen primitive break-ins in the movies. Those types of things hadn't been able to pick locks in almost 500 years.

She searched around her, looking for another way in. The glass windows of the entire office were bullet proof. She looked up and down for a spare key. A heat vent. Any way into a room that any classic action movie with Brad Pitt had taught her. Nada.

She paced up and down, knowing her time was running out. Out of the corner of her eye she saw a sign on a door: *Maintenance room.* She walked to it not getting her hopes up it would be open.

When the door opened with ease she was astonished. Someone had obviously forgotten to lock it. Which she knew was against Hemmer and Kane's protocol of locking all doors. They were almost paranoid.

The room was bigger than she expected. It was lines and lines of shelves with every tool and instrument you could imagine. Hadley grabbed a hammer and a screw driver. As she left she saw a mallet and grabbed it just in case. She hit the doorknob on the maintenance room as hard as she could with it. The doorknob fell to the ground and rolled away with a deafening ring. She had no intention of getting anyone eliminated for her own break in.

She went to Hemmer's office and started to try to break in with the screw driver. She fiddled with the screws but soon realized they were welded on. She exhaled and grabbed the mallet. She reached her arms above her head and brought it down hard on the lock. The sound echoed through the hallways. She hit it again, and again, and again until she watched to lock fall off, hanging by a single bolt. It took almost 50 swings before the fragile looking lock had broken. Then she pushed open the door and took a step into the office.

The sound of the alarm made her jump. Her heart pounded out of her chest. Her palms became moist as she frantically searched her pocket for the drive. She listened as the alarm echoed through the hallways and atrium. It was so loud it was making her head ache. She ran to the computer knowing backup would be here soon and plugged the flash drive into the side. Nothing happened on the screen but a little bar across the drive started to fill with green light. She smiled. *Elijah is a genius!* Her brain exclaimed. She made a mental note to tell him that when she saw him, if she got out of this alive.

Out of the corner of her eye she saw men running towards the bird's nest a few floors below. She dove under the heavy giant mahogany coloured desk and held her breath. A pair of feet walked up and stood right in front of her. So close if she reached out she could have touched them.

"Find them!" Kane yelled. He was the one standing right there. He tapped his fingers on the desk and waited. After a few minutes he sat down on Hemmer's chair and as he kicked his feet under the table his foot made contact with her nose.

This brought tears to her eyes but she didn't dare make a sound. She sat there letting the tears and blood run down her face. Then, someone came into the room.

"No sign of anyone sir. We've checked everywhere. They must have scattered when the alarm went off." It was Jeremiah's voice.

Kane swung his feet back and forth. Hadley pressed herself against the inside of the desk as far back as she could. "Smart move. It doesn't seem like anything was taken. The computer is still locked and password protected. For now, we will forget it as there is a lot to do tonight."

"Yes sir," Jeremiah answered.

"Is everything ready?"

"Of course. It will go as planned."

"I don't need to remind you of the importance of Hadley not meeting Katrina."

"No sir. We all understand."

"Good."

They left the room and the alarm and lights shut off. *Who is Katrina?* Hadley crawled out from under the desk and didn't bother to clean up the blood even though they would trace it back to her, it was too late.

She stood up and grabbed the flash-drive, surprised they hadn't found it. She tucked it into her sports bra for protection. She ran out of the room expecting the quiet hallway to be deserted but Kane was waiting.

"Get what you needed?"

"Kane!" She was scared and surprised. Her eyes went wide and they stood staring at each other for a moment. She backed up slightly.

"I knew you were under the desk, but I was scared Jeremiah might kill you if I told him."

"Why didn't you let him?"

"I don't want you dead, but this was something else Had."

"I thought everyone wanted me dead."

"How could you think that?"

Without thinking she whispered, "Don't lie to me. Haven't you two done it before?"

The colour drained completely out of his face. He was whiter than a ghost. He was not expecting those words to come out of her mouth.

"What?!" he whispered, his face emotionless.

Hadley studied him for a moment, betrayed she breathed, "You know. Don't pretend. He would have just killed me again. Like the first time in the video."

"But how do you know?" Hadley could see that his world was crumbling beneath him. She could see it. There was a swirling black abyss that was about to swallow him whole. She suppressed an urge to laugh in his face.

"Does it matter? You are a filthy lying scum bag. You disgust me." Hadley went to slap him but he grabbed her hand. His reflexes were faster than hers. She spat in his face. He let go of her and wiped his face clean with his sleeve. Hadley turned on her heel and walked away.

"Hadley, wait!"

Hadley paused for a moment, waiting.

"You're supposed to be with me. You always have been. Since you were just my student in a class."

Hadley didn't turn around but she replied, "You controlling piece of shit."

"You're everything to me, I've told you before and I'll say it again, I love you."

"You don't though. You love the idea of fucking one of your students."

She didn't even look back to see his jaw drop to the floor. The rage spread across his face. Luckily she had made him forget that she had been in Hemmer's office. He didn't follow her. He couldn't move; he was paralyzed and raging so he just watched her go. It was silent except for Hadley's echoing footsteps.

For once, she had beaten him at his own mind control game.

# Chapter Fifty-Two

There was a chill in the air, and the clouds were building up, preparing for the worst. The sky knew that the storm was coming, and that before long it would roll in with more power than ever before.

Hadley tucked the flash drive into a side pocket in her sports bra. She knew it would be safe there for the time being. She actually hoped it would be safe there until she had to give it back to Saul.

She hadn't let her guard down for a minute for fear of Kane or Hemmer showing up in her room. Instead, since she had gotten back to her room she had sat holding a handgun she had stolen from the armory on the edge of her bed.

But they hadn't come.

Kane hadn't run to Hemmer. He hadn't ratted her out, he hadn't run to his superior to tell him who had stolen his information. Looking back, she wondered how long he had stood there staring after her.

Hadley zipped up her eco-jacket, which was made out of a compostable material that was waterproof and bulletproof. Her pants and gloves were made out of the same material, both were completely dark grey with minimal pockets and stitching.

She walked into the kitchen. Her eyes were red and her wits on end. She looked around, frightened at every little thing. Jeremiah, Stephen and Pax were sitting at the table. They were talking in hushed tones. Hadley coughed to make her presence known. She didn't want to appear to be eavesdropping. Jeremiah would probably kill her for that, and she didn't even joke about it.

They turned to look at her, quieting their conversation.

"Hey," she said casually and went to the hot coffee pot. She opened the cupboard and grabbed a mug. She poured the coffee into it. She watched the ripples through the black liquid. She turned and leaned against the counter looking at the three men sitting at the table. She took a sip of coffee.

"Long day, Hadley?" Jeremiah growled

Hadley lifted an eyebrow and raised her mug to him as though to cheers. It took all her composure to act as though absolutely nothing was wrong, "Not at all, I was having a nap until the alarm went off. Any idea what happened?"

Jeremiah raised an eyebrow back at her, he was not buying it. She knew that she had hastily covered up her broken nose and black eye with some cover up and healing spray but she knew half her face still appeared blue. They were probably running the blood from the floor this morning and would be waiting for me at the rescue launch today. After that she didn't know what would happen. All she cared about was getting the thumb drive back to Saul, no matter the reason he needed it.

"Someone broke into Hemmer's office last night." Stephen said casually. He swirled his spoon through his bowl. She took another sip of her coffee, taking in the information and giving it a second to settle.

"How is that even possible?" she asked with a little too much surprise. Hadley looked down avoiding their eye contact.

Pax furrowed his brow and looked at her quizzically. "They didn't break in very well. They literally bashed the door in. Needed some strength to do that." Her heart skipped a beat; that might have been the out she needed.

"That's intense. I don't think I could ever break in a door." She looked at her arms and gave them a weak flex, almost willing them to look weak. Pax and Stephen laughed. Pax got up awkwardly, attempting to not give away their current disdain to anyone else.

Jeremiah was still staring daggers through her, but he left it be with a shake of his head. *At least for now,* she thought.

"All right lads, 20 minutes until take off. I'll see all of you in the courtyard." He gave a nod to Stephen and Pax and walked out of the room.

Stephen, looking awkward, grabbed his bowl and stood up. He walked past Hadley and Pax, avoiding eye contact. He gave Pax a slight punch in the arm and dropped his bowl in the sink. Then he hurried out of the room.

They stood in the kitchen, side by side leaning against the counter. Hadley took another sip of her coffee and finished the rest in her mug. She was so tired she turned around and poured herself another steaming cup. She looked sideways at Pax. "Ready?"

"You know it!"

She smiled at him, feeling the exhaustion sinking over her. Pax always had the easy air of confidence; he knew exactly what he was doing tonight. He looked at Hadley, completely head over heels with her. He could feel his heart pounding in his chest as he looked at her.

Hadley just yawned and took another sip of coffee. She was off in her own little world.

He grinned at her and side stepped so his chest pressed up against her back. He wrapped his arms around her stomach and she moulded into him. He put his head on her shoulder. "You're going to be careful tonight right?"

"Only if you are?" she yawned.

He squeezed her tightly. "I have to live a little on the wild side."

She took a sip of coffee and slowly turned around. She smiled at Pax holding her coffee mug with two hands in between their chests. She took another sip and held the coffee cup at her lips.

"You are so cute." Pax said. He leaned forward and kissed her forehead. She took her coffee cup and placed it on the counter. She wrapped her arms around his neck. He closed his arms tighter around her. She rested her head on his shoulder, almost falling asleep on his muscular shoulder.

It took her breath away. "Pax?"

"Yeah Had?"

"I'm sorry you know?"

"We don't have to talk about this now," he said pulling away.

"Is there anything to even talk about though?" The words escaped her lips before she could stop them. As she felt them slip over her tongue she immediately regretted them.

"Stop pushing me away Hadley."

"I can't let you in."

"Why not?"

Vanya, Jinni and Kirsten walked into the room. "Oh sorry didn't mean to interrupt!" Jinni taunted shielding her eyes dramatically. She threw herself backwards and peaked out from the corner. Pax took a step backing up even further. She blushed, picking up her coffee cup again embarrassed.

The three girls giggled as they walked in.

"You both have rooms here—" Kirsten said as if offended, but a smile broke across her face. Hadley gulped back a mouthful of coffee. She half coughed on it. Pax smirked at all of them. He knew how private of a person Hadley was but he liked thinking for a moment they were together if everyone else did. She, however, really didn't like that everyone knew about her and Pax. It was her own business not theirs.

"Midnight breakfast anyone?" Hadley said to cut the tension.

"Nah, we best get to the helicopters," Jinni said and they all walked out of the room. Hadley set her coffee cup in the automated ecofriendly dishwasher on their way out.

Soon they emerged onto the helipad. Three Super stallions were ready to go. Their propellers were already running. The large helicopters had been redesigned a hundred times but had kept the classic look and power. Though now they could travel over 3000 km before refuelling. Everyone was just waiting around. Jeremiah was standing near the walkway to the helipad. He was glaring at Hadley so she gave him a brilliant smile; she knew it would set his teeth on edge. She continued to walk past him with Pax and the girls. Jeremiah grabbed her arm and pulled her back. He pulled her into a corner before anyone could stop him, and Hadley could hear his heavy breathing.

Jeremiah shoved her up roughly against the wall and the air was pushed out of her lungs. She coughed trying to get her breath back. He just pushed his forearm against her chest harder.

"Hey!" she stuttered.

Jeremiah pushed his whole body up against hers and put his mouth against her ear. She tried to push him off but he was stronger and bigger than her. She felt his hand on her waist, it made her skin crawl. Her mind flashed to the video. Nausea washed over her entire body. He was shaking, he was so furious; there was a gleam in his eyes.

"You will under no circumstances mess this up. If you do one thing I do not ask you to do I will kill you. Slowly. I will kill you slowly. You have no idea what I'm capable of."

She did though.

He backed away from her but kept his arm on her chest. "Do you understand?"

She could feel nothing but soul crushing fear. wanted to give a sarcastic response that would make his blood boil but she had no response. She knew he would do what he said. They stared at each other both hearts pounding. She was sweating heavily and trying to calm herself down as she stared into his eyes.

Suddenly, Pax rounded the corner and upon seeing Hadley's predicament grabbed Jeremiah's shoulder and pulled him off of her roughly.

"Fucking get off of her Jeremiah." Pax was livid. Hadley had never seen him so mad. She wanted to take a step away from him but was stuck in the corner.

Jeremiah put his hands up by his shoulders and backed away from Paxton to avoid a fight. "I was just making sure she understood the mission." Jeremiah nodded with a wink and walked away. He had a spring in his step.

Pax grabbed Hadley's hand sharply and they walked to the helicopters. "I wish you were on the same flight as me Had."

She smiled at him, mustering all the energy she had she replied, "Don't worry; I can take care of myself." She squeezed his hand as they walked up to grab their guns from the case. Hadley holstered one at her hip, and grabbed an automatic machine gun. She wanted as much ammunition as she could get, who knew what the next 24 hours would bring.

"Come on Hadley! Everyone's waiting for you!"

She looked up to see Vanya waving at her. With one last glance to Pax, she ran towards the towering helicopter and pushed through the wind. She ran past Jeremiah who put his hand on her back as she jumped into the copter. Then with a wave to the pilot he followed her into the open cabin. He motioned for the pilot to take off, and then he grabbed a headset and mumbled something into it. Suddenly they were up in the air in an instant. Hadley sat down and strapped into one of the 50 or so seats that were crammed together. She pulled the straps across her chest and waist. She grabbed a pair of headphones and a mic. The noise disappeared to a dull roar in the background.

Vanya was sitting beside her. She leaned over and mouthed, "You and Pax are so cute." Hadley blushed and rolled her eyes. She had been avoiding her own brain when it came to Pax. She knew, after what Saul had said, that she should have ended it. Now she was going to have hours of sitting and thinking about how horrible she had been. She looked around and Kristen, Stephen, Jeremiah, Vanya, and a few others were sitting staring at each other in silence. The awkwardness was deafening.

***

The helicopter flew high over blackened plains and deserted cities. Hadley was breathless as she watched the landscape below her. She recalled faint memories of lush green grass and epic cities. Though she could never be certain those memories were real or just something she had seen in a book. The skylines should have been wonderful in the early morning sun. But the earth was black. It was barren and crumbling. The trees, or what remained, were dead and dying. The cities were just piles of rubble, like dunes in the middle of nowhere.

Hours, upon hours past. Everyone in the helicopter started to doze off, ignoring everything that was happening around them until they felt the helicopter start to descend. She looked below and saw a few standing buildings surrounded by a fortress of walls and as far as the eye could see destruction. A barren wasteland with one perfect complex in the middle. Hadley couldn't help but picture the earth exploding around here for years and then finally, when the smoke cleared there was this one unmarked spot.

In the distance the storm was coming, the grey sky billowing with magenta clouds and beneath them an impenetrable wall of white. The precipitation was starting and as predicted, it was a combination of snow and sleet. Hadley hoped they could get out of the area before the storm hit them or it would be a rocky and detrimental ride back.

The chopper landed and the pilot turned off the loud engines. They all undid their belts, took off their headsets and got off onto a large cemented parking lot. Even with the headsets protection, Hadley's ears were ringing in the quiet. She looked around and there was stillness in the air. She put on a fake smile, expecting the wave of people who thought they were coming to rescue.

However, as they all looked around the reality dawned on the group. There was no one there. It was silent.

Hadley blinked, confused. Jeremiah, looking disgruntled, motioned them all forward, "This way, stay close. They must be waiting inside the lobby. We were fifteen minutes behind schedule so they'd best be ready to go."

They all acknowledged Jeremiah's instructions and followed him towards the closest building. The building sat at the top of a long row of stone stairs that once had been expertly set to be perfectly smooth and even. Now chunks were blown out from each, which made stepping a cautious venture. Everyone walked up slowly, keeping an eye on their surroundings. Hadley looked around at the destruction that surrounded this building and its parking lot. It was overwhelmingly black charred earth.

Hadley kept her hands on her machine gun, which was across her chest. She inhaled slowly as they reached the top and saw the destruction before them. The glass doors were shattered and piles of glass scattered the floor.

They stepped through the frame of what used to be automatic doors and into an atrium. The vaulted ceilings framed double staircases that led to large doors at the top. One set of stairs laid in pieces while the other was perfectly intact. The atrium had glass cases aligned through it. Each had a placard and cased a stuffed dead animal. Many of the cases were shattered and the animals stared blankly ahead coated in tiny shards of glass. A sole desk greeted them. It was elegant and smooth with a sign reading "Welcome to the Museum and Laboratories of Extinction". Hadley tilted her head to the side trying to imagine what lay beyond but her thoughts were interrupted by a blood-curdling scream.

She turned sharply to see Vanya finish her scream. Jeremiah gave her a dirty look and a nudge. She sent him a death glare before focusing her attention back on what had scared her. Hadley followed her gaze, looking up and saw a man hanging from a noose beside a giant eagle hung up with a placard. The man's head was cocked to one side disturbingly, his neck clearly broken and his skin was yellowing. Dried blood across his chest read RFE. His lifeless form rocked gently back and forth in the breeze. Hadley inhaled sharply bringing her hands to her mouth in shock. No one moved for a moment.

Jeremiah stared dumbfounded, "See what the RFE's can do?" His voice cracked with anger. He turned sharply and looked at Hadley, ignoring everyone else, his gaze like daggers. He was pulsing with rage and couldn't understand how Hadley didn't understand how bad the organization could be.

She had no response. He raised his eyebrows and shoulders awaiting an answer from her. But she had nothing to say, she couldn't find any words to muster. So they just looked at each other for an extended moment but in the end, she still had nothing. It was like her brain was frozen in time. She looked away from Jeremiah and back to the man.

*Was I right to trust the RFE's? They might be bloodthirsty killers for all I know—* she thought. Neither side was completely right. If you look at any war or fight there is always another side to the story. Hadley's whole life everyone always taught them to put ourselves in the other side's shoes. But she didn't know who to trust. At that point she didn't even know what side *she* was on, or even if she was on a side.

Jeremiah turned on his heel and they all walked forward. They walked up the staircase that wasn't in broken pieces. At the top, they took a side door you couldn't see from the bottom of the atrium. It had a large red sign saying RESTRICTED on it. Jeremiah tapped his wrist across the pin pad and it clicked open. They walked into a breezeway full of doors. Everything here was perfectly intact.

Hadley felt sick; the image of the man's face was burned into her memory. She looked at Kirsten who was absolutely green. The gun she held shook in her timid hands. An overwhelming feeling of guilt rushed through Hadley.

*Could this be my fault?* She thought. Based on what she knew she had started RFE. So wouldn't everything the organization did reflect solely on her?

They continued walking. Keeping in a tight formation. Hadley kept her eyes on Jeremiah, afraid of his next move, afraid he was going to turn around and shoot her between the eyes. She imagined the bullet racing towards her, helpless to do anything, unable to move. She pictured the tiny spinning piece of metal hitting her and everything going black. For a moment, the fleeting thought that it would end everything passed through her mind.

She had to physically shake her head to get rid of the feeling. She didn't actually feel that way, she had to reassure herself.

They turned a corner and saw the path of destruction. It hit them like a wall, coming out of nowhere. The hallway to this point had been untouched. That was no longer the case.

The explosion went off like a bomb erupting beside them.

The sound rattled them before anyone realized what it was. Immediately they were running back the way they had come in. Hadley saw the walls around them explode into pieces. They were immediately covered in flying bits of drywall. The white powdery dust was engulfing them. They were running through a cloud of powdered drywall. Jeremiah scanned his wrist and they ran out the door. It slammed behind them with a deafening thud.

Hadley heard someone on the other side slam their fist against the heavy metal door and exclaim, a loud deep yell. They flew down the spiral stairs and back out the doors. Hadley's only thought was to get back on the helicopter and fly away, far, far away.

The whole group started to run through the lobby and towards the staircase. Their only thought was to get on the helicopter, fly away and regroup. They had no idea who they were even dealing with. Jeremiah made presumptions and he knew it was the RFE's.

Each and every one of them had to stop the instant the helicopter came into view. The dark cascades of smoke plumed into the air. The remnants of the helicopter were scattered around the parking lot. The flames licked at the sky 10 feet above their heads. Considering their height above the parking lot, it was just barreling smoke.

Hadley looked through the smoky rubble and saw someone staring at her. A woman. Hadley blinked and she was gone. She stared into the spot they were and looked frantically for any sign of someone, anyone.

Jeremiah was talking in frantic hushed tones to the pilot. He gave the pilot another nod and stepped in front of us all, shielding some of the wreckage behind him. The flames looked as though they were coming out of his head. In the craziness of the moment, Hadley started to giggle. She tried to hide it but it became uncontrollable. She covered her mouth with both her hands. Jeremiah shot her a look and she made herself cough to cover it up. She finally regained her composure. Jeremiah put his hand over his mouth, debating what to say. Hadley watched the grooves beside his eyes turn down, deep in thought.

He raised his hand. Thinking intently about what he was going to say. "Someone did this." He stated. Hadley raised an eyebrow expecting him to continue but realized he had nothing to say. He was as baffled at this chain of events. His leadership faltered slightly. He liked to be in control and right now, everything was out of his control. Everyone could see it in his eyes, his distaste and need to prove himself.

"We need to find anyone, anyone at all who might be alive here. So let's go." He pushed his way through the group and back to the door to the building.

They left the door we had escaped from and proceeded back up the stairs. They went through the main museum doors. Upon opening the doors, they were greeted by a nine-foot-tall polar bear. His marble eyes stared right through them. Hadley glanced at the placard and read "*Ursus maritimus.* Artic polar bear, extinct in 2064 due to increased northern temperatures and the elimination of sea ice." She stared at him, wondering how such a powerful animal could have been wiped out while humans had managed to survive.

"Hadley, keep up!" Jeremiah yelled back at her and she realized she was a few feet behind everyone.

They made their way through the first part of the museum, through what seemed like hundreds of taxidermy animals. Hadley glanced to her left and saw a woman lying in a pile of glass, a large shard piercing through her abdomen. She laid at the feet of a one horned rhino. "*Rhinoceros unicornis.* Extinct in 2053 after massive fires and droughts."

As they got deeper into the museum, the massacre became more apparent. There were bodies strewn about everywhere. Both those in government uniforms and those dressed as RFE's.

It was complete carnage.

# Chapter Fifty-Three

Stomachs grumbling and minds going wild they followed the signs to the cafe, hoping to find some morsel of food. They emerged into a large cafeteria that was fully picture windows with rows and rows of metal chairs and tables. Vanya gasped somewhere ahead of the group. As Hadley got further into the canteen, she saw a woman lying on the table. Her head was resting at an abnormal angle, a small drip of blood dried on the corner of her mouth. Her blond hair soaked with blood was strewn across her face and pillowing down onto the bench.

Hadley covered her mouth with her hand, disturbed. Jeremiah motioned for Kristen and the pilot to go look for food in the kitchen behind the cue line. The attack must have happened after hours because the cafeteria was pristine except for a spray bottle sitting under one of the food heat lamps. Hadley looked through the windows and saw the last bit of light disappearing over the horizon. They had spent the entire day looking around, rummaging through only a small portion of the complex. The people who had tried to blow them up were either long gone or were good at hiding. The sunset cast a yellow glow through the room. The reds and oranges reflected dramatically on the steel.

Suddenly a woman's scream echoed through the vast cafeteria room. The metal accents allowed an eerie echo to ensue. Jeremiah rushed into the back first and everyone else all followed on his heels. The pilot lay on the floor, a pool of blood around his head. Jeremiah reached down and grabbed his wrist. He held it for a moment before he looked up at them.

"He's dead." Jeremiah stated.

"Where's Kristen?" Vanya whispered. Everyone looked around an eerily empty room.

Then the lights went out. Everything went dark. They were thrust into darkness.

It took a moment for Hadley's eyes to adjust to the darkness. She focused on anything she could. Somewhere in front of her Vanya said, "What's happening?" her eyes strained to pick up anything, that's when the panic began to set in.

"I don't know! Head back to the main room." Jeremiah said, he turned on the light attached to his gun and they were able to see again, the panicked feeling in Hadley's chest subsiding.

They walked out of the storage room and back into the main eating area. Everything was dark except for the last glows of the sunset. All the lights were gone. A cold tingle ran up Hadley's spine. She shivered uncontrollably.

"Okay, we need to find whoever is here. Let's split up!" Jeremiah stated. His face aglow from the light he was shining. The shadows danced across his angry face. Hadley studied him for a moment, exactly in his element. This was what he was good at, it took him a while to get over the shock but now momentarily she saw the natural leader he was, not the monster she knew. Everyone started to go off, they were all in sync so once orders were given then they just acted. Hadley seemed to be the only one out of step.

Vanya grabbed Hadley's arm and they started out across the cafeteria towards a doorway on the other side. She had only taken a couple of steps before she noticed Jeremiah's light pointed straight at the back of her head. It cast the perfect shadow of her against the wall.

"Hey!" he shouted, "Hadley you are coming with me. Vanya go with Fred."

Vanya's face said it all; her expression matched perfectly what Hadley was feeling. They were the people they felt safest with and they were being forced to split up.

Anger washed over Vanya, but she didn't dare say anything. She instead turned on her heel and grabbed Fred's arm. Hadley watched them walk away. In two's everyone left in separate directions until Hadley and Jeremiah stood staring at each other, alone, across the body of the dead woman.

"Let's go." He walked towards her and grabbed her arm. He yanked her towards a door and motioned her to go through it with a push. "You first."

"How do I know you won't shoot me in the back?" She asked lightly, though completely serious. They never lost eye contact.

"You don't." He shrugged. Hadley had no choice and turned and walked. She had no other choice. The image of him shooting her flashed across her mind again. This time a little too real.

She knew Jeremiah's gun was pointed at the back of her head. She knew he wasn't looking at anything but her. He didn't care about anything other than her compliance. He was watching as her shoulders moved up and down as she walked, an urge to pull the trigger pulsating through him.

She kept walking, careful to catch any movements ahead of them. Jeremiah might not be looking at anything else but she was. She wanted to find the woman she had seen in the smoke by the helicopter.

Suddenly a shadow flashed across the hall for just a moment. Hadley barely caught it in front of her in the gleam from Jeremiah's gun. It was only there for a split second and then it was gone. But she knew what she had seen. She stopped in her tracks, evaluating, listening intently. She surveyed the walls. They were in an older part of the building. It was in desperate need of repairs. The brick walls were losing pieces. The metal doors had been painted a sickly orange, but it was peeling. Each door had a long window up the side. Lockers lined one side of the wall.

"What?" he hissed at her, hitting the back of her shoulder with the front of his rifle.

"Shhh, I saw something." Hadley said becoming increasingly frustrated; she lifted her hand to signal him to be quiet.

Jeremiah sidestepped beside her and they both peered forward into the darkness. A thin beam of light shone across the linoleum floor. They started to walk slowly towards the end of the dark hall with their guns up. Hadley's finger had the slightest pressure on the trigger, ready at any moment to pull it and shoot. The doors were eerily closed. She peered in one room and saw a man's face pressed against the window through the dust and debris.

She jumped back, her heart pounding. She looked back at him only to realize he was dead, there was no life left in his eyes. Jeremiah shook his head in disdain. Hadley took her eyes off the man and back to the task at hand.

They neared the end of the hall. There were double doors leading to a stairwell. Hadley reached out to open the door, shaking, but was distracted as something rolled in front of her feet. She looked down just as Jeremiah flung himself at her, trying to get them both out of the way.

The canister exploded in a cloud of gas. They coughed and everything went fuzzy in an instant.

# Chapter Fifty-Four

It took Hadley a while to refocus when she finally came to. Her nose and throat burnt as though they were on fire. She coughed and gagged. She desperately needed water but even more so she needed air. She gasped for breath as she was suffocating slowly. The inside of her lungs felt scorched.

Her surroundings slowly came into focus. She was exactly where the canister had gone off. Nothing had really changed. She looked to her side to ask Jeremiah what had happened but he was gone. There was a pang of fear throughout her and for the first time ever she was wishing he was there. She instinctively brought her hand to her holster, only to find it empty.

She looked around and saw three people talking in hushed tones. She pushed herself into a sitting position then took a deep breath, trying to fill her lungs. Her throat burnt as though it was covered in battery acid.
She pushed herself to her feet and started backing away from the people, careful to not take her eyes off of them.

To her left she noticed a steel pipe. She sidestepped and reached down for it without breaking her gaze on the trio. Her clammy fingers grasped it tightly and she stood up feeling the cold metal in her hand. She started to walk backwards faster. It was pure luck that they had not noticed her yet and she knew it.

She took a step back and ran into something hard and solid. Thinking it was a building post she looked back over her shoulder.

She immediately jumped into the air. It wasn't a metal pole; in fact, it was a man. He had to be almost seven feet tall and the biggest man Hadley had ever seen. She took a step away from him looking him up and down. She raised the metal bar to take a swing but he grabbed it out of her hand and threw it aside.

"Going somewhere?" He said with a southern twang. He reeked of tobacco, a banned substance that she only knew of from a distant memory she couldn't quite remember. He spat a mouthful of dark black liquid onto the ground. He raised an eyebrow at her. She was flustered and started to back away.

"Who are you?"

"The real question is who are you?" a woman's voice said behind Hadley, the trio coming over to them. Hadley looked at her. She was thin, her dark features were beautiful. She exuded confidence and grace. But she also held her gun too professionally. She had probably lost count of how many men she had killed.

"Who's asking?" Hadley shrugged. She took a tally of the two men behind the woman. Both were large and muscular with no characteristic features.

"I am Liani. I am the leader of the Eastern Americas RFE's."

"Did you kill all these people? Are you going to kill us?" Hadley asked plainly, immediately regretting the verbal vomit she had just mustered. She really needed to get that habit under control, it was as if she couldn't help but say every single thing that came to her mind. If the woman was going to kill Hadley though then she would no matter what anyone said.

"Oh yes, we did kill them. We have no plans to kill all of you though. Hemmer needs a message and we need a bargaining chip. You however will die here."

"Why?"

"That's what RFE does; we kill the government to save the people. It's war: we have to kill or be killed. Win or we will lose." She looked at Hadley as though that was common knowledge. Hadley couldn't help but raise an eyebrow.

"Where is Jeremiah?!" Hadley hissed.

"He's alive. He's Hemmer's man; he's our best bet of getting what we want."

"Why did you take him and not me?"

Liani looked Hadley over. She raised an eyebrow, "Because there was something about you, I can't put my finger on. I want to know before I kill you, because I'm not taking you with us. We have enough hostages and I don't have any information on you."

Hadley just studied her. Liani and Saul were completely different with completely different motives. Saul wanted to save the people whilst Liani was exactly the same as Hemmer. She was out to kill the GOVs whilst Hemmer was trying to kill RFEs. They both wanted the other group dead.

Hadley looked around desperately and then she saw it. Her escape route. To her left a door was slightly ajar, hanging off its rusted metal hinges and she could see the stairs leading down. Another staircase, another way out. She casually took one step to the side. They didn't grab a hold of her so she knew she had a small chance of making it.

"I'm not sure that was what RFE was supposed to do." Hadley stated, taking another side step.

Liani studied her for a moment and she took a step towards her, "Really? And who are you to tell us what our organization does. Aren't you just a little government rat?"

"I guess— technically—"

"Exactly! Now what's your name?"

Hadley contemplated for a moment. For some reason the only thing she wanted to do was tell her, her real name so she did, "Hadley Evans."

Her mouth fell open in awe. She was flabbergasted. Hadley had never seen a name cause such a reaction. She looked at her in wonder.

"You— you can't be— you're dead. I made sure of it." Liani laughed but there was difference in her tone. She was talking faster and higher. The words were getting caught in her throat and she was having difficulties getting them out. She was just staring at Hadley's face.

"No. I'm not." Hadley took another step and was within reach of the door. After a moment's pause, she went for it, knowing the four of them were reeling with her information. She felt the gust of wind as the 7-foot-tall man barely missed her arm as she bolted down the stairs. The hairs on her arm stood straight as arrows and a cool tingle ran slowly up her spine.

Hadley raced down the stairs and heard them running behind her, so she went faster and faster. She catapulted herself around the corners, grasping tightly on the rail, her feet leaving the ground. Two flights later, she crashed through a door into another hall.

Sprinting, she hurried down the narrow passage, which hadn't been entirely destroyed. She leapt over a man's dead body, glancing down at his torso, which had been severed in half. She took multiple turns, right, left, right, left and as she got to the end, she grabbed the door handle pulling sharply. She looked forward and could see the main museum, and her way out. It was locked. She pulled harder. But it wouldn't budge. She could hear their footsteps rattling after her in the distance.

She looked around and after a moment's decision flung herself into the nearest room, a large old fashioned chemistry lab, full of placards explaining what the traditional equipment was used for, Hadley noticed one sign dating to 2010. There was a closet in the corner and she pulled herself inside. The door squeaked as they walked in a moment later and she slowed her breathing as well as she could. Hadley placed her hand over her mouth to stifle her breaths. She looked out through the thin slit between the wooden doors.

Liani and a man walked into the room. They looked around.

"She can't be Hadley Evans!" Liani muttered angrily.

"What if she is?" The man said.

"Then we really have to make sure she's really dead this time." Liani stated as a matter of fact. They looked around the room but she could tell they were distracted. Hadley's name had shaken them. She frantically looked around the closet. She noticed a whiteboard pointer on the ground and grabbed it. There were lab coats hanging on old metal hangers, leaving spots of rust on the collars of the white linen. Broken vials lay misplaced on the ground.

There was a loud bang outside and a car honked its horn repeatedly. They frantically looked around, trying to figure out what to do. Liani threw her hands in the air in disdain. They were throwing everything around and they flung open cupboards and looked under desks.

"That's the signal Li." The tall man said grabbing Liani's arm. Liani looked out the window towards the billowing sky.

A glimmer caught Hadley's eye above and she noticed a ventilation shaft. The cover was already removed and sitting sideways over the shaft. She reached up but was too short to reach and her hand flailed awkwardly above her.

"Liani, we need to go." The man said, he had stopped his search and now was standing by the door.

Liani's eyes flashed crazily, "We have to find her."

She looked around like a maniac, pulling every cupboard open and pulling everything out in fail swoop. She was shattering equipment everywhere. She violently threw test tubes against the cupboards, spraying the room with shards of glass.

Hadley looked at her feet and saw a box hidden in the back corner. Liani continued with her destruction of the room and started screaming at the top of her lungs. Hadley took it as a sign and pushed the lab coats aside. She stepped up on the box with a squeak that was drowned out by the squeals in the room. Just so, she was able to reach the opening.

But the man heard her movement, "what was that Li?"

Liani stopped her rage in an instant and stood stark straight. She looked towards Hadley in the closet, though unable to see inside. Hadley watched Liani, her heart pounding and her breath caught in her throat. Liani started to walk slowly towards the cupboard.

"We might have her Ric." Liani said with a sly smile.

Hadley started to panic and quietly tried to pull herself up but only was able to get the top of her head through the opening before her arms gave out. She put her feet on the box and without a care jumped and using all the adrenaline and the strength she had pulled herself into the roof. Just in time too.

She heard the closet open just as her feet made it through the roof. She lay completely still. The only thing moving was her heart beat against the metal ventilation shaft.

Liani shuffled through the closet pulling the lab coats out and onto the floor. She screamed a primal yell before she slammed the door closed. Hadley rested her ear on the metal of the ventilation system, listening while her heartbeat pulsed through her ear.

"Liani, we have to go, we have all the rest of them. We will have to leave this girl. No matter who she is," Ric stated cautiously.

"Fine!" Liani huffed. Hadley listened to their fleeting steps as they left the room.

Then she reached down towards her pocket and pulled her phone out. She rolled into a sitting position and she expanded the phone holographically. She opened one of the GOV's satellite apps and zoomed in on her position. Then she watched the camera get closer and closer to the parking lot outside of the buildings.

There was a brigade of cars and she watched horrified as Jeremiah, Vanya and the other members of her team's limp bodies were drug out and thrown into the vehicles mindlessly like sacks of potatoes. Kristen's head was hit brutally against the corner of the trunk of one car.

Hadley tapped on one of the vehicles and placed a tracker on it. She leaned back and stared at the metal tube surrounding her. Her ears strained to hear any noise. But there was only silence. She closed her eyes, feeling every bump and bruise on her entire body, the pain settling to a dull ache, and her lungs burning from the gas.

What seemed like a second later, she opened her eyes. Her phone was letting off a quiet ping. She looked at it and saw the vehicles were stopped outside a hatch like structure. She copied the location and put it on a GPS route.

It was 200km from her current location. She mapped the storm. She would be going straight into it.

She sighed and shuffled back to the opening. She jumped down and left the closet.

The place was eerily quiet as she walked through the abandoned halls. Every once in a while she opened a door to gather supplies. Though she had no clue what she was getting into. She noticed a door with a well-worn sign and walked into a storage room. Fully stocked to her surprise. She looked around wide-eyed at the perfect rows of supplies. Maybe her luck is changing-- she thought hopefully.

Hastily she grabbed a backpack off a hook and threw in a sleeping bag, a knife and some food tablets. She cringed at them but knew six droplet-sized tablets would sustain her for a week. She ripped open a packet of water tablets and popped two in her mouth. She immediately felt the cool sense of hydration. She threw the rest into the bag. There was a cabinet of medical supplies and she opened it. She found an anti-chemical gas spray and inhaled it. The burning in her lungs almost immediately subsided. She grabbed handfuls of medical supplies and thrust them in her bag.

She was hoping she didn't need more than a few hours to find her team, but she decided to over pack just in case. Legitimately she packed everything that she could possibly need.

She went to the end of the room and saw a padlocked cabinet. She looked around and saw a hammer. She grabbed it and swung it above her head and brought it down hard so the lock fell to the ground. She dropped the hammer and opened the cabinet.

Before her, there was a large selection of weapons, all in perfect mint condition. She grabbed two automatic rifles and four hand guns. She shoved as much ammunition as she could into the backpack and her pockets.

Hadley's clothes were dirty and blood-soaked. She contemplated for a moment just wearing them as is, but decided against it. Even though she knew anything new would end up looking exactly the same. She undressed and grabbed a new pair of cargos and a tank top off one of the shelves. She grabbed a long sleeve top and pulled it over her head. There was a longer length waterproof anorak jacket, which she pulled tight around herself; it shielded her from the cold metal feeling of the room. A baseball hat sat on a shelf and she put it on, pulling her ponytail through the opening as she did. She looked around once more and spotted military grade combat boots. She browsed until she found her size. Then she sat down on the ground and pulled on the boots and laced them up carefully. Then she stood back up. She holstered two of the hand guns to her thighs. She tucked one into an ankle strap and grabbed a body strap off the wall to holster the last hand gun by her left rib cage for ease of access. She slumped the backpack onto her back and tightened the straps. Finally, she put the rifles' straps across her shoulder hanging it across her chest.

She caught her reflection in the metal of the cabinet as she was about to leave. She looked ready for battle, which made her smirk. Then without a second glance she left the room. She thought about what she had told Pax earlier. He had asked her to be careful and she was doing the opposite. But she knew she couldn't abandon Vanya and the others. She even felt a need to help Jeremiah. Though she wasn't sure he would ever accept her help.

She walked through the halls until she emerged into the parking lot. There were a couple cars but as she inspected them she saw the tires were slashed and no good. She looked around and saw a motorcycle. It was black and shiny in the glow of the streetlamp above. She walked up to it and saw the keys were surprisingly in the ignition.

She picked up her leg to swing it over the bike when she saw him. Lying on the ground was a man, and his empty blue eyes stared right through her.

Hadley shuddered. No wonder the keys were in the ignition. She pushed him the rest of the way off the bike.

She swung her leg over the seat and hopped on. With one last look at the man. She pulled the clutch, turned the ignition and started the bike. She felt the power around her and she rode into the impending storm.

There was electrical energy in the air.

# Chapter Fifty-Five

2228

Hadley desperately struggled against two large men as they walked down a deserted hallway, following the swish of Alice's ponytail, which was waving in time with her steps. Locked door after locked door they went through, the men scanning their clearance as they went. Hadley kicked and screamed, trying to get free. It really wasn't any use though, she was smaller and they barely blinked at her excessive struggles. Finally, they got to a large room with various boxes filled with liquid.

She gulped, almost melodramatically.

Cryosleep. She knew it the instant she saw the chambers, lying neatly in a line. Two people already

This was the second time she was going to be forced into a chamber where she would lay for years until someone decided to wake her up. The first time she was forced into this she'd been knocked out before it started and didn't realize anything until she woke up 120 years later. There was no way that she was going to let that happen again! She started fighting as though her life depended on it.

She had heard that in the first moments it felt as though you were going to die. It was peaceful after that as you lived in a dream world, letting time pass around you. But waking up was the hardest... She already knew that. She had done it once before.

One of the men let go of her and the other stronger one put his one arm around her waist. She kicked and struggled but it was no use. She stopped wasting her energy, instead looking around for a way out. The man who had let go of her had a shaved head and a tattoo covered his skull. She studied it while she watched him prepare various instruments and turn the machine on. His partner was just bald.

"Why are you doing this Alice?!"

"Purely orders Hadley!"

"Is that why everyone made me come here today? I knew it was a bad idea."

"Well, now you really know. There's a war coming Hadley and Hemmer can't risk your death right now."

"Let me fight!"

"We can't. You're too important to us even if you aren't on our side right now."

"Ever, Alice." She paused for effect, "I will never be on your side again Alice."

"We'll see about that Hadley, at least this way I keep you away from my husband for a while."

Hadley just scowled; she never wanted anything to do with Kane and didn't understand why Alice always thought that.

The men grabbed her and pushed her into the capsule. They attached her arms and legs to the bottom of the tank through leather restraints that they pulled too tightly. The circulation to her extremities was being cut off.

Hadley felt his hand before she could comprehend what was going on, and everything started going numb. The bald man's fingers trailed along her arm. "What the hell do you think you are doing?!"

He laughed. His partner paid no attention and continued fidgeting with buttons and vials.

"Just getting a little piece before we freeze you. Or would you prefer it after you are subdued when you know what's going on but can't fight back," he whispered in Hadley's ear. She was utterly speechless for once in her life. He breathed on her ear and nipped at it with his teeth. She struggled to get away, forgetting she was restrained.

Alice came over and smacked him across the head with her clipboard, but she didn't say anything, she just threw a glance at the man with the head tattoo, who came over and stuck a needle in her arm. She immediately felt the cold run through her entire body.

"You fucker, stop it. Kane and Hemmer will kill you for touching her. Just get her clothes off and finish the restraints."

Everything went limp for Hadley. She was trapped in her own body. Everything started going numb. The cloudiness started blocking her mind, though fight as she did against it.

The bald man undid the restraints slightly and started to remove her clothes, piece by piece, cutting them off as he went, and pulling them out from under her. Though he was no longer blatantly touching her, his slow motions triggered nausea. Hadley's stomach did somersaults; whether that was the meds or his touch, she'd never know.

To calm herself she started to look at her surroundings. It was tainted blue and filmy. She couldn't see through the box she was in. He took her wrists and bound them a second time in thick metal bracelets outstretched above her head. Then he moved to her feet, he tightened the clamps around them to the bottom of the plastic tank. He put a metal brace around her waist that attached to the bottom of the tank. Lastly, he placed a metal bracket around her neck, attaching her completely to the glass box.

"Don't worry," the man with the head tattoo said coming over and staring into her eyes, "the sooner you breathe in the sooner it gets better. See you in a hundred or so years."

She stared at him in shock. Her eyes were as wide as saucers. She couldn't speak; she could barely breathe with the restraints.

Suddenly her toes felt cold. She used all of her strength to peer downwards, straining her neck to see. A cloudy white liquid was pouring in around her. It flowed over her feet. Then to her legs, body, torso and arms. She lifted her head up as far as she could to stop it from going over her face. She was stuck in her own head, unable to speak.

The liquid flowed with the consistency of honey, slow and strong. Soon her whole body was under. The liquid rose slowly over her chin, she searched frantically for a way to stop it. She couldn't move. She couldn't do anything.

The liquid poured into the corners of her mouth. It was salty, like the ocean. She felt a wave of nostalgia, of times by the sea. She spat out as much as she could and pressed her lips tightly together.

But the liquid kept rising up. It burnt her nose as it crept up her nostrils like worms. It cooled her cheeks, which were hot from anxiety.

She held her breath.

She watched the liquid as it crept into her eyes; she blinked, trying to see through it. But it clouded everything. As it got hold of her hair, her head got heavy and it was pulled down. She looked up and saw the grey outlines of the two men through the cloudiness.

Still though she held her breath. Forcing her body to go against its natural response.

The need for air was consuming. Her chest was getting tighter and tighter. She was panicking. She started to thrash against her restraints, unable to get free, to do anything.

Then, almost worse, everything began to compress. The liquid around her froze into a solid. Her hands tingled as they were frozen in place.

She couldn't hold her breath any longer and took a deep breath of the liquid. She panicked as she did, her lungs wanted to expel the liquid. But then it warmed her lungs and suppressed her need for air. It was almost ethereal. She almost smiled. She wasn't dead nor was she dying. Just drifting into a different state.

The liquid around her torso started to freeze; it sent chills up her spine. The compression was painful but she was drifting deeper and deeper into sleep as her body was starved of oxygen.

\*\*\*

Then everything went away.

The last thing she thought about was what it had felt like the last time she had woken up, and she wasn't looking forward to it.

# Chapter Fifty-Six

2226

Waking up was sudden. Disorienting. Panic Striking. Hands clenched at Hadley's sides. Her eyes were wide, as she tried to blink away the liquid in her eyes. She tried to make sense of what was happening. Her eyes searched for answers but she only saw shapes and colors.

Her chest was tight and she realized that she needed to breathe but she couldn't take a breath. The bottom half of her body was in the slushy liquid that now remained from its frozen mass.

"Breathe!" Someone said gently.

She pulled in to breathe but her lungs were already full. She exhaled and felt the warm rush of liquid. It burned her throat and mouth. She coughed and sputtered.
Her body took over and she inhaled. She felt the oxygen rush through her body. Her heart slowed to a regular pace.

Hadley's vision started to return. She was able to focus on the scene around her. The first thing she saw was people wearing scrubs and surgical masks. It wasn't just her being pulled out of the tank. At least four other people were also still half submerged.

She looked down and watched as the ice shards surrounding her legs swirled in the moving water. Abruptly she was pulled out and set on her feet. She stood in shock, feeling cold and naked. A towel was thrown hastily around her. She felt like ice, though she didn't shiver. Late stage hypothermia, was all she thought.

"Get them to the heat chamber!" someone yelled in the room. Hadley was picked up like a baby and carried to the next room. She watched as the same thing happened to the others. She was sat in a large armchair that molded to her body before it started to pulse. She felt the heat move through her body from the slow pulses. Another blanket was laid over her and she felt the blood rush back to her fingers and toes. Feeling the tingling sensation through her whole body.

Anna was brought in after her. Followed by Pax, and then finally a man she didn't know. Anna caught her eye and looked away, "Anna! What's going on?" She tried to say but her voice was caught in her throat and it came out as a squeak.

"I'm sorry Hadley. I am. They froze me a week after you."

"They froze us all in the weeks after that—" Pax said.

"Do we know how long it's been?"

"120 years." The mysterious stranger said. His voice was deep and rich. Hadley noticed his tattoos.

"How do you know?" She asked, regaining her voice slowly.

"Hemmer told me right before he pushed my head under himself. He wanted to make sure we weren't affected," the man said casually.

Hadley was awake but not present for the next hour or so. Lost in her mind. She wanted desperately to know what had happened to the world in the time they had been frozen. It had been over a century, the world and everything they had known had long died.

Hemmer walked in and Hadley knew finally they were going to find out.

He started to talk, mainly mumbling and Hadley held on waiting for something that truly mattered. A great deal, but then again nothing had changed.

Hadley felt as though her life was exactly the same. Contained in the safe complex that was their military base.

Kane came to say hi, he and Hemmer had also been frozen.

In a way, she felt bad for the workers who had lived through the last century, waiting for the day when they could wake those frozen up. Hemmer had put a timer on himself and had woken up once a week for the last hundred years for a few minutes. Therefore, he had aged just less than five years. Though you couldn't tell.

Hadley got into her uniform and walked to the lab. She knew how to get there by instinct but she found her usual route closed. She looked at the large metal door, confused. She reached out and grabbed the handle but it was locked. The door didn't even budge.

She peered through the glass window in the door. She couldn't see anything or anyone. She stood on her tiptoes to no avail. She laughed at herself, because why would standing any higher give her a better view of nothing? She sighed and turned around only to find herself staring at the chest of a very tall man.

She looked up and saw the mysterious stranger from earlier. "Hi?"

"Hi Hadley."

She furrowed her brow. "Who are you?"

"Get a cup of coffee and maybe I'll tell you?" he said in his deep voice that could make any woman swoon.

She smiled at him. He stared at her determinedly. She was sucked into his gaze. After a moment, she embarrassedly looked away biting her lip.

"Coffee?" he asked.

"Sure."

He held out his arm and she put her hand through it. They walked towards the cafeteria.

# Chapter Fifty-Seven

She had been alone with her fleeting memories for the last couple of hours. Worst though, she was pelted by rain as she drove down the dark road. The assaulting dark sky meant the only light was from her bike. Beyond that, there was total darkness. The rain was slowly turning to sleet, and in the headlights, she could see the colours around her changing. The clear drops were turning an eerie white. It created a fog like appearance around her. The snow was coming. The storm was coming.

Terribly, she was driving straight into it.

She reached carefully into her pocket, trying to not wipe out on the gravel street and pulled out her table, which was in its coin size. She clicked the top of it.

"How much longer?" she asked it careful to keep her eyes on the road ahead of her. For a moment, she slipped and felt the tires zigzag below her, losing traction, and she tipped a little. But luckily, she was able to right herself.

"Two more minutes," the automated voice said.

She put the coinet back in her pocket and grabbed a hold of the other handle of the bike again. She turned the headlights to the daytime running lights. Everything around her became misty and unclear. She needed the subtle light, but knew she couldn't be seen or it would compromise everything. She felt as though she was being pulled into a black hole.

The road ahead of her narrowed, getting smaller and smaller until it was just wide enough through the remnants of burnt trees for a car to pass. Her body shook with the bike as it sped over the tiny rocks on the ground. The only thing she could hear was the hum of the motor.

She saw the vehicles in the distance and pulled her bike into the sporadic charred trees. She turned it off and kicked down the kickstand. Then she stepped off.

She walked towards the cars. There were no voices or sounds. But still she crouched low as she walked past the first of the cars. She kept her back to them to avoid any unwanted surprises. She looked around the bumper of a car and spotted a small shack. It had plain concrete walls, a flat roof and a steel door.

She pulled one of the handguns off her belt and tiptoed towards the door. She reached carefully forward for the doorknob and turned it slowly. She opened it with a quiet click. She pushed the door open just as the first snowflake landed on her face. She wiggled her nose as it melted and ran down onto her lips. She licked at it, immediately parched. The cold water left a spot on the tip of her tongue.

The warmth was overwhelming as she stepped through the door. Until that moment, she hadn't realized how cold she had become on the ride there. She had been so focused on getting here that nothing else had crossed her mind. But now inside, her fingers started tingling as they regained feeling. She looked at her hands and saw the pink returning to her blue nails.

She looked around and realized she was standing at the top of a long set of stairs. The stairs were uneven and descended so steeply she felt unsettled looking at them. They descended further than she could see and were only illuminated every ten or so feet by a tiny ball of light on the wall. She looked over her shoulder and saw the shack was illuminated by a large candle attached to the wall by a brass holder. The milky yellow wax formed dripping trails down the sides cementing the candle eternally in place.

Contemplating for a moment, she inhaled a deep breath and took her first large step down the stairs. Her foot squished into the inch of mud that had accumulated on the cement. The mud was flowing down the staircase and she struggled to keep her balance as she went. She practically slid from stair to stair and could feel her knees starting to ache from the impact. She kept her gun raised parallel to the ground, her eyes staring down the barrel.

She jumped back against the wall as something fluttered above her head. She looked up and saw a bat. She smiled and inhaled a deep breath, then kept walking down the stairs. Slowly the stairs got wider and wider until they became a gradually sloping tunnel. The air was getting stuffy and hot as she got deeper, though the ground became hard and crunched below her boots. She kept walking getting deeper and deeper below the ground.

Hadley turned a corner and saw light at the end of the path. The first real sign of life she had seen since coming through the heavy door, which seemed like an eternity before. She couldn't see anyone around and walked forward where she emerged into a well-lit room. It was empty. The candles flickered around the room. There were three doors leaving the room.

She went to the middle one and opened it. She peered inside intensely. The tunnel went about ten feet before it twisted and her view was gone; she decided to take it. She walked down the path and after a few minutes hit an intersection between three different paths. She spun around slowly giving each of the tunnels a look in the flickering candle light.

She heard footsteps approaching her and launched herself into a groove in the dirt wall. She was perfectly hidden by the shadows.

"I heard we are holding them in sector 8. I am on my way there now," a cheerful woman said, as she continued walking.

A man replied, "Yes, Liani got almost all of them. Their executions are to begin one by one in an hour."

"Almost all of them?"

"Yes, she killed a few and missed one live one. And guess what?"

"What?"

"Jones claims that the girl they missed was Hadley Evans."

"She's dead— We all watched her die, over and over again, everyone played it a million times on a continuous loop. It just created outrage at the GOVs. That's what started the rift between Saul and Liani. Stupid of Hemmer too, thought it would create peace, showing that they could kill our leader so easily." The woman was stating facts. Both the man and woman had awestruck faces at the possibility that Hadley might be alive.

Hadley smiled at their utter confusion, and continued eavesdropping on their conversation.

"Hadley, Saul and Liani had their differences before Had's death." The man stated simply, with a cock of his head.

"Oh right. I forgot that you'd know."

Hadley gave them a few seconds before turning to follow them. As they wound further and further into the labyrinth, she wondered to herself if she was doing the right thing.

She had almost turned back numerous times on her drive here, not due to fear but due to self-preservation. Which was selfish and she knew it. But she pondered whether she should have called for backup or waited. She knew it was stupid to try to save them alone. *Why did she always feel the need to be the hero?* She thought.

Unfortunately, all her other options were in the past.

Hadley stayed in the shadows just outside the door as the couple got to a room with low ceilings. She looked around the room and saw the entire room was lined with numerous 3-foot squares of bars stuck hastily into the walls, each just a few feet from the other. Hadley took a closer look and saw they were the entrances to cells. Dark, dank and tiny cells. She crouched down and looked into the closest cell she saw. Behind the bars, the cells were tall enough to stand in but just barely. The roofs were leaking water.

Drip, drop, drip, drop.

The water had created a small pool in the middle of the intensely dark cell.

The man and woman stopped in the middle of the room. They were looking anxiously around. There were footsteps behind Hadley and she slunk further into the shadows to avoid being seen.

Hadley watched as Liani and Ric, the beastly man she had met earlier walked forcefully into the room. Liani's hair was tied so tightly into a bun on top of her head that it pulled her whole face awkwardly backwards towards her hairline.

"Is the connection set-up?" Liani asked abrasively.

The woman nodded and took her phone from her pocket. She pressed a few buttons and a screen appeared on the far wall of the room. Hemmer's face appeared on the screen. Hadley gasped and quickly clasped her hand over her mouth. Her eyes were wide; Hemmer was the last person she'd expected to appear on the screen. Hadley held her breath waiting for them to come find her. But they hadn't heard her gasp between the hype of getting Hemmer on the screen and the buzz of the surrounding machinery.

The look on Hemmer's face scared her. It was pure rage. He looked as though he was going to jump through the screen and rip their heads off. He was glowing a bright burgundy.

"What have you done with her team?" He practically spat at Liani through the screen.

She chuckled, "Oh Hemmer, they are alive for now—"

"For now?" The colour drained completely from his face, leaving a pale and deathly Hemmer on the screen.

"Yes Hemmer, you aren't getting them back in one piece. Any of them." Liani just smiled, a sickly smile. Hadley's skin started crawling with the sound of joy in her voice. A shiver went down her back.

Liani was enjoying this more than a kid in a candy store.

"You are going to kill a group of innocent kids?" Hemmer was appalled.

Liani un-holstered her gun and held it in her hand. She looked at it, twisting it back and forth in her palm. "They aren't innocent Hemmer. No one is anymore. And they aren't kids anymore; they are grown adults who have been alive for centuries. They were the smartest people on the planet. They were your future, and I'm taking that away from you, like you did me."

"You are going to kill all of them?" Hemmer choked, the word barely made it out of his mouth. He looked older and older by the minute.

"Well all the ones we have—" Liani sighed. She was annoyed at not having everyone, at not having Hadley, who just reveled in that fact.

"The ones you have?" Hemmer asked cautiously trying to not show any emotion.

"Yes Hemmer. We ran out of time and energy and missed one. I killed two already as well."

"Who?" He asked in barely a whisper.

"The one who calls herself Hadley Evans. Good one Hemmer, brainwashing some girl to believe she is Hadley. But we all saw her die. We all watched Kane kill her after you told him to."

The immense relief that washed over Hemmer was so apparent. Somehow, though Liani missed it. "Yes, funny aren't I?" Hemmer said lightly, perfectly to cover up how he actually felt. Hadley looked at his eyes and knew that he almost couldn't contain his joy. He really needed her for something, of which she was unsure. He hated her so much and had threatened her more times than she could count but in this moment he was happy she was still alive.

"Get the first girl!" Liani chuckled to the others in the room.

The other woman went to one of the cages and unlocked it. The two men ducked inside. A moment later they pulled out a struggling Kristen. Half her face was covered in blood and cuts. Her hair was matted with mud. Her one arm was twisted in a weird way. She was gagged and tears were running down her face. She was pulling with all her might but it was no use, she wasn't as strong as them.

The men put Kristen on her knees in front of the screen with Hemmer. "Kristen—" He whispered in a fatherly tone, silently exuding how he felt. She looked up at him. Hadley couldn't see her face but knew they were sharing one last precious moment. It was odd seeing Hemmer show any paternal feelings, especially towards Kristen. Hadley didn't even think Hemmer knew Kristen's name.

"Kristen, honey I'm sorry," he said gently.

"Dad, it's ok. I knew what I was signing up for," Kristen cried.

Hemmer looked back at Liani. "Li, why her?"

"Uncle Hemmer, why Anna?"

"That was different."

"You shot her just to get Hadley to give you the code. How is this different?"

Liani had stumped Hemmer. Everyone in the room could see it all over his face. Liani was using his own twisted schemes against him, and it was working. He was fumbling.

"Li, I didn't ever want to do that."

"But you did Uncle."

"Li, that's your cousin."

"Hemmer, first it was my mother, next my sister. You left me alone. I shouldn't have talked my dad out of killing you."

Liani raised the gun to the back of Kristen's head. Her grip tightened on her gun and Hadley took a step forward. She wanted to help more than anything but retreated back into the shadows after a moment's pause.

She didn't know what to do. She couldn't think. She had to wait for the right timing to reveal herself and help the others or she would just end up in a cell too. There was too many of them.

Liani relaxed her body. She slowly tilted her head from side to side and planted her feet. Her finger squeezed the trigger. The small space everyone was in echoed the sound. A moment later Kristen's limp, dead body slumped to the ground. Her head tilted so her lifeless eyes stared right through Hadley. A small trickle of blood ran down her cheek from the black hole between her eyes, and onto the ground.

Hemmer stood up in his seat. "Liani stop this! There has to be some way—" He looked on the verge of tears.

Liani walked forward stepping over Kristen. "Give me the activation instructions and location."

"You know I don't have them! Hadley had them and they died with her!"

"So you say, but I can't help but think you are lying. I will call you back in an hour to kill another one of your people. So that gives you 60 minutes to think about what's more important to you."

"Don't you think if I had them I would have used them to wipe you out?"

"Fuck you Hemmer." Liani turned off the screen. She turned on her heel and walked back past Hadley's hiding spot and out of the room. Ric grabbed Kristen's body and dragged her out of the room on her face. Hadley had to just watch them go and after they had gone stared at the last place she had saw them. Frozen and despaired.

She studied the room and knew she needed a key to get into the cells. The man and woman were deep in conversation. The man nodded at her and also left the room. As soon as Hadley heard his footsteps fade away she stepped out of her corner.

The woman turned around and looked straight at Hadley as she heard footsteps approach her. Hadley pointed her gun between the woman's eyes.

"Hadley?" She was stunned. Blown away really, as though someone had dumped a bucket of ice water over her head.

"No. Open that cell!" Hadley commanded and motioned towards the cell they had just pulled Kristen from. The lady had no other choice than to open the cell. "Get in and leave the keys on the ground. Also any electronic devices you have,"

The lady crawled in and left the key on the ground along with her phone. This was too easy— Hadley kicked the door shut and reached down and grabbed the key. She locked the bars closed and put her gun into the holster, but she didn't do it up, she didn't know when she'd need it next.

"But you died. I've watched the video. My grandma told me about it. She was one of your most loyal followers," the woman said pressing her face into the rusted metal gate and looking intently at Hadley who was standing a few feet away. For a moment Hadley felt bad for this woman who was working for a psychopath. There was a chance that the woman would be shot, just like Kristen, for not keeping Liani's prisoners.

"Then I'm sure she's really proud of you," Hadley sneered through the gate, her pity expelled.

"Hadley is that you?" a voice yelled in the room, it was followed by various murmurs of her name.

"Yes?" she replied into the dark space of the room. Jeremiah's beaten face appeared at one of the sets of bars. Hadley went to it and unlocked it. He crawled out and stood up. His nose was shattered and he was limping. After watching the video of us it gave Hadley some pleasure to see him like this, but still—she pulled out her gun from its holster and pointed it between his eyes.

"They have Vanya. They took her somewhere!" He was hysterical. He started towards the exit completely ignoring the gun but Hadley stepped in front of him.

"We need to get everyone else."

He stopped and looked at Hadley as though she was insane. He couldn't understand why she was stopping him, he had seen what had happened to Kristen and adrenaline was pumping through his veins. "Fine."

Together, Jeremiah and Hadley got Fred, Zeek, Olive and Gunner out of their cells. They were in terrible condition and barely able to stand. Hadley looked at the gashes and bruises that the team was covered in. Looking around she had no clue how they were going to get out of this underground maze alive. Fred could barely stand and Olive was practically unconscious.

"We need to find Vanya!" Jeremiah practically screamed at Hadley as she was quietly assessing the group.

"Quiet Jeremiah! Someone will hear you," Hadley moaned. "None of you are in any shape to find Vanya. So let me do that and you get out."

Hadley explained to them how to get out, to the best of her memory, and asked them to find car keys on the way, stating the mass of cars outside. Jeremiah was about to put up a fight but the second Hadley handed him a handgun, he was quiet.

"I will find her Jeremiah, I promise," Hadley said gently, she gave him a look urging him listen to her and lead the team out.

He seemed to get the hint and decided to take the high road and be a leader.

# Chapter Fifty-Eight

Hadley took off the opposite way as everyone else at the crossroads. She had made it about 10 seconds when she felt a hand on her shoulder. She jumped and pointed her gun, putting pressure on the trigger; she was completely ready to shoot.

But she turned to see Jeremiah standing there.

"Dammit Jeremiah, I almost shot you!"

"I'm not going to sit in a car and hope you find Vanya. I'm coming with you."

Hadley sighed at him but she couldn't and didn't argue. They headed down the passage. The candle light was creating a glow on their faces as they walked. Jeremiah kept pace but he was limping and kept letting out grunts.

"Are you all right?" Hadley stopped and looked at him. He winced.

"Let's keep going—" he grunted and walked ahead of her. She kept her gun up and walked.

The caverns got more and more intricate and she was scared the deeper they got the harder it was going to be to find the way out, with or without Vanya. *I should have left a breadcrumb trail, Jack and Jill style.* She stopped and listened. There was running water. It reminded her of Saul's building, but decades older and less tidy.

Twist and turn, after twist and turn, they didn't see a soul. They just wound their way through the candle lit caverns dug into the hard rock. Finally, Hadley stopped before a doorway. She motioned for Jeremiah to stop. He came to a halt behind her. His warm breath on the back of her neck. The hairs on her neck stood up and sent tingles down her spine.

She pressed her ear against the door softly and held her breath. She could hear a faint buzzing but nothing else. She reached down and grasped the doorknob. She turned the doorknob slowly, one bit at a time until she heard the latch unhinge from the wall. Then she lightly pressed her weight into her shoulder and pushed the door open.

They emerged into a room filled with computers, that was completely dry walled a stark white. The room was floored with cement, unlike most of the paths we had gone through and was lit by large artificial lights implanted in the ceiling. The first artificial light they'd seen in these caves. Hadley looked around the room and saw one computer was on. It was buzzing and jumping between screens. All the other computers were black and cold. It was odd she thought.

She went up to it and saw a live feed of various rooms throughout the place they were in. As it jumped screens Hadley saw Vanya, tied to a chair in one of the frames. She barely recognized her before it went to the next screen. Jeremiah looked at Hadley in a panic. Without a word they watched the computer go until it looped around again. This time when they saw Vanya they were ready.

The box in the right hand bottom corner said 'A wing-area 32'. Hadley made a mental note of the number. She looked around the room and saw a large map on the wall, making it too easy. It was right beside the door they had entered through and Hadley almost laughed at having just noticed it.

There was a little blue sticker with: *you are here,* written on it. *Helpful.* Hadley took out her coinet and took a picture of the map. She traced her fingers along the wall and saw they weren't far from A wing. Slowly she found a path to room 32. Without speaking they set off. Jeremiah muttered to himself as they went. He was frantic and trying to calm himself down. The adrenaline had kicked in to take away some pain, but he was still grunting as he walked on a broken ankle.

After the third turn Hadley had to stop and look around. She opened her coinet and looked at the map. She could feel the heat of the candle she had stopped beside on her cheek. She peered at the map of which she had taken a photo.

"Well—?" Jeremiah whispered annoyed.

"Hold on." Hadley put her hand up to shush him and stared into the screen. A moment later she knew which way we were going.

Hadley motioned them both forward. A few feet later they had to stop, there were footsteps ahead. Hadley watched a group of men walk by. Once they had passed they kept on their route. Finally, after what seemed like ages, they got to a room marked 32.

Jeremiah pushed in front of Hadley emotionally and opened the door without checking anything. He was ready to fire on whoever was in his way. Vanya was sitting in the chair. Blood dripping from the corner of her gagged mouth. One of her eyes was so swollen that no one could see where it opened. Her ankle was twisted sideways. Jeremiah half ran, half hopped to her. She looked up in a daze. After a moment her look turned to panic and she started to shake her head furiously. Hadley furrowed her brow as she rushed towards her friend.

Jeremiah ripped off Vanya's gag and kissed her cheek. Tears running down his face.

"Oh my god, you're alive, thank God! I love you so much, I'm so sorry," Jeremiah rambled in a hurry.

Vanya didn't look at him though, she stared into Hadley's eyes and screamed, "Stop, get out!"

"Vanya. We're here to help," Hadley said calmly, thinking she must have hit her head.

"It's a trap Hadley— they knew you would come after us if you actually were Hadley Evans." Vanya whispered.

It was too late.

Hadley had fallen into their trap. She had done exactly what she always would have. She turned around just in time to see the giant needle plunge into her neck. The world disappeared in a fog.

The only thing she saw was the ground get closer to her face as she fell in slow motion.

# Chapter Fifty-Nine

Everything, and Hadley meant everything came rushing back. Every memory she had forgotten, every pain she had endured, every plan Hemmer had erased was back. All except one. The one she now remembered she had erased. She was liberated and confused as too many neurons in her brain fired at the same time.

She was beyond furious that she kept getting knocked out by everyone. Then again getting knocked out by people in general. But everything was back, and for that she was slightly grateful.

The nerve endings in her brain kept firing and she helplessly drifted in and out of consciousness as her brain was overloaded with information. She felt like a computer that kept trying to update but the hard drive kept crashing. She now knew what it felt like to be a piece of equipment. Useless, as though there was a bug.

She was just a piece in some game, and with her memories back she knew exactly where she fit in the puzzle.

Slowly she was able to focus on her surroundings. Her temples throbbed and she felt as though a bus had hit her. Every muscle in her body hurt. Her hands were shaking, her nails clicking against the metal bed she was restrained to. She was so cold that she was shaking. She was wearing a thin white tank top and hospital gown over her sports bra and panties.

She looked up and a large metal disk hung over her with a small incandescent light bulb in the middle. It was swaying gently. The ceiling was grey and cold looking. She looked to her side and saw a machine very much like the one in Dr. Emily's office, though this one was older. The rest of the room was bare. She glanced down and saw there were tubes and cords attached to her everywhere. They wormed their way like snakes from under her clothes.

The door opened somewhere above her head and she strained her neck back to see. But could only see the top of their head. Though, with a falling feeling in her stomach, she could see the dark hair.

"Hello Hadley." The person stood over her and looked directly down at her face. It was Liani. She pressed a button and the bed rotated to an upright position so Hadley's feet were firmly on the floor.

Liani pressed a button on the wall and a holographic projection appeared before them both slowly. It was Saul; he was sitting at a desk somewhere far away, safely in his compound. But Hadley felt as though she could reach out and touch him.

"What Liani?! I told you to leave me alone. I don't agree with what you're doing!" He was annoyed.

He rolled his eyes and raised his hand to slam it down onto a button to end the call. Then he saw Hadley, in her stark white against the metal bed in the background.
"What are you doing with her?" His voice was panicked; he didn't try to hide it.

"Do you recognize her Saul dear? The great Hadley Evans raised from the dead. And guess what?! I restored her memories." Liani was positively gleeful. She was grinning from ear to ear. Then she became somber, serious and menacing. "And Saul, I do mean all of her memories. Even that one about us— oops— was I not supposed to bring that up?"

Saul threw the closest thing he could grab. Hadley watched the clock sail through the air and shatter into pieces against the invisible wall. She just stared at him. Liani was practically bouncing around the room and Saul was ready to murder her, rightly so. Hadley could feel herself starting to get drowsy again. Her head lulled to one side. Her eyes closed for just a second before she snapped her head back up to focus on reality. The holographic form of Saul took a step forward and looked into Hadley's eyes.

"Everything?" He nearly choked on the word. It came out as a whisper.

"Everything," Hadley said breathlessly.

She immediately flashed to the image that had sent her marriage crumbling to the ground. The moment she had walked in on Liani and Saul in bed, the day she had woken up from decades of Cryosleep.

"How? You, Kane and I formulated the newest serum ourselves," Saul said to Hadley, breaking her away from the images running rampant through her mind.

"You three aren't as smart as you think you are, even if you did somehow manage to convince people to let you be in charge," Liani muttered looking at her nail beds.

"Liani, you were once my friend," Hadley stated trying to reach any part of her humanity she had left.

"You once told me what I needed to hear so I would be your friend," Liani hissed at Hadley. She was feral.

"Liani you were the deceitful one!" Hadley exclaimed.

"Everyone is deceitful. I used to worship Hemmer." Her statement radiated like it was the craziest thing in the world. But even Hadley knew that they had all worshiped Hemmer at one point. He had been the messiah, the saviour, the one who had turned out to actually be Lucifer.

"Hemmer is still your Uncle Liani!" Saul screamed rolling his eyes.

"But as of today dear old uncle's daughter is dead and gone," Liani cackled.

Saul looked at Hadley confused. "I thought Kristen survived."

Hadley just shook her head. She honestly couldn't formulate words. Flashes of memories danced through her eyes until they settled on Kirsten's dead blue eyes staring right through her soul.

Liani rolled her eyes. Her constant need to be in control bugged Hadley, and it always had. Hadley promised herself as soon as she was out of her restraints that the first thing she would do would be to punch Liani. If she could still move her arms that was. Everything was becoming strained Hadley noticed to herself.

"Now Hadley, I need a very important piece of information. I need to know—"

"How to activate it?" Hadley replied tiredly.

"Yes!" She was almost bouncing off the walls. She looked at Saul's hologram, "I just wanted to show you her one last time. Your perfect poster girl will be dead by morning." Liani clicked the button again and before Saul could say anything else he was gone.

Her face was smiling in anticipation. "I can't tell you." Hadley said. Liani's face fell, just as Hadley knew it would. The smile turned to anger almost instantly. Her gaze narrowed and her mouth became a thin line. Hadley just took a breath. Sick of explaining the same thing to everyone.

"I have ways you know—" She went to a wall and placed her hand on it. A drawer clicked open and revealed an assortment of torture devices. She picked up one covered in spikes and walked towards Hadley who struggled against her restraints.

She took a sharp breath in. Hadley didn't want that device anywhere near her. Liani raised her arm and brought it down as hard as she could into Hadley's stomach. Hadley screeched in pain. Tears pouring from her eyes. She looked downwards and saw the perfect rows of red dots form across her midriff, soaking the white linen clothing. The dots spread until her stomach was a large red blob.

"Liani I can't tell you because I didn't erase that memory. I killed it." Hadley had to get across what she was trying to say. The words barely making it out.

"What?!"

"Take a brain scan. You will see a spot on my brain where I permanently damaged a piece of my cerebral cortex. Permanently erasing that memory, so no one could do what you want, what Hemmer wants to."

Hadley's words hit Liani like a slap in the face. She stared at Hadley for a moment before turning on her heel and leaving the room. Then Hadley was all alone again and soon her head lulled to the side and she was out cold, blood running down her bare legs.

One thing was certain though her mind couldn't handle everything that was happening and she knew Liani would be back to play with her drawer of toys.

# Chapter Sixty

Hadley was moving. But not by her own free will or ability. At that point she really had neither. Her feet were being dragged down a hall, her knees scraping along the ground. Two men were on either side of her holding each of her limp arms. She had been tied up and tortured for hours in that small grey room and now she had no more willpower to fight.

Liani hadn't listened to Hadley's constant pleas about her brain. Liani had used every torturous tactic in the book, and now Hadley was a fragment of what she was.

At last Liani ended the torture and they had scanned Hadley's brain over and over. Finally, Liani had conference called both Hemmer and Saul. They reiterated what she had just found out. Now everyone who cared knew for certain that she had risked her life by frying a part of her brain to hide this secret. Even if she hadn't, she would rather die than tell anyone what she had known. She had made a mistake when she had created the program and it was a mistake she had proved over and over again that she would die to stop.

At that moment she was barely conscious due to the blood loss, her lungs were filled with water she kept spitting up and she had more broken limbs then she could count. But besides that she wondered about the safety of her team and whether Jeremiah, Vanya and the rest of them had made it out alive. If not, this had all been for nothing.

All she knew was that she was being dragged to her execution. Finally, it would all end.

Outside the storm was raging. Hadley could hear it whistling through the depths of the tunnels. There was a low buzz from the blowing wind. Through her semiconscious state she knew was going outside.

The buzz was getting louder and they were walking upwards. She could just picture how outside would look. The snow blizzarding around her. How her grey skin and the circles under her eyes would show what Liani did to her. The blood falling almost poetically in tiny drips from her body, making art in the snow. She imagined the peace most though, as she went in and out of consciousness.

One face kept coming back to her, despite Liani. The face of the man she loved more than anyone, no matter what he had done to her in the past. She hoped, actually prayed, that he knew how much she cared about him.

Hadley knew that after this, and after everything, her face would no longer be one of hope, but of disparity. It would teach everyone that fighting for what you believe would only end in ruin. She had tried, valiantly, and she knew that. She had succeeded according to her, but no one else would know that. She would take that to her grave. The only thing she could do is hang her head in shame.

She took her last bit of energy and tugged on her arms, trying to get them loose. She tried with all her might to break free. She thought about how running down the passage would feel. That last moment of freedom. But the men didn't even look down at her. They ignored the frail form she had become.

Then Liani opened the door to the blizzard that lay beyond.

The wind and snow hit Hadley like a train as they walked into the cold air. It didn't even make the men who were holding her flinch, they were wearing heavy clothes, and Hadley really only had a thin tank top on.

The door swung open and banged backwards against a wall. The sun was a small spot just over the horizon. It was blurred around the edges from the falling snow. Hadley stared into its tiny form breathing in the last moment of sunshine, of hope. The most powerful thing in this universe became no more than the glimmer in the distance every night. As though it was a distant memory. Though it reappeared every morning to bring new life and new hope. It gave the world a moment to realize why it needed it. The darkness brought out the evil and the hatred and the fear. The sun, with each new day, vanquished all that night had brought. But the sun couldn't stay alive always. It needed time to show what it was fighting against. So no one ever took it for granted.

Hadley had made it back from death time after time. Each time resurging the hope of a new and better world. But this would be her last sunset. This time was the absolute end. This time she wouldn't be able to be the light. She was vanishing forever into the darkness. Not only did she know that, she fully accepted it. In some ways she was tired of fighting.

They walked into an open area free of cars and debris. Hadley was pushed to her hands and knees on the ground. Her skin immediately froze from the cold. She pushed back to sitting, her hands fell limply to her sides, she could already feel the frost bite on her palms, and she was unable to lift her arms back up. Her head lulled forward and there she sat. Unable to move or think.

Quite a few others followed the group out. Hadley hadn't even realized they were walking behind them. She hadn't heard the footsteps. Everyone was dressed in snow gear. One of the women held a camera. She was focusing on Liani's face.

"To everyone who is watching. This is the ultimate end of Hadley Evans. Her revolution is over. You are either against us or with us. May fate take the GOVs to their graves." Liani made a dramatic solute to the camera. She reached into her jacket and extracted a hunting knife. It was long and jagged.

She ran the cool metal over her palm. Liani walked around Hadley overly dramatically. She was putting on a show. She kept circling, like a hawk. She stood behind Hadley's back and leaned down so she could whisper in her ear. "Goodbye Hadley. Die for good this time."
Liani cracked her neck and exhaled with an ecstatic moan.

Liani brought the cool metal to Hadley's throat. Hadley inhaled sharply. She was ready for the pain. Ready for the end. She immediately felt the tip of the knife bite into her throat. The warm trickle of blood ran down her chest and pooled on her breast. It just added to the red in which she was already covered. The knife was pressing against her airway and she was struggling for breath. Hadley wanted her to get it over with.
She just wanted it to end.

Hadley closed her eyes, took a breath of the cold and waited for the pain that didn't come.

"Put the knife down!" a voice blared over a speaker in the distance. It was deafeningly loud.

She opened her eyes hopeful. She looked up through her eyelashes and saw helicopters descending from the sky. Liani obviously saw them as well as she had lightened her hold of the knife on Hadley's throat, who was finally able to take a deep breath in. She felt like she was breathing in life.

"Hemmer—" Liani hissed.

Liani was dumbfounded. Hadley used the pause to reach up and push Liani's hand out of the way. She then rolled to the side and landed on the ground. The snow covered her face and body, burning her. She tried to push herself to her feet but she had no energy left.

Hadley was so weak and still losing so much blood from the torture. She watched the snow as her blood pooled around her.

Shots exploded. She felt bullet casings fall against her body. They landed in heaps across her back and head. The hot metal leaving little burns across her.

Then everything stopped and it was silent. Liani and her minions were retreating in the distance. One of them slammed the door behind them, locking it with a click that would only keep out Hemmer for a second. Hadley didn't know how far the tunnels led but she knew they had gotten away for this moment. Hemmer wouldn't find them in the labyrinth. He didn't even care to try.

Hemmer was the one who picked Hadley up off the ground. She just looked up at him dazed and confused. "Why are you helping me? You want me dead—"

"Yes but not just yet—" He raised his eyebrows and gave a curt laugh.

Hadley was pulled into the helicopter and as soon as they were inside it lifted off the ground. Hadley was shoved onto a stretcher and they were off. No one said anything but Jeremiah and Vanya were also sitting in the copter. Both were injured but looked all right.

"How?" The word came out as a garble from Hadley's mouth.

Vanya rested her head against Jeremiah's shoulder, "They all wanted to watch your execution. Gave us just enough leeway to escape."

Hadley tried to smile but it probably looked like she was oddly contorting her face. So she settled for a small yet noticeable nod. Dr. Emily came from out of nowhere and unzipped a large first aid kit. She pulled out a spray can and sprayed a mist around the entire cabin. Hadley was in a cloud. Then she started with the med bots. She placed them all over Hadley's body and they got to work with little buzzing sounds. They all watched as they zoomed around, fixing Hadley's body the best they could. Fixing all the holes. Emily placed one under Hadley's nose, it was the size of a pinhead and she felt it tickle as it went up her nostril. Hadley was scared of what it was going to do.

"What?!" she choked out.

Emily looked at her with pity, "It's just going to repair the internal damage. Don't worry Hadley."

Emily grabbed a steaming mug out of the bag and tilted Hadley's head up. Hadley felt her neck crack as she took a long sip letting the hot liquid warm her from the inside out. It tasted like chocolate and wine. In this moment it was the best thing she had ever consumed.

After that she drifted in and out of consciousness as they went. The storm was blowing snow in through the cracks in the helicopter. They went up and down. The turbulence almost took the copters down more than once.

Finally, they arrived and landed. Hadley felt warm and stronger. Though she still couldn't really shake the ill and wobbly feeling and she stumbled out of the helicopter and onto the ground, which seemed to be spinning.

# Chapter Sixty-One

She could only see six inches in front of her face because of the snow. She was dizzy and disoriented, and somehow lost hold of the helicopter and the people around her. She flailed her arms around searched, grasping for anything solid. All she got was air.

She stumbled forward unsure of which way to go. She looked around and she had lost sight of the helicopter and the others. Her knees were about to give out as she walked forward. Or what she thought was forward. She was hoping to get inside, away from the cold.

"Hello?!" she yelled into the seeming abyss.

"Hadley!" She heard a recognizable voice somewhere in the distance.

"Saul?!" she yelled back, remembering the thumb drive suddenly. Her hand instinctively went to her bra. One of the few things that Liani had left on her. The thumb drive had been tucked unnoticeably out of the way and she still had it.

"Follow the red light." He yelled. The wind whistled all around her. In the mass of white that engulfed her she saw a faint red light blinking in the distance. And she started towards it.

"FIND HER!" Hemmer yelled only a few feet behind her, she could hear his footsteps. She felt the energy of arms waving behind her.

She did the only thing she could think of and started running. She knew they were behind her but it didn't matter. She only needed to make it a few more meters. The red light was getting brighter. She could see dark figures around the red light. Her feet were sliding around beneath her on the icy ground. She looked down but couldn't see her feet or the ground.

The snow was suffocating her but still she ran faster and faster. She went as fast as her suddenly frail body could but it was the hardest thing she had ever done. She was getting closer to them when she heard bullets explode behind her, whizzing past her head. One of the figures ran towards her, it was Saul she was sure. She could see his outline against the vivid red dot. His arms outstretched trying to get to her faster.

The bullets rang past her ears. Still she kept running. They were so close when she felt a shot hit her thigh and then another to her stomach. The pain was blinding.

She fell to her knees and as she did so she pulled the flash drive out of her bra and held it out. She watched as Saul got closer to her. He grabbed her hand that held the flash-drive and pulled her to her feet. He tried to get her to go with him.

She thrust the flash drive into his palm and clutched both her hands to her stomach for a moment. She felt nothing, no blood pouring out of her. Something was wrong.

Without thinking she threw her arms around Saul. He looked at her stunned for a moment.

Then she kissed him. Their mouths pressed together familiarly.

"I love you." She said simply.

Tears filled his eyes. He started to shake and couldn't find the words.

"Go!" She said suddenly, urging him to get away. She was slumping over, everything was numb.

"I'm not leaving you again." He bent down to help her, trying to throw her over his shoulder. But they were losing time.

"Go Saul! I'm begging you. Finish what we started. Do it for me. You won't make it back with me"

Saul knew she was right. He needed the information on that drive to bring Hemmer down. Hadley was no good to him right now. He clenched the flash drive to his chest and stood up. "Fine. But I'll always love you Evans, and I will get you out of there."

"You better always love me Saul," she joked in a whisper.

With one last look and without hesitation he ran back into the whiteness towards the dot. Before Hadley knew it the dot was gone. They were gone, and safe. She knew after that her co-SPaDIs wouldn't be able to find them.

Hadley looked down and saw the blood pooling around her knees. *Finally*, she thought.

The bullets were still flying around her. She turned around and saw Jeremiah limping towards her just two feet away with the automatic rifle. She had to blink to make sure she wasn't dreaming.

She had nothing left and fell onto her side in agony, no longer able to sit up. The pain pumped through her whole body. Jeremiah took the last two steps towards her. He pointed his gun at her face. She blinked up at him as her vision started to go blurry. She glanced at her hand and saw it was covered in blood again from her stomach; Doctor Emily had only healed the top portion. They knew she would try something like this.

"I wish you had never existed, it would have been so much easier." The butt of Jeremiah's gun hit her across the face and she clutched her bleeding and broken nose. He dragged her through the snow by her hair. Their few moments of friendship dissolving into the snow.

They got to the complex and he threw her inside a room. He tied her roughly to a chair and left. The rope was digging into her wrists and ankles. She could feel her wrists becoming raw. She looked down and saw a drop of blood fall onto the floor. The sound of the drop rung through the empty room. All she could do was stare at the grey wall. A single light bulb hung over her head. It swung eerily back and forth in an invisible breeze.

Behind her she heard the door click open and briefly there was bright light. She watched as Kane and Hemmer walked in. They were followed in by the old man she had seen in Hemmer's office. He was still as frail as the last moment she had glimpsed him. He kept his head down and jumped every time Hemmer made a move.

"What do you know?!" Hemmer yelled in her face.

"Nothing!" Hadley spat back. She struggled against the restraints. She could feel the ropes become more soaked with blood.

"Hold it right there," Kane said putting a hand on Hemmer's shoulder.

"What Kane?"

"She won't tell us anything, no matter what. I can see that now."

Kane, for the first time ever understood Hadley. He didn't look at her the way he always had. He saw that she was stronger than he'd thought. He finally saw her as an equal instead of a subordinate.

Hadley looked him in the eyes with an intense fire. All she wanted to do was throttle him. Something inside her lurched and she put her whole body weight against her restraints but the chair didn't even budge.

"I told you we needed to get rid of her," Hemmer said to Kane. Kane just nodded slowly. He bit his bottom lip. In that moment Hadley almost smiled at Kane; he had finally figured it out. He knew that the planet was more important to her than her own life. Human decency was more important to her. Saving those who were innocent was more important to her. Everything was more important to her. Kane had just never seen it, even after all that time.

Hemmer took out a gun from his holster. He pointed the barrel between her eyes. Hadley inhaled, ready again to die for what she believed in. She wanted to stop running.

Then she saw something out of the corner of her eye. The old man held a small circular device in his hand. He pressed the button and electricity went through the room. Suddenly, she knew exactly who he was.

The barrel of the gun fell away from her face. She felt the electric shock up her spine. Every hair on her body stood straight up. She could taste the burning in her mouth. Smell it in her nose. Feel it on her cheeks.

Pax rushed into the room, grabbing her elbow as she faded out of consciousness.

"I'm not going to let you down this time Hadley."

"You'd better not Pax or I will kill you."

"I learn't my lesson last time Had."

Everything went black again. She practically rolled her eyes as it did.

# Chapter Sixty-Two

And after a nuclear war, a worldwide plague and at the beginning of an ice age, the corrupt government still hadn't won. The human race was on its way to multiple planets. But they were here, trying to save earth from them.

The revolution was still standing.

Hadley was still standing.

# About Bradlyn Wilson

Bradlyn Wilson is a multi-media content creator, blogger, writer, environmentalist and photography lover. After completing her BSc in Earth Science at the University of Alberta, she moved across the planet to finish her Masters degree in Media and Communications at the University of Sydney in Australia. Now, she spends her time travel blogging and using media to communicate science and scientific research. She enjoys winding real science with compelling content. Travel is one of her biggest passions, and like many people, dreams of working from a beach somewhere. She caught the travel bug a few years ago, she got on a plane to Europe and has slowly been making her way across the planet since, sharing her journey online and on Instagram the entire way.

**Social Media Links**

Facebook: https://www.facebook.com/bradlyncreative/

Facebook: https://www.facebook.com/earth2bradlyn/
INSTAGRAM:
https://www.instagram.com/bradlyn_wilson/
@bradlyn_wilson

Pinterest: https://www.pinterest.com/bradlynwilson/

Twitter: https://twitter.com/BradlynWilson
@bradlynwilson

Website: http://bradlynwilson.com/

**Acknowledgements**

The biggest challenge that human kind will face is Climate Change. It will be the hardest thing that people will have to overcome, and we have to do it for us. The planet will survive anything, the combination of water, rock and life will reset and start over, continuing to circulate the sun. This book explores, what could happen if we keep going how we are.

Thank you to everyone who encouraged me to keep writing this book even when I felt that I couldn't keep putting words on the paper.

To my family, who has dealt with my outbursts of creativity and frustration at having writers block. You helped me to pursue everything I have ever dreamt of, and have pushed me to work harder than I ever thought possible. Mom, Dad, Kenzie, Cole, you guys have made me be my best self. Your encouragement was how I was able to finish this project. You are the best family that a girl could ask for, and I appreciate everything from the moral support to tough love you have given me. Love you all to the moon and back.

To my best friend, my person, thank you for letting me write. Thank you for always pushing me towards being the best writer I can be, even when I didn't want to hear it. You are my world, and I love you so much.

And last, to everyone else, who has pushed me to be more than myself. To spend every day "doing good." Thank you. Know how much you mean to me.

88748040R00191

Made in the USA
Columbia, SC
03 February 2018